TROUBADOR PUB

Mary Cavanagh spent her childhood in the leafy climes of North Oxford. She attended St Barnabas Junior School in Jericho, and Milham Ford girls Grammar School. Being lazy, and academically challenged, she was grateful to show education a clean pair of heels. A hedonistic working life of sorts followed as an office clerk, graphic artist, barmaid, au pair, and various other forgotten nightmares, none of which she took at all seriously. She married Bill, and had two sons, Alastair and Rory.

She eventually undertook teacher training, and it was through her English course that she discovered the joy of creative writing. Wisely, or not, she chose not to teach, and spent the next twenty years being completely fulfilled in medical management and administration.

Her first novel *The Crowded Bed*, was published by Transita, in January 2007. Both this novel, and *A Man Like Any Other* have been born out of her two fascinations; the strange and secret life that is lived within the mind, and the myriad of changes in social and moral behaviour over the last fifty years. She has also contributed to two anthologies, published by The Oxford Writers Group (OxPens), *The Sixpenny Debt and Other Oxford Stories,* and *The Lost College and Other Oxford Stories.* Her writing has been compared to Susan Hill, Henry Fielding, Virginia Woolf, Anita Shreve and Pat Barker.

Her favourite authors, and influences, are George Orwell, Daphne du Maurier, Ian McEwan, and the Bennett boys, Alan and Arnold.

Mary is delighted to talk to reading groups, formulate workshops and attend literary festivals. In fact, she will do anything to perpetuate the continuance of quality fiction.

Updated information can be found on http//:marycavanagh.blogspot.com

Memory and Experience

One breaks us, one makes us, but I'm damned if I can decide which is which.

Father Ewan McEwan
2008

Life!
Life! I know not what thou art,
But know that thou and I must part;
And when, or how, or where we met,
I own to me's a secret yet.
But this I know, when thou art fled,
Where'er they lay these limbs, this head,
No clod so valueless shall be
As all that then remains of me.

Anna Letitia Barbauld
1743 – 1825

Acknowledgements

I would like to thank the raft of people who have supported and encouraged my writing career over many years. You were the ones who made it all possible.

Deborah Terry, my dear friend and first ever critic, who read all my first bizarre scribblings, and cheered me on regardless.

Yvonne Ruscoe and Pat Allen, who both generously gave up their time to read *A Man Like Any Other – The Priest's Tale* in its raw form, and to discuss it with me at length.

Caro Fraser and Sharon Stanley, for their generous pre-publication reviews.

The Oxford Writers Group (OWG), most especially Linora Lawrence, Jane Gordon Cumming, and Edwin Osborne.

Ruth Dowley, for her excellent OUDCE creative writing course.

And to those who have helped in so many other ways. Mark and Nicki Thornton of 'Mostly Books', Abingdon, Oxon and Simon Key and Tim West of 'The Big Green Bookshop', Wood Green, London. My fellow Transita writers, The Transisters. Lynne Moores (Molyneaux) and BookCrossers Worldwide. Sharon Goforth (Ex-Libris) and Mary Zacaroli. Peter Mole and Mark Brewerton. Karen Batchelor from The Oxfordshire Library Service, and the chief librarians (most especially Clare, Anne, Vikki, Gill and Dominique). Tony and Ann Butler, Audrey Lowe, Joan Godwin, and Pauline Brown.

Lastly to Jeremy Thompson, Julia Fuller, and the team at Matador for being so easy to work with, and for producing a book of such a high quality and visual appeal.

Mary Cavanagh 2008

Waldringhythe Abbey, the village of Monks Bottom, and the Strathburn Naval Base, are all fictitious places.

Genetic Sexual Attraction (GSA) is now a phenomenon recognised to affect parents and siblings who have been separated through adoption and subsequently meet, having spent the key years of adolescence apart.

'Embrace the Base' day took place at the Greenham Common Army Base in Berkshire, UK on Saturday, December 12th 1982, but the fictional events described are based on eye-witness accounts.

The passages relating to nuclear research during the Second World War in Scotland are all wholly fictitious.

The Prologue

SEPTEMBER 1984
WALDRINGHYTHE ABBEY, SUFFOLK

It's the afternoon of an Indian summer. The birds are silent, and the air hangs hot and dry. You're looking in through a window. It's not right to be a voyeur, but you can't help yourself. You're much too fascinated. You see a young man you know to be a priest, reclining in a chair. His eyes are closed, and his face shows peace, contentment, and a wry smile (as well it might). At his feet sits a woman. She's clearly some years older than he, but endowed with a rare and fortunate beauty.

'Now, I'm ready to talk to you,' she says.

'Then talk,' he replies. 'You may pause as often as you need to, but I won't interrupt. Just tell me when you've reached the end.'

She takes the priest's hand, and leans her cheek against his knees. He pulls her hand to his face, and kisses her fingers.

She begins to speak. You recognise gentle Irish overtones, but her voice is so hesitant and soft you have to strain to hear the words.

'The laughter became louder and louder, until it turned to helpless hysteria and clapping. Then a sudden lurch of the boat, a splash, and a shout of, "Child overboard."

Roger rushed from the wheelhouse and hurled himself into the water.

Toby followed him in nanoseconds.

Tim briefly stood transfixed before he dived in too.

Then all the other men, both young and old, tore off their ties, and jackets, and shoes, to join in. The women were screaming, but I was silent and calm, knowing it was just a question of the first good swimmer to reach her.

There was a real panic around the bow, with too many rescuers getting in each other's way, but Roger's strong crawl gained ground over everyone else. "Where was the splash?" he shouted.

"Over there! Over there!" thirty voices yelled back.

"Where for fuck's sake's over there?"

He dived under the water time, after time, after time, but it soon became stirred up into a muddy sludge. He tried, and tried so hard, but each quest became shorter and more desperate.

The women were now silent, and holding disbelieving hands over their mouths. The San Fairy Ann, with no one in control, slewed a wayward course and collided hard with the river bank. There was a cracking and crumpling sound, of glass breaking and metal twisting, and those of us left on board were flung on our backs.

No one wanted to be the first to admit it was a hopeless cause, but in the fullness of time, when Roger conceded failure, everyone in the water began to gasp and scramble for dry land. The women were now openly sobbing, and rapidly abandoned ship to assist their menfolk. I was left to stand alone.

The place she'd fallen in was now as still as a millpond, and the normal life of the river had already returned. A heron hooked a fish with the plummeting beauty of its large wings, a pair of swans led their cygnets in a slow, weed-trawling glide, and the wind swung the willows. It was only then that I screamed. I screamed so loudly I didn't make a sound.'

She stops speaking, slowly raises her head and looks up at the priest. 'My daughter was drowned. My husband was drowned. There's no more story to be told . . .'

Chapter 1

APRIL 2008
WALDRINGHYTHE ABBEY, SUFFOLK

Father Ewan McEwan. The name demanded perfect diction. A strange, quiet and serious man who never laughed, but whose face retained the softness of a permanent smile. A face that drew the eye to his peculiar, imperfect beauty.

Today he sat staring at a Howard Hodgkin print on his sitting room wall, but the bursting splash of its colours were faded to dullness. Earlier that day a phone call from Timothy Proudfoot had confirmed that Marina's death would come before nightfall, and thus, for the first time in his life, Ewan had cancelled his clients with the excuse of stress. The hours had passed in an empty silence, waiting for the phone to ring; his body moving only to prepare endless pots of coffee, and light numerous cigarettes. Now the light was fading, and he could delay his walk no longer. With an abrupt decision he laced up his boots, and flung his cloak around his shoulders.

His daily two-mile discipline along the Deben estuary bank was a strict, sacrosanct routine. It was his time for philosophy, reflection, and debate with all things spiritual, but today he found no room for anything beyond his misery. His feet followed their usual beaten path towards the marshes, but the thrash of his strides gave no relief. At the turn-back point he stopped to rest, sitting on a dry tussock of grass to overlook the lower reaches of the wide waterway. With the tide drawn out it was a flat stretch of wet, muddy sand, showing the criss-cross imprints of a seabird's wavering walk. He lit up, drew in deeply, and lowered his head in painful memory.

NOVEMBER 2007

From a vantage point, high up in the Abbey library, Ewan had watched her drive in. A chance broken moment he'd taken to rest his eyes from writing. To go to the window and absorb the autumn splendour of the grounds, basking in strong sunshine. It was the first time in nearly twenty-five years she'd arrived without an official appointment, and he knew instantly that something was different – something was wrong. Her normal entrances were consistent and legendary. The Aston Martin gliding to a smooth halt, and the widow emerging with the slow body language of depression; her face a waxwork of apathy, her eyes hidden behind dark glasses, and her head bowed to confirm the solitude she displayed like a medal. Today the car had swung into the carpark at speed, and the brakes applied so harshly the chassis rocked. There were no dark glasses, her normal tight chignon hung past her elbows in a thick, flaxen waterfall, and her traditional mourning black replaced by a sleek trouser suit in a wild shade of scarlet.

With a combination of apprehension and delight, he briskly descended the stone staircase and walked outside to greet her. Aware of a gardener, raking up leaves, he moved forward with his arm extended; the action of a professional, detached therapist greeting his patient. 'Lady Proudfoot. What a pleasant surprise.'

'Sudden decision, Father,' she said. 'I need to see you.' Her voice was pitched much higher than usual, and she displayed an excited edge; as if she'd consumed just one drink too many.

'Then if you'd like to go over to reception and book in, I can see you right away.'

As she swung away he nodded politely to the gardener, and hurried towards his house on the outskirts of the Abbey estate. But before shutting the front door he positioned the usual notice,

Father Ewan is in consultation
Please do not disturb

Marina flopped down casually onto a large Edwardian armchair, and slowly crossed her legs. With a lazy turn of the head, and a slouched, angled shoulder, she lowered her eyes and smiled. 'Well, at least say you're pleased to see me,' she said. 'You look as if someone's just nicked the altar silver.'

'I'm just thrown a bit off guard,' he replied. 'What's happened? There's something wrong, isn't there? I can tell.'

'Oh, fie! I just had an urge to see you. A fit of madness caused by this wonderful autumn weather.'

Ewan looked at his watch. 'The thing is, I'm a bit tied up. Father James is away and I have to say mass at six.'

She glanced at the clock. 'Well, it's only four. How long does it take to put your party frock on?'

The aftermath of orgasm can be alarming, alerting one to the fine line one treads between life and death. The disappearance into a black, hazy void where you're never so close to your lover, but never so blissfully alone. Ewan was sure he'd briefly lost consciousness. His heart raced, his head was filled with a blurred underwater sound, and his lungs were so restricted, speech was impossible. 'Can't breathe,' he choked, fighting to emerge from the shroud of her hair. She rose to her knees and he inhaled sharply. She laughed, crouched over him, and then, as was her custom, leaned down to run the tip of her tongue over the small scar on his top lip.

'You're beautiful, Ewan.'

She left the rumpled bed, pulled on her black satin kimono, and moved to stand before the life-sized facsimile of *Crucifix Man* that hung on the wall. The iconic anti-nuclear image of the late twentieth century, as renowned in the western world as the napalmed Vietnamese girl, running in pain and terror.

A dramatic sepia-wash showed a young dog-collared man shackled to a cross. Bare-chested, arms spread-eagled, legs encased in torn Levi's, and Doc Martens hanging heavily on crossed feet. Long wet hair obscured his face, and around his brow a barbed wire crown held a large medallion depicting the CND Logo. She stared at it for several seconds, as if it were the first time she'd ever seen it, then ran her fingers slowly across the youthful arms to the flopped, manacled hands. 'Why did you do it?'

'You know why. Love of man. Love of the world. The right to life.'

She fixed him with a steady gaze. *'Life, I know not what thou art, but know that thou and I must part.'*

He threw himself out of bed. 'There is something wrong, isn't there?'

'I've got a little problem,' she said. 'In fact, quite a big problem.'

Chapter 2

APRIL 2008
MONKS BOTTOM MANOR, OXFORDSHIRE

Marina Proudfoot's hands lay desiccated and yellowing on the French lace counterpane. Marina was dying. Perhaps the hands already had, but despite the weakness and confusion of extremis, she seemed irritated and impatient. Her fingers flickered into life, rasping and blindly tapping. She was attempting to make words, but her dry whispers were just a muddled slur.

Sally Fuller stroked her brow and whispered the usual comforting platitudes, wishing she could convey more than sympathetic noises. It was always the right of the dying to be understood and nurtured at the end, but somehow philosophy was anathema when time was seeping away. She could offer nothing but her professional nursing skills; to sooth, to ensure dignity, and monitor the demise. 'Listen, Tim,' Sally said. 'I'm sure she's trying to say something.'

Timothy moved closer to the bed and hovered anxiously over his mother. 'Mumma, it's Tim. I'm listening.' With a powerful effort the husk of Marina's body stiffened, her arms flailed, and a desperate gasp cracked from her parched throat. She then paused and spoke with perfect diction.

'Hat trick.'

Sally stared as the tortured face became calm and the rib cage dropped. She felt for the pulse, placed the stethoscope over the heart, and listened intently. She shook her head and stepped back. 'I'm sorry, Tim.'

Timothy clasped his face with both hands. 'Hat trick. You know what that means, don't you? The score of three. My father, Morgana, and now herself. She knew it was her last moment. God must have crept in at the end after all.'

Sally turned and patted his shoulder, knowing it was still her duty to be kind to him, but already feeling detached and anxious to leave. 'You need a few private minutes,' she said, pulling up a bedside chair. 'I'll go downstairs and phone Andrew. He has to sign the death certificate and arrange what happens next.'

The bereaved son and the nurse skillfully avoided eye contact, deeply aware that the hidden agenda between them was striding out of cover, shaking a hand-bell, and blowing a whistle.

When Sally had left the room Timothy retrieved his mobile from the windowsill, and pressed a number. 'Oh, Skipper. It's all over.'

Chapter 3

THE DOWER HOUSE, MONKS BOTTOM

Roger Fuller's ear had been sharp-tuned all day for the merry summons of his mobile's ring tone (the theme music from *The Magic Roundabout*) and Timothy's emotional updates had come in with regularity.

'. . . Oh, Skipper, having to cope without you is agony. . . She's drifting in and out of consciousness. . . Andrew Gibson called in at lunchtime and said it won't be long now. . . Sally says her pulse is weakening. . .'

As Roger listened his lips had formed the expected words of sympathy and concern. 'Angel, just hold tight. I'm with you every step of the way.' Now, at last, with the final pronouncement, Roger responded with well-rehearsed cooing tones, to convey deep compassion and understanding. 'Just hold on, honey. I'll be there.'

'Best give it an hour,' Timothy said. 'We've got to wait for Andrew to do the paper work. I'll ring with the all clear.' He rang off without further exchange.

Roger's hand gripped the goblet of white wine he was holding so tightly the stem broke from the bowl and the contents fell on his shoes. His heart thumped. His stomach lurched. He had a spontaneous erection. He thought with horror that he might actually cry, but Finnegan's noisy presence broke the moment, bustling at his feet, and lustily licking the spilt wine from the sturdy Lobb brogues.

Roger had known Marina Proudfoot for most of his life, and in decent terms of respect, he should have been sorry. But he had to admit that sorry wasn't the word that sprang to mind. Fucking, frigging, bollocking delighted was more apt. He fell on his knees with joy and clumsily embraced the slobbering Wolfhound. 'Oh, thank you, God,' he said aloud. 'I'm dancing with delight. Could relief ever be more glorious?'

He staggered to his feet, dizzy with happiness. At last she was gone. Hurrah! How he hated the cow. Forever the fly in the ointment, the spider in the web, swanning around like Lady Muck, and swamping Tim with her power. But (being trained and experienced in PR), he would act his part to perfection. Sympathetic noises and head-angled concern would be the order of the day. He'd be the listener, the hugger, the kisser, the lover.

Unable to shake off his euphoria he jumped up and down on the spot like a marathon runner on the starting grid. Finnegan, instinctively picking up the mood of his master, pirouetted with the grace of a foal, thumped his tail, and eyed Roger with a 'what comes next' look. 'I can tell you're as happy as I am, old boy,' Roger said to the bounding hound. 'You thought you were staying behind with Mummy, but I've decided you're coming with me. That's a surprise, isn't it? First thing we'll do is nip up to the petrol station and get some flowers for Tim. Coals to Newcastle, I know, but it's the thing to do. Suppose I'd better write a note.' Roger looked around for a pen.

Chapter 4

Andrew Gibson sat at Marina's dressing table, dealing with the officialese of death. He looked at his watch. 'Just gone seven, Tim. It's a bit late to call out the undertakers, but I'll give them a ring for you first thing in the morning. Her instruction was that she wanted a standard cremation, with no bells or smells of any kind. Are you agreed?' Timothy nodded, and Andrew continued. 'The only other thing I must do, as her executor, is to mention her requests. Firstly, there's the music she wanted played.' The doctor blew out his lips, as if in bewilderment. 'Just the one piece. A hit song from the nineteen-fifties called *'Twilight Time'* by The Platters. The other thing was a purple handbag she wanted Father Ewan from Waldringhythe to bless, and then to go with her. Do you know what she means?'

'Absolutely,' said Timothy. 'A huge, hideous plastic thing. Morgana used to keep all her little toys in it, and she hauled it every-where. It was rescued from the chaos of that. . . that horrible day. I told Father Ewan I'd ring him when. . . as soon as. . . I'll mention it.' Clearly agitated, he began to reverse slowly towards the door. 'Andrew, could you possibly inform Cora Feather for me? I'm not up to coping with her.'

The doctor nodded. 'Of course. I'll pop in on my way home. The old girl was very close to your mother, wasn't she?'

Timothy then turned to Sally, but before he could deliver an obligatory speech of thanks, she shook her head and held up a warning finger. He nodded in agreement and left the room.

Sally immediately set about clearing up Marina's bedroom with fast efficiency, heaving the debris of the sick room into a black plastic bin-sack. Andrew Gibson sighed, stretched wearily, and got to his feet. 'She was an incredibly beautiful woman, wasn't she?'

'She was,' Sally agreed. 'Stunning. Even now she still looks lovely.'

'I've always thought there was something a bit peculiar about her, though. Not an obvious psychosis, but an aura of... How can I put it? A part of her no one could fathom.'

'Surely that's natural after a tragedy like hers in the past? She talked quite a bit about the child towards the end. Said it was only Father Ewan who'd kept her sane.'

'That's another strange thing. She told me several times she had no time for God, so it's weird she had such a strong bond with a priest – especially one as sanctified as *Crucifix Man*.'

'He was essentially her grief counsellor, Andrew. Her harbour in a storm. His fame and following are just things that have grown up around him.'

'Well, I still think it's very odd. In fact, I think the whole set up was very odd. I mean, look at that wedding photograph over there. A lovely young girl on the arm of an old gargoyle. A fabulously rich old gargoyle, though.'

'She was no gold-digger,' said Sally. 'She idolised Toby. It was a real love match.'

Andrew shrugged. 'Oh, well. If you say so. She certainly led a very plain and sober widowhood, so you might be right.'

Together they drew back the bedding and stripped the skeletal body of its slinky, satin nightgown. The body that in health had defied time's march, and in illness had scorned the practical comfort of winceyette and long sleeves. Then the ritual performed. A perfunctory obligation carried out in a respectful silence.

With duties done they pulled up the lace counterpane to shroud the body. Sally's hands then dropped to her sides and she adopted a frozen attitude of her head. The fingers of one hand flexed, and the other tightened into a fist. She pressed her lips firmly together, sniffed loudly, and turned away. Dr Gibson smiled sympathetically. 'It's so difficult sometimes not to get personally involved, isn't it?'

Sally grabbed her coat and rushed from the room, scrambling for her car keys.

Chapter 5

Timothy's legs felt weak as he moved down the galleried landing and entered his own bedroom. Crossing to the window, he stood to look over the vast expanse of The Manor House gardens, where, in failing light, the ancient hardwoods showed their first flush of new season's growth. Clumps of daffodils nodded their bold yellow trumpets, catkins hung on the walnut tree, and a prowling cat (or was it a fox?) slithered furtively into the rhododendrons. In the gloaming, the lampposts that edged the long, curving drive were already lit, casting wide arcs of bright light over the lawn. His father had always called them the sentries; stationed to stand guard over the Proudfoots, but now Timothy stood gripped with fear. He shut his eyes. The bliss of hot June sunshine. The gentle lap-lap of the water. Roger's gaze and Gioconda smile. Loud, happy laughter. The boat's lurch. The muffled sound of a splash. Then silence. A child's arm held erect, as if waving. Waving, not drowning.

Turning slowly, he stared at two photographs on his bedside table. One of Lord Justice Proudfoot, studio posed in classic monochrome, his pickled-walnut face sombre beneath the curly sheep's ears of his wig. A wild Irish Celt of a man. A funny, talkative, extravagantly affectionate man, with a phlegmy cigar-smoker's voice and raucous laugh. The other, in faded Kodak colour, was a full-length shot of his parents' on their wedding day in the early autumn of 1965; their faces gazing besottedly at each other. His beautiful mother, then only a girl of twenty-one, but a joyful bride linking the arm of her bearded, paunchy groom, already approaching fifty. Her tailored Chanel suit, and pillbox hat, reflected sophistication, but her face shone with youthful vitality. How strange she looked with her hair a warm shade of auburn, and cut in a short, pixie-like style of the times. So different from her familiar golden-blonde waterfall. Timothy lifted the photograph and ran his forefinger over his mother's sleek pencil skirt. There was no sign of swelling, but he knew the kicking foetus of Timothy Tobias Proudfoot lay within; a proud parading of his parents' love and passion for each other. Timothy bit his knuckles. How much he'd been a part of their unity. One third of the perfect triangle; one strand of the perfect plait. And how apt that she'd chosen *'Twilight Time'* to be her exit music. As a child, when he'd snuggled down in bed, and she'd turned out the light, she would kiss him goodnight and move slowly out of the room, singing the familiar words, *'Heavenly shades of night are falling, it's Twilight Time'*.

Driven by an unknown force, he fell on his knees. 'Dear God, please make sure Mumma goes to Heaven. She was perfect, God. A truly perfect person, without flaw or sin of any kind. You must know of my own sins, God, but I accept all my guilt, and I deserve your punishment, but I beg your forgiveness.'

He had no idea how long he'd knelt in contemplation, but he was alerted by the slam of Sally's car door, followed shortly by the slow crunch of Andrew Gibson's heavy frame on the gravelled drive. He picked up his phone. 'Time to come, Rog. Please hurry.'

He then crossed himself and made another call. 'Father Ewan. . .'

Chapter 6

Sally slammed her foot down on the accelerator and careered recklessly out of Monks Bottom Manor. Without warning, heavy rain began to fall, and the high beam of the headlights illuminated a sheet of glassy shards. With rare aggression she flicked the windscreen wipers to fast speed and they sprang into action; swiping and parting the deluge as a parody of her own bitter rage. She knew that Timothy had left the room to phone Roger. Why not? It was the final scene in the mummer's play of silence they were all enacting.

How many crouching birds in the dry shelter of the beech hedges observed the hurtling silver Mini, seemingly intent on suicide? But it wasn't death she sought. Just a desperation to get home and plead her final case. To beg a change of mind and heart, no matter how much groveling and humiliation it cost. But as she turned into the drive of The Dower House, her bold power-surge collapsed. There would be no dramatic scene. Roger's car had already gone.

She ran through the teeming rain to the front door, waiting for Finnegan to perform his usual manic leaps of welcome, but as she turned the key in the lock there were no deep woofs, and no skidding scrapes on the floorboards. The house was holding itself in a dark, silent vacuum. She switched on the lights and walked through to the kitchen to see a note on the table; just a hurried note, written on the back of a junk-mail envelope that had announced an unmissable credit card deal.

Sally. Gone straight over to be with Tim. He needs me. I'll come back and collect my things tomorrow. I've taken Finnegan. I know we agreed he'd stay with you, but he knew I was going, and he looked at me so sadly I just couldn't bear to leave him behind. Speak soon, Love, Rog

She stared at the note. Just this? Only this? He'd gone, and Finnegan too had gone, when all she wanted was to wrap her arms around his big doggy body and seek his warm, uncritical devotion. The network of strings around her mouth tightened, and her eyes stung, but an inner voice screamed at her not to indulge in self-pity.

She walked upstairs and sat down heavily on the king-size. The bed bought in the 2005 January sales by a jovial couple who'd agreed their old one was worn out. Worn out by years of regular coupling, and the twists and turns of sleep. Three months later, finding out that for most of it she'd been sharing her husband's body and affections with Tim Proudfoot.

She'd been spring-cleaning the windows and paintwork in Roger's study. Stepping back, she'd carelessly kicked over a bucket of soapy water, followed by a panic of trying to save a large Numdah rug. Crawling to mop up beneath the narrow confines of his desk she hit her sweaty head on a firmly taped, padded envelope. A hidden video! She smiled. In fact, she nearly laughed out loud. Oh, well. Roger was no different from the average man. She just had to take a look. Porn wouldn't shock a nurse. Might even do her some good.

Tim was lying naked on a giant-size brass bed, his eyes wide open, and his beautiful, neo-classical face set with an actor's pose of wickedness. With knees drawn up, he displayed a slow self-stimulation, whilst looking at the camera with complicity. Then Roger's large hairy body lumbered into view, like an ungainly brown bear, to wave a female satin thong at the camera.

Gradually, they slithered and entwined, like two netsuke wrestlers, to begin the deft manoeuvres of time-served lovers. After many skilful delays the moment was loudly agreed. Roger thrust with the sound effects of a sworded bull, while Timothy, with the thong gripped firmly between his teeth, bleated like a lamb.

Roger's sobbing admission revealed that a passionate affair had begun long before he'd met Sally. Terminated the year before they'd married, and re-kindled when Louise was four.

'Who took the video, Roger? You must know it's a criminal offence.'

'I set it up on a tripod. No one else was there. I swear to you, Sally, there's not another single soul who knows.'

'Don't be stupid. Marina's not deaf, dumb and blind.'

'We're very careful. We only show our affection, or make love, when she's away. Honestly. Tim's neurotic she doesn't find out. You know how special their relationship is. Even I have to take second place a lot of the time.'

'Oh, poor you! I actually thought our relationship was quite special too.'

'It is, Sally. It still is and always will be. You're my wife, and I love you. I really do love you, but I can't help the way I am.'

'The way you are horrifies me.'

'I can't help it. Tim's an obsession.'

Sally had turned away, crying softly, but Roger came up behind her and gently touched her shoulders. 'Are you going to throw me out, Sal?'

She'd shaken him off, and rounded angrily. 'No. In fact, I forbid you to go. Louise is *fifteen*, Roger. How can she cope with a gay father!'

'Will you still share a bedroom with me?'

'Of course. But that's all I'll be sharing with you.'

'Have you stopped loving me?'

'No. That's the most miserable thing about all this. I do still love you, but right now, I hate you. How many Monks Bottom wives have to have HIV tests?'

'There's no need.'

'Why should I believe you?'

Memories of that brutal encounter now forced Sally's tears to break through. Rising from the bed she kicked the carpet, realising that the whole sordid story would now hit the village fan. OK. She would have to admit defeat, but it wouldn't be a pathetic tail turning and creeping away like a kicked cat. A feline anger she didn't know she had, drew her claws. 'So, Roger dearest,' she thought. 'You'll be back for your things tomorrow, will you? Well, great expectations, lovely. I'm off to pastures new. All you'll find is a pile of ash and an empty house.'

Chapter 7

Ewan returned from his waterside walk, removed his boots and hung up his cloak. He entered his sitting room, and as he moved to warm his hands at the slumbering log fire, his mobile phone sang out its silly, demanding jingle. He grabbed it, and threw it to his ear, his voice so tight he could hardly force a response. Timothy's statement was short, with no preamble of greeting. 'Father Ewan, my beloved mother has just passed away.'

The term used in the grief counselling profession is anticipatory death; something widely thought of as a buffer to the pain. Not true. Ewan shook. Invisible hands clutched his limbs and poked alien fingers into his flesh. The space behind his ribs turned to a block of ice that dropped to his bowels, and the room blurred. With a steely effort he compelled himself to full concentration, determined to absorb the sounds and senses of the moment. Lucifer, his cat, mewed loudly at his feet, the old station clock ticked with enhanced resonance, and the fire crackled. She'd made perfect, nut-brown toast for him at that fire, sitting cross-legged like a schoolgirl, and holding forth the slices with a long brass fork. Then, with thick butter and lashings of her home-made damson jam, they'd devoured the whole loaf.

Forcing himself back to the moment he mustered up his usual polite, priestly script; a kind and soothing tome that threw in God's good grace and eternal love. 'Timothy,' he concluded. 'Please be assured that I'm here for you, at any time of the day or night, should you feel the need to talk. That's not just an empty promise. I really mean it.'

'Thank you, Father,' Timothy replied graciously, 'and thank you for everything you did for my Mother. Her life was wholly enriched by your wisdom and support.'

'She was a brave and gracious lady. I shall mourn her passing intensely.'

'Father Ewan, were you planning to attend her cremation? I know she asked you to bless Morgana's old handbag and to make sure it went with her.'

'I most certainly will attend, and carry out all her wishes.'

'Thank you, Father. I'll contact you in the fullness of time.'

'Goodnight, Timothy, and God bless you.'

'Goodnight, Father Ewan.'

Momentarily Ewan swayed. After pouring himself a slug of neat whisky, he stumbled over to his American rocking chair and howled, unashamedly, like a wolf. He raised the glass, swallowed hard, and rocked gently back and forth. What exactly had she done to him in that chair on that hot September afternoon so many years ago? Seduced him? Torn up his vow of celibacy? Stolen his virginity? No. It had all been complicity. He'd beamed his message as brightly as the Southwold lighthouse, and she'd answered. For what must have been the hundredth time, he opened Marina's last letter to read again her rare, written words:

4*th* March 2008

My adored Ewan,

It's a sunny, frost-sharp afternoon and although Andrew Gibson has insisted on bed rest, I continue to defy him. Instead I'm here in the drawing room, sitting by a slumbering fire, and looking out over the beauty of The Manor grounds. At my feet Anthea is curled up on the hearthrug in a comatose feline bliss - no doubt Lucifer is doing the same. At the bottom of the long lawn I can see the swans gliding serenely on the lake. Hundreds of daffodils are in tight bud, and the tops of the bare oaks are bent low by a vicious wind. How lucky I am to be spending my dying days in such luxury, but what would I give to throw myself on the wings of that wind and be transported to your arms? Today Tim has driven up to the Cotswolds to pick up a dozen Garrya Elliptica trees to plant as my final memoir. Dear old Cora has just left, so with a rare afternoon alone, it's a perfect time to write to you. Not only to write to you, but to start a painful journey I've decided to make to the inside of myself.

These written words must surely be my last to you as my hands are getting weak. Speech too is becoming difficult, and soon the time will come when we can no longer talk on the phone. I'm slowly being completely removed from you. I've never written to you before to tell you how much I love you, but please allow me to do so now. Ewan, I love you, but there are no words that can do justice to its width and depth. My love for you is without parameters. Not only have you given me so much love in return, you've given me your beautiful young body and have never rejected me, despite the tick of the clock.

The purpose of this letter is simple. Throughout the years you've patiently put up with my manic changes of mood, and given free rein to my selfish behaviour. You tried so gently to decipher my mind, but I was tiresome and flippant. Can I tell you why? Ewan, everything you know of me is one long con trick, but now that I'm poised for the final retreat I can't go to my grave (urn, actually) withholding the deception. At last I feel strong enough to apply your wise, unique therapy.

When I'm gone you've promised to bless Morgana's old bag, and to make sure it's burnt with me. Before you do, you'll find something inside it to read. My confession. My story. Why now, you may ask? The answer is that it's only now, when I don't have to look you in the eye, that I can do it. You may find yourself reading muddled ramblings because I haven't started yet, and I don't know how it's going to come out. All I know is that I've not much time left and I won't waste words.

I love you, Ewan. 'Til we meet again, and I hope we will. (No - that's not really a change of heart, but it's something I want to believe in today.)

Marina

Clumsily he returned the letter to its worn envelope, unable to concentrate on her strange talk of confession. She was gone, and in terms of life itself, he too, might as well be gone. The irony was almost laughable. Who could give bereavement counselling to a sinning priest and fellow counsellor? His only choice, apart from drinking from the poisoned chalice, was to apply his own tough methods to survive.

The McEwan School of Grief Therapy was based on a simple text:

> *Grieving is an arduous journey to find peace, and the stages are thus: disbelief, pain, anger, healing and acceptance. Your journey will be one of perseverance and fortitude, and can only be achieved through discovering your identity. To know yourself is to understand yourself, and memory is the only key. To go back in time, to the beginning of your life, and work forward in strict narrative order.*
>
> *It's like a route march that has to be endured, but there are no points or penalties. Remember the allegory of the tortoise and the hare. Gradually, as you begin to find yourself, acceptance will overcome you. Days will become weeks, weeks will become months, and months will become years. The threads of normal life will be picked up, and slowly plaited together, until a seamless time comes. Your grief at last becomes painless, but your memories remain, forever after, as an indelible, golden time.*

His consulting room was a bright, warm conversion of the Abbey's Chapter House, and although an intrinsically religious setting, it held no depictions of apostles, virgins, lambs or infant kings – the early Cistercians believing that artistry and ornamentation distracted the mind from duty and devotion. Therapist and patient faced each other at a seated distance of exactly six feet, and his initial session ran for two hours. Whilst seeming brutally long, his skill was such that the anxious interviewee always emerged feeling as if time had suddenly run out.

Marina Proudfoot had been the worst failure of his career. In their first session he'd stilted through thirty minutes of her bland expression, and monotone replies, before asking her if she wanted to stop. She shook her head and turned away to avoid his questioning face. . . But this sort of remembering her was a nonsense. He couldn't dwell on individual episodes of their relationship. For God's sake,

Ewan, stick to the script. '*To go back in time, to the beginning of your life, and work forward in strict narrative order*'.

Thus, he closed his eyes and fought to cross the Rubicon.

Every night, in the blind black hours, he crept into the darkest corners of his childhood and dredged up the memories. Fragmented and detached, they barged their way into his senses like the poorly tuned crackle of a cheap radio. A limping nun and a hump-backed priest. Mr Toad, who knew how to talk big. A damp, basement room in a place called Jericho. The whistle and steam of a train journey. But these were just the ephemera of a confused mind. It was the big one that assured his insomnia. The boomp-boomp of a body bouncing down the stairs was no invention?

In confusion he would lie there, sweating and turning, assuring himself that in the morning he'd take that quantum leap to further knowledge, but knowing that in daylight he'd be too cowardly to pursue it. Perhaps, as the years had passed, he'd embroidered the scenes with the threads and stitches of fancy, but whatever the memories were, he knew them to be true.

JANUARY 1965

His name was Patrick. Patrick O'Dowd. His Mammy said that now he was five, it was time for him to go to school. The nuns said he wasn't allowed to go to the school in Jericho, so he had to go St Clement's on the bus. 'It's a bloody long way,' Mammy said, 'but if we don't behave ourselves, that's my poxy job and their shitty old food vouchers down the pan. It's a real pain in the neck.' He thought it must have been the cold wind at the bus stop that gave Mammy the pain in the neck.

When they got to the school they had to wait a long time in a freezing corridor before a limping nun appeared, hobbling towards them like an injured black crow. Mammy bobbed, and touched her titties. 'Good morning, Sister Evangelica.'

'Take his mac off, Miss O' Dowd, and hang it over there,' the black crow snapped. Mammy took off his gabardine raincoat, but then the old hag picked up his pullover at the shoulder, and hauled him up on his toes. 'And what, pray tell me, do you call this item of filth?'

'They gave it to me at Notre Dame,' Mammy said, whirling her head so sharply her thick, silver-blonde hair flew round her shoulders like the flop of a mop. 'It was spanking clean on this morning, same as all his clothes. Can I help it if he spilt his Farex and I didn't notice?'

'In the name of our sainted lady, Farex is baby food.'

'Well, Patrick likes it,' said Mammy. And he did like it. Mammy made it with evaporated milk, and she put a big dollop of golden syrup in the middle. He swirled it round and round with a pudding spoon, and drank it off the plate.

'Miss O'Dowd, five-year-old boys don't eat Farex.'

'Well, this one does, and I'll thank you to call me Mrs O'Dowd.'

'Oh, to be sure you are, and I'm Princess Margaret. Now off you go to your work. We'll expect you to be standing outside at half past three, and don't be a minute past. We've more to do than entertain your son after the bell.'

Mammy kissed him, and hugged him tight, and told him to be a good boy. He didn't feel like crying so he couldn't understand why he did. 'Don't cry, my lovely,' said Mammy, 'or you'll start me off, and I can't go to work with two big red eyes, can I?' She looked at her watch and gasped. 'Heavens, look at the time. I can't be late. Don't worry. It'll all be fine, and home time will be here in a flash.' She ran down the corridor clicking her high heels.

When she'd gone the old nun grabbed him again, holding onto his wrist with two white, bony fingers, and led him up the corridor to a classroom. Nun's skin was always white, and waxy, and papery thin. Mammy said it was because the priests sucked all their blood out of them. 'This is a new boy,' Evangelica said to the class. 'Patrick O'Dowd. Not only is he wearing a filthy jumper, but it's grey. Now what colour are our jumpers supposed to be, just in case Patrick hasn't noticed?'

'Green,' shouted the class, all happy and beaming in their clean, green jumpers.

The teacher was an old priest with a humpty-back called Father Ignatius, and he showed him to a seat at the back of the class. 'There you go, son,' he said. 'You sit by Brendan and Sheila, and it doesn't matter a tiddlers what colour your woolly is.'

Halfway through the morning the tinny clang of a brass hand-bell rang out, and Evangelica re-appeared. 'Get your coat on, child,' she ordered. 'Go out and get some colour into that pasty face.' He followed the other children to the playground where Father Ignatius was handing out little bottles of milk, but he was jostled to the back of the queue by a gang of hard-faced boys, and by the time he got to the front, there were none left. Nobody asked him to play. Sheila called him specky-four-eyes, and said he smelled of piddle. Brendan said he was evil and ugly, because his top lip was slanty and scarred, and if anyone looked at him they would be struck dumb and die.

At dinnertime the serving ladies in the canteen were huffy, and said he couldn't have anything to eat because they didn't know he was coming, and in any case, his mother hadn't paid. 'This is Patrick O'Dowd,' said Evangelica in very loud voice. 'He gets free dinners because his Mammy's a right good for nothing. Isn't it obvious she never feeds him? I've seen more meat on a butcher's pencil, so you'd better find him something in case he faints.' They found him some cold carrots and gravy, and some soggy rice pudding with loads of skin.

Just before home time he sat with his head on his hands, dreaming dreams, while Father Ignatius read a story called *The Wind in the Willows*. The words were lovely, and he was swept up by the adventures of Ratty, and Moley and the Badger. He laughed at the doings of Mr Toad, and wished he was brave enough to talk big. Father Ignatius was nice. He looked as old as God and his nose dripped. He wore one normal boot, and one boot with a big sole, but he didn't limp as badly as Evangelica. 'If it's not too icy tomorrow,' he said, 'we'll go over to Angel Meadow. I'll take you all along the backwater, and through the rushes tall, and we'll try to find a real water rat in the river.'

When home time came ice-cold rain was spitting, and Mammy was outside, stamping her feet and drawing her coat collar up over her face. Evangelica called out to her, 'I think a pair of fur-lined boots would serve you better than those silly shoes in this weather, Miss O'Dowd, though why I care escapes me.' She handed over a brown paper carrier bag. When they were on the bus Mammy took out a pair of clumsy, fur-lined ankle boots, with thick rubber soles, and brass zips up the middle. 'If she thinks I'm wearing those hideous things she's got another think coming,' she said, putting her tongue out and making a face. 'See me clumping around like some old granny. They'd think I was doing a Father Ignatius!' Mammy burst out laughing. He laughed too. Then Mammy flung her arms around him, and pulled him onto her knee, and they laughed and laughed. . .

The second day he remembered was the day his Gran went off her head. Gran lived in Circus Street, and they used to go to see her on Tuesdays. Mammy always said, 'We're going to be very busy today, darlin', and I think we'll give that old school a miss. We'll go up to Gran's and see if we can wheedle a sub out of the old bag.' Sometimes the Nuns came knocking on the door, looking for him. 'Patrick's been ill today,' said Mammy. 'Terrible tummy pains.'

'You're a liar, Molly O'Dowd,' they said. 'You'll rot in hell, you wicked girl.'

Every time they went to Gran's there was a quarrel. Gran called Mammy 'a scrubber' once, and they had a fight. A real fight. They were always fighting like boys do, but it was true. Mammy *was* a scrubber. She went to the Convent of Notre Dame on the Woodstock Road every morning, and she'd get a tin bucket of hot soapy water and a brush. She tied some cloths around her knees and spent all morning scrubbing the floors. On Fridays she got some money in a small brown envelope. 'Old cows,' said Mammy. 'All week with my hands in suds for a piggin' pittance.' Sometimes they gave her a bag of clothes for 'the boy.' 'They can stuff their hand-me-downs up their tight arses,' she said, but he always ended up wearing the clothes.

On the day they went to Gran's for the last time, Mammy sat down at the kitchen table. It was a cold, quarry-tiled kitchen that smelled of gas and Jeyes fluid. She took out a mirror from her bag, and started to powder her nose, but Gran came up behind her, and shoved her shoulder, and called her a vain little tart. The mirror flew out of Mammy's hand, crashed down on the quarry tiles, and smashed into a thousand pieces. 'There! That's seven years bad luck you've given me now,' she yelled.

'You make your own bad luck, Molly,' Gran said, pointing a finger. 'That little bastard, for instance. Pity you don't know the difference between a lucky black cat and a randy Tom, and even more of a pity you couldn't finish off his face properly. Hares only cross the path of the wicked.'

Mammy suddenly jumped up with tears running down her face. She made a lunge at Gran, and screamed so loudly his ears hurt. 'I'll kill you,' she yelled. 'I swear to God I'll kill you. How dare you belittle him? He's a beautiful child. Isn't his life going to be tough enough without you rubbing salt in the bloody wound?'

It all happened so fast. Mammy picked up a saucepan and tried to hit Gran over the head. Gran ran up the stairs, and Mammy ran after her. They started struggling with each other on the landing, snapping and snarling like two dogs in the street, but he wasn't afraid. It had happened so many times before he thought it was quite exciting. But then Mammy's foot and Gran's foot got all muddled up. Gran toppled over and came tumbling down. Boomp-boomp-boomp.

Mammy flew down the stairs two at a time, but at the bottom she had to jump over Gran. 'Come on,' she yelled. 'We're off.' She grabbed her bags, and pushed him by the shoulder through the front door. She slammed it so hard behind her the windows wobbled, and then she turned round and shouted through the letter box, 'Don't expect me back this side of Christmas, you vicious old bitch.'

Mr Bradshaw next door was sweeping his path, but he stopped and his mouth hung open. 'Blimey!' he said. On the other side Miss Primandproper was polishing her doorstep and she jerked up sharply.

'Fishwife,' she hissed. 'Now I've heard it all. That really takes the biscuit.'

'You buggers can both shut your faces,' bawled Mammy.

She then shoved him out into the street so hard he fell over on the pavement. 'Oh, for God's sake, child, get up!' she yelled, and marched down the road talking to herself. She went so fast he had to run to keep up with her.

'What's the matter with Gran, Mammy?' he asked.

'She's off her head, darlin'. Completely and utterly off her head, and that's the God's honest truth.'

When they got home Mammy said. 'Well, we didn't get our sub after all, did we, so it'll have to be fishcakes and spaghetti again.' He didn't mind at all because it was his favourite tea. She then got out his colouring book and crayons. 'Would you like to do some colouring in now, sweetheart?'

'Please, can we have *The Wind in the Willows* first?' he asked. He'd become such a good reader he could read nearly every word himself, but it was much nicer to sit on Mammy's lap and listen. She said the words just like she was a *really, really* posh lady off the wireless, and she made it all so exciting.

'... 'The Rat, much excited, kept close to his heels as the Mole, with something of the air of a sleep-walker, crossed a dry ditch, scrambled through a hedge, and nosed his way over a field, open and trackless and bare, in the faint starlight. Suddenly, without warning, he dived; but the Rat was on the alert and promptly followed him down the tunnel to which his unerring nose had faithfully led him to. It was close and airless, and the earthy smell was strong...'

'Oh, darlin',' Mammy sighed. 'Mole's house sounds a bit like this place. A damp dump in the bowels of the earth. How I wish we could close our eyes and be whisked away out of it.'

'Toad Hall!' he said, sitting bolt upright on her knee, flushed and smiling with excitement. 'One day we might live at Toad Hall.'

'Do you know what I'd like, lovely?' she replied. 'I'd like a great big house in the country, with a whopping great garden, where you could go out to play, and you could run, and run, and run, until you were so puffed out you couldn't run any more, and when you stopped to get your breath, you still wouldn't be able to see the end of the garden. Fat chance of that happening because your Mammy's a fool.' She sighed again. 'Oh, Patrick, your Daddy could have been so many things. A Texas millionaire, or an English Lord, or an Indian Prince. Why did he have to be a fishporter from the Covered Market?'

He'd heard this story so many times, but he couldn't understand it. His Daddy didn't go to America and make a lot of money, he failed to become a member of the Royal family, and he didn't change the colour of his skin and wear a turban, so why, if he had so many other choices, did he hump fish?

'Miss Primandproper called you a fishwife today,' he said. 'Perhaps she knew my Daddy,' but then there was a hard knock on the door. It was a man wearing a belted raincoat and a trilby hat. On either side of him stood two big policemen with serious faces, poking their tongues through their lips.

'Miss O'Dowd,' said the man. 'I'm Chief Inspector Butler. I've some very grave news. Your Mother's been found dead at the foot of the stairs. Her neighbours, Mr Bradshaw and Miss Lamb, said there was some sort of domestic incident this morning, involving yourself. Could we possibly have a little chat?' One of the policemen took the puzzled little boy out of the room to sit at the bottom of the stairs, and after a while Inspector Butler came out to talk to him, on his own. 'How old are you Patrick?'

'Five.'

'It's sad about your Gran dying, isn't it?' He nodded. 'You saw her this morning, didn't you?' He nodded again. 'You and your Mammy were probably the last people to see her alive. Now Patrick, do you know what happens to people who don't tell the truth?'

'They rot in hell.'

'That's right. But you're only a little boy. Little boys don't go to hell. Do you know what happens to them?'

'No, I don't know.'

'The nuns eat them for their tea. Now I don't want anything horrible to happen to you. I want you to grow up to be a big boy. So tell me the truth, Patrick. What was your Gran doing the last time you saw her?'

Mammy appeared in the doorway. She was crying. Her head was wobbling, and she was twisting a hanky in her hands. She was looking really frightened so he knew he had to tell the God's honest truth. If he didn't, he would be eaten by the nuns. 'She was completely and utterly off her head,' he said.

Mammy then told him he was going away for a holiday. 'It won't be for long,' she said. 'Just until I get things sorted out.'

'Where am I going, Mammy?'

'Somewhere lovely. There'll be other boys and girls there, and you'll have lots of fun. Father Ignatius is coming over to get you.'

'Will it only be for a little while?'

'Just a holiday, my lovely.'

'Why are you crying, Mammy?'

'I'm not. I've got something in my eye. Now you've to be a very good boy.'

Mammy packed his bag and Father Ignatius came to collect him. She said she had to give an extra big kiss and cuddle to her very grown-up boy who was going on a holiday. 'Here,' she said. 'You can take your colouring book, and when you get back home you can show me what you've done. And make sure you take care of your glasses. You don't want to go over the edges, do you?'

He couldn't remember the holiday, but he remembered two nuns taking him to a noisy train station and meeting two jolly, smiling people on the platform. He'd met them lots of times before, and they were called Mrs and Mrs McEwan. They'd taken him to the London Zoo, to see Guy the gorilla, and to a teashop called Lyons Corner House, where he had a big ice cream called a Knickerbocker glory. They spoke with gentle Scottish voices, and they were very nice. The nuns said he could now call them Mummy and Daddy. Mummy McEwan kissed his cheek and Daddy McEwan ruffled his hair. They told him that his name was now Ewan McEwan, and wasn't Ewan a really nice name, and a much nicer name than Patrick?

'Well, goodbye, Ewan,' the nuns said as he got on the train. 'Make sure you're a good boy, and say your prayers, and look after that new puppy that's coming for you.'

The train wheezed and whistled when it moved off, and Mummy McEwan lifted him up to sit beside her on the seat. 'It's going to be a long journey,' she said, 'so I've brought you a book to help pass the time. I've been told you can read very well.' He'd soon finished the book, and he said that although he was very fond of Rupert Bear and all his friends, he would much rather read *The Wind in the Willows*. 'Well, we've a child prodigy here all right, Duncan,' she said.

'I'm not prodigy,' he said. 'Sister Evangelica said I was so skinny she'd seen more meat on a butcher's pencil, and my Gran said I was belittle.'

'Then we better get cracking and fatten you up,' Daddy McEwan said. 'Look, we've bloater paste sandwiches, a fine pork pie, a Battenberg cake, and a flask of hot tea. Tuck in, laddie.'

At the end of the journey there was a lot of noise and clatter, but when they got off the train, and the whistle blew, and the last carriage had disappeared out of sight, there was a perfect stillness on the platform. He could hear a blackbird singing, and someone whistling, and in the background was the hum of a tractor. 'This place is called Woodbridge,' Mummy said. 'Your Daddy is to be the head of the English department at a school near here called Waldringhythe Abbey. We've a lovely house to move in to, and it's near the seaside. That'll be fun, won't it? And here's another thing that's going to be alot of fun...' A station porter was walking towards them with a basket.

'One puppy, madam. One rather damp puppy, madam.'

'He's for you, Ewan,' said Mummy. 'He's your very own doggy, and you can choose his name.'

He thought carefully. 'Iggy-Piggy,' he said. 'It's what my Mammy called Father Ignatius.'

A smiling, waving priest then appeared to meet them, and there was a flurry of handshaking and words of welcome. 'You must be Ewan', the priest said to him. 'I'm Father Paulinus. My, that's a fine pup you've got there. I can just see him racing up the banks of the Deben.'

They got into a big black car called a Humber Hawk, and the soft, warm puppy scrambled up over his chest and shoulders and licked his face.

No one knew he remembered any of it, because he knew no one wanted him to.

Chapter 8

Timothy sat at the top of The Manor's wide, sweeping staircase, holding the flopped, purring body of Anthea, his mother's cherished Persian cat. Although he'd heard no ringing, the ansaphone downstairs began to broadcast the strident tones of Cora Feather, the daily help, who grandly referred to herself as the housekeeper. Clearly, her intention was to leave a message of condolence, and to offer the usual, 'Is there anything I can do?' but her courage failed when faced with the vexation of a recording facility. She rang off mumbling.

As Timothy waited he began, with something of a sense of failure, to wonder why his mother's death hadn't induced the dramatic flood of tears and hysteria he'd anticipated. His only sensation was of a breath-holding suspension from time, and a conviction that her last words, 'Hat trick', were some sort of celestial link to heaven and the afterlife.

At last he heard the low, regular hum of the Mercedes Estate and leaped to the landing window. It was raining heavily. He watched Roger park in front of the columned portico, haul himself out of the car, and reach inside to the back seat. He emerged holding a small bunch of flowers, a razor pouch, and a duvet. Why a duvet? But when he lifted the tailgate the answer leapt out. Finnegan! He'd said nothing about custody of the dog! The agile Wolfhound sniffed the sodden air, twisted his huge, hairy body, and barked with brainless pleasure.

Timothy crashed down the stairs, threw open the heavy oak front door, and ran out with his arms wide open. 'Skipper!'

'Angel,' Roger gasped, but any tender scenes of sympathy, and their first kiss as outed lovers, was foiled by Roger's arms being full of things, the teeming rain, and the chaos of a neurotic dog inspecting his new quarters. Finnegan rushed ahead into the house, leaping like a

29

springbok, and splodging his wet, muddy paws all over the cream Wilton. However, in the muddle of the moment, they both failed to notice that a terrified Persian cat had been hounded out into the black hole of the night.

'I passed Cora Feather by *The Dog and Duck*,' Roger said. 'She was in full flight on her way up to poke her nose in, but I steered her off. Firmly said I was coming up to take control.'

'Thanks. She means well, but I only want you tonight.'

'Well, for better or worse, you've got me for every night now.'

Moving into the house, and with all arms free, they kissed gently to reflect the sadness of the occasion. This moment was the watershed point; the moment they'd long planned: all conventional ties severed, and their lives united. 'I can't cry, Skipper,' Timothy sniffed. 'Tears won't come.'

'They will, honey-pie, they will,' Roger assured him, 'and when they do, I'll lick up every one. Now, let's go down to the kitchen and I'll get you something to eat.'

'I'm not hungry.'

'Nonsense. You've got to keep your strength up.'

Roger, preceded by Finnegan, steered Timothy down the long corridor to the kitchen, and guided him to a seat at the table. After directing Finnegan to lie down in front of the Aga, he banged about in the larder and the fridge, only to discover there was actually very little to prepare. All he could find was half a packet of Cream Crackers, a chunk of old Cheddar, a plastic bag of tired salad and some super-market bottles of wine. 'Can't find much,' he said. 'Shame. I'm actually quite hungry.'

Roger realised that he was, indeed, ravenously hungry, having had nothing since a bowl of Weetabix just after dawn. Lunch had been spent at *The Groucho* with a famous geriatric comedienne, supposedly to plan the publicity for her ghost-written autobiography, but no one had warned him she was an alcoholic. The session had turned into a long, foodless piss-up, culminating with the funny lady slipping slowly under the table, and having to be carried in his arms to a taxi. Dozily inebriated himself, he'd sobered up on the train, but he now had a gnawing desperation for food. 'Is this *really* all there is?' he said plain-tively, his disappointment a little too obvious.

'What do you mean, "Is this really all there is?"' Timothy answered. 'I haven't exactly had time to go to Sainsbury's this week, have I?'

'Well, how about I ring for a pizza then?'

'Oh, Rog, please! Mumma only died five minutes ago. How can I scoff a pizza?'

'Sorry, old chap. Didn't mean to sound gung-ho. Cheese and biscuits'll do nicely.'

Roger sat down to eat, but Timothy's face had set in hard, sulky lines. By way of appeasement Roger offered sympathetic facial expressions and hand-patting, but nothing raised a flicker of response. Undaunted, Roger polished off the meagre left-overs, and poured out two glasses of a cheap Chardonnay. 'Come on,' he said, 'get this down you. Please, Angel. A little toast. To us and our new lives.'

But as Timothy sipped, the long-awaited tears arrived. He gave in to grief, got up and eased himself onto Roger's lap, not quite knowing what sort of comfort he was seeking. 'Skipper, you know I don't believe in God, don't you?'

'Absolutely.'

'Well, Mumma's last words were really odd. She said 'Hat trick'. You know – like in cricket. I know this sounds crazy, but I'm sure it was a sign she *knew* she was going to the Kingdom of Heaven to join Pa and Morgana. Like she was the last of the three of them. Seconds later, she was gone. It's really spooked me. I spoke to Father Ewan earlier on and he said he 'was there' for me if I needed to talk. I think perhaps I'll phone him in the morning, to talk things through.'

'Not a good idea. Far too drastic. The last thing we want is that Creeping Jesus poking his oar in.'

'But he's a good, wise man, Rog. He gave Mumma great strength in her life.'

'Look, things'll seem much better after a good night's sleep. You've got me now and I'm all you're ever going to need.'

'Oh, I do hope so. You are here forever, aren't you? No going back?'

'Nope. Honest Injun. It's all sorted with Sally and my moccasins are coming tomorrow.' He picked up Timothy's hand and ran his tongue over his palm. 'Now, why don't we go to bed? I think a nice early night's just what the doctor ordered.'

Ten minutes later Roger was laid flat on his back in the dark, his head on the pillow, and his eyes wide open. Timothy was lying beside him, screwed up in the foetal position, rocking with prolonged sobbing, and mumbling incoherently about the existence of God.

Chapter 9

Sally was grateful when Father Ewan's recorded message facility clicked in. 'Father, this is Sally Fuller. I'm sure Timothy will have already phoned you with the inevitable, sad news. I'd like to confirm I'll be arriving at Waldringhythe before lunchtime tomorrow.'

She replaced the receiver. Now it was time, and like an Olympic weightlifter she grew, both mentally and physically, to steel herself. With the resolve of a Samurai she armed herself with a roll of black bin liners, went up to the bedroom, and gathered up every piece of Roger's clothing. Minutes later she dropped a dozen full bags out of the window, to land with muffled thumps on the stone terrace below.

The room now echoed with a tangible emptiness, but in her heart she felt another sort – the emotional emptiness of the lonely, only child of parents whose marriage had been no less a sham than her own. In those days she'd used attention-seeking histrionics to express her frustration, but that had been a complete waste of time. Her mother's poker-faced retort was always the same: 'Sally! Behave! Stop making an exhibition of yourself. What will people think?'

She entered the garden wearing a padded jacket, and the fleecy balaclava she wore to walk Finnegan on cold mornings. It had stopped raining, and although the ground was sodden, the sky was now clear and pinpricked by starlight. She formed a high pile of Roger's effects in the middle of the lawn, and found a can of paraffin in the garage. Sprinkle, sprinkle. A thrown match, and a *woomph* that nearly threw her off her feet. But she was elated by the danger.

Having endured years of centrally heated desiccation, the clothes were tinder dry, and a sudden wall of licking, yellow tongues forced her to stand back. The destruction was exciting. The cotton items quickly disappeared, the woollens slowly singed, the man-made fibres melted into a bubbling, gloopy mess.

The life of the fire was far too brief. She took a hoe, hooked and pushed a few remainders into the centre, and watched as the last throes flickered. Little remained. The metal teeth from the fly-zip of some jeans; the cuff of a leather jacket; a congealed trainer. She walked away without further contemplation, feeling suddenly exhausted. Was this the start of the collapse that usually follows euphoria? The emotions cocking a snook and shouting, 'Sucks, I fooled you! I let you think you were strong, but guess what? You've been had!'

She showered, dried herself, and got into bed, but immediately she was missing the old routines of bedtime. She and Roger, in their shared but detached bed, straining to hear the current *Book at Bedtime* above Finnegan's noisy breathing. A short discussion on the progress of the book, and Roger prompted to pass on any gossipy anecdotes from the undercurrent of London publishing he'd picked up that day. Turning to each other for a traditional goodnight kiss, both knowing they would make love again the minute she gave the word. But her pride just couldn't allow surrender.

Now, faced with final separation, she began to wonder if being 'in love' with him had really been another sort of love: the fierce love indulged on one's children, or the emotional love for a pampered pet. How about the binding love reserved for parents or favourite relations? Had she loved either of her deceased parents? She certainly hadn't had a shred of affection for her cold, miserable mother, and she found it really difficult to remember her army officer father, blown up by an IRA bomb when she was fifteen. Her mother had anticipated his death with no apparent emotion. 'Army wives wait for it to happen,' she'd declared, so every time he went off on a tour of duty, she waited patiently. When it did happen she was stoically prepared – even though he'd been blown apart in a rural booby trap massacre, with only half his body weight remaining. Somehow Sally had never managed to brace herself for the inevitable loss of Roger.

She soon found she was too elated for sleep. A couple of stiff gins might have been the answer, but she'd never used drink to mask misfortune. Neither had she been a pill-popper, or a pothead. She sat up, thinking that something to read might calm her, but the only thing on her bedside table was the handbook to Waldringhythe; a glossy, expensive pamphlet that show-cased the Abbey's history from its first sketchy medieval map, to a glossy shot of a Royal visit in 2004. The frontispiece showed a photograph of Father Ewan seated on a small chair, dressed in a traditional double-breasted cassock, and holding a prayer book. But it was a strange depiction. His face was cast in shadow, making it impossible to define his features. She was suddenly both excited and fearful at the prospect of meeting the famous, reclusive priest.

Feeling an urge to get close to his ethos, she got out of bed and went to find her much-thumbed copy of his most famous publication, *Hand in Hand With Your Inner Self;* a slim million-selling volume, known throughout the world for its life-changing spiritual philosophy. She brought it back to the bed, and turned to the flyleaf.

Father Ewan McEwan was born in 1960. He was educated at Waldringhythe Abbey School and ordained into the Catholic Priesthood in 1983. Under his leadership and direction, Waldringhythe is now known throughout the world as the definitive centre for grief therapy and bereavement counselling.

This book is dedicated to Everyman who seeks to understand the enigma of life and death, and to the eradication of nuclear weapons.

Below the quote was printed the famous photograph, *Crucifix Man;* the iconic depiction of Christ on the cross that had caused such hysterical furore when it was first released to the media back in 1982. Memories came back of the scuffed, giant-sized poster stuck on the wall of the nurses' home common room. The naked upper body covered in ballpoint tattoos, and the borders graffitied with bubbles of vulgar sexual suggestions. For Sally, looking lustfully at men's bodies had never been the spectator sport it was for some women, but she had to admit to being intrigued by this one. She also conceded, with something of regret, that she'd led a sheltered life. As a nurse the human male form had no mystery left, and her shyness was long gone, but as Roger had been her only sexual partner, her experience of it was limited. Before she'd married her mother had warned her, with her usual lemon-sucking expression, not to expect too much. 'All men are animals,' she disclosed. 'It's a woman's lot in life to grin and bear it.' But Sally had found that with the discovery of passion she'd grinned most happily in the arms of her adored young husband. Now, the smell of the marriage bonfire wafted through the window and the bed was. . .What was it? Half empty or half full?

The loud pit-pat of rain started again and she was filled with a comfortable security – as if the wild weather was offering her some protection. Despite many previous reads of *Hand in Hand*, she snuggled down to begin her revision from page one.

Chapter 10

Timothy came-to abruptly in the dark, aware that he didn't feel well. His nose was swollen, his eyes smarted and his ribs ached. A peculiar screeching noise had woken him, but whatever it was had faded. Beside him, Roger was snoring, but it was only the low decibel on-his-side version, and from somewhere else in the room came the braying sound of Finnegan's sleepy wheezing. Surely, the monstrous dog wasn't going to have to share their bedroom? However much Roger might dote on him it was most unhygienic, and he emitted a smell rather like congealed grass cuttings. He'd have a tactful word in the morning, but it wasn't Roger's septum or a dog's lungs that had woken him. There it was again; a clear, baying yowl. A dog fox perhaps, or a muntjac that had strayed onto the lawn? No – something much more familiar. He threw himself out of bed in horror. Anthea!

He threw on his dressing gown, stumbled down the back stairs to the kitchen, and unlocked the scullery door. The vain Persian slunk in with her belly to the floor, her thick, pearly fur lying flat-soaked and filthy, knowing she looked as plain as a feral moggie. She looked up, giving him a brief glance of sheer disgust. 'Oh, babyboofs,' Timothy said, whipping a warm tea towel from the Aga rail and gathering her up in his arms. The snooty cat, despite her misery and self-loathing, didn't appreciate capture. She hissed, extended a spiteful claw to Timothy's exposed bare thigh, and fled to the boiler room for sanctuary.

Timothy dabbed his wounds with the wet tea towel and crept back upstairs. As he moved to cross the galleried landing, a theatrical shaft of moonlight was shining onto his mother's bedroom door. He tried to deny the need to enter, but already he ached for the sound of her voice, her affectionate hugs, her concern with all his problems and the genuine, undivided attention she'd always given so freely on demand. Now, by the cruelest paradox, he wanted her to be with him, to salve the pain her death had brought on him. He found his fingers turning the heavy brass handle.

Fumbling in the dark, he switched on a bedside lamp. He'd braced himself for the sight of her shrouded body, but was shocked by its abnormally long, thin shape. He inhaled sharply, and shivered with cold, but steeled himself not to run away and abandon her like a coward. In the soft muted light he recalled how this room had played such a large part in his childhood happiness. His earliest memories were of his accident nights; waking in a cold, wet bed, and stumbling in to his sleeping parents, grizzling loudly. Both of them immediately rising, without complaint, to give their affection and understanding, followed by warm soapy-flannelled washes, a pair of freshly ironed pyjamas, and a set of clean sheets. The bliss of Sunday mornings, diving in and snuggling down between the two of them. His father making up funny, exaggerated stories about a bird called a Peckerpecker, that pecked off little boys' willies if they told fibs, while he lay back in childish innocence, pressed against the puffed pigeons of his mother's breasts. In later years, taking his ageing father breakfast in bed, and staying for long, easy discussions of this and that, and the planning of his future life. It was to be in horticulture, they decided. A fine career, and so suited to his quiet, artistic disposition.

After the birth of Morgana it had become a busy, noisy place of night crying, and the night feeding demands of the lusty, red-faced infant; the infant who rapidly turned into a demanding toddler, and woke them all from their slumbers, in distress from her own wet bed. Then, after the tragedy, the painful, echoing silence of the room, broken only by the muffled tears of the single occupant.

As Timothy lowered himself to sit carefully beside the stiff effigy, a loose finial on the scrolled brass bed rang out with an innocuous ting-a-ling. Was it really thirty years ago that he'd stood outside the door, with his ear pressed close, to hear the merry music of its jingling in the night? Listening slack-mouthed and dizzy with adolescent fantasies, as his parents rough-housed their passion. The next morning, seeing his father's hypnotic gaze on his mother, and her returned complicit smiles. 'Angel,' he called her on those mornings. 'My beautiful Angel.'

As he sat there he tried hard not to move. But he had to. He had no strength to deny himself. Like a magnet he moved to a rosewood tallboy, and with shaking hands, opened his mother's underwear drawer. Advancing years had never sent her to the sensible section of the Co-op or Marks and Spencers. Her breasts had always been loaded into the underwired satin of Janet Reger and La Perla, and her girlish flat abdomen was still enhanced with lace-panelled thongs. He pressed a silky, red G-String to his lips, but despite its sensuality, the sight of a small, square cardboard box tucked away at the back sidetracked him. Clearly, from the primary colours of its cartoon decoration, it held a child's toy. He opened it, and carefully withdrew a wind-up tin chicken in pristine condition. He was sure he'd never seen it before. It must have been Morgana's. He turned the key, set it down on the glass top of the dressing table, and watched it jerk and whir in a ferocious display of mechanical pecking. Gradually, it ran down to slow motion, and flopped onto its side. He carefully put it away, in the way he always treated Morgana's memory; taken out of a box, motivated with clockwork, and carefully replaced without painful philosophy. It was so hard to remember that an animated, boisterous little girl really had existed. There were no photographs of her in the room, nor in fact anywhere else in the house, but he could still see, with crystal clarity, her soft, dark curly hair and pretty teeth. It was time to leave. He rose, stared with misery at the stiff, shrouded mound, and turned off the lamp.

Roger's snoring had now become the flat-on-his-back version; a shuddering, dragon-fired roar, with overtones of a pneumatic drill. The flopped broadness of his dead weight was always too much for Timothy to turn over, despite placing his foot behind a shoulder and pushing hard. The only thing he could do was to sidle quietly in beside him, and pray for sleep. He lifted a corner of the duvet, only to find it was weighed hard down by a firmly installed Finnegan. The determined dog dug in his anchors and refused to budge, so Timothy edged into the free six inches of the bed. Half an hour later, as a pale dawn crept into the room, Roger noisily turned over and Finnegan's ninety pounds jumped out, using Timothy as a springboard. A cold nose immediately searched under the duvet, and truffled a pair of warm buttocks to alert his new mummy that it was time for walkies.

Chapter 11

FOR EWAN – THE TALES FROM THE PURPLE HANDBAG

Dearest Ewan

You're reading these words so I must be dead. Thus, from the other side (or from nowhere at all), I send you my eternal love. All you have to do now is take your seat in the confessional box and draw the curtain. Are you sitting comfortably? Then I'll begin.

I'm not Marina at all. I'm Molly from Limerick, born on April 1st 1944, officially a fool, and saddled with the name of Maureen Immelda Dympna O'Dowd. Baptised into the Holy Roman church and proudly paraded as the first child of Attracta, a scullery maid, and Declan, a farm labourer. A respectable, but dirt-poor, married couple. A couple of years after my birth Declan went off to America to forge a new life for us, but he must have suffered memory loss. We never heard from him again, so my mother became a tragic victim who'd been abandoned by a feckless bounder. Thus, she became a bitter woman who never missed an opportunity to tell me what a millstone around her neck I was.

In the mid 1950's, like many others, we crossed the channel for England where there was full employment. We settled in Oxford, my mother found work as a college servant, and we rented a small college house off the Cowley Road. You'd have thought that the change in our fortunes would have jollied my mother up, but it had the opposite effect. The only thing that gave her any pleasure was her devout subservience to our church, but all that bobbing about and mumbling wasn't for me, and I failed to toe the party line. I refused to attend Mass and I was rude to the priests and nuns when they turned up to give me pep talks. So you see, even in those far-off days, I was deemed to be a heathen.

In Limerick my education was more than a bit lacking, so everyone assumed I was as thick as brick. Oxford was supposed to be the seat of learning, but dumb Molly spent her school days sitting in a corner being ignored. I didn't give two hoots. I became swept up in the magical world of cheap romantic magazines and the cinema, convinced I would marry a millionaire, or become a famous film star. Trouble was, my fanciful life made real life boring, so in defiance I threw out all the rules of chastity that we girls are forced to absorb like the drip from a leaking gutter. In simple terms, I became a tart.

So there I was, Ewan. On my back, with legs akimbo, piping anyone on board who cared to climb the gangplank. Subsequently there were many, many men in my life, but only four had any real importance. A fishporter, a Rabbi, a Judge and a Catholic Priest. Sounds like the cast of a dirty joke, doesn't it? Ha! Just you wait to hear the punch lines.

1959 – THE FISHPORTER'S TALE

I left school the minute I was fifteen. Girls like me did in those days. You just left school and studied the 'sits vac' column. My first job was in a handbag shop in the Oxford Covered Market. After a few weeks I was bored out of my skull, and that old market was freezing cold, even in summer. I really wanted to be one of those girls who sold perfume and make-up in Elliston and Cavell's department store. You know the sort. All snooty, and posh, and refined. I went for an interview. I pretended I was eighteen, I snooted and poshed and refined my way through it all, and I got the job. 'Well, here's you arrived, Molly,' I thought. 'That's showed 'em. Five pounds a week, a little black dress, and free lunches.'

The owner of the handbag shop was old Stavros, a Greek in his fifties; a lonely, childless widower, who wore expensive shoes and stank of garlic. When I gave in my notice he said, 'Me very sad, Molly. You lovely girl. Me miss you. Here. A present for you to remember old Stavros.' He reached up to a shelf and handed me a huge purple handbag. 'For you, my flower of Olympus, and remember, if all go down drain pipe, there always job for you here.'

Anyway, I started selling make-up on the Monday, and on the Wednesday I fell in love on the stockroom floor with the manager of fancy goods. Some blabbermouth found out, and that was me out on my ear. Without a reference I had no choice but to sink my pride and crawl back to old Stavros. Of course he took me back, but with strings attached. I had to blindfold him, and give him hand jobs, but it didn't take up much of my time and he was very grateful.

Then I met Nico, the fishporter. God, did I fancy Nico! He used to ride around on a bicycle with a big metal carrier on the front. Every day, when he passed the handbag shop, he always made an excuse to stop and check his tyres, and make big eyes at me. Stavros told me, 'You stay away from that Nico. He Albanian. They bad family. He worse than all the rest. He no good for you.' But of course I took no notice. Well, you don't take any notice of anything when you're fifteen, do you? In any case, all the other girls chased him, so I had to make sure I was the one who caught him, and caught I truly was. In those days most blokes who got a girl up the duff did the honourable thing. At least with a shotgun pointed at their heads, they did. Anyway, my baby's father disappeared off the face of the earth before you could say wedding cake.

I've no need to tell you about society and attitudes to my

pregnancy in those days, have I, Ewan? Our great and almighty Catholic Church, thundering in like Visigoths to tell my fortune; ranting, and raving, and threatening hell and damnation, and making me feel such disgrace for the tiny life I'd created. The poor child doomed to the terrible tag of bastard, and his mother worse than dog dirt. But shall I tell you something, Ewan? The church can drop dead for all I care, but thanks to their bigotry my baby was saved. Today I'd have tripped off for a quick-fix abortion in my lunch hour with no conscience at all. All my prayers answered, and straight out to re-offend again. But my baby stayed locked in, and for that I'll kiss the Virgin's feet.

When I told my mother she smacked me round the head and called me a dirty little trollop. She made the nuns arrange for me to go off to one of those mother and baby homes, and 'it' would be adopted before my terrible sin put further blight on her life. Did I have a choice? Well, it may not have been a choice, but a solution turned up.

Stavros caught me crying at work, and he put his arms around me. 'Tell old Stavros what the matter,' so I did. 'You can move in with me,' he said. 'I have lovely cottage at Cuddesdon. You tell all those nosey parkies that you have home for your child. I never blessed with children, so you can take care of house, and take care of me, and maybe when you old enough we get married.'

Patrick was born two months prematurely, just after midnight on 1st January 1960. I sweated and cursed my way through it all, and when the baby finally slurped out there was just silence in the room. You know what it's like when a baby's born. It starts to cry, and everyone whoops around, oohing and aahing as if it's the first time it's ever happened. No one said anything for what seemed like hours. Then the midwife spoke, but she had to keep clearing her throat, and she couldn't look at me. 'You've a lovely little boy, Molly,' she said, 'but he's got a wee hole in his face. It's called a cleft lip, but don't worry. They'll be able to do a little operation on him, and he'll be as handsome as his Daddy.'

It was a shock, but a mother's love doesn't reject. I turned my soul inside out and found that elusive something that's inside all of us. It doesn't have a name, but it soars up to the surface with the power of a depth charge. I held him in my arms and I fell in love. I was little more than a child myself, but as I lay there, sweating from the pain and exhaustion of his birth, I had to find the strength and protection of a tigress. I simply had to grow up.

My mother didn't come to see me, but a flock of black nuns, and the old bitches from Social Services, descended to stare at us both. The nuns said his affliction was God's punishment. The old bitches said he deserved better. They all tried to persuade me to give him up, but Stavros was there. 'I am Miss O'Dowd's fiancé,' he said. 'We get married soon. Patrick will want for nothing. I will be proper father to the boy. I will adopt him. I have money. He will have private education. I pay for finest surgeon in London to fix his lip. Now go away and leave us alone. We family.' They went away.

When Patrick was six weeks old he was admitted to a private hospital in London to be operated on by the most eminent plastic surgeon in the country. A few months later Stavros said, 'Now you are sixteen, Molly, we get married. Eat up and get some colour back in those cheeks. Draw your chair nearer to the fire, and take a little glass of wine with me. Here, dear, take as much money as you want. Go buy yourself a nice new outfit and get your hair done. Come, my little honey bee, here's the blindfold.' Trouble was, blind man's buff was the only party game Stavros wanted to play, and it didn't do much for me. A few weeks later, he caught me in bed with the insurance man. He said I'd broken his heart. He said he loved me as a daughter, and as a wife, and he loved Patrick like a son, but I'd betrayed him. He was sorry, but he couldn't marry me after all. He found me a couple of basement rooms in Jericho, and gave me fifty pounds. I packed my bags and gathered up Patrick.

Here endeth the fishporter's tale.

Chapter 12

Ewan awoke in his rocking chair, well after dawn, with Lucifer curled up on his lap. His neck was stiff, and his mouth so dry he could hardly swallow. The room was still brightly lit by two large table lamps, but the fire had sunk to a pile of grey ash and the air was cold. He was vaguely aware that the hours had passed in a whisky-induced confusion, recalling both a frequent jerking awake to ease the position of his head, and nebulous dreams of his early childhood. The cruel face of an old nun, the jeering of hard-faced boys, and the boomp-boomp of a body falling down the stairs. But, as he slowly regained full consciousness, the last image to disappear was the one he hated above all others; the bearded man at the door. The scene remembered with such sharp focus it could have been yesterday, and in some ways even more disturbing than the booming of the body. The man wore a dark suit, and a strange kind of hat with a curly brim. He hovered within the sides of a doorframe, smelled strongly of cheese, and spoke in a foreign way that was more gesture than accent. Many times in the past Ewan had strained to go deeper inside his brain, to seek a back alley that might lead to the scene's enlargement, but all he knew was that the man's presence evoked a miasma of fear. He found his body shaking, both from the cold of the room and from the residual anxiety of the dissolving dream.

His first routine upon waking was to pray, but today he shook off the cat and reached for his mobile phone. 'Good morning, Sarah. I'm so sorry I didn't ring yesterday. How is Jacob this morning?'

'Some sweating and pain in the night, but he slept again.'

'Is he asleep now?'

'No. He's having a Zero Balancing session.'

'Then I won't disturb him. I hope he spends a comfortable day.'

'If he's up to we're going to watch a DVD of *Cher's Farewell Tour* this afternoon.'

'Will you give him my love, and tell him that my news has come?'

'What news is that, Ewan?'

'There's been a death in my family. Jacob knows the details.'

'I'm so sorry to hear that.'

'I'll phone again this afternoon. Goodbye, Sarah.'

Ewan now dropped to his knees, but instead of putting his hands together, he found himself crawling to a corner, with his arms outstretched, calling Marina's name. Blindly flailing he sought to find her. To take her in his arms. To hear her husky voice and throaty laugh. To see her smile. . . But it wasn't just the beauty of her soft lips and even teeth he desired, but the sparkling lights in her eyes, and the lift of her high cheekbones. To kiss that open, smiling mouth. To move to her ears and slide his tongue around the plain, gold-ball earrings he'd bought for her in Capri ten years ago, and she'd never since removed. His mind closed and retracted, knowing that his mental state was one of temporary madness, but one he never wished to return from. With his eyes tightly closed he continued his journey.

1965 – 1978

From the moment that five-year-old Patrick O'Dowd entered the insular world of Waldringhythe Abbey, he began a golden life as Ewan McEwan. His parents (and how quickly they became his parents) created a stable, busy life of learning, laughing and being loved; a wholly unselfish love, proffered with both guidance and tactility.

For the first two years he attended the local village infants' school, with gentle country children who knew no malice, and the kind, slightly dippy Miss Dingle as the only teacher. At the age of seven he was enrolled into the discipline of Waldringhythe Preparatory School; sliding with bright, well-adjusted ease into this new regime to find, that again, he was treated as a boy like any other, with no ridicule or reference to his facial affliction, or weak eye-sight. Now his days were divided into well defined areas dedicated to religious life and scholarship. Rising early for the daily Eucharist, absorbing the Latin texts and words of service until he was mumbling every prayer and response with the familiarity of a second tongue. In the classroom, throwing up his arm like a flagpole, knowing he was always one of the brightest in the class without much contest. Trying hard with games, and although not making the first teams, never made to feel inadequate. Being happy – oh, so supremely happy! – in the long-lost world of good manners, gentlemanly fair play, and dedicated career teachers.

On weekend afternoons, as a non-boarder, he was allowed the luxury of being at home. Having fun and fresh air on the long bank of the Deben Estuary, running in mock competition with the big, boundy Labrador Retriever that the puppy, Iggy-Piggy, had become. Then his mother standing with her hands on her broad hips, saying in her soft Highland tone, 'If you think you're coming into our house in that state, Iggy-Piggy McEwan, you can think again,' but he always did. His gritty, saturated coat briskly towelled down, followed by the inevitable wet doggy-shake. Cries of, 'Oh, Iggy!'

Afterwards, high tea. The washing of hands, and the saying of Grace. Sliced corned beef from a viciously sharp square tin, a lettuce leaf, radishes, half a tomato and a dollop of salad cream. Home-baked bread, fruitcake, and scones washed down with scalding cups of Ty-Phoo. The early evening devoted to the serious completion of his homework, and then an hour of Ludo, or Snakes and Ladders. Towards eight o'clock watches were looked at, and faces got serious. 'Wooden hill time, Ewan. It's gae late.'

'Please, Mummy. Just *one* more game and this time I'll beat dad.'

'Oh, all right, but only the one, mind.'

'Yea!'

Bedtime was always preceded by a list of his daily achievements, however small, but his shortcomings were never mentioned. A last-minute examination of his teeth and fingernails, followed by his child's hands pressed hard together in statutory prayers. Skimming the Rosary beads between his small fingers. '*Hail, Mary. Full of grace. . .*'

'Which Saint shall we pray to tonight, Ewan? You choose.'

'St. Francis, because Father Aidan's rabbit is sick.'

Thereafter there followed strangulating hugs, and smacking good-night kisses, first from Mum and then Dad, and Mum again, followed by a final, 'Good night, and God bless.' Thanks to these two exceptional and truly Christian beings, Ewan travelled a stable passage from childhood to adolescence with no inner turmoil or anxiety.

His mother: a big-breasted, rosy-cheeked Earth Mother, who laughed and sang, and pedalled around the school grounds on her bicycle, wearing swirly peasant skirts, broderie anglaise blouses, and Jesus sandals. Although one of only six teachers' wives, and one spinster nurse, amid six hundred males, she neither noticed nor complained about the narrowness of her environment.

His father: known throughout the school as Aberdeen Mac, the hawk-faced head of the English department. Feared throughout the school as a strict disciplinarian, but at home, an affectionate and patient father who made further education within the home such fun. 'Now, Ewan, I want a thousand words starting, 'The Berlin Wall was hidden in a mist,' ending up with, 'and that was how Margot Fonteyn lost her ballet shoes.'' On reading his son's lively and animated compositions, he never failed to be impressed. 'Jean, he really is exceptionally talented. It's not just the twists of the narrative but his use of words. The disguised puns, the rhythm of the sentences, and the imagery. He's certain to be Oxbridge material.'

Throughout the years his Father read to him daily, moving up through an eclectic mixture of Noel Streatfield, Frank Richards, Anthoney Buckeridge, Richmal Crompton, J.R.R Tolkien and C.S Lewis. Later, the breath-stopping pathos and drama of Dickens and Hardy, and the helpless, giggling hilarity of P.G.Wodehouse. In near adulthood he was encouraged to take on the heavyweights, with father and son reading a book in tandem, and discussing at length together. The blushing at D.H.Lawrence. 'You must never be afraid or ashamed of sexuality in serious literature, Ewan. Life's a big picture, and far too short for prudery. Vulgarity is one thing, but being well-read and open-minded is a completely different matter.' Finally, the screwed-up Catholics. The comic irony of Evelyn Waugh, and the cynicism of Grahame Greene. No laughing matter, but leading to long, philosophical discussions, concerning the calling to the priesthood he thought he was beginning to hear.

'Of course, if it's what you want,' his Father said, failing to disguise his disappointment. 'I'd rather set my heart on you reading English

Literature, but it must be your choice. We'll be gae proud of you whatever you decide to do, but don't worry your mother yet. I think bootees and rattles might be her distant dream.' At that, Ewan blushed puce and turned away. He knew he would never get married. He didn't know any girls, and even if he did, they wouldn't like his face. Girls only liked boys who could curl up their top lip like Cliff Richard and Elvis Presley.

At the age of eighteen it was Ewan who found his Father on the kitchen floor, swinging happily into the house after Sunday afternoon cricket, having bowled one and caught two; a rare achievement for one with no real sporting ability, and poor eyesight. Dad was flat on his back. Crashed to earth on the stone flags, his face blue, a slice of homemade Victoria sponge screwed up in his palm, and a smashed cup at his feet. Iggy-Piggy was sitting beside him, confused and whining, having lapped up the spilt tea. Ewan had fled in panic, searching for his mother, and yelling for the help of anyone.

Father Paulinus immediately took charge. The doctor was called but all he could do was confirm death and order the body to be ambulanced away to Ipswich for a regulation post mortem. After a delay of five days coronary infarction was confirmed, and a death certificate issued.

Ewan's life had then become a brutal bewilderment of trying to grieve on his own account, and to understand the alarming changes that immediately affected his mother. The open-armed, chattering woman turned into a husk of tearless depression. Her fast, enthusiastic movements became heavy, resigned plods, her healthy roundness deflated, her apple cheeks paled, and her hair became dry and lifeless. Politely refusing offers of help she single-handedly organised the funeral, and supervised school catering to provide a tasty spread for the mourners to move on to.

Ewan had received his 'A' level results on the morning of the funeral. Three straight 'A' grades, in English Literature, Religious Knowledge and Latin, but there'd been no whooping and leaping round the kitchen. 'Dad would've been pleased, wouldn't he?' he said, trying to include the presence of his father, but she made no comment. 'Good enough for St Scholastica's,' he added.

'More than good enough' she agreed. 'So you're still determined on priest training?'

'I must go, Mum. I've been called, but you don't want me to go, do you?'

'I've got to want what you want.'

The funeral service was held in The Abbey to a full congregation, but the burial entailed a journey to the Waldringhythe cemetery, half a mile away. Once the sad ceremony was completed, his mother gave clear signals that she wanted to walk back to school, despite the extravagance of funeral cars. 'Mrs McEwan,' called the undertaker, 'I've reserved the lead car for you and your son,' but the sad-faced woman moved off on foot, ignoring the polite stares of those still mouthing quietly at the graveside.

'Come along, Ewan,' she ordered him.

The fleet of shiny black limousines slowed down as they passed them, the occupants not knowing whether to wave, nod respectfully, or ignore them altogether. 'Well, that's that then,' she said when they'd all disappeared out of sight. 'Now we're forced to go back, and eat and drink and be brave, while well-meaning people brace themselves to say something kind and sympathetic. I've had to do it myself so many times. You try to look meaningful, but it's gae hard work trying to find all the right moves and words.' She paused. 'Ewan, I've something to ask you.'

He was anxious to talk to her. After enduring days of her sad silence, he was aching to resume their close, idle conversations, and the simple normality of their lives. They stopped walking and leaned their backs against an old field gate. The summer air was dry, a dragonfly shot past, and high above their heads two red kites circled gracefully on a hot thermal. 'I want you to think very carefully, and tell me the truth. How far back can you remember to your childhood? What are your very earliest recollections?'

He pretended to think very precisely. 'It was a day at Southwold,' he said. 'We were spending the day in a beach hut on the front. The sun was hot, but there was a cold wind off the sea. I was shivering, so you brought out a bright red fleecy top for me to wear. It had a Ladybird on the label. You said it cost five and six, and although it was a lot of money for a jumper, I was worth every penny. Iggy-Piggy was a puppy. I know he was because he still had a soft pink belly, and we all laughed at him when he bobbed down and did a pee-pee on the sand. I sat down and held him in my arms while you took a photograph, and you said, 'That's the one. That's perfect.' Then you burst into tears, and Dad came over and cuddled you. I think I started crying too, but you both began to laugh, and Dad threw me onto his shoulders, and ran around the beach playing aeroplanes. Later on in the afternoon you brought a cake with candles out onto the beach, but every time I got ready for a big puff and a wish, the wind blew the candles out, so we had to go into the hut.'

'We'd just come to Waldringhythe,' she said. 'September 1965. New job, new puppy, new everything. We were really happy. So you don't remember anything before that?'

He shrugged. 'Like what?'

'Oh, I don't know. Anything. Anything before coming here.'

'No, nothing before that.'

'Are you quite, quite sure?'

'Yes.'

She scrambled in her handbag for a handkerchief, blew her nose noisily, and began to sob; the first tears she'd shed since his father's death. Her face twisted into a hideous grimace of misery, but Ewan's most profound memory of that day was the shock of her angry retort. The blasphemous words that he'd only rarely heard, and never imagined could be in the vocabulary of his mother. 'Fuck it. Just fucking, fuck it.' She stamped angrily up the dusty lane for a few yards, then turned and shouted at him as if he'd done something terribly wrong. 'That day. That day you had a birthday cake. It wasn't your fucking birthday, and I'm going to have to tell you *why* or I'll go even madder than I'm going.' She stood clenching her fists and shaking. 'Ewan, I love you so much, and don't want to go and face all those people, and just when I need God more than ever he's deserted me, and when you hear what I've got to tell you, you'll desert me too.'

Ewan ran to put his arms around her shoulders, and to hold her manfully in the way he'd seen so many stiff-necked film stars comfort their leading ladies. 'Mum, I lied. I know what you're going to tell me. I'm sorry, but I thought I was saving you the pain of me knowing. I've only got very hazy memories, but something dramatic happened and I was taken away from my first life. I remember a couple of nuns taking me to meet you and dad on a train, and the journey to Woodbridge, and getting Iggy-Piggy. It doesn't matter what the truth is, because you're my mother. I know I had another one, a birth one, but you're my real mother, and dad was my real dad. Please, Mum. Please stop crying. It doesn't matter. It's never mattered.'

At his confession, she threw out her words like stones. 'But it *does* matter. I tried to do something about it, but the bastards fobbed me off. It was only your dad who stopped me from trying again. Now I canna live with it any more. The sin's eating me up, but it's not my sin. Oh, no. It's those buggers. You've got to hear the truth. I want you to tell the whole world and make sure they're punished. I hand the baton on to you. You're my only hope.' She began to throw her arms around, as if she were using semaphore flags, but then her eccentric behaviour suddenly calmed. She dropped her shoulders, and gave him a look of blank hopelessness. 'Take me hame, Ewan. You'll have to tell Daddy I'm very sorry, but I'll no be going to his wake.'

Ewan guided his mother back to the house where she walked up the stairs like an automaton, and removed her clothes. It was the first time he'd ever seen her undress, and he looked away with embarrassment. Wearing only a full-length pink petticoat she got into bed and pulled the covers up to her chin. 'I wrote it all down,' she said. 'It was the truth, the whole truth, and nothing but the truth, but your dad made me lock it away. Only because of you, Ewan. Only out of love for you, you see. He wouldn't let me keep the battle up, because you'd have found out you weren't really ours. I knew he was right, but there was so much anger left inside me because I wanted justice for all the others, and especially for my poor wee boy.'

'What boy, Mum? What are you trying to say? Did you have another child before you got me?'

'Aye. He was a bonny boy but he died when he was four. He had the leukaemia.'

'Was he called Ewan as well?'

'Aye.'

'I think I always knew there was something odd that hovered over us, but it wasn't anything to do with my blurred memories. When I was twelve I went to Rome on a school trip, and when we applied for my passport you must have used his birth certificate. I knew it wasn't mine. It said Ewan Duncan Anderson McEwan. Born in Edinburgh on September 9th, 1960, but I knew I wasn't that boy. I knew I'd been called Patrick in my other life and my birthday was in cold weather.'

'Aye. You were called Patrick. The adoption was arranged by a charity called *The Crusade of Rescue* and you were being cared for at the St Pius's Children's Home in London. In Camberwell. On the day we went there to meet you for the first time the Mother Superior had to turn away, to find something in a filing cabinet behind her, and I tried to read a letter that was on her desk. It was upside down, of course, so I didn't have time to find out much, but I made out the name Patrick O'Dowd. Your surname was O'Dowd.'

'I knew that, Mum. I've never forgotten who I was, but it makes no difference at all. You're the best mother a son could ever ask for, and dad was a perfect father.'

'And you're a wonderful son. How blessed we were to have had the gift of you. You've made us very happy, and very proud.'

'But you really don't want me to be a priest, do you?'

'It's just my selfishness. Wanting you to have what I wanted for myself. A family.'

'Mum, the whole world will be my family.'

'Let me sleep now, son. When I wake up we'll have another blether.'

But later that afternoon, before he had any opportunity to talk to her again, she awoke with strange mutterings and yelling about 'the buggers'. Followed by periods of muddled soliloquies, and intense teeth grinding, her behaviour became even more abnormal. She took to patting the walls in search of microphones, and crying out that she was being persecuted. Ewan rushed to find Sister Wagstaff, the school Matron, and her close personal friend. The well-meaning nurse sat at her bedside, holding her hand and talking about rests, and holidays, and time being the greatest healer. The senior priests arrived to gather at the foot of the stairs in a worried huddle, assuring Ewan that she would be as right as ninepence within a few days. But then the sound of screaming was heard from above, and they all surged up the stairs. His mother had punched Sister Wagstaff very firmly in the mouth, jumped out of bed, and put her head through a pane of the bedroom window.

The doctor immediately arranged for her to be admitted to a close-care psychiatric unit. Later that evening she was sectioned, and officially detained under the Mental Health Act.

Chapter 13

As Sally woke up slowly she could tell it was far too early for Monks Bottom to be awake. It was a myth that village life was quiet. The tranquillity of the sleepy hamlet seemed to act as an echo chamber, and even the most mundane sounds of the day coming to life broke the silence. Engines revved, doors slammed, and dogs barked. Children chattered, mothers scolded, and the early morning deliveries of post and papers resounded with banging gates, and merry whistles. This morning, Sally only heard the cacophony of garden birds. She lay cozily under the duvet, completely forgetting the brutal changes in her life, but then reality smacked like a rock in a sock. Her leg reached into an empty space, and the smoky waft of the marriage bonfire hung heavily in the room.

She rose, drew back the curtains, and stared out of the window. The pain of having to tell Louise that Roger had finally gone lurched to the surface, but to Sally's relief her daughter was on a student trip to France, researching Flaubert, so the agony could be delayed. But Louise knew the call was coming. She knew Marina was dying, and her Daddy was leaving them to live with Timothy, but even as a fully paid-up member of the unshockable, new millennium generation, she'd been unable to accept her father's sexuality.

Sally and Roger had told her the truth of their situation together; a brave and selfless act, stage-managed and planned by them both, last Christmas. In front of a blazing fire in the inglenook, amid the usual chaos of presents, and wrapping paper, and the opiate of a traditional turkey roast pressing on their ribs, they'd linked fingers. A bottle of red had breathed, and the glasses filled, but a toast wasn't raised. 'Lulu,' said Roger. 'I. . . That is, Mummy and me. We've got something to tell you. Marina Proudfoot's dying. She's got terminal cancer. . .'

'Oh, no,' said Louise, with a genuine look of sorrow. 'That's so tragic. She's really lovely. Far too young to die.'

Roger had continued a stumbling explanation of his future plans to conclude, 'So you see it's going to mean really big changes for all of us.'

Louise lifted her head, stupefied, but then she slowly began to smile widely, and laughed out loud. 'This is a joke. A wind-up. It's got to be.'

Her happy face was only met with the kind, blank faces of both her parents. She ran from the room and hysterically attempted to phone for a taxi, but with none to be had on Christmas day, Sally had been obliged to drive her back to Cambridge. As Louise walked stiffly out of the house, Roger held out his arms. 'Lulu, don't do this. I'm still your daddy. We can talk about this,' but she ignored him.

The journey was suffered in an atmosphere of frost and silence, but after travelling for thirty miles, Louise eventually spoke. 'How long have you known, Mum?'

'Three, maybe four years,' Sally admitted.

'Must be pretty kinky sharing your husband with a faggot?'

'We haven't made love since I found out, but I still love him.'

'You might be HIV.'

'I'm not. I've been tested twice. Daddy swears that neither of them have ever had anyone else, anyway.' Since then Louise had refused to speak to Roger, or come home, and all Sally's attempts at reconciliation had been stonewalled.

Sally pressed her head against a small Tudor windowpane, welcoming the coldness on her forehead. It had rained again in the night, and the charred mess on the lawn lay black and sodden. Momentarily, she felt guilt; the stern hangover from a life being led by a nose-ring down the straight road of order and convention. But hadn't the same life dealt her a cruel loser's hand? Surely she had the right to a backlash?

Abruptly, she turned and walked to the bathroom, trying to summon the mental strength to muster her withdrawal. On the wall hung an old art deco mirror – the same mirror she'd first looked into as brand new wife. On that day she'd been a classic pre-Raphaelite sylph, with a profusion of fiery-red ringlets she could sit on, freckled alabaster skin, and shining green eyes. Now, everything had changed. The slim, girlish body was now perhaps too thin, and her face was stripped of its bloom. Her eyes were edged with grids of finely maturing crow's feet, and her hair, now shoulder-length, was faded and coarsened. The changes had crept up so quietly they had never troubled her, but she now stared back at herself. 'Remember Marina Proudfoot's saying,' she instructed. 'Standing behind the old woman in the mirror is the real you. Make sure she always has pride of place, at the front.'

Sally straightened her shoulders, and held her head regally. From her wardrobe, she selected some rarely worn items; a short, boxy Aran cardigan to reveal her small waistline, tight-fitting black jeans that enhanced her long legs, and a pair of leather Chelsea boots. She fastidiously applied a rare full make-up, and applied electric straighteners to the desiccated corkscrews. With a proud toss of her head she admired her enhanced face, and swung her unaccustomed silky hair. Perhaps it was possible to arouse the girl she used to be from her sleeping corner.

With a lightly packed bag she walked down to the kitchen to write a good bye note to Roger. Hers would be an official, refined declaration. She selected a sheet of their bespoke headed notepaper, and unscrewed her fountain pen.

Dear Roger

1) *I'm going away, and won't return for some time.*

2) *You'll be hearing from my Solicitor with divorce papers soon.*

3) *I'll be instructing an Estate Agent immediately, so please arrange to transfer the deeds to my sole ownership (don't mess me about on this).*

4) *I'll contact Louise, and inform her of current events, though I feel sure a letter from you would be more appropriate.*

5) *Turn off the electricity and make sure you defrost the fridge and freezer. Don't forget to clean them both thoroughly, and dispose of the contents.*

6) *Double lock the front door and put the keys through the letterbox.*

7) *I'll make arrangements to re-direct all mail to The Manor House, so keep anything for me until I give you a PO Box number.*

8) *Cancel the papers.*

9) *Finnegan's inoculation record book is on the dresser behind the cow creamer. He's due for worming. Remember he's allergic to potatoes.*

10) *Don't bother to look for me, because you won't find me.*

I hope you and Timothy will be very happy.
With fond memories of our long marriage,

Sally

It was 7.00 a.m. She climbed into her silver Mini and headed for the Suffolk coast, to disappear, like another type of Alice, into another type of looking glass.

Chapter 14

At 8.30 a.m. Cora Feather trudged up the long, sweeping drive of Monk's Bottom Manor with a strong sense of purpose. She didn't usually do Saturdays, but this was above and beyond the call of duty. She owed it to dear Lady P to pitch in and help Timothy (who else was there anyway?), and it was going to be a very difficult day for him, what with the phone going all the time, and people calling round to pay their respects. She envisaged that she would be indispensable, but as she rounded the bend by the ancient oak, and the facade of house was revealed, her enthusiasm turned into full-scale fury. As she suspected, Roger Fuller's car was parked smack bang at the front door. Her hackles rose. Say no more. Dear Lady P not even cold, and Mr Big had swanned in with his toothbrush. Well, he could sling his hook. She wouldn't be laying out the red carpet for the likes of him and his pompous la-di-da.

On reaching the house she shaded her eyes from the sun. At the bottom of the long lawn she could see Timothy moving about on the edge of the lake, doing something with a weed pole. 'Oh well, Cora,' she sighed. 'Go and say your piece, but it won't be easy.'

Over the years she'd evolved a decided fondness for Timothy, even though village opinion had declared that he was a bit of a nerd; innocent, introverted, and with the social skills of an earthworm. On hearing that Marina Proudfoot was terminally ill a wave of profound sorrow had circulated the community, followed be a second round for Timothy. 'Poor bugger,' they all said. 'What's his life going to be like without his mother? How on earth will he cope?' It was fair comment. The only window the shy bachelor had to the outside world was the modest organic market garden he ran from the vast grounds of his home. His only regular visitor was Roger Fuller, an old

Monks Bottom pal, who helped out in the greenhouses, as a respite from his stressful publishing career. There wasn't an inkling of suspicion, or innuendo, as to the true nature of their relationship. In fact, some commentators referred to Roger's presence in terms of social work, being his only real friend, and supporting him steadfastly since (mouthed silently) 'the tragedy.' If only they'd known the truth.

Cora had sussed the situation many moons ago. It had been a terrible shock, but as a lifetime reader of the tabloids, she knew such things went on. It was the one case of 'the wine glass under the bed, and the watch under the pillow' about four years ago that had given the game away. Monday mornings she did the bedrooms. All nine, with proper wax polishing. None of your slovenly Mr Sheen on the antique mahogany. She knew Timothy slept on the right-hand side of his double bed. His silk Harrod's pyjamas were always neatly folded beneath the right-hand pillow, and the adjoining bedside cupboard was adorned with his things: an alarm clock, a gardening encyclopaedia, a beaker of pens, a notebook, a pencil torch, a wooden bowl to hold his small change, and several family photographs. That morning she'd swept up the fancy brocade valance to hoover, and there it was! An empty wineglass tucked underneath the *left-hand* side of the bed. Lady P was off at that retreat place, keeping her gob shut and bobbing about with the monks, so that *had* to be the evidence. Timothy had a secret lady friend! Then, on lifting the pillow on the same side to plump and arrange it, she found a watch. A fancy *man's* watch, and it certainly wasn't the one Timothy wore. Her legs nearly gave way. No doubt it had been taken off and slipped underneath the pillow before. . . Oh, my good Gawd. . . But apart from seeing a picture of Timothy, and whoever it was, sitting up in bed like Morecambe and Wise, she couldn't have been more convinced that a bit of rumpy-pumpy had been going on. She slipped the watch into her apron pocket and later produced it with careful indifference.

'Timothy, I found this in the downstairs cloakroom. Is it yours?'

'Oh, Cora,' he beamed. 'It's Roger Fuller's Rolex. He's been looking for it everywhere. He even had the whole of the compost heap out. He'll be sooooooo thrilled you've found it.'

Cora had gone hot and cold. Surely not that Roger Fuller! He was so big, so manly, and the dead spit of his father who could never keep his hands off anything in a skirt. And what about his lovely wife and daughter? Did Sally Fuller know what he was up to? But her lips were sealed. It was too embarrassing to repeat anyway, but with the art of a natural voyeur, Cora kept her eyes open. Their full dirty weekends always coincided with Lady P's absence, and the black rubbish bags in the wheely bin contained the confirmation. Beer cans, wine bottles, boxes that had held super-whammy-King-sized-thick-crust pizza Margarita's, or endless tin foil take-away cartons. In Timothy Proudfoot terms (who had no other life apart from his mother and his vegetables), this was decadence indeed.

As she approached Timothy she noticed the Fuller's famous Wolfhound was bounding around. Its size terrified her, but thankfully the mad animal suddenly caught sight of a rabbit, and shot off like lightning, its body motivated by a hound's thrust, and complete lack of grey-matter. 'That's Roger's. . . er, Mr Fuller's dog,' Timothy said, by way of a halting explanation. 'He, er. . . stayed here last night. Moral support and all that.' Despite Timothy being gifted with the male version of his mother's beauty, he looked wrecked. His blue eyes were red-rimmed and puffed, and his mouth dropped down like a dead salmon.

Cora pursed her lips, looking serious and gimlet-eyed. 'Your mother was a truly wonderful and courageous woman,' she said, moving forward to pat his hand. 'I've come up to get you through the day, and to start planning the funeral reception. Chin up, ducky. You can rely on old Cora. I was here for you all those years ago, and I'm here for you now.' Timothy, stifling back tears, thanked her with a flowery sentence. Cora thanked him for thanking her, but when she got back up to the house she wished she'd saved her breath. What a mess to walk in to! Kitchen table a complete schlitter of cracker crumbs, buttery plates and dirty knives. Glasses and empty bottles, of course. Had to drink their fancy wine, didn't they? As much as she had sympathy, this would *not* be tolerated. If this was a signpost to the future, she would say ta-ta.

A small bunch of orange rosebuds sat in the sink, no doubt being the first of many floral tributes that would arrive, so she placed them in a glass tumbler, and gathered up as many vases as she could find, in readiness. She then contemplated doing the washing-up, mulling over an excuse of extenuating circumstances, but decided that she had to make a stand – it was a Manor House tradition that the family always loaded up the dishwasher themselves, and that was certainly the way things would stay. With no other pressing duties she decided she would get on with the ironing while she had the chance, and went to fetch the laundry basket, but was incensed to find the hideously spoiled cat stretched on top, playing the *femme fatale* card. Its blue eyes opened languidly, trying to convey hardship, but a broad hand gave it a firm order to scram.

In the room directly above Cora's head, Roger stood at the window, watching the exquisite figure of Timothy twirling the weed pole in the lake; a job they traditionally spent the whole of the Easter weekend doing together. He looked normal enough, so it was fingers crossed for a speedy recovery. Strange he hadn't heard him get up, though. Pity. He was feeling more than a smidge randy, and a good hard ruck would have set him up for the difficult day ahead. He moved to the adjoining bathroom, peed with the resonance of Shire horse, and headed jauntily down the back staircase to the kitchen.

As he bounded into the room Cora stared, but unlike most women, the sudden sight of a naked man didn't faze her. She looked him up and down as if he were for sale. 'Mr Fuller,' she said. 'I'd be grateful if you could cover yourself up, and don't be long about it. I think there's the little matter of a table for two to clear up from last night.' Roger, stunned like a rabbit in the eye of a poacher's lamp, had automatically crossed his hands to hide his accoutrement and made to flee, but at that precise point, Timothy walked into the kitchen, preceded by four bounding legs dripping wet, muddy sludge. 'Not in here!' Cora shrieked, flattening herself against the sink, but Finnegan, was dancing in anticipation of his breakfast. Seeing Roger, he imagined it must be somewhere close at hand, and leapt about, smearing a marl of toe-shaped splodges on the pristine cream walls.

'Sorry, Mrs Feather. He's a bit confused,' Roger said, but with both hands fully engaged, he was unable to attempt any practical restraints.

'Well, I've got a darn sight more to do than clear up after disturbed dogs,' Cora expounded. 'Oh, for heaven's sake go and get some clothes on, and you, Timothy, capture that animal.' There was a flurry of activity. Roger fled from the room and Timothy shooed Finnegan back out into the garden. The traumatised dog shot off, squealing from the attentions of a hissing cat, who was beginning to realise that all normality was draining from her life. In accompaniment to the pandemonium the front door bell rang, with three short bursts. The undertakers had arrived.

Chapter 15

Sally's map-reading skills were being seriously challenged by the maze of gorse-filled lanes, unique to the Suffolk heritage coastland. Having driven twice around the same six-mile circuit, she stopped at an old garage workshop for directions. 'It's down there,' an old mechanic said, pointing in the opposite way she'd come from. 'Straight over at the staggered crossroads, and first left.'

'Down there,' looked just as empty and misleading as before, so with no real confidence she nosed the Mini as directed. After several long minutes of despair the joy of a signpost guided her to, 'Waldringhythe Abbey'. She joined a single width lane, edged with high trees, and peppered with sandy passing places. At ground level pheasants jaywalked unperturbed, and above her head, wavering, whippy branches of bright spring green were interspersed by sharp, glittering sun.

Without warning the lane suddenly ended, to reveal a wide sweep of low farmland, and on the edge of the distant horizon she could see the glinting water of the Deben estuary. Before her a simple, black-painted board, with gold lettering, announced, '*Waldringhythe Abbey. Please drive slowly*', and to her right hand side, between a distant group of oaks and beeches, Sally caught her first glimpses of 13th-Century perimeter walls.

She turned into a wide drive, flanked by black metal railings, and ignored on either side by grazing sheep and bleating spring lambs. She was already feeling a sense of reverence, but when the full majesty of the Abbey loomed up before her, she slammed on her brakes with a sharp intake of breath. Why was she unprepared for such ancestral beauty? She'd studied the official handbook many times, and was familiar with its colour plate photographs, aerial shots, and professional blurb:

An outstanding and perfectly preserved 13th-century Cistercian
Monastery. . . a rare example of early English Gothic, with both
Tudor and Victorian additions. . . pointed arches, rib vaults, flying
buttresses, Mediaeval Great Hall, carved stone tracery, historic tiles,
early stained glass, wood panelling, ornate plaster work. . . extensive
landscaped gardens with panoramic views over the upper reaches of
the Deben estuary. . .

Her conclusion was that no abstract could portray the overpowering magnificence of Waldringhythe, but despite her shock and
humbling amazement, Sally sensed there was nothing intimidating in
its splendour. The gentle pastoral landscape of East Anglia gave up no
natural hewn stone, and thus the Cistercians, seeking to estrange
themselves from the Benedictines, had built the core of their sanctuary
using the only materials available to them: an endless supply of palm-
size elliptical stones endemic to the sweeping coastline, some five
miles down-river. The black and grey mottled flints had been soaked
by early morning rain, and now, full face in sunshine, threw up minute
diamond-bright flashes. Sally could picture bowed and silent ascetics,
patiently assembling layer after layer, hand over hand, toiling for
perhaps the whole of their short working lives to perpetuate their
blinding faith in God, and denial of physical comfort.

What struck her most powerfully was the stately-home opulence of
this mediaeval, religious institution. 'The Church' (as the body politic)
had never paid much part in her life. Being the child of a serving army
officer she'd been duly christened into the Church of England, but any
faith she'd been educated to had evaporated when her father was blown
up in a Christian war. Certainly, her extravagant white wedding had been
nothing more than a dressing-up excuse, so why on earth had she chosen
to work in a religious retreat? The answer was that one's denomination
was of little consequence at Waldringhythe. Father Ewan was a modern
and pragmatic priest, who recognised that experience and qualifications
superseded orthodoxy, and on business terms, an exclusively Roman
Catholic clientele couldn't balance the books. Thus Catholics, Anglicans,
Sikhs, Hindus, Muslims, Buddhists, Jews, and atheists flew in from all
corners of the world to this centre of excellence. He asked only that the
non-Catholics accepted the routines of those that were.

At the end of the drive a clear notice directed her.

Welcome to Waldringhythe Abbey
All visitors must book in at the Reception Hall
We request that you turn off your mobile phone for the entirety
of your stay
Thank You

Sally was met. As she drew up in the reception car park a young, black-frocked priest emerged from the front door, extending his hand and smiling warmly. 'Welcome. Welcome. I'm Father James.'

'Sally Fuller,' she said. 'You may not be expecting me. It was rather a rushed decision to come today.'

'Ah, Sally,' he said, with genuine pleasure. 'You're certainly expected. Father Ewan told me this morning you might be coming to work with us. I do hope so. We've a large team of counsellors, but Father Ewan's workload is far too heavy. He was off sick with exhaustion yesterday. The first time I've ever known him to cancel his list. I saw him this morning, and he looked very pale and drawn, so I had another nag at him to ease up a bit. Not that he'll listen – he's impossible to organise. Now, if you'll come with me, I'll take you over to your accommodation in the Prior's Lodgings. It used to be the Matron's quarters when the Abbey was a boarding school, so there's all mod cons and some lovely views. Can I take your cases out of the car?'

'I've only this one small bag.'

'Ah. Does that mean you're not stopping after all?'

'Oh no, Father James. I hope to stay for quite a while if I pass muster with Father Ewan. I've just decided to leave my old life behind and start afresh. It's going to be a complete make-over for me, and it won't just be mental.'

'Crumbs! Not the life and loves of a she-devil, I hope.'

'Not quite. Let's hope for the life and loves of a born-again angel.'

They laughed. How nice he was. How good it was already to be in the company of new people. How lifted she felt as they walked together, in easy conversation, through an archway of high cloisters.

'Have you ever met Father Ewan, Sally?' he asked.

'No,' she replied, 'but I've spoken to him on the phone several times. I don't know if he told you but I was Lady Proudfoot's Macmillan nurse.'

'No, he didn't say.'

'I kept him informed of the situation from time to time. She sadly died yesterday evening?'

He shook his head, sighed, and crossed himself. 'Word was that she was terminally ill, but I had no idea her death was so imminent. I'm so sorry. In all the years she came here she insisted on total seclusion, so the rest of us didn't know her at all. But of course that was her prerogative, and we all respected it. I'm sure Father Ewan will mourn her passing deeply.'

Father James then stopped abruptly and clapped his hands together. 'What perfect timing! It's himself!' He lifted up on his toes and waved with both hands, smiling broadly, showing an extension of the genuine person he was, and his obvious fondness for his mentor and fellow priest. 'Father Ewan,' he called. 'Father Ewan. Here's Mrs Fuller.'

Sally's first sight of the famed cleric was something of a shock as he bore no resemblance to the shadowed picture from the handbook, or the iconic youth of *Crucifix Man*. He walked wearily towards them; tall, lean, bearded, and bespectacled, wearing a long, voluminous brown velvet cloak. His hair was completely white, bald on the crown, with the remainder pulled into a thick ponytail at the nape of his neck. Conversely his eyebrows, beard and Zapata style moustache were dark, but surely. . . Yes. . . Hardly noticeable. An extremely successful cleft lip repair, but the imperfection enhanced his face with a compelling attraction.

He approached and nodded to Father James, but when he took Sally's extended hand, he bowed and kissed her fingers. She resisted the urge to laugh, or even smile, at his unexpected behaviour, as the reserved expression on his face clearly offered no invitation of warmth or friendship. The colour of his eyes was indefinable behind the smoked lenses of designer frames, a small gold hoop earring in his right ear carried a pearl droplet, and on the third finger of his left hand was a plain gold band. He seemed to shiver, and as he adjusted his cloak, she noticed he was wearing black leather trousers and bright red rock-climbing boots. Were these strange affectations of dress a deliberate psychological choice to appear as an eccentric rather than a standard, cassock-clad priest?

'I'm pleased to meet you, Sally,' he said quietly, 'but I was actually expecting your Wolfhound too.' His voice was temperate, and essentially English public school, but with the slight nasality of those who have endured surgery to lip and palate.

'Finnegan's staying with my ex-husband,' she said. 'I thought it best that I settled myself in first.'

'I'm rather sorry,' he said. 'I like dogs. I haven't had one since I was a child and I was looking forward to it. Anyway, I'm glad *you're* here, and I warmly welcome you to Waldringhythe. Can I talk to you later on if it's convenient? Say eight o'clock at my house? James will give you directions. Now you'll have to excuse me as I'm due to take an outreach class.' He bowed slightly and moved away, but almost immediately turned back. 'On second thoughts, Sally, perhaps you'd like to join me. It'll give you an insight into the diversity of methods we use here.'

'Of course, Father Ewan. I'd be most interested.'

'Excellent. James, can you organise a cup of tea for Sally and bring her to the Long Hall for 11.30?'

Sally joined a quiet, mixed-sex group of about twenty apprehensive counsellees, waiting with aimless detachment from each other. Father Ewan entered with a positive flourish, now wearing his conventional priest's garments, but he offered the group no cheery greeting. Without preamble, or ceremony, he started the session.

'For those of you who haven't taken part in an outreach session before, can I briefly explain what we hope to achieve? Salvation to your grief is not solely centred on your journey to know yourself. You must be able – and this is probably the hardest test of all – to re-create a detached memory of your loved one without emotional context. Can I ask that you have no conversation with anyone else? Empty your mind. Try to concentrate fully without distractions, and to evoke a feeling of inner peace and tranquillity. Now find a partner.'

Not since school days had Sally heard the dreaded words 'find a partner.' Memories rushed in of all the established best-friend bondings, flapping their hands and scanning for each other, and there was she, the army child, who'd been to six schools before she was eleven and had never stayed in one place long enough to become anyone's best friend. Relief was found as Father Ewan's hand touched her shoulder.

'Stand and face each other,' he instructed the group, 'Press your palms together with your partner's, and close your eyes. I want you to concentrate fully on your departed one, and try to visualise them through your hands. Focus positively on an occasion when they were especially happy, vigorous and full of life. Tell yourself, and them, that forgetting is not an option. You will always carry them with you in your heart, but your future life must be lived, and you can only do this by memorising without anger and sentimentality.'

Although Sally was aware that this type of grief counselling was unique to Father Ewan's ethos, her own training course had rejected group therapy. She had thus been a little sceptical of its value, and she fractionally opened her lids. Father Ewan's eyes were tightly shut, he was deeply committed, and his lips moved silently. With a compulsion to co-operate, she did the same.

After a few minutes he instructed the class to separate. 'Open your eyes but don't make eye contact with anyone. Try to maintain the images you've created, and the peace within yourself. Think about the growth of spring, and your own inner growth. Go now quietly. If you wish to communicate with your God, it's a good time to pray. Have a hot drink and a short rest, followed by a brisk, solitary walk in the grounds. As you walk, try to focus on any advances that outreach may have given you. Write them down and bring them to your next individual session. God bless you all.'

'I'll see you at eight o'clock as arranged then, Sally,' Father Ewan said quietly. Hanging his head, he slipped rapidly out of the room.

Chapter 16

'Jesus Christ, that'll be the bloody undertakers,' Roger shouted, dithering on the stairs. 'Mrs Feather, hold the fort until I'm dressed. Tim, just stay calm.' Cora, still simmering from her altercation with a naked man and a mad dog, immediately switched from dragon to dove. As Roger fled she grabbed Timothy's arm with matriarchal compassion, and with slow-footed solemnity, steered him up the long kitchen corridor to the front reception hall. Through a side window she could see an immaculate Volvo estate (special order with smoked blackout windows, reinforced floor, and nine inches longer than the norm) parked strategically distant, with its open tailgate to the fore.

'It's them all right,' she mouthed, lurching forward to open the door.

Three grave-faced men were standing in stiff line. They were all of equal height, equal shoulders being the prime requirement of coffin bearers, and apart from radiant white shirts were dressed in traditional black. Their patent leather shoes shone like glass, and Cora thought they resembled three elderly tap dancers. With perfect co-ordination all three stood at ease and clasped their hands behind their backs. Mr Sidney Fullylove, the proprietor himself, was placed centrally, and announced his superiority with a gold tiepin depicting the Fullylove logo; a flying dove with an olive leaf in its beak. He moved forward, massaging his gloved hands with Uriah Heep-like subservience. 'In respect of the departed, Mrs Maureen Proudfoot,' he simpered with hushed, oily tones, and proffering a small, black-edged card.

Fullylove and Fullylove
Family Funeral Directors, Est 1914
Saying goodbye to your loved ones with reverence and dignity

As Cora examined the card she pursed her lips, and was compelled to correct him. 'It's actually *Lady* Maureena, what's pronounced Marina,' but before she had a chance to officiate further, Roger walked confidently down the front staircase, fully dressed and sporting a sombre, authoritative face.

'Thank you, Mrs F, but I'll attend to this. Please don't let me keep you from your normal duties.' Cora, being ungraciously dismissed, had no choice but to return to the kitchen. As she moved off glowering Roger turned his full attention to the undertakers. 'Good morning, gentlemen. Please follow me upstairs.' The trio entered the house without comment, wiping their feet fastidiously and examining the carpet.

Once in Marina's bedroom they carefully unfolded a light chromium trolley, of the type a magician uses when he elevates and vanishes the lady, but sadly, despite the fairy lightness of Marina's body, there would be no dignified exit. The three chorus boys puffed and groaned with ruddy faces, demonstrating that their short arms, thick waistlines, and advancing years had robbed them of any artistic ability. After much struggle and effort the corpse was transferred to a zipped mummy-shaped bag, secured by straps to the trolley, and manhandled down to the front door.

'Such a joy to have a wide-staircase,' Mr Fullylove said, with unrequired familiarity. 'We usually only get the two-foot turn round of a standard semi to work in. It involves a complicated vertical manoeuvre that's less than ideal.'

Roger, in the role of stoical family supporter, accompanied the working party to supervise the transfer to the Volvo, taking a full military stance as the black car crunched slowly down the drive, and out of sight.

Timothy, who had watched the proceedings from his mother's empty bedroom, sat in the window-seat, his head bowed with depression. Was it only a week ago that she'd lain back in heroined comfort and idly reminisced? At first, recalling the happy memoirs of himself as a rewarding, loving child, but then, with half-closed eyes and a sweet smile on her face, she'd begun to talk of Morgana. 'She was a feisty little madam, wasn't she, Tim? Do you remember that pull-along Snoopy she called Hoggyponk, and how she used to shout at him, and tell him off, when his little clicking legs got stuck? I'm sure she wished she'd been a boy. She had no time for teddies and dolls – she'd much rather kick a football with Pa on the lawn. Do you remember that huge purple handbag she hauled everywhere? I've asked Father Ewan to bless it, and make sure it comes in the box with me. You'll find it in her room and you must make absolutely sure he gets it.'

Yes, Timothy well remembered his little sister. Her insistence that her big brother Timfee carry her everywhere on his back. Her moodiness, her thumb-sucking, her calling in the night for nothing at all, and her stroppy little foot stamps when she was asked to do something she didn't want to do. Did either of them really remember Morgana, or had they created another child out of snatched enlargements from her short life?

And his mother had also talked lovingly of his father. 'Toby loved Yeats, you know, Tim. At our wedding we had a full reading of *Men Improve With The Years,* and indeed he did. *'O would that we had met when I had my burning youth!* There were so many years between us, but the older he got the stronger our love became. He was the darlingest man, a wonderful husband, and a devoted father to both of you.' She'd then closed her eyes and disappeared into a short sleep. Thankfully, Timothy had been able to turn away, and press his face into a cushion.

Roger came back into the room cracking his knuckles. 'Mission accomplished, old chap. They said they'll try to arrange the cremation as soon as possible. A week's about the average delay. No longer than that.' Cora's strident voice was then heard calling up the stairs, to tell them that she was off to Mr Bhatti's, because they were clean out of milk and biscuits, and you had to offer tea and biscuits to all the people who would be coming round to pay their respects, and actually it would be a very good idea if Mr Fuller could do a full shop at Sainsbury's when he could find the time.

Mr Fuller, in unseen sanctuary, raised two sharp fingers. 'Tim, do we really have to put up with that old hag? She gives me the shits.'

'I'm afraid we do,' Timothy replied. 'You'll get used to the old feather duster. She might seem grumpy, but she means well.'

'Well, I've got something to tell you that might remedy the situation.' Roger smiled for effect, his eyes dancing up and down like a naughty schoolboy's. 'A surprise! I'm going to pack up work.'

'What? But you can't!'

'Yes I can. Sandridge Fuller can do without me. I won't give up my directorship, but I intend to become a sleeping partner. Stuff it. I shall really enjoy domestic life so we won't need the housekeeper from hell.'

'Oh, that's wonderful. We can expand the business. Get some more greenhouses put up. There's a huge demand for butternut squashes.'

'We're going to be really happy, Angel.'

'Skipper,' said Timothy, gingerly. 'At the cremation. We *are* going as an item aren't we? You know – like we talked about. Come out. Show the village.'

'We most certainly are, honey,' said Roger confidently. 'Gay pride and fuck it will be the order of the day.'

'And is it really all sorted with Sally?'

'Yes, Tim. Once and for all, it's all sorted with Sally. I love *you*. All those years ago we wanted it to last forever, but we were young and the world was a different place. Things went wrong. We were both to blame, but we can't spend the rest of our lives wrangling with 'what ifs.' You're still that beautiful boy I fell in love with on that awful day, and. . .'

Timothy dropped his head and screwed his hands into fists. 'That day. We don't talk about it, do we? We put it away, like you pack things away in a box and hide them in the loft, but it's always been there like a black shadow. It's been over twenty-five years, Rog. I thought I'd learned to live with it, but the minute Mumma died, the horror came marching back. All the old wounds are being opened up. Hold me, Rog. I feel so weak and peculiar. You will get me through this nightmare, won't you?'

''Course I will, love. Come here.'

As Roger put his arms around Timothy he found, that although his own memories of the day were more horrific than Tim realised, it was the day *after* Morgana and Toby were drowned that came more readily to mind. Marina, standing straight-backed, hideously controlled, and icily acerbic. His father, having identified the bloated body of the child, being forced to stumble through the worst afternoon of his life, and himself sitting there like a big moronic dummy. The events that later culminated in his first blissful seduction of Tim. He'd forgotten that Cora Feather had also been there.

JUNE 1982

Roger and his father stood at the front door of Monks Bottom Manor, stooped with diffidence, and sweating with anxiety at the scenario to come. It was opened by Mrs Feather, the lumbering, pigeon-breasted woman, famed in the village for her sumptuous cricket teas. 'Yes. What can I do for you?' she demanded, with the challenge of a security guard.

His father spoke with quiet respect. 'We'd like to consult with Lady Proudfoot.' Cora nodded covertly, conveying she was 'in the know' to every single micro-detail of the situation, and that she gave her approval to the request.

'She's in the garden room. She's very shaky but Doctor Devlin's just given her something to help. I'll take you through.'

Marina was standing alone, dressed in long black garments, within a tableau of tropical green plants. Her usual classic chignon tumbled in golden-blonde chaos to her waist, and her face was that of a stranger. Her lips were pale, twitching and thinly compressed. The linings of her eyes were inflamed, emphasising the stunning bright blue of her irises. Her nose was florid and shedding skin, having been blown, and sniffed, and rasped, by a great many fine linen handkerchiefs. All Roger really wanted to do was to run away, but at the age of twenty-three, and being (as he was then) a Captain in the Grenadier Guards, he was expected to behave like an officer and a gentleman.

The widow turned with the grace of a prima ballerina. 'Toby was a great admirer of Larry Adler, you know,' she said, but it was obvious she was expecting no further small talk about jazz harmonicas. Roger's father moved forward jerkily to take her hand, but she backed off with a writhing body movement that said, 'don't touch me!' She gestured for them to sit on two large wicker armchairs, but she remained standing.

'Positive identification,' Alex continued. 'It *was* her.'

'Of course it was her, Alex. How many other children were drowned yesterday? And where exactly was she found?'

'In a weir near Hurley Lock.'

She nodded. 'Thank you, Alex. It can't have been pleasant.'

'Marina, you know I'd give my own life to turn the clock back. What else can I do to help you? Surely, there must be something?'

She stared at him, in a pose of cynicism. 'To make *you* feel better, or to make *me* feel better?'

'I *am* grieving for you. Please believe me. . .' but the conversation had reached the immediate truth that Alex wanted a quick release from any indictment.

'Alex, be assured there'll be no charges, or seeking of compensation. The fact that you own the *San Fairy Ann* doesn't mean you're guilty of any crime. The police are satisfied that the boat was correctly certified, and all the required safety standards were in place. It was my fault for not ensuring she wore a life jacket. Now they're gone, and I must live my own death sentence.' Her eyes shut tightly, and her jaw tensed.

Roger's father was a successful man of business, but of so little sensitivity that he was floundering like a hooked trout to sound profound and wise. 'Marina, perhaps you might be able to find some support through your religion?'

'No chance. I'm hopelessly lapsed, but Toby was devout. Father Joseph would come and drink our sherry, and they talked philosophy together, but the old bore had no time for me.' She turned her head away and addressed the garden. 'Like everyone else, he thought I was no more than a dumb blonde. A trophy wife. I'll tell you what I am, Alex, or rather what I was. How many times, over the years, have you made me a filthy little offer behind the salad dips, and how many times did I fall for a bit of fun? Never. That's how often. No one could ever believe it, but I was a faithful, loving wife. We had to wait sixteen long years for. . . for our daughter. Sixteen years! I know the village was rife with vile rumours that she wasn't Toby's child, but she was. She was our miracle. Now they've both gone and I'm bereft.' She swung back to look at them fiercely. 'I can't help being bitter,' she raged, 'but I've their funerals to get through, and I must be strong enough to support Tim.' She paused, sighed deeply, and became becalmed. 'I'm so sorry I flew at you, Alex. It was very undignified. Please forgive me.'

Suddenly, seeming to remember Roger's presence, she walked over and placed her hands on his shoulders. 'Roger. Dear Roger. I'll never forget how hard you tried to save my little girl. You put your own life in such danger, and you're truly a hero. But then you saved Tim's life, and for that I truly thank you. Now you really must go up and see him. If there's one thing he needs it's some young company. He heard last week that Kew has accepted him as an RHS student, and I so want him to go. Perhaps you can support and encourage him?' With sudden strength she tossed her head back, and ran her fingers through her hair. 'Now, Alex, there *is* something else you can do for me, after all. I've wreaths to choose. Will you take me into Henley, please?'

Cora Feather preceded Roger up the stairs and knocked on Timothy's bedroom door. She called him Mr Timothy in those days. 'Mr Timothy. Here's Mr Fuller to see you. Mr Roger. He'd like to come in if it's all right.' The door opened and Roger entered the room, darkened by closed curtains against the bright sun of the afternoon. Cora hovered but Timothy shut the door against her. She tapped at the door again. 'Would you be wanting a tray of tea, because if not I'm just off?'

Timothy made a gesture as if he were tightening a knot. 'No thank you, Mrs Feather,' he called. 'Goodbye. Your kindness is truly appreciated.' He then sat down on a small padded chair while Roger took to the floor, leaning his back against the sharp protrusions of an ancient metal radiator. 'Thank you for saving me,' said Timothy. 'A million times thank you, but it should have been them, not me.'

'It was just chaos,' said Roger. 'Everyone was splashing around the bow and shouting. I tried to find Morgana so desperately. I went under the water twenty or thirty times, but it became so stirred up, it was as black as night and as thick as soup. There was just no point carrying on. Then, when I emerged for the last time, I could see you were in trouble.'

The Fuller Jaguar was heard spiriting the widow away to the florists. The front door banged, and Cora's flat, heavy feet were heard crunching away down the drive. Roger swallowed and fixed eye contact with Timothy. He got up, moved across to him and knelt down. He took his hands and focussed on his face with soft concern. 'How *are* you, Tim? You must be feeling lousy?'

'It's so bad. So bad. How can I ever live a normal life again?'

Roger began to massage the inside of Timothy's wrists with his thumbs. 'Tim. Everything's going to be all right. I can help you. You do like me, don't you?' Timothy nodded. 'And you do like me in another special way too, don't you?' Timothy nodded again. 'As special as this?' Roger rose up, leaned forward, and kissed him on the mouth. 'I love you, Tim. I'm *in* love with you, and I want to make love to you, but I want to look after you as well. My love can help you to survive all this.'

'I've been in love with you for years,' said Timothy. 'Do you remember all those village sports events the vicar's wife got together in the school hols? I went to all of them if I knew you'd be there. I followed you around like a pet dog, but I know you never noticed me. You were always captain of cricket, and you looked so splendid in your whites, and in the winter, when it snowed, there were those toboggan contests on the common. One year I sat behind you, and I held on to your waist, and we bumped all the way down Abbot's Hill together. It was magic. The moment I knew. . . You know. When I knew for sure what all my dreams were about.'

'What a stupid blind bastard I was. I'm sorry I didn't notice you, but you were only a kid in those days. It was yesterday that did it for me. The sight of you sitting there on the boat with the sunlight on your face. And it was the way you looked at me, too. I just knew. I was trying to concentrate on steering the boat, but all I wanted to do was look at you.'

'I was looking at you all the time, too. You looked so fantastic in that Ark Royal hat'.

'It was only something whacky. Good old Rog, playing the clown as usual.'

'I thought it made you look so. . . you know. . . so important. So powerful. You were the Skipper, and I was the naval rating. I wanted to be your slave.'

'Call me Skipper, then.' Roger began to slide his lips down Timothy's neck, and his hand reached out to lie on his thigh. There was a short silence, both knowing that within the next few seconds the commitment would be made. 'Have you ever made love, Tim?'

'No. Never. Have you?'

'Only a few times,' Roger lied. 'Boy at school. Innocent fumbling. Not love like this.'

'Ever with a girl?'

'Never,' he lied again.

Roger began to pull Timothy's T-shirt over his head. Gradually, they undressed each other, moved to the bed, pulled the duvet back, and lay on the cool sheet facing each other. 'I want to make it good for you, Tim,' Roger cooed. 'I want to make you fly. Tell me your fantasies. What are they? You must know.'

'I can't tell you.'

'Yes, you can. No thoughts are wrong. Thoughts are only thoughts and they can never do harm. I must share your secrets. Tell me, honey. Tell me.'

'Their bed used to ring like a bell. It called out in the night, and so did they. I wanted to be in there, with them, between them. He called her Angel. You have to call me Angel.'

'Then come here, my Angel,' Roger said.

Chapter 17

Ewan found that taking the outreach session had left him drained and exhausted. He'd participated so deeply in the class himself he felt like a gagged cat; desperate to yowl but compelled by his own instruction to an ordered dignity. He'd tried to follow his own edicts to the letter, but all he felt was pain. How demanding and tough the McEwan School was. It hurt. It hurt so much he needed morphine. He wanted to clear his desk, to run away, and disappear forever into the Deben mist.

But he knew, without doubt, that his methods were successful, and the whole purpose of Waldringhythe stemmed from his innovation and direction. At Christmas and Easter he received hundreds of cards from past patients, each with personal messages of thanks, and stories of an enriched life. All of them from Joe Public, the root and branch of life, toilers in the field of the ordinary, who had gritted their teeth and got stuck in, without any prior knowledge of navel-gazing. They'd struggled like drowning sailors, but for the most part, had endured the pain barrier and been brought to peace. He looked at his watch. Just after four. He produced his mobile phone.

'Poznanski,' a weak, dry voice answered.

'Jacob, it's me.'

'My dear boy. My poor boy. What can this old wreck do to comfort you?'

'Just tell me you love me.'

'*Ikh hob dikh lib.* I give you the Yiddish words of my mother.' Ewan failed to answer. 'Are you still there, my lib?'

'Yes, but. . .' He paused again.

'My people have a word for your sadness. *Farklempt.* It means too emotional to talk. I will leave you, but my arms are reaching out to hold you. We will talk again soon. *Lila Tov.*'

The phone clicked dead. Ewan ran the heel of his hand inside his eyes, and across his running nose. Rising from the chair he stumbled out of the room, and shakily climbed the staircase to his bedroom. There, he prostrated himself on the floor before his Madonna, and began to intone his usual words. *'In the name of the Father, and of the Son, and of the Holy Spirit...'*, but he had to stop. He opened his eyes and looked up at the image of *Crucifix Man* hanging on the wall. The means that had, forever, set him apart from the rank and file of the priesthood, and had ensured his place in twentieth-century history. A brave pioneer with the audacity of youth and the resolve of a warrior. Was that young man really this broken heap of weakness and despair? Rising up onto his knees he tried another traditional prayer. *'Behold, O Kind and most sweet Jesus, before Thy face I humbly kneel'*, but trying to continue was pointless. His purpose on earth was shot away like a clay pigeon; blasted into sharp fragments, and falling fast to ground. His palms, and the small of his back, ran with sweat as his own words intoned; *to know yourself is to understand yourself, and memory is the only key.* With fainting spirit he continued his odyssey, now knowing his faith was no longer with him.

SEPTEMBER 1978

Ewan had visited his mother daily in the psychiatric unit, but due to his youth and inexperience, he found them excruciating to endure. The unit purported to be bright and relaxed, with cheerful staff cracking jokes, and treating their charges as if they were all completely normal. But in reality, the smell of dried urine, and the unpredictable behaviour of the patients, made Ewan nauseous. They rocked, they gaped, they dribbled. They slept, they snored, they wet themselves. They wailed, they screamed, they spat. They argued and they fought. They twisted their hair to baldness, and occasionally exposed themselves.

Mostly, she wouldn't recognise him, sitting wordlessly rigid with her head stuck firmly into her neck; pop-eyed and fearful, as if menaced by a terrifying spectre. Some days she would be distressed and agitated, shouting about 'the buggers', and slapping the arms of the chair in frustration. On others she was fairly lucid and animated, greeting him with a wobbly-headed wave, and demanding news of the Abbey people. Days like these gave him hope that she would soon 'be better', and she could return to Waldringhythe, but her consultant psychiatrist explained that these mood swings were consistent with a deep psychotic illness. Although she was undergoing a regime of medication, psychotherapy, and social rehabilitation, discharge would only be considered if she could be meticulously medicated, and under constant supervision. Ewan had thought, in his simple and naive way, that Sister Wagstaffe and the local district nurse, would be able to cope with her, but it was only when he discussed this possibility with Father Paulinus that he heard the bad news.

'Ewan. This may come as a shock to you. We're being forced to close the school, and I'm ashamed to say that the blame must fall squarely on the shoulders of the senior priests, including myself. We know now that we've been introverted and blind. Far fewer parents are looking towards a strict religious education these days, and registrations have been seriously falling off. Added to that, the majority of us are on the point of retirement, and young Catholic teachers, even if we could find enough, are looking to teach a much more modern curriculum. Your father was a terrible loss to us, Ewan. He'd actually been trying to open our eyes to the situation for a long time, but it was only at the beginning of this last academic year that we realised how right he'd been. He became our driving force in trying to prevent closure, and he'd been working on all sorts of schemes and plans. Like getting local authorities and the diocese to fund scholarships, taking students from overseas, and developing summer sports camps. He even suggested that we should take girls and non-Catholics, but the Archbishop vetoed that as far too radical to our traditions.'

'My mother and I hadn't heard a whisper,' Ewan said.

'That was typical of your father. Loyal, discreet, and wholly professional. He'd formed several committees, and worked on report after report, but the intake for next year is far too small to continue. We're deeply in debt, and the school must close immediately. I can only pray that the Abbey's magnificence is saved for the nation.'

'Father Paulinus. Do you think this stress contributed to his heart attack?'

'Undoubtedly, Ewan, undoubtedly, and in view of this, the Bishop has agreed to fully fund your mother's care for the rest of her life. We've just heard that The Sisters of Mercy in Spitalfields can offer her a permanent home.'

'That's such good news, Father Paulinus. It's a great relief to me. I'll write to the Bishop and thank him.'

'Will you still take up your place at St Scholastica's?'

'Definitely. Now I know my mother's future is secure I can accept the place. Studies commence in three weeks.'

'I thank God that you will be joining us in the priesthood, Ewan, and we welcome you with all our hearts.'

Ewan had dreaded telling his mother that she couldn't return to Waldringhythe, but he'd been supported by the Bishop, the kindly Mother Superior from The Sisters of Mercy, and Father Paulinus. 'So, I'll be near you in London then, son?' she asked gruffly.

'Yes, Mum. I'll be able to pop in and see you quite a lot.'

'And is there a garden to sit in? Can I wear my own clothes? Can I make a cake? Can I knit? Can I take Iggy-Piggy?' The spirited Sister Concepta took over, giving out an enthusiastic spiel about all the home comforts they would provide for both her, and her elderly, arthritic dog. 'And is there a typewriter? I must have a typewriter.'

'I'm sure we can find you a typewriter, Mrs McEwan.'

'Good. Ewan and I have a gae lot of work to do.'

'And what sort of work is that, Mum?'

'You know what we've got to do,' she screamed. 'We've got to nail the bastards. Get something done. Bring the buggers to book.'

The gentle nun soothed her with well-meaning words, and talk quickly turned to recipes and knitting patterns, but she wasn't to be distracted. 'You all want me to keep my mouth shut, but I won't. Ewan knows what I'm talking about, don't you, dear?' Unseen by his mother, he shrugged, but she turned round and grabbed his hand. 'Read it,' she pleaded. 'I wrote it all down. You'll find it under the bed, in a suitcase, and every single word is true.'

On returning to Waldringhythe, Ewan reached under his mother's bed and withdrew a battered leather suitcase. Inside, there was a cardboard folder, labelled '*Strathburn*', that contained some neatly

typed pages. He sat on the bed, and with a sense of dread and respon-
sibility, began to read:

29th July 1966

To Mr. Archie Dungannon, the Member of Parliament for
Strathburn
This report is a truthful record of my own personal
experiences and I am willing to testify this in a court
of law. .

My name is Jean Morag McEwan, (nee Anderson). I
was born in 1929, and brought up in Ardneath, a small
town on the west coast of Scotland. During the war, a
great many local people were employed at the
Strathburn naval base near the town, and in the summer
of 1944 six girls, including myself, were recruited
as a team. We were all school-leavers aged around
fourteen or fifteen years old. The work we were
attached to took place in three very large concrete
buildings, situated in a wooded area, a mile up the
coast from the naval base. It was obvious we were
working for civilian scientists, and the most senior
was called Dr Frydenberger. We called ourselves lab
assistants, but all we did was wash glass and metal
ware, so we were really just domestic helps. Apart
from us, no other outside personnel was employed. We
had to report to the naval base to be signed in, and
we would be driven up to the site in a truck. We had to
sign a paper to say that we wouldn't talk about our
work, but a lot of that went on in the war and we
didn't think it was odd. None of us knew what was
going on anyway, and nor were we interested. It was
just boring war work, and we got on with our jobs. All
it entailed was to go around with metal trolleys,

83

collect up the dirty equipment, and take it back to a washhouse. Some of it was so big it took two of us to load it up, and for those things we had to use a hose and a broom.

A year later the war ended, and of course that was the end of our jobs. My parents sent me to finish my education at a boarding school near Stirling, and I then got a place at a teacher training college in Glasgow. In 1951, a couple of years after I qualified, I married a fellow student, Duncan McEwan. I became pregnant straight away, which we were delighted about, but I lost the baby. For the next nine years I suffered miscarriage after miscarriage, but we never gave up hope. Eventually, I carried a child to term, and our son, Ewan, was born on September 9th, 1960.

Shortly after his birth my husband was offered the deputy headship of a boy's Roman Catholic School, near the city of Auckland in New Zealand, and we left to start a new life. We settled down as a happy family, but when Ewan was four he suddenly became ill. He was diagnosed with a vicious form of leukaemia, and died three weeks later. His death was a horrible tragedy for us, but we bore our grief with great support from our religious beliefs and church community. However, we came to feel very isolated and homesick, so we decided to return to the United Kingdom. A few days out on the boat journey back, I became very ill. My medical condition was so acute I was airlifted and hospitalised in Australia. I was diagnosed with an ectopic pregnancy. It was then that the surgeons discovered my other ovary was cystic, and I would thereafter be infertile.

Once back in England, knowing we would never become natural parents again, we applied to adopt a child. Last year we were delighted to be offered a five-year-old boy, whom we re-named Ewan. Just at this time my husband was appointed head of the English department, at Waldringhythe Abbey School in Suffolk, where the three of us happily live today.

Earlier this year I returned to Strathburn, to attend the funeral of my mother, my last surviving parent. Whilst there I became re-acquainted with Mrs Rhona Patterson, the mother of Janet, one of the girls I'd worked with during the war, and who had been my best friend from school. Naturally, Mrs Patterson had heard of my son's death, and was very sympathetic, but was delighted to hear I had now adopted a little boy. Our conversations took us down memory lane, but it soon became clear that happy stories of domestic bliss were not to be exchanged. It is the information she gave me that form the basis of my report.

In the twenty years since the six of us girls had worked together, three had already died, one of thyroid cancer and the other two of leukaemia. Janet, now living in Canada, had had multiple miscarriages like myself, but had had no live births. Another of the girls, Rhona, now living in London, had been unable to conceive. We agreed that these experiences were more than co-incidence. Mrs Patterson said she 'smelt a rat' and wondered if we'd been 'poisoned' up at the naval base. It was then I formed the conclusion that we must have been exposed to radiation through our wartime work.

We would thus like the following points to be the subject of a public enquiry.

1) Due to their working as domestic servants at the Strathburn Naval base, between 1944 and 1945, six young women were exposed to nuclear contamination .

2) That three of the girls have already lost their lives to cancer, and the surviving three, Janet Black (née Patterson), Rhona Ellis (née Cuddy) and

Jean McEwan (née Anderson) are living under the future threat of it.

3) Janet Black suffered multiple miscarriages and Rhona Ellis has been unable to conceive. This in turn has been responsible for them not being able to enjoy the normal rewards of family life.

4) I myself, Jean McEwan, also suffered multiple miscarriages, before my only child, Ewan Duncan Anderson McEwan, was born. This child died at the age of four from a vicious form of leukaemia, and I believe him to be a victim of radiation, congenitally transferred to him by myself.

I attribute all of the above to be directly caused by Dr Frydenberger's wartime work, which must have been ordered and funded by our own government, or by the allies.

Please, will you respond to this report in writing? I would be grateful to you for an appointment to meet and discuss the contents of this report.

Jean McEwan.

Ewan had read the unworldly, simplistic report and allowed the sparse pages to drop from his hands, thinking that they should land like concrete slabs onto his knees. He knew that some sort of radical reaction was required of him. That he should leap up, with fire in his belly, and a metaphorical gun in his hand. To rush out like Che Guevara, and blast at the establishment, until what he'd read was heralded in six-inch headlines on the front of every newspaper in the world. But although he knew what he should do, he also knew, with a sense of failure, that he would never be able to behave in the way his poor troubled mother wanted him to. All over the country the voices of his own generation were heard, either in the crazy clothes of glam rock and punk culture, or in the irreverent lyrics of pop songs. Life was a gas, and drugs were cool, but he didn't belong to this normal, happy band of fun-seekers, who thumbed their noses at authority and challenged the establishment. The only concession to his peer group was to grow his hair to his shoulders, but he wasn't really one of them, and never would be. Fashion, and music, and the exaggerated holiday shenanigans of his school-friends were just things that happened to *them*. He listened, and smiled, and joined in the fun of laughing at their exploits, but he had no feelings of jealousy, or that he was deprived in any way. Reading the report had certainly made him feel something, but it wasn't for revenge or confrontation. He just wasn't a radical. His only response was of humanitarianism and altruism, of a priest-in-waiting. Priests didn't hurl bombs. Priests pacified. Priests loved. Priests offered support. Priests forgave.

When his mother had talked to him in her muddled, incoherent way about the report she'd screamed at him to, 'Nail the bastards. Get something done. Bring the buggers to book'. He now felt as if he'd been saddled with an inescapable burden, and being her only link to the sensible outside world, was duty bound to do something. The only problem was that 'something' was all or nothing.

Clearly, in its present form, the report was useless. There was no scientific or medical evidence, no detailed research, and no copies of archived government papers documenting any sort of wartime nuclear activity in the area. In her unworldly way, his mother had prepared the report as an account of the truth as she knew it. In her innocence, she probably thought that this would be enough to engage the enthusiastic interest of an elderly Liberal backbencher, who had no desire for controversy, and rarely showed his face in the House of Commons. The only reply she'd received was from a civil servant thanking her for her letter, and that the contents 'had been noted'.

He contemplated for days what his response should be, and if he could possibly fulfil any sort of promise to his mother, but his procrastination brought no decision. No decision meant that he would do nothing, and thus, he put the report back under the bed. If his mother mentioned it again, as inevitably she would, he would have to pat her hand, and appease her with the sin of a white lie. That he was doing what he could.

Chapter 18

Roger dreamily returned from his reverie of Tim's first seduction, to middle-aged reality, feeling both a sense of sweet nostalgia and the inevitable erection. Timothy, in need of emotional comfort, tightened his arms around Roger. 'Kiss me, Skipper.'

'I like to do a lot more than kiss you,' Roger mumbled, producing the usual shorthand of puffs and pants that preceded foreplay, but Timothy immediately tensed and jerked away.

'How on earth can you think of *that* at a time like this?

'What do you mean, "at a time like this"?' Roger snapped. 'I seem to remember our first time was *exactly* at a time like this. You were as randy as a jackrabbit. Couldn't get your kecks off quick enough from what I remember, so don't go all precious on me.' But, any thoughts of coitus were brutally interrupted, by a hideous howling of Baskerville proportions, emanating from the garden.

A wet and thoroughly miserable Finnegan was found hovering on the scullery doorstep, not quite knowing if he was welcome or not, sheepishly turning his head in a canine version of spinning the sympathy vote. 'He missed his breakfast', Roger said. 'He's starving.'

'Is he really?' replied Timothy. 'Well seeing as I'm not *au fait* with his dietary requirements, what might he like to eat?'

'He normally has a tin of tripe dog food, and a bowl of sweet tea.'

'Well, surprise, surprise! We're clean out of tinned tripe. It wouldn't have occurred to you to bring some with you, I suppose? He'll have to have some Weetabix, and from what I remember there's only a couple left. We haven't got any milk either, until Cora gets back, so he'll have to have them soaked in water. I think someone's going to have to go to Sainsbury's and it isn't going to be me!'

Donning the mantle of the mood, Roger sat silently on a kitchen chair with unaccustomed anxiety. Everyone who knew Timothy had to admit he was intrinsically sweet-natured and easy-going. Any sign of aggression, or even mild irritation, that could (in the loosest terms) be called attitude, was non-existent. Roger could thus, only watch with bewilderment, as he banged about in full tantrum, angrily preparing a mush of cereal in a Coalport soup tureen. When he cloncked it down carelessly on the kitchen floor Finnegan dived in with gusto, slurping like a sump pump.

'He needs it on a stool or he might get bloat,' Roger said carefully.

'What's bloat?'

'His stomach fills with air and he blows up. It's life threatening.'

'Good. I hope he explodes! I hate him.'

'You really *don't* like him, do you?'

'Oh, well done, Einstein!'

'Well, I don't like that revolting cat, if you must know. I never know if she's coming towards me or going away.'

'You're a pig! What a cruel and heartless thing to say. I adore Anthea. What's the matter with you? Why are you being so vile to me?'

Timothy, although parading aggression, didn't feel aggressive. He felt tired and miserable, and above all he wanted his mother. Oh, how desperately he wanted his mother. He wanted to believe that she wasn't dead – just away on her usual monthly trip to Waldringhythe. That she'd be home by the time the shadow was over the yard-arm, bustling in with smiles and gasping for a G and T. He moved to sweep out of the room, but Roger barred his way. 'Bloody hell, Tim. Calm down. If you feel that bad I'll take him home. Sally was expecting to keep him anyway, so no bones broken. I've got to pop back for some clothes soon, so I'll drop him off. Then I'll go to Sainsbury's, and stock up on all our favourites. Come on, Angel. All better now?'

'No. I feel weird.'

Timothy's weird feeling wasn't just attention seeking. Something really *had* started to change in the way the world appeared. His sight was distorted, his hand-eye coordination wasn't quite right, and something dream-like was happening in his head. A collection of cubes and triangles swung like mobiles, and turned into a burst of rainbow colours. He began to hear a loud hum, like the chorus from *Madam Butterfly*, and looking up to the ceiling, he was sure he saw the fluttering shadow of wings. 'I need some fresh air,' he said. 'That dog stinks like a tramp's pants.' He strode forcefully into the garden, pounded up into the middle of the side lawn, and slumped against the trunk of the old walnut tree.

Roger followed. 'Look, I'm sorry I insulted Anthea. It was only a knee-jerk. Why the hell are we quarrelling? This is stupid.'

Timothy looked up to the sky, seeming not to hear. 'Rog, she was such a perfect person, but she didn't confess or receive the sacrament. It has to be God's choice to take her soul to heaven, or she'll be left in Purgatory.'

Roger lay both hands on Timothy's shoulders. 'Honey, what *is* all this God stuff? Please. You've got to cut it out. Get grounded. It was your mother's choice to reject it all. Just leave her be.'

'But I can't just trust to luck, can I? Will you pray with me?'

Chapter 19

THE TALES FROM THE PURPLE HANDBAG

1965 – THE RABBI'S TALE

Right. So old Stavros found me in bed with the insurance man, and threw me and Patrick out on our ears. In half a day I went from the comfort and stability of a lovely, comfortable old cottage, to a miserable basement flat in Jericho. These days Jericho is a very fancy place to live, but in those days it was a tight knit community of old families, and proud working class values. The reputation of young Maureen O'Dowd came before me, and I found I was far from welcome. Just a teenage slut in a mess, far too fickle to be part of the young wives club, and I had a funny looking kid to boot. I was treated as a pariah, so for the next five years, I grubbed my way from hand to mouth, determined to prove my worth as a mother. I impressed no one, but they were the most precious five years of my life having Patrick to share it with me; an angel of a child who I adored. A kind, chattering, and companionable little boy, who accepted the poor limitations of his lot without complaint.

The Social Services turned up from time to time, snapping at my heels like Jack Russells, slamming their supremacy in my face, and poking their noses into what they called 'Patrick's welfare'. Callous spinsters, with poker faces and tweed suits, who had no idea what it was to be a woman, let alone a mother. I was honest enough to admit that his life wasn't ideal, but they never managed to dig up enough, or invent enough, to take him away. They must have seen that I was devoted to him, and did my best for him, however inadequate I was. He made my life. He *was* my life.

Eventually my mother grudgingly accepted me back, but it was only a surface tolerance. She remained what she'd always been; a bitter, disappointed woman. She ignored Patrick's presence completely, and I can never remember an occasion when she actually spoke to him directly. Just referred to him as, 'that little bastard.' She dropped me the odd quid when I was desperate, but it was given with a lip-curling grudge, and a lecture to remind me what a loathsome disappointment I was. I had to take it all on the chin, though – I needed the quid – but that was small change compared to what I really had to do to survive. Courage, Marina! Out with it! Forget the nausea that's rising in your throat. Press that pen down and release your disgust.

No matter how hard I tried I could never make ends meet. I was so young. So foolish. So trapped. Forever vain. Forever a spendthrift. I scrubbed floors, and pulled pints, and got a pittance from the social, but I was so useless at managing I was always in debt. I kept thinking that next week I'd try and put a bit by, but I never could. In the end the debt was so massive I had no hope of ever getting straight.

Mordechai Weisenbluth, the local Rabbi, was also my landlord. Every Thursday night, on the dot of six o'clock, he knocked on the door. 'Good evening, Miss O'Dowd.'

'Good evening, Rabbi. Please, come in.' He was in. The door was shut, and he produced the rent book. We then began the ritual that precluded our business arrangement.

'The rent of three pounds, fifteen shillings is due today.'

'I've only two pounds, four and six, Rabbi.'

'Can I assume you still don't have the arrears of fifty-eight pounds, plus nine pounds, three and eight pence, for the gas and electricity?'

'I'm so sorry, but I haven't. I've tried to economise this week, but I've had some hopeless expenses.'

'Like new shoes, Miss O'Dowd?'

'Like new shoes. My old ones were leaking.'

'And of course, you had to have your roots bleached.'

'I did. I can't go around looking like a tramp, can I? I'm sneered at for looking up to myself, but I'd be sneered at all the more for looking a mess.'

'So it's fish and chips again for Patrick?'

'It is. Patrick, darlin'. You've to run straight up to the chip shop, and don't talk to strangers. Stay in the warm, and tell them you're waiting for your Mammy. I won't be long.' Patrick left, and no more words were exchanged between the Rabbi and me.

He removed his hat and his black jacket. The putrid smell of dried perspiration wafted towards me. He moved nearer and his face leered up close to mine. His long, grey beard was encrusted with particles of food, his teeth were coated and decaying, and his breath so foul my throat retched. My blouse was unbuttoned, my breasts exposed and slobbered over. I closed my eyes as he fumbled with the buckle of his trouser belt. I gritted my teeth, and retched again, as the stench of the farmyard puffed up in my face. He guided my hand to excite him, but he suddenly turned me around, forced my head hard down on the kitchen table, and threw my skirt over my head. A searing dagger of pain, one hand pinching my inner thigh, the other gaining purchase with my hair. I was forced to hold in my cries, and silently beg for his end.

It was consensual rape, I suppose. He had no need to be so bestial and cruel, but it was an underlining of his contempt for me, and his hypocritical un-Godliness. 'Until next week, Miss O'Dowd,' he said to the back of my head. 'Perhaps you might have found the arrears by then.'

'Until next week, Rabbi,' I said without moving. 'Thank you so much for your understanding.'

When he'd gone I sank down on the floor, quietly sobbing. I didn't just think I was filth. I *was* filth. When I'd cleansed myself I went up to the chip shop to find Patrick, and he always knew I'd been crying. His little arms would reach out, and beg me to pick him up, so he could cuddle me. 'Beardie Vicebloof stinky, fat bad man,' he'd say, but I'd just laugh, and tickle him, and tease him, and sit him up on the counter so he could choose his own piece of fish.

What Rabbi Weisenbluth did to me was a hideous violation that sickened me with shame. Was it prostitution? I don't know. You tell me. The dictionary says '*a woman who engages in sexual activity for payment,*' but I didn't do it for money in my pocket. If I'd done that I could have really gone on the game, and cleared my debts in a week or two, but I could never have sold myself. I wanted the thrill of love – I've already told you how free and easy I was with my favours – but allowing men to buy my body was abhorrent, even to my own pathetic standards. The only whoring I ever did was to buy a roof over our heads. Eviction meant the hovering vultures would swoop and grab Patrick, so I had to do what I had to do.

Here endeth the Rabbi's tale.

Chapter 20

Sally left Father Ewan's outreach class and found her apartment in the Prior's Lodgings. She'd expected its stone walled interior to be Spartan, but it was warm and welcoming, fitted out with modern Swedish furniture, and soft furnishings in bold, primary colours. Two long mediaeval windows overlooked a far-reaching landscape of lawns and shrubs, edged with a row of old Scots pines that fronted the flowing estuary.

Her first taste of Waldringhythe's unique ethos had filled her with a mixture of sensations; freedom, discovery, intrigue, anticipation, and a peculiar feeling that she was being touched by spiritual forces. Her fingers seemed to tingle from the warm touch of Father Ewan, and on lifting her hand to her nose, she realised that the acrid, smoky smell of the marriage bonfire still lingered under her nails.

She ran a bath, and sank down into the comfort of the water, reflecting that although the outreach session was only intended to be an observation, she'd been alerted to search deeply within herself. Was she in grief, or was she boiling with anger? What was she feeling, apart from confused? Father Ewan's closed eyes, and murmuring lips, had directed her to copy him, and to her surprise an image of Roger had immediately risen before her, but it wasn't selfish, mean Roger who hadn't even bothered to say a proper goodbye to her. The scene was from last summer, on Louise's eighteenth birthday party. In the garden at The Dower House, celebrating with old friends and neighbours, and a tribe of teenaged children they'd known since they were babies. He'd been wearing a chef's hat and apron, showing off with his normal over-the-top performance as mine host, and laughing loudly. Tossing a huge salad, filling up glasses, and turning spitting sausages on the barbecue. Later, chock-full with pride, his genuine and emotional speech, when he presented the birthday girl with his great grand-mother's diamond choker, and asked the assembled revellers to raise their champagne flutes. 'A toast, everyone! To Louise, our beautiful daughter, who came of age today. Happy Birthday, darling.' The three of them had embraced and exchanged kisses. But then, Sally's nostalgic musing was abruptly replaced by a harder analysis.

'Face facts, girl,' her complex new self instructed. 'You're a dumped wife. A pathetic, humiliated, dumped wife and the bastard isn't worth a backward glance. Oh, I know you've got very strange and unique circumstances, but there are hundreds like you. Thousands, in fact. Men can be absolute bastards, can't they? They marry you for better or for worse, and when worse comes along, be it the inevitable weight gain or flagging libido, the bull herd bellows off to look for fresh, green grazing, and a comely heifer. The poor old cows are left behind with only two options. The first is to become hard-faced, embittered battleaxes, who can't trust or enjoy any more. They sneer, and deride, and blame, and whine. They develop broad backs and carry on like martyrs, forming a cold second skin, with every new line on their faces etched with hate and the need for revenge. Or, alternatively, they acquiesce and collapse. Go all wanton and girly, and lie back with their arms and legs in the air like immobilised ladybirds, desperate to catch the first man who falls on them. But once they've caught their prey, they forget to ask themselves if being back on the treadmill is really what they want.'

Get a grip, Sally, she ordered herself. Take deep breaths, clear your head, and re-discover yourself.

Chapter 21

Cora wearily hauled her way up the long drive, carrying a string bag laden with emergency supplies. As for biscuits, all the village shop could come up with were chocolate bourbons, pink-iced wafers, custard creams, and Jammy Dodgers; an insult to Lady P who always had a class selection from Fortnum's. Above the sound of her own heavy breathing she heard a benign rattling, and turned to see an old Morris Minor slowly grumbling up behind her. When its even older driver emerged she recognised him as Father Joseph, the Proudfoots parish priest. 'Front door's on the catch, Father,' she called. 'Go on into the drawing room.'

She carried on, making for the tradesmans entrance, but then. . . What on earth! Timothy was in the middle of the side lawn, leaning against the walnut tree. His chin was on his chest, Roger Fuller was standing beside him and. . . oh, how disgusting! Today was a serious day of mourning, and there they were, in broad daylight, touching each other up! Fat lot they cared about decorum, and thank the Lord Father Joseph hadn't seen. She put the bag down and attempted a version of jumping up and down on the spot. 'Timothy,' she yelled, crossing her arms like an air traffic controller, and bawling full megaphone. 'Father Joseph's here. I'll put the kettle on.'

'Steady the Buffs, Tim,' Roger ordered. 'Leave this to me.' In smiling public relations mode he guided Timothy firmly into the drawing room, but was knocked sideways, both physically and mentally, when Timothy rushed forward, dropped to one knee, kissed the priest's hand, and began to recite an intense prayer. *'My Jesus, by the sorrows Thou didst suffer in Thine agony in the Garden, in Thy scourging and crowning with thorns, on the way to Calvary, in Thy crucifixion and death, have mercy on the souls in Purgatory, and especially on those that are most forsaken; do Thou deliver them from the terrible torments they endure; call them and admit them to Thy most sweet embrace in paradise. Amen.'*

The priest crossed himself, and after dropping stiffly down to join Timothy on the floor, intoned a Latin response. Clutching each other, they rose to their feet (completely ignoring Roger), sat down on the sofa, and began a long philosophical discussion concerning the possible meanings of Marina's last words.

'Father Joseph,' Timothy said, 'Her last words were 'Hat trick'. Surely that was a reference to her death being the third in the family? I'm convinced she knew, that at that *exact* moment, she was leaving to join Pa and Morgana because she immediately breathed her last. She must have known God was with her. I must have reassurance that this means she received absolution to enter the Kingdom of Heaven.'

Roger, forced into the uncharacteristic role of silent observer, had no choice but to listen politely to a conversation he found as baffling as astrophysics. Even when Cora broke the intensity, by bustling in with a carafe of freshly brewed coffee, and a plate of the nursery biscuits, they didn't seem to notice. 'Perhaps you could be Mother, Mr Fuller?' she suggested.

Roger looked at his watch for the fortieth time in five minutes. Nearly one o'clock and Father Joseph was seriously outstaying his welcome, but to his relief, there was another welcome tap on the door from Cora. 'I've made some sandwiches for your lunch,' she announced, 'but I'm afraid they're not up to standard. All I could get at Mr Bhatti's was a tin of tuna, and some yellow plastic they've got a cheek to call Cheddar.'

Timothy rose. 'Thank you so much, Cora.' He then turned to the priest and extended the invitation to his guest. 'Would you like to join us, Father? You'd be most welcome.'

The priest beamed. 'How kind, how kind.'

The polished mahogany table in the dining room was set with three places, and the low-grade lunch stretched out, with bowls of crisps, on several pretty Worcester plates. 'A glass of wine, Father?' enquired Timothy.

'How kind, how kind. But I don't drink red. I find it rather indigestible.'

Roger was despatched to get a bottle of white, and a lowly super-market Chardonnay was found at the back of the fridge. When most of it quickly disappeared down the clerical throat Roger went to the wine-cellar, and brought up a worthy red, carefully ensuring that he drank most of it himself. To his fury the religious conversation endured, and after a further half-hour he leapt to his feet, looking theatrically at his watch, 'Look, I'm awfully sorry, Father, but we really have got to get on, you know. Arrangements and all that.'

The doddery old man nodded sagely, and hauled himself to standing. 'Perhaps one last prayer, then? *Our Father, which art in Heaven. . .*' More delays followed that involved a trip to the lavatory, and (the real purpose of the visit) the receipt of a cheque large enough to immunise several hundred African children. ('How kind, how kind.') Roger, on the point of screaming, steered the old bore to the Morris Minor, pressing him down into the driver's seat before a stroll around the garden could be mooted.

Cora cleared the table, wiped it down with a waxy duster, and rattled the Ewbank, sadly reflecting that the day had lost its focus and energy. She'd expected, if not a party atmosphere, at least a show of village solidarity. Was an infuriating old priest all they were going to get? From the end of the corridor, to add to her chagrin, she heard the raised voices of two grown men who had no more idea of managing themselves than two spoiled toddlers.

'. . . your fucking fault.'

'. . . not my fault at all.'

'. . . if you hadn't. . .'

'. . . I didn't. . .'

'. . .fucking Sainsbury's.'

'. . .you promised.'

'. . .bollocks did I.'

'. . .that horrid dog.'

'. . .then we'll both go. Right.'

The door of the Mercedes banged, and the car leaped away, throwing up a skid of shingle, and leaving a deep, muddy gouge. Ten yards later there was a shuddering emergency stop that caused an even deeper furrow. A red-faced Roger stomped out of the car to open the tailgate so a seriously confused Wolfhound could jump in. In full throttle he sped down the long drive, and sheered left, with squealing tyres, into Manor Lane. 'Don't go so fast!' Timothy screamed.

'Shut the fuck up,' Roger bawled back. 'We're doing exactly what *you* want to do, remember.' But, as he slewed the car around the next junction into the village High Street, he failed to notice an approaching motorbike. The biker, being forced sharply onto the other side of the road, lost control, skidded for fifty yards, mercifully lost speed, and slithered into the empty car park of *The Dog and Duck*. 'Blind cunt!' Roger yelled, gesticulating the V sign and flattening his foot on the accelerator.

As Roger drew into the drive of The Dower House he felt like a sailor returning to the sanctuary of harbour. Swathes of scarlet tulips nodded in the warm sunshine, anemones and primroses covered the borders, and shiny bronze leaves were beginning to burst from the copper beech tree on the front lawn; the beech that had been planted by his grandfather, Lord Wilfred Sandridge, on 6th June 1956, to celebrate the publishing house of Sandridge Fuller he'd just formed with Alex Fuller, the man who had just married his daughter. It was the first time that Roger had ever felt any nostalgia for The Dower House. It was just his family house, but it held no happy memories of his childhood. The continuous rows concerning his father's serial infidelity. Boarding school from the age of nine, and returning in the holidays to see his domineering father bullying his sad, plain mother. His mother getting sadder, and plainer, and eventually, with the death of his grandfather, becoming paramount as the company's major shareholder. Thereafter, his parents' pantomime of truce, resolved only by his father's premature death. Then, on his marriage, being bequeathed the house by his mother, and moving in with his glorious, red-haired young wife.

Sally's car was missing. 'She's out,' Roger said. 'Are you coming in or are you going to sit there with a face like a sow's chuff?'

'Sally won't want me to come in.'

'Sod what Sally wants. She's got it all, or had you forgotten that I'm signing the house over to her? Just to remind you, petal, that's well over a million quid's worth. I live with *you* now, you ungrateful bugger, so just try and remember what I've given up for you. I'm even prepared to pack up my career to look after you because you're such an inadequate little tosspot.'

'I'd rather sit out here. Listen to my breathing. I'm having an asthma attack.'

'Bollocks! You've never had an asthma attack in your life. God, you're such a drama queen.'

'I'm not like that. You know I'm not like that.'

'Well, you are today. Shift your arse and give me a hand.'

Roger slammed the car door shut and walked to the front door. Timothy followed; his face showing a tight, pained expression, and holding a hand to his chest. Thirty seconds later, on walking into the kitchen, Roger found Sally's goodbye note. 'She's left me!' he yelped. 'Gone. No address. No nothing. Wants an instant divorce. And she's going to sell up right away. She can't just piss off!' He flopped down at the kitchen table with his head in his hands, waiting for Timothy to console him, or at least pour him a drink, but Timothy, obsessed with his own problems, was anxiously pulling on his lungs.

'I'm going to collapse, Rog. It's like a vice round my chest. It's even worse in here. I must be allergic to Finnegan. This place just reeks of him.'

'Then go in the garden and get some fresh air. And don't be so bloody rude about my house. It does *not* reek, thank you very much. The Manor might be a sanitised little palace, but my house is a real home, where real people live. It seems very convenient to me that my dog gets slagged off big time, and you live with that ghastly cat's crapbox in the boiler room?'

'It's Fuller's Earth. It doesn't smell.'

'Ha! It ronks to high heaven, but I've never been so honest as to mention it.'

'I'm really ill, Rog. We'll have to go home.'

'Well, that'll have to be the royal *we*. I've just told you, Sally's fucked off. I can't leave Finnegan here on his own, can I? For God's sake go outside and take some deep breaths.' But at that moment, Roger chanced to look out of the kitchen window and noticed a large charred heap in the middle of the lawn. 'What in the name of. . .?'

On reaching the garden Roger immediately came full face with the sodden remains of the bonfire, and various fragments of his recognisable clothing. 'Oh, Jesus Christ! She's burnt my stuff! Look, Tim. Oh, the bitch! Oh, the cow!' He turned and rushed inside the house, but was back within thirty seconds. 'Wardrobes empty. Nothing left. Not a stitch. She's burnt every bleeding item of clothing I own. Even my shoes.' Timothy wasn't listening. He was leaning against the garage wall, making a dry sucking noise, and holding his mouth.

It was into this scene of angst and disorder that two uniformed policemen walked around the corner of the house. Please could they to speak to the owner of ROG 666 in connection with a recent traffic accident involving a motorbike? Seconds later a breathless and green-faced schoolboy appeared. 'Where's Mr Fuller?' the schoolboy puffed. 'A lorry's just splatted his dog.'

Chapter 22

Sally, promptly for eight o'clock, walked up the garden path of Father Ewan's house. Built in the latter half of the nineteenth century, for Waldringhythe's head gardener, it was situated on the far periphery of the Abbey grounds, affording total privacy and seclusion. Whilst too large to be a cottage, and too small to be a villa, it was heavily gabled, with traditional Victorian features of a slate roof, prettily carved soffit boards, and multi-paned windows; the type of house that buyers would kill for in Monks Bottom. Its mellow red bricks were grown over with flowering climbers, and to the rear, a long rambling garden overlooked the panorama of the estuary. It was a wild, brackened place, where its shrubs and trees had become overgrown and blousy. A place that would be foraged at night by shy, nocturnal creatures, and invaded at daybreak by a hundred rabbits.

He opened the door wearing the leather trousers, a black, collarless Indian-style shirt that hung to his thighs, and thick-soled clog mules. He shook her hand warmly, kissed her fingers again, and hung a *'Do Not Disturb'* notice on the front door. 'Welcome, Sally. Give me your coat and go on through to the sitting room.'

She entered a large, high-ceilinged room, prettily enhanced with its original embellishments of decorative cornicing, picture rails, and a tiled, black-iron fireplace. It was tastefully and appropriately furnished, with a button-backed Chesterfield, two deep-seated Edwardian armchairs, and an ornately carved American rocker, but the walls were conversely hung with the contemporary prints of Chagall, Dali, Klee and Hodgkin. Surprisingly, there were no crucifixes, no Madonnas, and no religious pictures – in fact, no signs at all that this was the home of God's disciple. Soft lighting came from a selection of large table lamps, an old station clock ticked evenly on the wall, and a high-piled log fire slumbered in the grate. He offered her an armchair at the side of the fire, and as she sat down she noticed a small velvet bed in the hearth, on which a black cat lay sleeping. It woke up briefly, and blinked its yellow eyes. 'That's Lucifer,' Father Ewan said. 'He's the devil incarnate. Keeps me well in order. Now, before we start, how about a glass of wine? Or any other drink? Fruit juice? Coffee? A cup of tea?

She accepted a glass of Pinot Grigio. He took a seat opposite her in the rocker, pausing to light a cigarette without the usual courtesy of asking her if she minded. 'Well, Sally. It's good to meet you at last, and I must immediately thank you for your superb care of Marina Proudfoot. Over the years she'd become something of a personal friend, and her loss has saddened me deeply. We spoke frequently on the phone until her voice gave out, and she talked at great length about you. How perceptive and kind you were, and how your support exceeded the bounds of your professional nursing contract.' He paused to lift a file containing her application and references. 'So, let's get down to business. Career-wise you've been working as a Macmillan nurse, but two years ago you completed the London University Course in Grief and Bereavement Counselling, under Freya Godberg. You qualified with distinction, and I congratulate you. Freya's course is very demanding. We've never seen eye to eye on a professional level, but I spoke to her earlier today and she told me you were an outstand-ingly sensitive pupil. On a domestic note you're separated from your husband, your daughter's in her first year at Cambridge, and you seek a new beginning. Sally, I'll get straight to the point. Your qualifications and references are first class, and I'd like to offer you a situation here as a one-to-one counsellor. It'll be a six-month initial contract, with an offer of residency. After that we'll appraise the situation, and discuss how you see your future career. I'm really looking forward to working with you, and hopefully you'll accept my offer.'

'Thank you, Father Ewan,' Sally said, smiling. 'I accept with pleasure.'

'Excellent,' he said. 'I sincerely hope you'll be very happy here, but can I now use this opportunity to talk to you a little more deeply on a personal level? You may think it's none of my business, but I really need my counselling team to be at peace with their own lives. Are you at peace, Sally?' The leather of his trousers creaked as he raised his right leg and rested the ankle on his left knee. He leaned back and rocked gently, awaiting her answer.

Her tutor, Freya Godberg, a committed feminist, had called this position the 'Chanticleer'. Confident, controlling, and in full cock display; the body language of the male in domination It incensed the vitriolic Freya, and all men in her presence who affected this position (both students and patients) were asked to sit up straight. Sally wished she had the courage to be so bold with Father Ewan, but she had to think very quickly. Body language, or in any language, she'd been thrown off guard.

'Roger and I have been emotionally estranged for many years,' she replied. 'Louise is well established in her degree course, and we both feel it's now time to go our separate ways.'

He raised his head in question. 'So you have no conflict within yourself about this sudden change?'

She nodded her head confidently. 'Absolutely none.'

'Are you sure?' Father Ewan was showing himself to be exactly what he was known to be. A skilled and intuitive interviewer, choosing his words, pauses, and physical gestures to great effect.

'I can assure you, Father Ewan, my life is in perfect harmony.'

'And I can assure you, Sally, that I know exactly what you've just left behind you. Over the many years Marina came here we talked a great deal about it all. Firstly Tim and Roger, then Tim, Roger and Sally, then Tim, Roger, Sally and little Louise, and finally, full circle to Marina and Sally and Uncle Tom Cobleigh and all.'

'But how did she know?' Sally asked quietly. 'It was a closely guarded secret.' But as she spoke, she realised that Marina, knowing she wasn't supposed to know had, like herself, securely masked the truth. She suddenly felt very angry with the cool, cocksure Father Ewan; as if he'd suddenly exposed her as a pathetic victim. Obviously, he must have encouraged Marina to reveal anything in her life she was at odds with, but by the same token, he wasn't at liberty to break her confidence. She was tempted to challenge him aggressively; something Freya Godberg would have called, in professional terms, a volley, but in private, a powerful smack in the balls. But the voice of her mother deflated any brief thought of attack. 'Always be a lady in company,' she'd ingrained into her. 'It's most common to raise your voice.'

'I really had no idea she knew,' Sally said, now holding her head and expression like a superior headmistress. 'But surely, Father Ewan, you had no right to break the confidence of a patient?'

'Sally, once Marina's final prognosis was known we were able discuss it without fear. I told her that you'd applied to come and work here when she died, and she gave me full permission to reveal that she concealed the facts only as a protection to the *status quo*.' He shrugged. 'What other choice did she have?'

Sally sighed. 'To think I lived in ignorance for so many years of my marriage, and all the time a perfect stranger called Father Ewan McEwan knew everything.'

'I'm afraid it's the burden of being a Father Confessor,' he admitted. 'I saw Marina at least once a month for over twenty-five years, and at the start of every session she always relayed the latest details of her home life. She jokingly called it the Monks Bottom version of *The Archers,* and it helped her enormously to unwind. Please be assured there was no voyeurism involved on my part, and forgive me if I've upset you.'

'And I'm sorry for being so caustic. It's you who should forgive *me*.'

'Sally, can I help you to overcome any anger or sadness you may be feeling? No real counselling or analysis. Just some plain, old-fashioned talking.'

'Thank you. I'd really appreciate the opportunity.'

The conversation had come to a halt, but he didn't seek an opening gambit. He stared into the fire, seeming to disappear completely into his own thoughts, while Sally listened to the tick of the clock, the occasional fizz from the log fire, and the cat's low purring. But then he spoke. 'Sally, there's something else, but please don't think this is a huge mountain to climb. Your C.V. says you're an atheist. I'm never going to stuff religion down your throat, but on the other hand, I'd like to know why.'

'It's very simple. I was brought up as an observing Anglican, but my father was a Major in the British Army. He was blown up by a bomb in Northern Ireland. Lured into a trap by a minor roadside incident. It's a sure fact that the people who made that bomb called themselves Christians. I'm so sorry, but doctrinaire Christianity has little appeal for me.'

'I didn't know, of course. I'm so sorry. You sound very bitter?'

'I'm not really bitter.'

'Another lie, Sally,' but his face was kind as he looked at her. 'You'll know that Marina was a card carrying atheist too.'

Sally nodded. 'I expected her to capitulate, and ask for the last rites as she neared the end, but it didn't happen. Tim was convinced she had some sort of heavenly vision at the precise moment of her death, but I'm sure he was looking for it. He adored her to the point of stupefaction, and her existence in the afterlife must have been a salve to his misery.'

'I've prayed for her soul,' he said. 'I shall miss her greatly.'

'She was devoted to you, Father Ewan. She said you saved her from madness.'

'Perhaps I saved her on that level, but a part of her remained frozen. I was never able to thaw her completely. Our reputation here at Waldringhythe is built on success in helping the bereaved come to terms with their loss. All races and creeds and non-believers are welcome, but as you well know, different cultures address loss in different ways. Take Asian religions and even European Latins. They grieve publicly. They wail in the streets, and their mental anguish is spewed out in a noisy explosion of release. It's not the Anglo-Saxon way, but I believe it helps. I've always regretted that I didn't encourage Marina to yell and scream.'

'Freya Godberg rejects this theory as a quick fix. A dramatic window dressing that denies examination of true interior feelings.'

'Do you believe that?'

'Oh, Father Ewan, I don't know. All I can say is that Freya treated grief counselling as a pure, personal therapy, and found the religious aspect superfluous.'

'Let's be honest. It's not my religious beliefs she can't come to terms with. It's what she sees as my innocence and subservience. As if I'm buried down here in the dark, like a little Hobbit, with no real knowledge of the world outside the confines of Waldringhythe. It's very near-sighted as I really do try to research the human condition. Every summer I take a short holiday in Capri, and then I go out for a month into what's laughingly called, 'the community'. I go to learn. I've worked in prisons, hospices, psychiatric units, women's refuges, and hostels for the homeless. This year it'll be an HIV centre, so you see I'm not entirely blinkered and ignorant.'

'Well, whatever professional jostling exists between you, she had all your books on the curriculum reading list. In teaching the course she might have tried to steer us towards other schools of theory, but... we... well... this is rather embarrassing. We rather deified you.'

'Thank you. I'm most flattered, but please don't think I'm conceited or always wholly successful. I still have terrible struggles, and even the odd complete failure. Maybe Marina was one of them.'

'Father Ewan, last week she could only speak in a whisper, but she told me that every bone in her body was at peace because she'd loved and she'd *been* loved in return. She knew it was a clichéd conclusion to her life, but she said it was the epitaph she wanted, and what had given her the strength to face death. I feel sure it was her admission of spiritual fulfilment.'

'Then perhaps I didn't fail completely.'

'Rest assured you did not.'

He nodded and leaned forward to attend to the fire. He rattled with a poker, and added another log, disturbing Lucifer who screwed his face up, and stretched his claws. After touching the cat's head with affection he sank back down again into his rocking chair. Leaning back he removed his glasses, rubbed his eyes, and stared ahead of him in a studied mask of thought. One side of him was illuminated by a large lamp, and the other by high, yellow flames. In this unusual mix of light Sally was able to examine him closely.

His bare crown was tight and shiny, stretching over a perfectly shaped oval skull; a feature that could have aged him, but actually gave him the regal essence of an ancient King. His residual hair was pure white, of a thick, coarse texture, and without its restraining band would probably fall past his shoulders. In stunning contrast his eyebrows and beard were of the darkest brown, perhaps black, and his large eyes a pale, clear blue. With his high cheekbones, and firm jaw, it was a face of intense beauty. But this was a man born with a hole in his face; the only tell-tale sign being a small diagonal scar in the upper lip line, softened into disguise by the curl of his moustache. What pain had his affliction caused him? How often had his blight forced him to be singled out for the second look of momentary pity?

Within seconds he replaced his glasses, and normality returned to the room. After a few minutes of trivial exchanges, they produced diaries. 'On Sundays breakfast is served in the Refectory from nine,' Ewan said. 'Father James is designated with all the ecclesiastical duties, so would ten be civilized?'

She agreed. 'It'll give me time for a good walk. If there's one thing I know I'll miss about my old life it'll be my early morning rambles with Finnegan.'

He got up, saw her to the door, took her hand, and again pressed her fingers to his lips. Was this the way he treated all women? If so, he was wasted on the priesthood. 'Good night, Father Ewan.'

'Goodnight and God bless, Sally. Oh, and by the way, it's just Ewan. All my friends and colleagues call me Ewan.'

'Good night, Ewan.'

She returned to her room but she was far too agitated for sleep. She pulled back the curtains to see dark, fast-moving clouds flying across the sky, and tiny spots of moving light glinting on the estuary water. Her mind meandered back to Father Ewan's isolated house. She looked through the kitchen window. She saw him rinsing two wineglasses under hot running water, and pouring a saucer of cream for his cat. She followed him up the staircase, and watched him ease the band from his ponytail. His fingers rubbed and soothed the nape of his neck, and his hair fell like a shroud around his shoulders. He removed his shirt to reveal his lean *Crucifix Man* shoulders and taut upper body. His leather trousers creaked like an old gate as they fell from his narrow hips.

Chapter 23

As darkness fell, Roger had stood alone in The Dower House kitchen, staring out of the window, recalling the events of the afternoon as a farcical blur. He'd knelt on the side of the village green, cupping Finnegan's limp, bloodied head, and one of the policemen, a fellow member of the Monks Bottom cricket team, had laid a firm understanding hand on his shoulder. 'Carry on, Rog,' he said, 'the motorbike thing can wait.' But just as they were about to lift up the lifeless carcass, the other policeman had rushed out, holding Timothy over his shoulder by way of a fireman's lift.

'Bloke's collapsed,' he shouted. 'Asthma attack. He needs casualty. No time for an ambulance. We'll have to take him.' Clearly, it was an emergency, and with Roger being given no further explanation, consultation, or chance to accompany them, they loaded Timothy into the rear seat of the police car and shuttled him away.

Roger knew he should have followed on, but his immediate duty was to deal with the remains of his adored, capricious Wolfhound. The dog's dead weight was too much to carry, so in a state of sheer exhaustion, and something that could only be described as a zombie-like state, he'd been reduced to dragging him by his collar up the drive and into the back garden. He found a spade, and with a weird feeling of revenge, began to dig a hole in the centre of the charred mess of the bonfire. With the hole dug he went to the garage, to find something to wrap the body in, but all he could find were two redundant coal sacks that had probably survived since his parents' day. Deciding he couldn't bear the indignity of such dirty, utilitarian items being Finnegan's final shroud, he went indoors for something soft and clean. He returned with Sally's long bridal veil that had always lain, wrapped in tissue paper, at the bottom of her wardrobe. After swathing Finnegan with the white netting, he carefully laid him to rest; his sad grave loudly announced by a hump of bright brown soil that contrasted loudly with a perimeter of black and grey ashes. Roger felt as if he should be crying, but his stiff upper lip resolve would only concede a firm salute, and a silent farewell. 'Goodbye, old friend. You're better off out of this fucking mess anyway.'

An hour later, the cricketing policeman returned alone. 'Your mate's been admitted for observation,' he said.

'Yes, I know,' said Roger. 'I rang the hospital. Diagnosis of panic attack. No visitors allowed. I've got to ring in the morning for an update.'

'He was in a right old state, but A and E did the business and he calmed down. I didn't realise he was Timothy Proudfoot. Haven't seen him for donkey's years. I heard through the tom-toms that Lady P had just passed away, so I gave them the info. Might have been relevant. I put you down as first point of contact. Hope that's OK?'

'No probs. I'm an old family friend. Look, do you fancy a drink?'

'Sorry, Rog. I've got to be a copper now. You can drink the barrel dry after you've breathed into this bag for me.'

'Come off it, Colin. I haven't had a smidge.' Despite Roger's protestations the bag was passed over, and he reluctantly huffed and puffed.

'Well, no smidge actually amounts to more than a smidge over the limit,' the bobby said, 'but I'll turn a blind eye. You've had enough bad news, what with your poor dog copping it. It's not enough for me to make a case out of anyway. I'll be back in the morning to get a formal statement.'

'I'm completely innocent. That bloody bike was going far too fast.'

'It's an official complaint, mate, so I've got to see it through. Sorry.'

Roger now stood in the kitchen as dusk fell. Wife-less, dog-less, clothes-less and lover-less, feeling as lonely and abandoned as his nine-year-old self on his first day at prep school. That day, nearly forty years ago, but recalled with the clarity of yesterday. His father's insincere words of the chin-up variety, and making loud, jokey small talk with the other parents. His mother fussing about his trunk, and pennies for the phone box, and instructions to clean his teeth and eat up his vegetables. Promising to send him *The Beano* and *The Dandy,* and a giant bar of Cadbury's Fruit and Nut, every week. Kissing him on the cheek, taking great care not to display too much affection, knowing his father would bombard her in private with vitriolic reprimands for 'turning the boy into a pansy'. The feeling of being unloved and abandoned had never left him.

He sighed deeply. What in God's name was up with Tim? He thought their new life was going to be so easy. A confident statement of, 'Well, here we are. Tim and Roger, bursting with gay pride. We're in love, and have been for years, actually. Unbelievable isn't it?' But was it really – *really* – now the crunch had come, what he wanted? Wouldn't his life become just a tad dull? What if he wanted to buzz off for a little fling occasionally? The compass point in his head swung towards a new life with Tim, and retirement from Sandridge Fuller; a gentle day-in-day-out sameness, and a slow, green-wellied plod into old age together. Then it changed its mind, and pointed back to the cut and thrust of publishing life. The fast moving between trains and taxis, the long lunches, casual office affairs with an endless line of up-for-it career girls, and faceless gay-bar pick-ups. A cynical definition of 'wanting your cake, pigging out on it, and going back for seconds.'

He looked at his watch. A long, lonely evening loomed ahead, with none of the familiarities of a Dower House evening-in. No Saturday evening menu of a classic *Delia* digesting nicely, no log fire roaring in the inglenook, and no DVD of an old movie. But hang on! Sod the curfew! He looked at his watch. Only eight o'clock. Getting up to town at this time of night was a breeze, especially. . . Yes! Especially behind the wheel of the bitch-mother's fabulous DB5. He just felt like getting his right foot down, and feeling some G-Force in his guts. There was even private parking round the back of his office in The Haymarket. Bollocks. Why not? A valedictory farewell to his old life called.

Just after nine-thirty Roger found himself wandering up and down Jermyn Street, wondering what to do and where to go. The classy venues, such as *The Camp David Club,* and *The Cockatoo Bar,* were always good for guaranteed action, but things didn't get going properly until after midnight. There was also the various (so-called) health and sauna clubs, where twenty-four-seven decadence was guaranteed, but he didn't really have enough energy for marathon athletics. To his great surprise he found himself being drawn to the Argonaut Hotel. He entered and perched on a barstool. 'Good evening, Danny. A large whisky and American dry, please.' He passed over a twenty-pound note, with a practiced nod, and an instruction to keep the change.

Ten minutes later an elegant young woman, as regal and well groomed as royalty, slipped gracefully onto the next stool. Roger smiled. 'Can I buy you a drink?' They moved to a small table where his requirements, and a price, were quickly agreed. He would have gladly paid extra to talk to her, but it was obvious that the Polish Princess's command of English extended no further than was necessary for business.

Thirty minutes later, after a bland, condomned missionary, he was back at the barstool, with another scotch in his hand, wondering why he felt even more depressed.

Chapter 24

Ewan had stared into space, chain-smoked five Marlboro', and drunk three cans of Carlsberg since Sally had left. In the haze of slight inebriation he envisaged her silhouette still sitting opposite him. Gentle, quietly spoken, unhurried. A perfect nurse. The ministering angel at Marina's death, and whose hands had been the last to touch the living body of his love. He could think of nothing but those long-fingered, lightly freckled, ringless hands. He felt them resting, with cool Madonna-like tenderness on his brow, in a pathetic attempt to absorb the spirit of Marina's departing life. How his heart ached, how numb his spirit, how grateful he'd be for the oblivion of hemlock. He lifted his phone. 'Sarah, I apologise for the lateness of the hour. Is Jacob asleep?'

'Sound asleep. He had a morphine shot about an hour ago.'

'How's he been today?'

'Not good. Distressed. Rambling. He's been terribly affected by your sister's death. I'm so sorry, too. I had no idea you had a sister, or that she was ill.'

'Thank you for your kindness. Should he wake, tell him I love him. I'll pray you both have an undisturbed night.'

'It's all too rare these days.'

'I'll speak to you again tomorrow. Goodnight, Sarah.'

He climbed the stairs wearily and undressed, reprising Marina's sweet epitaph that Sally had quoted. *'She had loved and she had been loved in return.'* Where had he heard that before? His tired mind told him it was something to do with *Lolita*, or was it someone called Annabel Lee? It was now well past midnight, and he was too tired for any more thought. Neither had he the desire to even pretend to pray. He slipped quickly into bed, easing his naked body onto the cotton sheet, and pulling the duvet up around his shoulders. He always felt the cold when he got into bed, and he shivered for several seconds. 'Warm me, warm me,' he'd cried, and she'd thrown her legs around him, and gathered him in her arms, and within seconds the air between them was moving and blowing warm like a hairdryer.

He lay flat on his back and placed the palm of his right hand over his penis. It was shrivelled, ice-cold, and paralysed. Flamed by their passion it had quickly leapt, but it wasn't only powerful lovemaking she'd given him. It was the whole wrapped-round experience of *being* in love. The acrobatics were just a journey to pleasure, but love was the unquantified emotion that superseded bodily craving. Love was something that dyed his soul gold. Not the hard, monetary metal of gold, but the yellow, shining aura she radiated into him. To live again their holidays spent at Jacob's villa on Capri, high up on a rock face that overlooked a sheer drop of craggy grey cliffs, and the dark blue Mediterranean. Two weeks a year filled with long, slow, hand-clasped walks, and of stopping every ten paces to kiss her under her large straw hat. Shopping with lazy, time-wasting ease to buy bread, olives, tomatoes, cheese, pasta, and local red wine. The evenings spent in dreamy companionship, on a garden swing under the stars, while cicadas chirped, and the air wafted the scent of lemons and ripe grapes. The nights spent making love to exhaustion, and hearing the low hum of her sleeping body.

But then he remembered the rare frustrations of her character that she had no more control over than the weather. From wild flirtatiousness, to aggressive, business-like debate that bordered on the quarrelsome; from helpless laughter when watching *One Foot in the Grave,* to painful, purse-lipped sadness; from selfish, demanding passion, to the rare bewildering occasions when her emotions were frozen, and her body stiffly rejected him. He wanted to overturn the rules, to skip the painful years of his own journeying, and reprise the glory of their love affair, but that was deception. The rules remained.

SEPTEMBER 1982

Ewan, at twenty-two-years old, was still a dedicated priest-in-training and had never wavered from his calling. He rarely mixed with his fellow seminarians, and had made no close friends, but he didn't see this as a failing. He was simply leading the life of his own choosing, with complete happiness and fulfilment. Becoming exactly the person he set out to be; a devoted disciple of God using His goodness as a therapeutic tool to salve the misery of his fellow man, and forgive the sins of the world.

His mother remained in the care of The Sisters of Mercy, and although she was only in her early fifties, was growing into a frowning, round-shouldered old age. It was now four years since his father's death, but she still talked to her beloved husband, muttering vague, rambling soliloquies about what he fancied for his tea, or chiding him for some minor misdemeanour. Iggy-Piggy had died of natural causes at the grand old age of fifteen, but her hand still dropped to the side of her chair to pat his absent head, and to tell him he was a good boy.

The pattern of her life was muddled and incoherent, but she spent fairly long periods of medicated stability when she knitted, and baked, and pottered in the small walled garden, whilst telling any audience (either real or imaginary) that she had lots of tasks to complete, and she had to 'get on.' But there were also many serious lapses into the black hole of her condition, when her single topic, delivered in short angry blasts, was for Ewan's plans 'to get the buggers,' and 'to seek retribution for their sins.' The nuns took very little notice, thinking that it was just a feature of the delusion she brought up from time to time.

Every visit Ewan made to her had its own unique atmosphere, and anyone meeting her for the first time would have been somewhat frightened by her wild eyes and manic stare. Sometimes she sat with intense concentration, talking about a wide range of unconnected things, without expecting any reply. Sometimes she stared out of the window, hunched up in silence, muttering gruffly to herself, and ignoring him completely. On rare occasions she was coherent, but these times were announced by a strange anomaly. She sat retracted, pulling herself into the body of a chair, with her chin on her chest and hiding her face behind a pulled up cardigan. Her voice was barely audible, but if Ewan sat up close to her, and didn't interrupt, she would talk in a normal and lucid way. Today was one of those days.

As he entered her bed-sitting room her face was already concealed behind the fine wool of a pink Pringle cashmere. 'Hello, Mum,' he said.

She replied with her refined, articulate, Scottish inflection. 'Helloo, son. How are you getting on, then?'

Having very little opportunity to talk to her about his life, Ewan launched into an animated description of the current stage in his training. 'Working hard, Mum. Father Ronald makes sure of that. My ordination's only a few months away, and I've got an audience with the Bishop next week. The Anglican Historic Preservation Society has nearly finished renovating Waldringhythe, and we're going to discuss the possibility of my being appointed Chaplain. I'm enjoying my work with the bereaved, and it's a strange thing to say but I really enjoy it. . .'

'You know what I mean, laddie. I don't need all that day-to-day stuff. What are you doing about Strathburn?'

Her normal Strathburn outbursts were usually delivered with an abstract meandering, and appeased by a quick response that she neither listened to, nor understood. But this time she spoke in an ordered and articulate fashion.

'You must do something, Ewan. The more years that go by, the less chance you'll have finding folk who'll remember.' She suddenly pulled down her cardigan, revealed her face, and looked at him with concentration. 'He died when he was four.' Ewan, completely unprepared for a direct reference to her dead child, remained silent. 'He was such a lovely wee boy. Dark like you, but his eyes weren't blue like yours. They were hazel. A real hazel. More like amber. We reckoned he got them from your dad's granny. We'd joined a Scottish ex-pats club in Auckland. We had to make a fifty-mile round trip every Sunday afternoon on a bus, but it was worth it. What gae fun we had! He was learning a bit of Highland dancing, and we'd bought him a wee kilt. It was on the bus going home one day in October that he started to feel ill. He'd had a big tea. Jelly, and cake, and all the things bairns love, so we just thought he'd over-eaten. We put him to bed, but then he went a bit sweaty, so we put it down to the 'flu, or some childhood thing that he'd get over in no time. After a couple of days in his bed, he developed a high fever. The doctor said it was an infec-

117

tion, and gave him penicillin, but he just got worse. He couldn't eat, he was losing weight, and his joints ached so much he cried all the time. Then he broke out in bruises and his gums bled, so the doctor sent him into the Children's Hospital in Auckland. They did tests, and a few days later they said it was the leukaemia. The most vicious type. They tried all sorts of treatment, but he died six weeks later. I killed him, Ewan.'

'No, Mum. You didn't kill him. It *wasn't* your fault.'

'Oh, it was. Those evil bastards poisoned me. These people you talk to. The ones who've lost loved ones. When you talk to them, remember me and your Dad. We never stopped grieving for him. When we got the gift of you, we still had so much love to give, and we transferred it all to you, but we never let him leave us. Please help me, son. It's not revenge I want. It's too late for that, but we need to find out the truth.'

Ewan took his mother's hands. 'I will do something, Mum. I promise. But I must ask God to help me. Let's pray together. Let's ask God for his blessing.' Holding her hands he intoned a heartfelt prayer. 'Jesus, my Lord and my God. The time has come for me to try and reveal the secrets of Strathburn. Please can I ask for your help, and approval, that everything I do is solely to bring my mother to peace?'

His mother reached out and patted his head. 'Your real mother, Ewan. The one you had before me. We were sure you were taken away against her will. As far as she was concerned, you might as well have died too. Whatever her sad circumstances were, she had you, and she looked after you, for just a wee bit longer than I had my laddie. Five years of memories. So many happy memories. Somewhere in the world, God willing, she's still out there, and I bet not a day goes by when she doesn't think a wee thought about you. Her bairn. Her Patrick. Do you remember her at all?'

'Like in a dream, Mum. Scenes that never change. Her name was Molly. She was kind, and gentle, and fast moving, and funny. I can't remember her face, but she had long silver-blonde hair that tickled my cheeks when she read to me.'

'Bless her,' his mother said. 'Bless her.'

Ewan found himself crying. Not just a smarting of the eyes and sniffing, but streaming tears that fell down his face, and dropped off the end of his nose and chin.

His mother suddenly sat up straight and spoke boldly. 'Would you ever think of looking for her?' His sobbing prevented him from answering. 'If you did look, you've got my blessing. It's only right and fair a woman knows her own bairn. No one could have loved you more than us, though. Now, go to the drawer of my bedside cupboard. I've got something for you. It's not much, but it's yours. It's time you saw it. A little bit of your old life that came with you. The only bit they gave me.'

Ewan withdrew an envelope that contained some flimsy, yellowing sheets of paper.

Medical Report on Child Ref: 6543M D.O.B 1/1/60 (Five
years, seven months)

I visited male Child 6543M at St. Pius's Children's Home on 28th June 1965, in my role as medical officer to The Catholic Children's Society, (Crusade of Rescue).

He is purported to be of Irish-Albanian extraction. He has straight dark hair, is pale-skinned and blue-eyed. Despite the affliction of a unilateral cheiloschisis he is an extremely attractive child. A cheilostomaplasty was undertaken at The London Clinic, at the age of three months, by Mr Joseph Terry, an eminent reconstructive surgeon. The top lip shows a neat, diagonal LH scar, and although there remains an inevitable split to the lip line, the cosmetic result is (as expected) excellent. He is able to eat and breathe normally, his naso-passages are clear and all his milk teeth are present. His voice has a slightly nasal sound, but this should improve with maturity. He has a minor speech problem with pronouncing the letters P and W, but this too will probably improve in time as his jaw grows. Please advise his adoptive parents that he should be seen on a regular basis by a maxo-facial surgeon, an otolaryngologist, and an audiologist, as he may need further corrections or specialist dentistry. Otherwise, his limbs, body and genitalia are all of normal appearance, and he has attained a height consistent with his age. He is a little underweight, but despite this, he presents as strong and healthy. Tonsils and adenoids are not enlarged, and his hearing test was normal. Heart and lung functions are sound, and he has no problems with either bowels or bladder. I'm informed there has been no bedwetting, but he has had the odd bad dream. His skin is clear of all dermatological rashes and parasites, as is his hair. He has been fully immunised against diphtheria, whooping cough, tetanus, and poliomyelitis. A Heaf T.B. test has been done. (Negative) He wears spectacles due to a degree of myopia, and I have arranged a formal eye test with an Optician to ensure his lenses are correct. Medical notes, sent on from his former GP, state that his attendances at the surgery have been minimal, and only for the usual childhood ailments of fever and upper respiratory viruses. I'm pleased to report that he has no medical conditions that require treatment, and I pronounce him to have a clean bill of health.

I'm very impressed with this child. He presented as an extremely polite little boy and seemed well adjusted, despite his previous and current circumstances. He responded very intelligently to my questions, and has an excellent vocabulary. His I.Q test was subsequently found to be extremely high, corresponding with that of a child of seven years and four months. The Mother Superior tells me he already reads very well, and even chooses story-books in the 7-9 age range. His only negative points are that he

seems to have had no experience with organised games,
or physical activities, and is shy with his peers.
Bearing in mind all of the above, I see no reason for
him to have a formal psychological assessment. I'm
positive he will be an ideal and rewarding child when
placed in better circumstances, and I would even go as
far as to recommend that he be placed in an academic
environment.

Dr William Randon
MB ChB (Cambridge 1950) MRCGP

Ewan dropped down on his knees to the floor so he could look into his mother's eyes. 'Let me give you a hug, Mum. Let me give you my love, and Dad's love, and God's love', but as he did so, she stiffened, withdrew back into her usual detached silence, and pulled up her jumper.

Ewan returned to his own sparsely furnished room at the Seminary, and stood at the window, overlooking a small, empty courtyard. Clearly, someone in the past had attempted to plant some shrubs in pots, but they stood bare-branched and completely dead from lack of attention. Every spring, for the last four years, he'd vowed he would re-plant and create some colour, but thoughts were all he ever achieved. His room, he knew, reflected the same sort of detachment. The single bed was made, and the sheets were clean. There were no gaudy posters on the walls, and no heaps of clutter. No strewn items of dirty laundry, empty beer cans, half-eaten packets of chocolate digestives, or pop music tapes. His study table was stacked with his Bible, prayer books, textbooks, writing pads, and a pencil case. The only personal items displayed were his Madonna, and a small framed photograph of his parents with Iggy-Piggy. He was aware of its soullessness, but his mind-set was of Godliness, and minimalism, and an assurance to himself that it was a reflection of being a good priest. To anyone else it could have seemed a cage, but on winter evenings a small, hissing gas fire, and an Anglepoise lamp, created an atmosphere of security. On summer nights, the rays of the sinking sun threw blasts of fiery light onto the walls, filling the room with a comforting warmth. Within this confine, he could honestly say that he was happy.

As he sat down quietly at one end of the bed he reflected on his strange, rare conversation with his mother. He loved her as his real mother, and he thought of her as his real mother, with no feelings of second-best or replacement. His birth mother had also loved him, of that he was quite sure. But what of his father? Had the silver-blonde loved the man, stated as an Albanian, who was his real father; the fishporter that she'd mentioned from time to time? What did he, himself, know of love between a man and a woman? A strange feeling had come over him recently when he'd visited a Falklands widow who, at only twenty-two, was the same age as himself. She sat in pale light, serene and miserable, with a sleeping, flush-faced toddler on her knee; a scene like so many depictions of the Virgin and Child from the brush of Murillo, or Botticelli, or Michelangelo. He tried to comfort her with a priestly, theoretical formula, but he suddenly became tongue-tied. He was overcome with a singing in his head, a loud beating of his heart, and a pleasure surge in his loins. On leaving her he promised he would come back, but he knew he never would. The sight of her composed face had never left him, and neither had the rush of emotion he felt as he walked away from her small, sparse flat. A feeling that he could scale the top of Big Ben, or sing the lead in an opera, or dance down the street like Gene Kelly.

It was a romantic notion he'd tried so hard to forget, but he now wanted to think that his real parents were in love, and that he was created by their love. Whatever the circumstances of his adoption he was convinced that he wasn't given away because he wasn't wanted. He realised now that Molly's presence in his head had only ever been like scenes from a play, and her role had been that of a character. Why had he never thought of her as a real person, or recognised her emotional part in his life? 'Somewhere in the world, God willing, she's still out there, and I bet not a day goes by when she doesn't think a wee thought about you. Her bairn. Her Patrick.' His guilt gripped him like a vice, and he clasped his hands in prayer again. 'Dear Heavenly Father. I have asked so much of you already today, but might I ask for your understanding again? I have so many memories. Strange fragmented memories, like pieces of a puzzle that have no hope of fitting together. If I should find the courage to look for my birth mother, please will you support me in my quest, and give me the strength to shoulder my findings?'

Chapter 25

Roger, with a feeling of unaccustomed apprehension, entered the hospital ward at midday on Sunday morning. 'I've come to collect Mr Proudfoot,' he said, making eye contact with a pretty young nurse in pale blue theatre scrubs. She smiled and dropped her eyes; a reaction Roger induced in many women who met him for the first time. On closer inspection her badge said, '*Dr Julia Redmond. Senior House Officer.*' Roger thought she'd be ideal for one of those DIY programmes on the telly. The bursting enthusiasm of the seriously brainy, but highly fuckable Dr Julia, introducing a money-saving series on *Kitchen Table Surgery.* 'How to strip varicose veins,' ending up with the full monty of a triple heart bypass.

'He's much better,' the pretty doctor said, 'but the panic attack was fairly severe. I understand he's just lost his mother, so some bereavement counselling would be useful. Oh, and he took Holy Communion earlier. It seemed to help, so it might be a good idea to contact his local priest. Here's a letter for his G.P., but I'll ring him as well to put him fully in the picture. Make sure he keeps his fluids up and eats properly – Mr Proudfoot that is, not his GP.' She was now clearly flirting with Roger, but she didn't get the usual playback. He was far from wanting to joust with her. His friend, the cricketing policeman, had returned just after nine. This time he was accompanied by a hatchet-faced female colleague, and within ten minutes they'd formally charged him with dangerous driving. So much for the Old Pals Act that Roger regarded as his birthright.

Timothy was sitting ashen-faced in 'the day room'; four soulless, grey walls containing two regimented lines of scruffy, leatherette chairs, and a heap of torn magazines. Other dischargees, all with the same pallor, were sitting silently, or walking up and down with the repetitive ritual of caged zoo animals. For the two gay men there could be no public display of hugging and apologies, but it seemed neither of them was in the mood anyway.

'Oh, at last,' Timothy snapped. 'I've been sitting here for hours. This place is absolutely ghastly. Get me out of here before I have an action replay.'

Roger leaned down and whispered in his ear. 'If I have any more of your nonsense you'll see an action replay on the end of my fist.' But he took careful control of Timothy's arm, and guided him to the car park.

'Why are you driving Mumma's car?'

'It's a tad zippier than the Merc. Got a problem with that?'

'No.'

'Then shut up and get in so I can tell you the good news. You'll be delighted to hear Finnegan's dead. Run over by an oil tanker, but you were too busy collapsing to notice. Don't say a word. Not a word, or I might just strangle you. It was all your fault. You must have left the front door open.'

Timothy knew he *hadn't* left the front door open. As he'd been feeling so ill he'd gone straight to the kitchen to get a glass of water, while Roger had turned to pick up the post from the doormat. He guessed there was no point in reminding him. 'I'm sorry. I really am. I'm so sorry.'

'No, you're not.'

'I am, honestly.'

Silence.

The drive home passed in prickly hostility, but, as soon as they were through the front door of The Manor House, they fell gratefully into each other's arms. 'Oh, Skipper. I'm so sorry about Finnegan, but I didn't leave the door open. Please don't blame me. It wasn't my fault.'

'I know it wasn't your fault.'

'But you said it was.'

'Well it wasn't, was it? It was mine.'

'I'm sorry about the panic attack as well, but I really couldn't help it. My life's gone upside-down, and fighting with you was the end.'

'We mustn't quarrel, Angel. We really mustn't quarrel.'

'No, we mustn't quarrel.'

'Tim, the two coppers who whipped you off to the hospital. They came about that motorbike I nearly hit. I've been charged with dangerous driving. Bastards.'

'Well, that *was* your fault. Is the chap injured?'

'No, thank Christ. Just a wrecked bike and scuffed leathers. And it was *not* my fault, actually. He was going far too fast.'

'It *was*, and you know it was. You were in such a foul mood.'

'And why was I in a mood? Oh, don't start again, you petty-minded pillock.'

'You just can't be nice to me, can you? We've only been through the door two minutes and you're being vile again. You're so selfish. You've done nothing to help me. I bet you haven't even been to Sainsbury's.'

'Sainsbury's! My dog's been slaughtered, my wife's burnt every item of clothing I own and vanished off the face of the earth, you've gone doo-lally, and I'm still expected to go to Sainsbury's! Why don't you stick a broom up my arse and ask me to sweep the floor as well. Right, Sir! I'll go shopping. Right away, Sir, but it'll have to be Tesco's, or somewhere else that sells clothes on a Sunday. I've had the same socks and pants on for three days, and don't even bother to offer me a loan of those crack-slicing pouches you're so fond of.'

With the mention of underwear Roger's anger was immediately distracted. He smiled wryly, and placed his hand on the back of Timothy's thigh. 'Let's calm down, honey.' He moved forward with gentle, puffy breaths to kiss him, but Timothy's head veered sharply to the side, his face showing an expression of disgust.

'You were wonderful to me when Pa died,' he whimpered. 'I'd never have got through it without you, but now you're just being a pig. How can I love you when you can't be nice? I'm going up to bed, but you mustn't go out and leave me. I couldn't bear to be on my own.'

'Tim. A minute ago you said I had to go shopping. Now you tell me I'm not allowed to leave you alone. What in the name of the bollocking devil *do* you want?'

'I want Mumma. She'll be back from Waldringhythe just after five. Can you make sure we've got plenty of ice? She can't bear her gin and tonic without ice. You can go out as soon as she gets back.' He slowly began to drag himself up the stairs, but turned round lazily when he was half way up. 'I can hear a car coming up the drive. Whoever it is, don't you dare bring them anywhere near me. It's only Mumma I want.'

Chapter 26

Sally arrived precisely on time for her Sunday morning appointment with Ewan, but when he opened the door she was shocked to see that he was dishevelled and unready. He stood rubbing his wet hair vigorously with a towel, wearing a pull-on jogging suit. As he held his arm above his head his navel was briefly exposed, revealing dark, crunchy, body hair that certainly wasn't present on *Crucifix Man*.

'Sally, please forgive me for being unprepared,' he said. 'I had a bad night and then seriously overslept. I do apologise, but I hope you're well rested.'

'Unfortunately not, Ewan. I didn't sleep well either.'

'Then I'd better get some strong coffee on the go.'

Sally's night had been one of tossing and turning in the alien single bed; her head filled with the mental fallout of her sudden life change. She'd finally slipped into a light sleep around dawn, and come-to a couple of hours later with a thick head and a parched mouth. As predicted she immediately longed for her usual morning routine. Being woken early by the bouncing presence of Finnegan, throwing on her leggings and fleece, grabbing his lead and ball, and heading out into the fresh country air. But this morning, even if she'd wanted a bracing walk in the Abbey grounds, it was more important to shower and attend to her new beauty routine. For some reason it was imperative to appear attractive to the strange, enigmatic priest.

So now she was sitting again in the roomy Edwardian chair, and although she was obviously in the same position as the night before, things were very changed. It had always been a mystery to her how the clock, and the weather, affected ambience. Last night she'd been interviewed by a professional priest, in a style which purported to be friendly and informal, but was in fact a controlled and challenging probe. The interview could have soured, but the warmth of the log fire, and the diffused lamplight, had seduced her into compliance. This morning there was a harder atmosphere. Sharp sunshine pierced the room, illuminating a diagonal shaft of dancing dust, and the log fire, although lit, was at the cold, smoky stage. The only thing that remained of the night before was a rust-red velvet cushion on Ewan's rocking chair, still dented from his sitting position.

She watched him leave the room, dreamily confused with mixed messages of reverence and fascination for him. Last night his contours had been hidden beneath the stiff confines of leather, but now the soft jogging suit accentuated the loose, swivelling flow of his movements. He seemed to hold himself in two halves; his upper body held regally erect, while his hips and legs moved with the skilful manoeuvres of a salsa dancer. She leaned back into the comfort of the chair, recalling the fleeting glimpse of his navel, and the dark, furry line that led below.

Ewan returned carrying a tray, his long, mussed hair now drawn severely back in a band. 'I'm really sorry for the chaos. I only have myself to manage, and sometimes I can't even do that.' He placed the tray on a low table, and sat down in his rocker. 'Sally, can you just excuse me for a brief moment while I settle myself into order?' In the same way as he had withdrawn last night he removed his glasses, and stared straight ahead. It was a perfect opportunity for her to re-examine him in the bright light of morning. His face revealed a man who looked as if he really *had* passed a very troubled night. His eyes were puffed, his complexion pale, and the shaven areas around his neat beard were heavily shadowed with a night's growth. Despite the ravages of his insomnia she found him even more beautiful, and the voice of her subconscious began to whisper in her ear again.

'You fancy him, don't you?' it said, 'but don't think you're the only one with a void to fill. There's not a woman through the doors in this place, no matter how old or bereft they are, who hasn't given that icon a hot thought. Let's face it, he's got everything going for him, hasn't he? He's famous, successful, sensitive, and clever. Also, he's boyishly lean, and that poor broken lip doesn't half bring out the mother instinct. The safety valve for all these other sad admirers is that he's a pipe-dream; an unavailable celibate priest, so they can fantasise to their hearts content. But you're different. You kid yourself you've come here to re-invent yourself, but have you really? Isn't all this 'pastures new' stuff an excuse for trying to find new love? You really are looking for something, Sally, so be careful you don't make a complete fool of yourself.'

Ewan exhaled, opened his eyes, served the coffee, and then lit an inevitable cigarette. 'Sally, I won't slip into formal counselling mode, as you'll soon recognise the format, but can I encourage you to try and establish your feelings for Roger? Once you've done that, to complete truthfulness, you must confront them and work out a way of dealing with them.'

'My feelings for Roger fluctuate,' she said. 'One minute I'm wallowing in nostalgia and affection, and the next, gripped with fury. On Friday night, when I got home, and found he'd already left me, I was so bitter I made a huge bonfire of all his clothes. I burnt the lot. Now I'm really sorry and ashamed.'

'Did you want to punish him, or was it a need to create your own drama?'

'I have to confess to punishing him. Revenge, I suppose.'

'Would you like to tell me how you met Roger, and a bit about your early life together?'

'We met when I was twenty. It was late 1982, and Roger had just left the Grenadier Guards to join Sandridge Fuller, his family's publishing firm. I was a student nurse in my final year, working on intensive care, and his father had had a massive stroke. Alex was unconscious for three weeks before he died, so I saw a lot of Roger and his mother. For me, it was love at first sight, and he said it was for him as well. I had no reason to suspect his feelings for me weren't genuine, because I think they were. We married eighteen months later, and his mother gave Roger The Dower House, and her shares in SF, as a wedding present. She moved into a cottage in the village and died five years ago. She was so nice. A great friend, and I still miss her.'

'So in financial terms you and Roger have always been very well set up?'

'Yes, but it wasn't all plain sailing. When Roger joined the firm he knew nothing about publishing, and he had to work with some very powerful cousins. The firm was taken over in a merger ten years ago, and he was actually quite relieved. SF is part of a huge consortium these days. Roger's a director but he has very little influence. He does stuff that he's quite good at. Mainly hospitality and publicity, but he's built up good contacts over the years and he's very well liked. "It'll see me out," he says.'

Ewan leaned back and nodded. 'It must have been just before the merger when I was looking for a publisher for *Hand in Hand*. My agent approached Sandridge Fuller, but they turned it down. Did you know that?'

'No! No, I didn't. I doubt Roger knows as he's never had any involvement on the contracts side. What mugs they were. They might have been able to hold off the takeover if they'd had your sales.'

Ewan shrugged. 'I'm really sorry if that's the case. My current publishers tend to roll out the red carpet for me, but I'm not the rich man everyone imagines. As a priest I'm not allowed to pocket any extra income. I draw generous expenses, and enjoy some fruits of success, but most of my royalties are gifted to Waldringhythe's Trust Fund.' He paused to light another cigarette. 'Sorry to digress, Sally. Enough about me, as they say. Can we talk now about your daughter? Am I right that you have no other children?'

Sally was suddenly fearful. The sad history of her lost family was a unique and private bond that she shared only with Roger. A part of their past that was sacrosanct. Something that could never be part of Roger's life with Timothy, or her life with any future partner. Would discussing it be deemed a violation? Could she, should she, in the current tempest of her emotions, reveal all?

The fire had begun to crackle, the intrusion of the sharp sun disappeared, and the warm seduction of the room was returning. 'No. No other children,' she said, 'but can I be brief? Just basic facts. We both wanted a big family, probably to make up for our own lonely childhoods, but it took me five years to conceive. The confinement was completely normal, but Louise was born, with high drama, two months prematurely. Needless to say she came through as a perfectly healthy baby. Eighteen months later we had a full term boy, but he had a congenital heart defect. He only lived for twelve hours. A couple of years after that I lost twin girls at twenty weeks. We both really wanted to try again, but I was exhausted and despondent. After a lot of soul-searching we decided to call a halt.'

'This time was obviously a very sad and emotional part of your life,' said Ewan. 'How did it affect things between you?'

'We became really close. Our whole focus was on our daughter, and each other. We made lots of friends, and took part in village activities. I ran the local playgroup, and Roger was captain of the village cricket team. It was then that he began to spend quite a bit of time with Tim in his gardening business. I really encouraged him as he enjoyed it so much. Little did I know why. It was exactly at that time they... they resumed their love affair. They'd been lovers before he met me, but you might not have known that.'

'I did know that, and obviously so did Marina. How long was it before you discovered the truth?'

'Oh, getting on for eleven years. It was such a shock. Roger was a wonderful husband and father, and I was still very much in love with him.'

'And did you find that violence and anger spilled out?'

'No. After the initial shock we made a pact to bottle it all up for Louise's sake. She could tell we'd had a big row, but we just laughed it off. Took her on holiday to Cyprus, and made a big show of lovey-dovey stuff. Roger and I agreed to remain friends, but we spent months in a miserable sort of limbo. But then he bought Finnegan, our Wolfhound. It was a brilliant move and united us all. Like caring for another baby.'

'Then can you see your anger now as the repression of that time, bursting out like hot lava? I'd be very surprised if Roger isn't feeling some serious confusion too.'

Sally nodded. 'The most difficult thing I have to face now is my relationship with Louise. She's got no idea I've run away. We told her the truth last Christmas and she had a very powerful reaction. Something between disgust and heartbreak. I know one thinks that the youth of today are wholly accepting of all the quirks and vagaries of the human character, but I guess having a bi-sexual father extends the limits. She's in France just now, but I'm bracing myself to tell her I'm selling up our home and starting a new life. She won't be homeless, though. I intend to buy her a flat in Cambridge.'

'So, that's the whole story,' Ewan said, fumbling on the tabletop and lighting his third cigarette of the interview. He paused briefly to inhale and continued. 'I see things like this, Sally. Psychoanalysis is never the brief of a counsellor, so I can only suggest things to help your interaction with each other. Your anger is the manifestation of repression, but it'll diminish with time as you forge into your new life. I think you need a concentrated time of reflection, say another week. Then you should go back to Monks Bottom and arrange to meet Roger. He'll be well into his own period of adjustment, and it'll be a good time to talk in a calm, analytical way. Try to remain the friends you've always been. You're both really in a sort of mourning, you know, in exactly the same way as experiencing a death. Not just for the living presence of each other, but for the security you know you've lost. The day-in-day-out humdrum of life, but something we all need as a cripple needs a crutch. It'll take time, but Waldringhythe will offer you the sanctuary and support you crave. You have a future, Sally, and somewhere in that new, untravelled land lies an exciting challenge and a peaceful relocation.'

He then abruptly stubbed out his cigarette, and brought the interview to a close. 'I'm sorry, Sally, but this must be enough for today. I must confess to a pounding headache. I want you to go away, think deeply, and try to decide how you intend to focus. Can I see you here again tomorrow? Would nine o'clock be all right? Mondays are always manic, and it's the only time I have.'

She stood up and confronted him with a level gaze. 'You *must* stop smoking.'

'I know I must, but I. . . I too, need a prop.' He deliberately avoided her scrutiny by dropping his head, tightening his hands around the arms of his rocker, and skewering himself to his feet. Her eyes fell. Briefly, beneath the fine wool, and loose cut of the jogging trousers, his genital mound shuddered; a loose-hung scrotum, and the glorious outline of a thick, diagonal shaft. 'Goodbye, Sally.'

'Goodbye, Ewan. I'd go back to bed if I were you.'

'I will.'

'Just one more thing. *Crucifix Man.* Do you have a spare copy?'

'Yes, of course I do, but it's not something I parade like a family photograph. It's very much a part of me, but a part of me I must refuse to discuss.' He went to a small walnut bureau, opened a drawer, and withdrew a large postcard; the type found nationwide in galleries, museums, and shops related to culture and the arts. He passed it to her and she contemplated it.

'It's stunning. Twenty-five years on, and the emotional impact's never failed, has it?'

'That's the genius of Jacob Poznanski.'

'Until tomorrow, then.'

'Until tomorrow. God bless you.'

Chapter 27

As Timothy disappeared around the top of the stairs to his bedroom Roger heard the sound of a car door shutting. When the doorbell rang loudly he dithered, not wanting to answer, but Andrew Gibson, Sally's colleague, was seen waving through a side window, and he was compelled to open the door. 'Ah, Roger,' Andrew said. 'I've just heard that Tim's had a crisis, so I thought I'd better come straight round to check up on him. Is Sally here?'

'Come in, Andrew. Sally's gone away for a few days so I'm keeping an eye on Tim. Proudfoot relatives are a bit thin on the ground, so I've been drafted in.'

'I'm glad he's not alone. The HO was extremely concerned. How is he?'

'He's just dragged himself up to bed, and I'm seriously worried too. He's just told me to organise the gin and tonics because his mother'll be home soon.'

Andrew knitted his brow. 'Oh, dear. It all sounds very much like post-traumatic stress disorder, but it's far too early for his mother's death to be the cause. It's got to be something triggered by a past trauma, and I don't think we need to look very far, do we.'

'You mean the drownings?'

'Yes. It must have been an horrendous experience to go through.'

'It was. I was there myself on the day. Truly horrendous.'

'Well, it's likely that the terror of that day has returned, and psychologically he's drowning too. Ah, well. Let the dog see the rabbit.'

Roger carefully opened Timothy's bedroom door, but the room was empty. 'He, er. . . might, er. . . be in another room,' he said. The two men then cautiously shuffled into Marina's bedroom to find Timothy, in the vast brass bed, propped up by pillows, and wearing his mother's black satin kimono. The exotic Anthea, who was nestling under his arm, looked up possessively, wriggled closer in, and her blue eyes glowered. 'Tim, it's Andrew Gibson,' Roger said carefully. 'He's just popped in to have a chat.'

Timothy turned his head languidly. 'I need to contact Patrick,' he said.

Roger shrugged. 'I've no idea who Patrick is,' he whispered under his breath. 'Best I leave you to it, Andrew.'

After the doctor had spent half an hour with Timothy, trying to coax some sort of exchange or outpouring, he admitted defeat and came downstairs. 'All he wanted to talk about was this Patrick' he sighed. 'It was such a muddled story. All I can deduce is that he must have been a childhood companion, real or imaginary. I suspect there's some serious regression going on, and it's all very worrying. I've not medicated him, but I may need to give him something later on.'

Roger reached into his trouser pocket and produced a crumpled envelope. 'Just remembered. The hospital gave me this letter for you.'

The doctor read it slowly, and placed it in his medical bag. 'Nothing I didn't know, apart from the fact that he took Communion this morning, and it seemed to help. Strange, that. I was sure religion didn't ride too high in this household.'

'You're right, it doesn't, but he's certainly become seriously God-struck all of a sudden. Their parish priest was here yesterday; a silly old buffoon called Father Joseph, but he'd be as much help as a chocolate poker.'

'Are you OK to stay on here for a bit?'

'No problem. Happy to help.'

'Then I'll come back around six to update the situation.'

After letting Andrew out Roger walked wearily to the kitchen, and slumped down at the table. The cold, lonely feeling of yesterday evening was creeping back, and he realised, that without Tim's normal easy presence, The Manor was a hostile place. A pristine, visual perfection that only reflected the shed loads of money that Lady Fucking Muck had thrown at it. The 'what if' scenario came into his head. What if he and Tim had run away together in 1982, and cut all their family ties? The patterns of memory and events swirled like the sleek plaiting of Celtic knots. One thing was certain. He wouldn't be sitting here being tortured by Tim's strange behaviour, Finnegan's death, the dangerous driving charge, and Sally's bewildering disappearance. His grandmother had had a stock phrase for anyone who expressed even a passing regret for any disappointment in life; *'If ifs and ands were pots and pans, there'd be no need for tinkers,'* but this philosophy held no answers. With white knuckles he twisted a tea cloth into a tourniquet.

JULY 1982

Being a crowned champion in the art of sexual conquest, Roger had always taken his opportunities wherever and whenever possible, but the silver birch wood, on the outer reaches of The Manor House grounds, was quite the most magical place he'd ever removed his clothing. On a soft, tartan blanket he lay with Tim, while dancing butter-kissed light dappled their faces, and garden birds sang. With silly, smiley post-coital contentment the two besotted lovers pressed their bodies hard close, exchanging words of the *I love thee more than* genre. Roger sighed heavily, and stared into Tim's beautiful neo-classical face. 'I'm sorry Angel, I've got to go. Just a quick show of my face, and I'll be back.'

It was a Sandridge Fuller tradition that all new authors were invited to The Dower House for lunch with the managing director and his family. Roger was thus required to hand around food and drink, and make witty conversation. Sadly, he could make no contribution as a literary expert. Marching around with a bear skin on his head, and seeking sexual encounters (of both skirt and shirt variety), were the main claims on his life, but his father was so excited about the firm's new political thriller, he'd been instructed to read the advance proof. Despite a month's notice his obsession with Timothy had been so all-consuming that he hadn't quite got around to it.

'Promise you won't be long,' Timothy pleaded.

'Promise faithfully, but I'm commanded to attend. You know what my old man's like. Armchair General. I have to wave the family flag.'

'You're lucky to have a flag to wave, Rog.' Timothy leapt to his feet, and threw himself into Roger's arms. 'Oh, Rog, I can't bear it. I miss Pa so terribly. Mumma tries to comfort me, but she's sunk in her own grief. Hold me, Skipper. Tell me you love me.'

'I love you, Angel. I love you. Come on. Put your arms round me, and hold me tight. There. Tighter. Squeeze the life out of me. We're going to be together for ever. When you finish at Kew I'll resign my commission. Then we can go anywhere. New York, San Francisco, Rio. We're a couple.'

Timothy suddenly released his grip, and jerked back sharply with a look of complete amazement on his face. 'I can't leave here. I couldn't possibly leave Mumma. Look, I've made a big decision. She doesn't know yet, but I'm not going to Kew. I'm going to stay here and get some greenhouses put up. Real commercial ones. I'll grow exotic vegetables, and get to grips with this huge wilderness down here. Maybe start a market garden. The soil's brilliant, and we've got acres going to waste.'

'No, Tim,' said Roger carefully. 'We can't just fuck in the garden for the rest of our lives. While you're at Kew we can get a discreet little flat nearby. Then, when you've finished, we'll move away and make a new life together.'

'But I can't *ever* leave Mumma. I couldn't possibly.'

'Hey, come on. It's early days yet. Time's the greatest healer and all that. She'll recover, just like you will. Bet your socks she'll get married again. Men go gooey over her, and she's rolling in dosh. She'll be snapped up.'

Timothy stared at Roger, his face as innocent as a three-year-old's. 'Don't be ridiculous.'

'Look, Tim, I must go, but when I get back we're going to have to have a serious talk.'

As Roger walked up the long lawn to leave, he saw 'Mrs Perfect, Faithful Wife' standing outside the garden room, wearing a long, black, floaty dress. Her feet were in the third ballet position, and she was holding her head at a 'Grace Kelly-at-her-most-beautiful' angle. Certainly shaggable, and his father had obviously tried to get some action, but the thought of the fat and florid old Toby, grappling on top of her like a dung beetle, made him feel quite queasy.

'Hello, Roger,' she said sadly. 'Have you got to go?'

''Fraid so. One of Pa's business lunches, but I'll pop back later if it's O.K.'

'Of course it's O.K. This place isn't exactly awash with visitors. Nobody calls. They're all too afraid of dealing with me. Except you, Roger. You've never shirked. You've been invaluable.' She sighed, and wobbled her actress's head. 'Oh, Roger. Tim's so lucky to have a friend like you. You really are so sweet and kind.'

Roger ignored her emotion, and saluted playfully. 'You can rely on Captain Fuller, Ma'am.'

Two months later the salute fell from grace, but it hadn't got into the papers. No glaring headlines, *'Guardsman's Immoral Act In The Gents.'* It had all been hushed up by establishment protection. Roger was offered the choice of resigning, or being transferred to the Royal Engineers, but it was no thank you very much to getting his hands dirty. Instead he chose the firm handshake, from a firm hand that had shaken him many times. His Guards tie was safe. All re-unions were safe. Honourable discharge.

His mother had patted his hand kindly, with stoical, loving support, but his father was silenced with disbelief. Being caught *en flagrante* with a girl, or even a hooker, would have been a dining-out story in his club, but in 1982, homosexuality didn't breathe its name in polite circles, least of all if one's son was the butt of the joke. Alex suddenly groaned, and marched about, roaring that he wasn't daft, and he wasn't born yesterday. He'd just twigged. Oh, the disgrace and humiliation if Monks Bottom found out. 'Everything's just fallen into place,' he bellowed. 'Now I know why you've been spending so much time with that namby-pamby Tim Proudfoot. So *he's* as queer as a nine bob note as well, is he? Well, I can't say I'm surprised. Marina asked for it, and Toby too, I dare say. Fussing and farting over the darling boy like he was some rare specimen in a zoo. Roger, us Fuller's are a family of men and you can bloody well shape up!'

'But, Dad. I'm in love with Tim.'

'Oh, are you really? How sweet. Does being in love include

getting arrested in a stinking men's urinal? Your career's collapsed and your mother insists I'm morally obliged to find you something to do at SF, but let's get one thing clear. You'll do exactly as you're told, you'll keep your nose to the grindstone, and there's to be none of your malarkey in the office.'

'Actually, Dad, I like. . . you know. . . with women as well, but I like men just as much. It's the way I am.'

'The way you are sickens me, Roger. You can damn well come to your senses and find a nice girl. For the moment, though, you can get right away from that mincing little poofter, and bugger off out of my sight. There's a vacancy for a tea boy in the New York office, and you can start from the bottom, like I did.'

'Please, Dad. Don't make me go. I can't leave Tim. He hasn't got over the tragedy yet. He's still in a terrible state.'

'I don't give a flying fuck what state he's in. You saved his life remember? The sooner that awful business is forgotten, the better. Roger, I don't think I need to remind you that you're unemployed. You've been thoroughly spoiled, and you're used to a very privileged standard of living. If you want to turn down being feather-bedded by the family firm, just say so, and you can make your own arrangements.'

'All right, Dad. I'll go. I really don't have a choice, do I?'

'Well spotted.'

'I'm really sorry for everything.'

'Not half as sorry as I am. Now piss off.'

Informing Timothy had been very quick and mandatory. 'Tim, the old man's guessed what's going on with us, but don't worry. He won't blab. He's far too ashamed, but I've had my marching orders. I'm leaving the Guards and joining the jolly old firm. Got to go off to the States right away.'

Timothy had cried. 'Please Skipper, don't leave me.'

'Tim, I really do have to go, but it won't be for ever. Just short-term, until we sort ourselves out.'

'You won't dump me, will you?'

'Never. Never, never, never.'

'Please don't go.'

'Tim, the only answer is to run away together. I mean now. My mother's cousin lives in Paris, and she's always been very fond of me. It would do for a start. Let's do it. Pack a bag and we can get off tonight.'

'I can't. You know I can't. Mumma needs me.'

'I need you.'

'I can't leave her.'

'Then I have to go.'

Chapter 28

As Sally shut Ewan's front door quietly behind her, she knew she'd been possessed by a sort of madness. She strode straight down towards the estuary bank, with a drunken smile on her face, feeling a surge of inexplicable power. Her back was strong and straight, her booted feet swung out with determined purpose, and the unbuttoned sides of her wax raincoat flapped like canvas sails. A strong, salt-laden wind lifted up her sleekly straightened hair, and within minutes her corkscrew curls had returned. The flat, wild marshes of coastal Suffolk were alive to the sound of marching music, and she was in love. High on beta-endorphins, the muscles and sinews in her legs hardened and flexed. She whispered his name, she said his name, she shouted his name up to the wide, empty sky, and whirled around, cackling like a Macbeth witch. 'I'm in love. I'm in love. Oh, my God, I'm so in love. I'm dizzy, I'm cow-eyed, I'm maternal. I'm sexy, I'm beautiful, I'm smug. I'm generous, I'm loving and giving. I think I'm going to explode, I'm soooooo in love.'

This time it was not her inner consciousness that spoke, but her true outer self. She was having what she thought was called a catharsis; a release as strong as an exploding firework, and permission to indulge in both physical and mental freedom. A revelation that she was, at last, crossing the barbed-wire boundaries of her inhibitions, and feeling no shame. All her tensions evaporated, and her old life spread its wings. Roger would become her ex-husband, with no conscience or sentimentality; a nonentity, unhitched like a caravan, and allowed to slide backwards down the hill behind her. She would now be as a stranger to herself; a detached and controlled new person, with no hang-ups, or angst, or guilt, or nostalgia for her former life. The place she now belonged to was of chopping grey water, swishing reeds, and the plaintive cry of seagulls.

A vision of her mother's sour, disapproving face briefly appeared, but she shouted away the lifetime of shadow it cast over her. She thought of the three long years of chaste loneliness she'd endured, lying beside Roger in their shared but detached bed, and what a fool she'd been to have given him so much protection. She thought of her reflection in the mirror, and the colourful, pretty woman who was beginning to replace her lonely, forgotten self. She withdrew the postcard of *Crucifix Man* from her raincoat pocket, ran her fingertip across the low-slung waistband of his jeans, and vertically caressed the button fly. Say it, Sally. Say it. Shout it across the water, and tell the seagulls what you want. My ankles are wrapped around his back. His hands are raising my arse up into a new, unbelievable contortion of submission. His long white hair is falling all over my shoulders, and he's telling me he loves me. His thick, hard cock is inside me and we're powering into each other with the G-force of a warplane.

Whilst Ewan had been searching in the bureau for the postcard she'd secreted one of his dog-ends. She now shredded it between her fingers, and inhaled its perfume. Its scent was so delicious, she could have eaten it.

Chapter 29

Ewan's headache was pounding, with a series of vibrating thuds to his skull, but he lifted his mobile phone. 'Hello, Sarah. How's Jacob today?'

'He slept for most of the night, but early this morning he was in so much pain I had to call out his doctor. She gave him a morphine shot, but it didn't work very well. He's not exactly asleep – sort of drifting – but I know he's feeling rotten. He's still really worried about you, and rambling a great deal.'

'I must visit. Will it be all right to come tomorrow afternoon?'

'Of course. We won't be going anywhere. Are you feeling a bit better in yourself today, Ewan.'

'I can't lie, Sarah. I'm not.'

'I'm so sorry.'

'Will you kiss my dear Jacob for me? I'll see you both tomorrow.'

He pulled off his hair band and massaged his head with all ten fingers. His grief was becoming an inner clawing of misery as Marina's presence manifested with vivid scenes of memoir. The noise and fluster of her arrivals at his house. Swooping in with the panache of a leading lady, unpacking her cool bag, and stuffing his fridge with food containers. 'Wait till you taste the chicken pate with brandy and nutmeg, darling. It's fantastic. The Moussaka's made to a real Greek recipe, and the lemon syllabub's got far more cream than's good for us, but who cares? Oh, and I've brought some cracking Stilton from the best deli in Henley. Now, let me pour you a lovely cold glass of champers.' Whilst she was removing the wired cork they'd chattered on like two schoolchildren, updating each other on the trivia of their lives, especially the naughty things their respective cats had got up to. Later, after they'd eaten in candlelight, the slow lowering of her hooded eyelids, pulling him to his feet, and the hard pressure of her forearms on his ribs. Her fingers pinching his shoulders, and a gentle biting of his neck. 'Make love to me.'

No, Marina. Not yet. Your time will surely come, but not yet.

The pain in his head was making him feel seriously nauseous. It was tempting to throw down some paracetamol, and dormouse down in front of the fire, but the discipline of exercise pulled him as a form of imposed penance. Donning his red rock climbing boots, and familiar brown cloak, he headed out into the raw April elements for a heavy-footed walk across the wet, lumpy marshes.

As he joined the estuary path he saw the distinctive figure of Sally Fuller, some twenty yards away. She was standing on the edge of the water, with her head held high, and although her back was towards him, it was obvious her arms were folded across her chest. A squall of wind whipped up her wild red hair, sending it to fly behind her like a bunch of russet seaweed; a parody of a mythical goddess, empowered with energy and domination, yet projecting the tenderness of an earth mother. He thought again of her long-fingered hands; hands that right now would be chilled by the cold air, and would lie like marble stones on his temple. He knew that Freya Godberg, her therapy tutor, taught finger pressure to the cranium as one of the grief-healing arts, and he felt a sudden desire for it. He was tempted to go down to her, and confess his need, but discipline overruled. The distance between them had to be maintained. He walked on by, swiftly and quietly without alerting her to his presence.

Ewan was now at Waldringfield, a small waterfront village some two miles up the coast. Seated at a bench, in the garden of *The May Bush* public house, he overlooked a small harbour, where tethered yachts bobbed, and a shrill wind rang their chandlery like discordant bells. Behind him a steady stream of Sunday patrons trooped past, crowding inside to enjoy the fine food and cosy warmth. Feeling an intense need for solitude he was grateful to find that the chill of the outdoors attracted no one but himself. A pint of ale, and a Ploughman's lunch, sat on the table before him, but he had no taste for either. He lit up, drew in deeply, and began the next stage of his journey.

October 1982

Dear Frances Flanagan

I am twenty-two-years old and soon to be ordained as a Roman Catholic Priest. I mention this to assure you that I'm wholly truthful, and can be trusted to be of sane mind. I'm writing in the hope that you can help me to investigate the wartime activities of the Strathburn Naval base, situated on the northwest coast of Scotland. I enclose a photocopy of a simplistic report, compiled by my adoptive mother in 1966. Sadly, she is now suffering from a debilitating depressive illness, and will have to be considered an unreliable witness. This report was sent at the time to Mr Archie Dungannon, the Liberal MP for Strathburn, and I also enclose a copy of the brief reply she received that was effectively dismissive.

My mother's long-term neurosis began four years ago, after the death of my father, and centres on the fact that she thinks herself to be solely responsible for the death of her natural son from leukaemia in 1964. Whilst I'm sure she understands very little of the world around her, she has always shown a desperation that I try to find out more about her wartime work, and if there could have been some form of radiation damage to herself, and her friends.

Miss Flanagan, I'm quite unable to progress any further with my investigations without help. I cannot access government papers, nor can I produce any proper scientific reports. I wondered if you might be interested enough to talk to me, with a view to starting an investigative campaign in your newspaper. It would, of course, be impossible to publicly reveal myself. If you would like to meet with me I will be in St. Gregory's Church, Clerkenwell, every Friday night at 7.00 p.m. for the next four weeks. I will be sitting beneath the painting of St. Anthony of Padua.

Yours sincerely

EM

A week later, as he sat hopefully under the doleful painting of the revered saint, a sharp, irreverent clicking of heels echoed around the high-buttressed roof of the church. He looked up to see a tall, attractive woman of around thirty approaching. She wore a short, tight skirt, high heels, and a low-cut cheesecloth blouse that failed to contain most of her large breasts. Swathes of dark wavy hair fell around her shoulders, and she was smoking a cigarette. She nipped the burning tip out with her fingers, and dropped the stub in her handbag. 'I'm Frances Flanagan,' she said, with a strong Liverpool accent. 'I think we have a date?' Ewan silently shook her hand. She then looked around her, inhaled the cold, holy air, and wrinkled her nose. 'Mother Mary, this place brings back memories. My guilt complex is about to overwhelm me so stand back in case I prostrate myself.'

'So you're a Catholic? That's a surprise.'

'Merseyside's full of us paddies, but I'm afraid I'm completely lapsed. No offence. Just the way things are.'

'I wasn't expecting you to have a northern accent either.'

'What were you expecting, then? Radicals like me are rarely public school posh like you are?'

'Is that what I am? I've never thought about it before.'

'You certainly are. What's your name anyway? I can't call you EM, can I?'

'I suppose you have to know. Ewan McEwan.'

'OK, Ewan. You can call me Fanny. It's what everyone else calls me. To my face anyway.'

They found a quiet corner in a small pub nearby, and she handed him a ten pound note. 'Mine's a double Bushmills, and you can have what you like.' When he returned with her whisky, and his own fizzy lemonade, she offered him a cigarette. He didn't smoke, but he took one, suddenly realising that she was treating him like a schoolboy, and not wanting to be seen as one. 'So. Why me?' she demanded.

'Your anti-nuclear articles are the most exciting and subversive in the British press. You're active as well. You go on demos, and you write all the time about CND and the Greenham Peace camp. I lead a quiet life and I don't know anyone like you.'

'Well, Ewan, I'll be honest straight away. I'm not sure I can offer you any help. The reason I'm here is to tell you that there's been very strong rumours circulating about Strathburn for years. Your mother's story *is* likely to be the truth, but the hard facts are that even people like me can't get their hands on any evidence. There will be evidence, of course. Masses of it, but it's firmly chained up in the vaults of Whitehall. The only people who would know anything are naval chiefs, selected members of the cabinet, high-ranking coppers, and our old friends MI5. Naturally, they're all gagged.'

'Have you any idea what really went on there?'

'Only hearsay. What do you know about nuclear development in the war?

'That all allied research and production was headquartered in New Mexico in 1940. 'The Manhattan Project'. A top-secret venture involving an enormous breakneck effort to smash Hitler.'

'That's right. It involved vast resources, and the best scientific minds in the world. O.K. They got a result. Horoshima and Nagasaki. End of war. But what if? What if the British government had been secretly developing their own research project? It's highly likely they were trying to develop a version of a bomb, or rocket warheads, that might beat the allied project and regain world supremacy for good old Britannia?

'Could that really be possible?'

'Well, something nuclear was definitely going on. I got my hands on an off-record medical report last year that shows a large cluster of leukaemia and thyroid cancer around the Strathburn area. Much, much higher pro-rata than in any other area of the British Isles. It's far too much of a coincidence.'

'Then why isn't this public knowledge? Why hasn't there been an enquiry?'

'Well, if you'll excuse my flippancy, in this case points don't make prizes. As far as your mother's medical claims are concerned no matter what statistics are produced there'll be a stone wall of denial. Currently there's admittance that female eggs can be destroyed, or damaged, by direct exposure to nuclear radiation. There's also proof that progeny conceived at the time of exposure can be born with handicaps, such as Down's syndrome or limb deformities. As for defects turning up years after the exposure, there's only admittance that leukaemia can be caused through affected male sperm. We know all this, chapter and verse, from the Hiroshima statistics. However, there's no proof that the mother can congenitally affect her children born years afterwards – in your mother's case nearly fifteen years – even though lab research has proved it can happen with animal experiments. The most interesting thing with your story is that with the deaths and fertility problems of six young women, we have the basis for a study. That is, if we can find the other survivors after all this time.'

'We could try and trace them. Then you could write an article in your paper.'

'Ewan, from a personal and journalistic point of view, an exposure of the Strathburn scandal would be the scoop of a lifetime. Mind-blowing news, and the history books re-written, but you don't really understand the limits of my freedom at *The Courier*. I'm a just a glorified hack. I write what I'm directed to write; newsworthy, highly politicised stuff. I have to get my head down with Greenham, the White House, the Kremlin, and the IRA.'

'Surely there must be something you can do?'

'The case would need to be built up with several layers of public concern, and the first proof would have to be the admittance that Strathburn was used as a nuclear research station throughout the war. Have you approached Greenpeace or Friends of the Earth? What about CND and that religious organisation of yours, the Pax Christi?'

'I'm too scared to get involved. My circumstances strictly forbid any sort of political activity.'

'Sod your circumstances. How come Monsignor Kent is the Secretary of CND?'

'Father Kent's only able to do what he does because he has no chaplaincy or office. I can't do anything to jeopardise my ordination.'

Fanny sighed loudly and stubbed out her cigarette. 'I came here tonight because I'm very interested, but you've got to turn yourself into a radical. Look, there's a huge gathering being planned at Greenham on December 12th. It's called 'Embrace the Base'. The plan is to link hands around the whole perimeter of the army base, and all the heavyweights will be there. Father Bruce and CND. Pax Christi. The environmental organisations. Politicians. Students. Famous faces from the media. Come and join the women and get stuck in.'

'I can't. I just can't.'

'Yes, you can. Either get involved or throw the whole story in the bin. Join the heartbeat of the country. What interaction with the rank and file of society do you get? Not much, I'll bet.'

'I have a wonderful, enriched life. I'm training to be a grief counsellor, and my days with the bereaved are full of joy and rewards. You're a Catholic, Fanny. You know all about the life I've chosen. Surely you're not suggesting that I have to sin to make life worthwhile?'

Fanny let out a loud groan. 'You don't have to commit the seven deadly sins, or take drugs, or swing from a chandelier with a live frog in your mouth. Just mix with vibrant people and hear conversations. Join in with lively debate. Even laugh a little, for God's sake! Do something that helps to make you grow. I can tell you're sweet, and kind, and intelligent, but your brain's completely saturated with cant. God sucks, Ewan. OK, I don't really know you, but it's obvious that all your emotions are going into your ordination. But what then? You'll get a parish and an elderly housekeeper. You'll spend night after night on your own in front of the telly, with a packet of fags and a six-pack. You'll end up like all priests end up. A sad, lonely old soak.'

Ewan sat still without comment. He didn't want to hear her words of reproach about his dedication, or what she thought he should, or shouldn't do. In situations such as this, when being berated by proudly lapsed communicants, he'd been taught to find the inner strength of God's love and forgiveness. He sat still and composed, and looked around the room, as if searching for it. Having found it, he also found some honesty. 'As a priest, I'm going to have to accept that sort of flack, but it hurts.'

'Then take my advice. It's 1982, for pity's sake! Become a new type of priest. Come out of the Middle Ages. Help your fellow man to fight Regan, and Gorbachev, and all the other bastards. Fight the cold war, and the arms race, and the IRA and the Berlin Wall. Battle for a new order.'

'But what can I do, Fanny? I can't shout, or push, or shove. I can't rant and rave on street corners.'

'Of course you can't, but it's the age of peaceful protest. The Greenham women are united in a wholly passive movement. There are no knives, or stone throwing, or verbal abuse. The only tactic they use is tying themselves up together with wool. Wool, for God's sake! It only seems like violence when four plods are needed to haul up the limp body of an eight-stone woman. Why don't you come down and join us? Of course, it's a women's enclave, but anyone else of support is welcome. If you make some effort, you can take up the Strathburn challenge and lead from the front.'

He shook his head. 'I can't.'

She rose and slung her bag over her shoulder. 'Oh, well. Your choice. Get in touch if you change your mind.' But as she began to walk out, he jumped to his feet.

'O.K. I *will* come down to Greenham and embrace the base.'

'Good man. I'll give you a lift in *The Courier's* van.'

Chapter 30

TALES FROM THE PURPLE HANDBAG

It's quite true what they say about digging up memories. You only bury the ones you really want to forget. They stay in the ground so long they develop huge, long taproots, and anchor like dandelions to the subsoil. Today, Ewan, I don't have to worry about the strength of my weeding skills. I have to tell you this horrible story, and everything is bursting out of the ground, marching to the front, and waving black flags. The whole thing lasted less than a minute. It was like this:

My mother insulted Patrick's face.
My hatred and fury exploded like a hand grenade.
I grabbed a saucepan to hit her with.
She ran away up the stairs, but I chased after her.
I caught her on the landing, but I dropped the pan.
I screamed abuse at her, and grabbed her by the shoulders.
I began to shake her, and my ankles locked around hers.
I pushed her hard.
Boomp-boomp-boomp down the stairs she went.
She broke her neck.
She died.

JUNE 1965 – THE JUDGE'S TALE

After spending a couple of nights in a cell at the Oxford police station, I was taken to Winchester prison. 'Some sight you look now, my lady,' said a toad-eyed prison wardress. 'When you get in the witness box they'll all see what a common little baggage you are.'

'Well, at least I haven't got plastic teeth, and my legs weren't put on upside down,' I spat at her. What a bitch she was. Was it my fault my hair had become like a ball of straw, and I had dark roots an inch long? With no face cream my skin had become dry and sore. I suffered from dandruff and cold sores. My armpits and legs grew fuzzy. The red Lifebuoy soap gave me a rash, so I stank, but perhaps I smelled marginally better than carbolic anyway.

When the Prison Governor came to see me he told me I was very lucky. 'Lucky!' I said. 'My mother accidentally falls down the stairs, and I'm charged with her murder. My little boy has been taken away from me for his own care and protection, and you think that's lucky. Well, I'd hate to have bad luck, Sir.'

'Now stop this nonsense, Miss O'Dowd. How many times do I have to tell you? The charge is not murder, but manslaughter. I'm trying hard to do my best for you, and the legal aid scheme has done you a great favour. There's a barrister, a Roman Catholic gentleman like yourself, who has just heard of your predicament. He's a kind and caring man who wishes to defend you. Now, don't get your hopes up, but not all's lost.'

The wardresses brought the important barrister to see me, and in awe of the severe man in the immaculate black pin-stripe, they left the room. He was just a middle-aged man. Short and overweight, with large features, and a neat chin beard, but his eyes were kind. He shook my hand and we sat down, facing each other across a small wooden table. 'I will call you Molly, and you will call me Mr Proudfoot,' he said. I immediately recognised that he spoke with the comforting tones of south-east Eire, but he didn't comment that we were both clearly born to the green, and had a common bond. The relationship was obviously to be professional and detached. 'I'm acting in your defence, Molly,' he said. 'That is to say, I'm going to try and prove your innocence, or at least minimise any sentence. You're going to be tried by jury, and it's my job to convince them your mother's death was accidental. As far as I can tell all the evidence against you is circumstantial anyway. You may find that I accentuate points that seem to bear no relation to the case. Do you understand what I mean?'

'Yes, M'lud.'

'I'm not M'lud, Molly. I'm Mr Proudfoot.'

'Yes, Mr Proudfoot. I understand exactly what you mean. You'll over-egg the pudding, and bend the truth, to make me be seen in a good light.'

'Precisely, Molly. It wasn't a wise move to run away, and leave your mother in a heap, so I shall portray you as being a little simple-minded. You mustn't be offended as I can tell you're highly intelligent, and clever enough to recognise all my tricks. However, most of your critics won't need much convincing.'

'If I'm found innocent, will I get Patrick back?'

'No, Molly. I'm so sorry to have to tell you this, but the powers that be have decided he's to be legally adopted. The wheels are firmly in motion and there's nothing I can do to stop the proceedings.'

I laid my head on my folded arms and wept. A vacuum inside me sucked away my life's air, leaving a big collapsed hole. Mr Proudfoot reached across the table, and placed his broad, stubby hand on mine. 'I'm so sorry, my dear. I wish I was a magician, but I'm only a servant of the legal system. Rightly or wrongly, you've been deemed an unfit mother, and his permanent removal from you is considered to be in his best interest.'

'But I'm not an unfit mother. I love him. I really love him, and he loves me. I've tried so hard to do the best I can for him. Surely he can't just be taken away?'

'I'm afraid he can. The 1949 Adoption of Children Act allows adoptions to take place without parental consent. Furthermore, local authorities have specific powers to arrange these adoptions, and to include third parties as respondents. The rights of the birth parents have, in tragic circumstances such as yours, been virtually eradicated. In simple terms, this means that the Social Services, our Church representatives, and the Police are authorised to make judgement against you. They have assessed, that even if you should survive this terrible blight on your life, your bad character has been unequivocally proved. Had I been involved right from the start I could have intervened, but now it's too late. I'm so sorry.'

'Do you know where he's gone? Are they good, kind people?'

'The details of his new home are strictly *sub judice*. That means that no one is allowed to know, not even me, but I'm told the boy is to be placed with a good Catholic family. Professional people. He'll be brought up very well, and want for nothing.'

'Mr Proudfoot, do you think Patrick will be better off with Mr and Mrs Perfect? Mr Perfect will be honest, and sensible, and serious, and bring him up to be honest, and sensible, and serious. Mrs Perfect will be rosy-cheeked and loving. She'll make her own bread and cakes, and knit him jumpers, and teach him how to say his prayers. He'll sleep in his own little bed, in his own room, with a Mickey Mouse light and lots of toys and books. He'll put on weight, and get an education, and he'll be a real somebody in the end. That's true isn't it, Mr Proudfoot? It's not the best for me, but it'll be the best for Patrick?'

'Molly, I'm assured that five-year-old children have very short memories, and he'll adjust well. All I can do for you now is my professional best, and there's much work to do. I'll return tomorrow with my junior and make a start.' He rose. He wasn't much taller standing up than he was sitting down, but his presence was so over-powering, he filled the room with authority and prominence. 'Is there anything you need, my dear? Anything my secretary can get for you?'

'I've no photograph of Patrick,' I said. 'I could never afford a camera, and even when one was around no one thought it was worth taking one of him.'

'I'll ask the Prison Governor to contact your Solicitor. He'll be able to convey your request to the Social Services, and thus to his new parents, but there's no guarantee they'll comply. I'll do my very best. Goodbye Molly.'

OCTOBER 1965

There was a knock on the door of the small bed-sitting room in Wandsworth I'd been taken to. Mr Proudfoot was standing there, shifting shyly, and wearing an unfamiliar brown tweed suit. He was carrying a trilby hat, and a stiff carrier bag from Harrod's Food Hall. 'Molly, now the trial's over and you're free. . .' He seemed unable to say more. 'May I come in?'

I stood aside for him to enter. 'Thank you, Mr Proudfoot,' I said. 'Thank you so much for saving me. I wasn't allowed a chance to speak to you. They just bundled me out of court and brought me here.'

'That's why I've come to see you. I. . . . I wanted so much to see you again. I've some more good news for you, and sharing that news is very important to me.' He withdrew a small envelope from his breast pocket. 'Open it, my dear.' I withdrew a coloured photograph of Patrick. He'd grown so much. He was sitting on a sunny beach, with a fawn puppy in his arms. He wore new glasses, a cherry red fleecy top, and yellow shorts. He was smiling. Really smiling. I felt he was looking into the camera, and trying to convey to me that in his new life he was being loved, and looked after, but he would never forget me. I stared at his image for several minutes, looking at every millimetre of the photograph, trying to form some sort of clue as to where he was, and where he belonged now, but there were no answers. I kissed his face and placed him back in the clean envelope without sentiment or tears. I knew I'd never see him again, but I had to be strong for his new baby brother or sister. At that exact moment, a tiny foot flicked within my belly. Mr Proudfoot placed the back of his hand on my cheek, and I twisted my neck to enjoy its comfort. 'He's going to be all right, isn't he?'

'Yes, Molly. I'm sure he is. Would it be apt then to break bread together, and offer a toast and a prayer to the future? Not only for Patrick, but for yourself. I'd be most honoured if you would. We are, after all, fellow natives. I'm a Waterford man myself.'

'Limerick,' I said.

'Then to be sure there's a good main road to join us across the Galty Mountains.'

He withdrew the contents of the Harrod's bag. Soft bread rolls, best butter, several cheeses, a glazed open fruit tart ('Tarte Tatin' he said) and double cream. He'd also brought a bottle of red wine, and had been wise enough to bring a corkscrew and two wineglasses. I fetched some plates and cutlery, and followed his gentlemanly etiquette. Gentlemen clearly didn't make large, filled doorsteps with the rolls. The bread was broken with the thumbs, and buttered. The cheese was cut into small individual pieces, and placed on the bread with a knife. The wine was sipped, and not sloshed back like beer. The tart was cut, placed on flat plates, topped with the cream and eaten with small forks, not pudding spoons.

'You were my last case, Molly,' he said, 'and it's grand to go out on a high note. I'm now known as Lord Justice Proudfoot. That means I'm a High Court Judge, but I'd be pleased if you'd call me Toby. I was baptised as Eugene Lorcan, but all my friends call me Toby. I'd like us both to be. . . well. . . friends too. Your real name's Maureen, isn't it?'

'Maureen Immelda Dympna O'Dowd.'

'Then can I call you Maureen?'

'Marina,' I said. 'Call me Marina. It's a much posher way of saying my name.'

'Marina then. Lady Posh. It might be a good idea to change your identity anyway, now you've got this sad business behind you. Your Solicitor gave out a short statement to the press about you going to Australia to start a new life. Is that true?'

'Fat chance of that,' I said, smoothing my hand over my belly. 'Does it show? I lost so much weight in prison, but it moved just now for the first time.'

'Is the father aware?'

'No. Nor will he ever be.'

'Were you in love with him?'

I thought of Mordechai, and the filth and degradation of the conception, but I knew that the child inside me was clean, and pure, and innocent, and would have no contamination from his evil father. 'Not a shred of affection passed between us,' I said. 'I'm just a tart, you see. A whore of the highest order.'

Toby clasped my fingers. 'You're not. Please believe me. You're a beautiful, sensuous woman. God gave us making love as a pleasure, but we've been brought up to believe that our desires are sinful. I'm a single man who's never married. I'm ugly, I'm ageing fast, and I meet no women in the nice, polite society I move in who would dream of sleeping with me. So what do I do? I pay for it. In France, it's legal, but this is England. Men like me, the pillars of society, have to be very careful. One afternoon a week I go to Curzon Street, to Mr. Montefiore, the Dental Surgeon. I walk in, go past the dentist's door, and on up the stairs to find high-class call-girls, who charge more than a working man earns in a week. They call me darling, and pretend to find me attractive. I do the deed, I get dressed, and I pay the maid. I make another appointment and furtively leave. That's the sad life of a pathetic old bachelor, Marina.'

I looked at the red-faced man so placidly pouring out his heart and protecting my morals. I owed the freedom of my life to him. The sight of him in his confessional had softened me to affection and understanding, but it was obvious what he wanted with me. The same as all the others. 'I won't refuse you,' I said. '*Quid pro quo*, and you've really earned it.'

'No. No. It's not like that at all. Of course I want to make love to you, but I want to do the right and proper thing. I'm in love with you, and I've come today to ask you to marry me.'

I swallowed and stared at him in disbelief. Love? Marriage? Who in the past had ever wanted *me*? 'Say it again, just so I'm sure I heard you.'

'I love you, Marina. You're the most stunning young woman I've ever met in my life, but it's not just your beauty. You're sweet, and gentle, and sensitive. I want to take you on my knee and comfort you, and spoil you like a child, but you're bold and exciting as well. You fill me up with so much energy I feel like dancing on the table, and playing the trumpet. Over the weeks I've fallen deeply in love with you. It's never happened to me before, so. . . forgive my embarrassment but. . .' He stood up, took my hand, and spoke in the sweet, old-fashioned way he would always use with me. 'Will you do me the honour of becoming my wife?'

'But I'm pregnant,' I said. 'How can I possibly marry you?

Toby pulled me to my feet, reached out and lay his palm on my abdomen. 'I've always wanted to be a father. The child will become our child. I promise to love it, and care for it, and be a devoted parent to it. I've a fine old house near Henley, with lots of land, where I rattle around on my own like a recluse. We'll turn it into a real family home. If you're willing we may even have our own children in the fullness of time.'

'Then we'll marry,' I said, with no second thoughts, 'but how will you explain me to your friends? I might be recognised from the dock.'

'Changing your appearance won't be difficult. A brand new hairstyle, and lighter make-up, is all that's needed. I'll pass you off as a young woman I've long courted from Ireland.' He reached out and held up a handful of my long, desiccated, bleached hair. 'Can I take you to the best hairdresser in Knightsbridge? How about an auburn tone? Then, perhaps, a short and feathery style like Audrey Hepburn's? You'll look even more beautiful. Then I'll buy you some fine clothes, starting with Dior or Chanel for your wedding outfit.'

I sighed deeply. 'Toby. There must be no lies, or deception, or any shadows between us, so we'd better get one thing straight. I hated my mother. She insulted Patrick. She accused me of not finishing his face off properly. I really did mean to kill the old trout.'

'I'd worked that one out for myself,' said the clever judge, pulling me towards him. He kissed me gently on the lips. His breath was sweet. My tongue found his. I pulled his short, portly body into mine, and held him tightly. There would be no more Curzon Street for this wonderful man. Thus began our long and truly indelible love-match.

Here endeth The Judge's Tale.

Chapter 31

Andrew Gibson returned to check on Timothy just after six. 'How's he been, Roger? Any improvement?'

Roger pursed his lips together, and shook his head. 'I'm afraid not. He's been talking to himself a lot. Turning his back on me one minute, demanding my attention the next. Playing with a kid's toy. Waffling on about God and sin. Looking for his mother, and this Patrick character. Biting his fingernails.'

'This isn't sounding good.'

The concerned doctor found Timothy in his mother's bedroom, still wearing the black silk kimono, and playing on the floor with a small, wind-up tin chicken. 'Would you like a go with the chicken, Andrew?' he said, smiling with a child's innocence. 'I found it in Mumma's drawer. It must have been Morgana's. Look. You wind it up and it goes peck, peck, peck. I'll sprinkle the corn and you can watch.' His face fixed in an expression of wonder as the toy furiously jerked. As it wound down, and fell on its side, he got up. 'I'm going back to bed now so I can go to sleep and forget my sins.'

'What sins, Tim? I need to know so I can try and help you get better. I really care about you.'

'Roger doesn't.'

'I'm sure that isn't true. He's most concerned.'

'No he's not. He's being really piggy.'

'Tim, you're going through a very unsettling time. Now, come on and get into bed. Then you can tell me what's really troubling you. Is it the boating accident that's getting you all churned up again? You can tell me. Just talk about it.'

'Andrew, she was such a perfect person, and I loved her so much.

I know she loved me, but I've never deserved her love. I've been a very, very naughty boy and it's all *his* fault.'

'Whose fault?'

Timothy opened the kimono and exposed himself, unaware that he was doing something shocking. 'His,' he said, pointing to his genitals. 'My sinful serpent. God came to Mumma with her last breath, and now I know He really does exist I've got to confess everything, or the Peckerpecker bird will get me. Can you get Father Ewan from Waldringhythe to come down and see me? He's a truly wonderful man. Mumma talked to him for years. He put her right, so he'll put me right too. Please, Andrew. Make sure he comes.' With the lethargy of a sleepwalker he got into the brass bed and pulled the counterpane over his head.

Andrew left the room, looked at his watch, and descended the stairs. Only seven minutes from start to failure. He found his way to the kitchen and shook his head. 'Complete no go, Roger. From experience, I'd say we really are looking at a fairly serious sort of breakdown. He's just exposed himself to me, and rambled on about being a naughty boy and confessing his sins, so it looks very much as if there's some sort of psychosexual involvement. He's adamant he wants to confess to a priest, and he's asked for Father Ewan. The famous one Marina saw at Waldringhythe.'

'Confession!' Roger scoffed. 'Sorry to be so ratty but what sort of confession is he likely to waffle on about in the state he's in? Bugger the God Squad. It's far too over the top.'

'Normally I'd agree. I'm not sure a priest's the best person to help either, but his mother set great store by this chap. I'll contact him personally and see if he'd be willing to do a pastoral visit in the circumstances.'

'I rather you didn't. It's only a load of old mumbo jumbo.'

'That's a very odd statement coming from the husband of a grief counsellor.'

'I'm entitled to my personal opinion. Sally doesn't know anything about publishing, actually.'

'Point taken, Roger, but with the greatest of respect, the effects of bereavement can be as real as a physical sickness. Headaches, anorexia, nausea, bowel disturbance and palpitations. The term 'broken heart' is used, and to a large extent it's true. The heart pumps harder, and thus mimics exhaustion, but it's the mental effects that are always the most obvious and painful. Despair, depression, loneliness and fear. I'm sure you're doing everything you can, but Tim said you were being. . . well I'd better use the word he used. . . a bit piggy. I know it's a reflection of the confused and childish state he's fallen into, but I'd be grateful if you don't interrogate him, or get cross. We must treat him with kid gloves if he's going to be able to attend his mother's cremation, and I've got some news. I rang the undertakers, to find out the state of play, and believe it or not they've had a cancellation. No – not a misdiagnosis on the slab. A Will found from another deceased person requesting burial in the Scilly Isles. Mr Fullylove has slotted it in for this coming Tuesday morning at ten-thirty. Would that be acceptable?'

'Best get it over with as soon as possible,' said Roger. 'Then things may improve.'

'There's no established pattern with this disorder. We can only hope the crisis peaks and gradually simmers out. I'm so sorry if all this is baffling, but I must reiterate that patience is the order of the day.'

Roger sighed with undisguised irritation. 'Andrew, I can assure you I'm doing my level best to cope sympathetically, but my eye's more than a bit off the ball. I'm sorry to have to involve you with the trivia of my own life, but our dog was run over and killed yesterday afternoon. A petrol tanker on the village green. I'm quite shot to pieces.'

'Oh! Oh, Roger, I'm *so* sorry. That really is awful. He was such a beauty. You *have* got a lot on your plate, haven't you? Are you quite sure you're OK to stay the night?'

'Yes, of course. There really is no one else.'

'That's a relief, otherwise I might have been forced to admit him. At the moment he's not showing any signs of being a danger to himself, but his emotional state is on such a knife-edge there might be a rapid deterioration. I've left a couple of tablets upstairs to help him get through the night. Just mild sedation, but he really should have something to eat and drink first. Something simple like soup and a sandwich. No alcohol, of course. If you have any concerns I'd rather you by-passed the normal on-call service and contacted me direct.' He wrote down his mobile phone number, and gathered up his black bag. 'Good night, Roger.'

'I suppose you don't fancy staying for a quick drink?'

'Not tonight, if it's all the same. I've got choir practice.'

The only food that Roger found to hand was the remainder of the cheap, village shop biscuits. He made a pot of tea and carried the tray upstairs to where Timothy lay, prostrate and flushed. Although Roger had absolutely no religious beliefs he suddenly felt like falling down on his knees, and praying for recovery. His relationship with Tim had, for so long, followed the same pattern. No real highs or lows. No quarrelling or diffidence. A predictable, comfortable and samey blueprint that needed no analysis. They knew each other's likes and dislikes, wishes, hopes and dreams. It had all been so easy. Sometimes on Sunday mornings, they'd lain together, salt-caked and stinking, and sung the Commodore's song together, *'Cause I'm easy. . . easy like Sunday morning. . . Cause I'm ee-ee-ee-ee-easy, easy like Sunday mor-or-or-or-ning. . .'* They both knew the words, the notes, the syntax and the rhythm. Suddenly it was dyslexia and two left feet.

'Angel,' Roger whispered. 'A little snack.'

Timothy lifted his head from the pillow, and stared hard at the tray. 'You haven't been to Sainsbury's, have you?'

Roger swallowed hard. 'No I haven't, honey, but I'll go first thing tomorrow morning, I promise. Now come on. Sit up. At least have a cup of tea. Andrew's left a couple of pills to help you sleep.'

Timothy sat up obediently, swallowed the tablets, and drank the tea. 'Why are you being so horrid to me?' he said.

'I'm not being horrid,' Roger replied. 'Look, the strain's getting to both of us. I'm just a bit tired.'

'Are you worried about Sally? Do you miss her?'

'I don't miss her as such, but I'll be very relieved when I know where she is.'

'But you won't go back to her, will you?'

'Good God, Tim, I've no intentions of going back to Sally! I've already told you. I'm giving up work, and I intend to devote the rest of my life to you.'

'And you still love me, even though I'm wicked and evil? Father Ewan's coming to see me tomorrow, and I shall confess everything.'

'Tim, all this confession stuff is really pissing me off. If you've got anything to say, say it to me.'

'I can't tell you because you'll hate me, and you won't ever speak to me again. I think I need to go to sleep now, so will you kiss me goodnight?'

Roger leaned forward like a parent and kissed his lips. 'Goodnight, Angel. You'll feel better in the morning. There's nothing like a good night's kip.'

'Night, night, Skipper. Is Cora coming tomorrow?'

'Presume so.'

'Then will you ask her to make some of her scrummy fairy cakes? Mumma'll be so annoyed if we don't have a nice little tea party to offer Father Ewan.

As Timothy fell into a deep sleep, Roger sat at the bedside trying hard to be understanding, but he was beginning to feel seriously claustrophobic. The ambience of Marina's bedroom issued a smoky, oily emanation of her; an invisible reminder of the stranglehold she'd had on Tim's life. He stared at her wedding photograph. A young peach-skinned bride, on the arm of the creased old Toby; her face completely unadorned and natural, glowing with a unique and fortunate beauty. Her pregnancy didn't show, but he knew she was well podded with Tim. Just a bimbo on the make. An old man's shag-bag. Granted she'd done Tim's libido no end of good, but Roger's own hatred for the bitch mother was something wholly detached from their sex games. Yesterday she'd been up-ended and ferried out as a cold corpse, but her power was still a threatening domination over Tim's psyche. Everywhere he looked he could sense her ghostly presence. Finding constant vigilance impossible, he left the bedroom and descended the stairs.

He slumped down again at the kitchen table. His body shivered, and an anxious tightening pulled his gut. His nickname at school had been Fuller-Confidence, but now he felt as weak as a faltering faun. On Tuesday, at Marina's cremation, his pact with Tim would have to be bravely verified. Their 'outing' they had to call it, as if it was as normal as taking the village playgroup to Legoland. At his feet the hideous Persian cat appeared, yowling pitifully. With something much less than tenderness he searched for a tin of cat food, found something called Felix, and donated the whole tin to its demands. Another vile reminder that this place was NOT home. The walls of The Manor House shifted to close in on him, and he lifted the telephone.

'Mrs Feather, it's Roger Fuller speaking. I was wondering if I could ask a big favour. Old Tim's not had a good weekend. He was admitted to hospital on Saturday afternoon with a bit of a breathing problem. Stress, they said, but it's quite a normal reaction in the light of things. He's home now, and having a bit of a confidence problem, but Andrew Gibson's firmly on the case. Problem is, I've just *got* to go into work tomorrow and he really needs someone to. . . well. . . just keep an eye on him until I get back. Could I ask you to stay on a bit longer? Double time, of course. I'll have to leave here at eight, and should be back by seven at the latest.'

Cora ummed and aahed. 'Oh, all right,' she agreed, 'but not a minute past, mind you. It's bingo night at the village hall, and I'd like the money cash in hand. That'll be five hours at twice £8.00. £80 by my addition.' Roger mumbled his thanks, and replaced the receiver. Eight quid an hour! For cleaning? Overpaid old bat!

He looked at his watch. Just gone six. Another long, alien evening on his own loomed up, but as something of a face-saver, he convinced himself he was tired enough for an early night. He took a long, hot shower, scoured off the sour-pig smell of his neglected body, and threw his rancid clothes into the washing machine. Then, donning Tim's towelling dressing gown that failed to meet in the middle, he dialled for an extravagant Lebanese take-away. It arrived just as he awoke from a delicious catnap. After mopping up every morsel, with the appetite of a wolf, he grubbed around in the wine cellar and found two very impressive bottles. Being rendered unconscious for most of the evening, it was well after midnight when he stumbled to the kitchen to transfer his small laundry from the washing machine to the tumble dryer. It was then he discovered that his navy blue socks, and red boxer shorts, had danced in biological delight with his dazzling white shirt; the latter now assuming a dull shade of pinky purple.

Fucking Persil Performance. Fucking life. Fucking Tim getting all fucked up. Fucking Sally fucking off. The fucking, fuck-awful face of his dead dog, and the fucking Gestapo police fuckers, and as for fucking, there was no fucking chance. Tim had asked him, 'Do you miss Sally?' Well, did he? He'd denied it, and he probably thought he was telling the truth, but twenty minutes later, he found himself still slumped at the kitchen table having thought of only her. The dearest constant in his life. His lovely Sally of the old days, who slept in his arms, and made cracking roast potatoes, and danced a mean lambada, and spread her womanly presence as thick as honey. For years he'd dreamed of being with Tim, but now the thought of not being with Sally filled him with a feeling that could only be described as fear. Where the hell was she? He would forgive her for burning his clothes. He would forgive anything, and give anything, for news of her return.

NOVEMBER 1982

Roger had been exiled for three months in the New York office of Sandridge Fuller when the news came. His father, having keeled over in his club, had suffered a serious, debilitating stroke, and was not expected to live. Roger now stood with his mother in a hospital ward, staring at the unconscious, impotent husk of the man who could no longer control his life. The feeling of relief had been greater than the effect of alcohol, or any narcotic. Tubes and leads were attached to various bleeping machines, and his bully's face was obscured by an oxygen mask.

Roger slid his arm around his mother's shoulders and went on staring, as mother and son stood dry-eyed, six feet from the bed. They didn't admit their lack of love, or any form of concern that he might not survive, but it was obvious. A nurse, graceful as a dancer, walked up to check on her patient. She was tall and slender, with heavy tendrils of crinkly red hair scraped into a twist under a circular white cap. Long neck, long arms, and long fingers. Long black-stockinged legs below a knee-length hem. Heavily freckled skin. No make-up apart from dark mascara on her lashes. Green eyes. A true shade of buttery jade. A colour rarely seen, and when seen, magnetic and unbelievable. Although she wore a shapeless nurse's dress, and an untidy plastic apron, the cello-like proportions of her body were obvious. Her breasts would be firm and small. Her shoulders wide and white.

Her badge said, *Nurse Kenton-Browne. Third Year Student.* She turned and gave them a hopeful smile. 'No change, I'm afraid, Mrs

Fuller, but no deterioration either.'

'Thank you, Sally,' said his mother, and then, turning to Roger, she introduced her. 'Sally, this is my son, Roger. Roger, this is Sally. Daddy's personal nurse.'

Roger said hello. 'The tea trolley's on its way,' the gentle nurse said. 'Can I get you both a cup?' Mother and son both nodded their acceptance.

'Such a kind girl,' his mother said, as the elegant figure glided away.

'She looks like those paintings,' Roger said. 'You must know the ones I mean?

'Ah, that'll be the Pre-Raphaelites, dear. Yes, she does. Actually, she's a perfect image of Rossetti's, *The Beloved Bride*. It's in The Tate.'

As he was handed a cup of tea, Roger fell in love.

Chapter 32

Ewan had retreated so deeply into his personal journey he suddenly came-to with a jolt. His pint of ale, and plate of lunch, were still untouched. All the bars in *The May Bush* were empty, the lights had been turned out, and the beer pumps covered over with tea towels. The jolly throng of lunchtime customers must have come out behind him at closing time, but he'd heard no voices or footsteps. Breathing deeply, he rose to his feet, surprised to find that his headache had completely cleared. It was now late afternoon and he began a slow-footed drag back to Waldringhythe.

By the time he entered his house, dusk was closing in. Normally, when he returned to the sanctuary of home, his compulsion was to draw the curtains, light the lamps, and stoke up the fire, but he had no desire to create a cosy comfort. He turned off his mobile phone, pulled the land-line socket from the wall, and slumped down into his rocker. But this time his misery was not an overhang of grief, but another kind. Hours then passed in darkness, cocooned inside a time capsule of vacancy.

It was well after midnight when he threw on his cloak and left the house. He walked out into a light, hazy fog that blurred the moon and stars: a night atmosphere so endemic to coastal Suffolk as to be the norm for muggy nights in mid-April. His feet followed the same winding gravel path he'd used as a short cut for over forty years, but with a restricted field of vision, he was forced to take cautious steps. Emerging from a small copse of rhododendron he came upon a wide lawn, covered over with an ankle-high layer of mist, resembling dry ice. Before him a row of strong floodlights illuminated the frontage of the Abbey, and its mediaeval magnificence loomed up as a mighty rock face. Ewan entered through the heavy oak door, and as he closed it carefully behind him, a loud creak from its ancient hinges bounced off the transepts. He walked slowly down the nave, breathing in the cold air, each footfall following him with a ghostly, split-second time-delay of echo.

The main body of the Abbey, compared to the ruined, but more famous, Abbeys of Tintern and Rievaulx, was of very modest size, and little of its original cruciform floor plan remained. Having been converted to a dwelling after the turbulence of the sixteenth century abolitions, its original east-west divisions (that strictly segregated the monks and lay brothers) had been removed, but the Cistercians' selfless display of worship remained, perfectly preserved due to the investment of The Anglican Historic Preservation Trust. Every stone, and piece of plasterwork, was conserved in its original pristine elegance: the moulded tracery arches, the elegant lancet windows, and the hooped wonder of the flying buttresses.

He sat down in the choir stall, recalling the many years that this powerful place had been part of his life. His first frightening visit as a five-year-old, where the grown-ups he was coming to know, as friends and neighbours, took on a serious and somewhat bewildering trans-formation when carrying out their religious duties. They spoke with tongues, performed elaborate body movements, and sang with loud responsive discords. Before long, he'd absorbed the knowledge that to be a Roman Catholic little boy was something special. Later, he'd carried out his own modest duties as an altar boy, and for the last twenty-six years had performed his own role-play as honoured custo-dian. He got up and picked a white lily from a vase. On the third finger of his left hand he wore a plain gold band, as a sign of his devotion to the virgin, but he was no longer in love with her. He moved to the altar, which was plainly adorned with only a single, heavy silver cross and two goblets. He removed the ring, slipped it over the flower's stem, and laid it carefully on a white linen runner. Returning to the choir stall, he continued his journey.

DECEMBER 1982

On the morning of the 'Embrace The Base' demonstration day, Ewan rose at 5.00 a.m. Never before had he had such an experience. To get up before dawn to go to a place where hundreds, perhaps thousands, were gathering with the sole purpose of protest. As he dressed he was elated, but apprehensive. All assurances were that the aims were of peace and sobriety, but with the possibility of dissenting factions losing control, violence might break out. But he was undeterred. Fanny had advised him not to wear his dog-collar, so he wore blue jeans, Doc Martens, and a fur-hooded anorak: clothes that were uniform to his generation, but he'd only recently bought as part of his transformation. 'What you need to do is mix with the crowd and absorb the heartbeat of the movement,' she said. 'If they see you're a priest you'll be treated with detached politeness, so turn up in mufti. Do the rounds and talk to people. Don't be shy. They're all there because they care, and they want to do something, no matter how small. Just try to enjoy yourself.'

He wound a scarf around his neck, slipped on his gloves, and left the seminary.

A mini-bus sat beneath a streetlight and was decorated with a banner; *'The Courier Supports Embrace The Base.'* A ragged posse of reporters and photographers stood in a quiet group, sniffing from the cold, and clearly disenchanted with the early start to their day. Fanny smiled with genuine pleasure when she saw him, and introduced him. 'This is Ewan, a friend of mine.' They all nodded impersonally. She was the only female present, but clearly in authority as she outlined what she wanted from them.

'The perimeter fence is a circuit of between twelve and fourteen miles, so I want proper coverage from right around the place and not just what Julie Christie's wearing. I want interviews from those who are far away from the spotlight. Who are they? Why have they come? What action do they intend to take in the future? How will they vote at the next election? As for photographs, Jacob will, of course, lead the field. I want clear images of the young, the elderly, and the tearful. I want you to point your cameras inside the base and snap whoever's looking back, but most especially, I want armed soldiers, no matter how blurred. I want police presence, but I don't want the laughing policeman dancing arm-in-arm with a punk LSE student. I want emotion.'

As the mini-bus set off, sleet blasted intermittently, and the interior quickly warmed up to a discomforting fug. Once out of London the conurbations of the suburbs gave way to long arterial roads, and as they neared the county of Berkshire, Ewan saw that every petrol station they passed was full of coaches. Large groups of women were seen talking, or stretching their legs, and everyone was wrapped in warm, shapeless clothes. Anoraks, duffle coats, hooded raincoats, and sheepskin jackets. Woolley hats, scarves, and boots. Some wearing the dull khaki of the army surplus store, and some in the rainbow colours of thick, hippy hand-knits. Most carried bright ribbons, bedecking themselves with the unity of neo-suffragettes.

On approaching the main entrance of the Greenham Common Army base, he drew in a short, hard breath of anticipation. The darkness glimmered with a hundred bobbing lights, and as they got nearer he saw they were hand lamps and torches, carried by a throng of the protest women. Two of them at the front, the obvious leaders, moved forward holding a clipboard, and Fanny produced her press pass. 'There's allocated space for your vehicle just over there,' one said. 'You'll see a notice board that says Press and TV only. Can you give us good coverage of the main gate, and all the big noises. You know, the MPs and the actresses turning up for a photo call, but we need them, don't we? There's even an old suffragette in a wheel chair coming – Lady Olga someone – so can you try to get her featured? Do your best anyway.'

'We'll do more than our best,' Fanny said. 'I've been promised an interview with Tony Benn, and my editors are reserving space on the front page. I can't see much police presence, though.'

'There's two coach loads of them parked up out of sight, plus a load of Black Marias and dog-handlers. They're all just having a brew, and relations are cordial. I can guarantee they won't be needed, or if they are, it'll be rent-a-mob and not us.'

The mini-bus turned to park on a stretch of wet, grassless mud where fellow journalists, and TV crews, were setting up for the day. Professional nods were exchanged between opposing newspapers, and there was an atmosphere of nervous expectancy. When the soft light of dawn began to appear from behind the trees, the hidden scene before them was then gradually revealed. 'Jesus!' Fanny gasped.

The peace camp women were revealed as tired, unkempt, and de-feminised, dressed in shapeless, mud-caked clothing. They stood as a large, morose group, holding banners and placards depicting CND slogans. One had sewn baby clothes all over her long shawl, one wore her wedding dress held with safety pins over a thick Aran sweater, and another was wrapped in a vast Peruvian blanket. Two women were handcuffed together, and displayed the sign, 'United' on their hats. The perimeter fence was covered with bows of yellow ribbon, dolls, toys, white towelling nappies, photographs of the women's children, bunches of chrysanthemums in varying stages of dying, symbolic pictures of spiders webs and snakes, and posters showing the huge mushroom cloud of the Hiroshima bomb.

Protesters in their hundreds were swarming the area, stretching away into the far distance as a great marching army of turned backs, seeking to make claim to a space on the perimeter fence. Alongside them a slowly moving trail of cars, coaches and vans searched for parking, and tooted their horns as a sign of support. A group dressed as troubadours banged drums, and played recorders, and a decanted coach load of female Oxford University students began to sing, *We will overcome*. Another group of portly Women's Institute types linked up their tweed-coated arms, marching their sensible winter boots up the road, and giggling like teenagers. A feeling of enthralment grew in Ewan's chest, and he was impatient to join in.

'My day's going to be one of hard work and constant interruption,' Fanny said, 'but I've got a job to do, and a job to do well. I won't be able to spend much time with you, so why don't you find the Pax Christi and Christian CND as a start-off point?'

'I'm going off on my own,' he replied. 'No dog-collar today. I'm just Ewan, peace-protester.'

'Meet me back here at two o'clock sharp then, and not a second after. If you're late we go without you, and that's not a threat. My copy's going to take hours to produce, and we must hit the road before the exit scrum.'

Ewan walked off and almost immediately came across a group of nurses who were organizing themselves to collect for the local kidney dialysis unit. With noisy exuberance they were jumping up and down on the spot, and as he passed them they called out to him and flirted.

'Oh, my God, it's a man on his own! Hi, gorgeous. We could do with an assistant.' They surrounded him, laughing. 'Will you carry a tin for us?'

He spent the morning with Olivia, an upper-crust home-counties type, and Doris, a tiny Hong Kong Chinese. As they trailed and propositioned their captive donors, the girls talked without pause, telling him funny stories of their nursing experiences. An hysterical story, told with tears of mirth running down their faces. Doris had helped to lay out a body; a procedure that required all orifices to be packed and plugged. But just as they'd finished, the ward sister rushed to tell them that the patient was an Orthodox Jew, and was only to be touched by another Orthodox Jew, so they had to quickly pull everything out of him before the Rabbi arrived. Then the time that Olivia climbed through a window into the nurses home at midnight, to find that she'd entered the bedroom of the snoring, hair-netted matron, sound asleep with her false teeth in a glass at her bedside. Would they have told him these stories if they'd known he was a priest? Would they even have asked him to walk with them?

In time the collecting tins became heavy and full, and as they'd travelled a couple of miles from the assembly point Ewan flagged down a passing police car. The nurses got in, giggling and cheeking the policemen. Before they parted he and the girls exchanged phone numbers, each of them promising to keep in touch, but he gave a false number. It was, after all, only a rare day off from his normal life. As the police car drove away they threw their heads and arms out of the windows to wave, and blow him kisses.

Just before mid-day, a van circled, announcing from a public address system that it was time to link hands. After an initial loud cheering there was a respectful silence, and a unique feeling of comradeship. The crowd turned to face the fence, two perfect strangers extended their hands to Ewan, and with a feeling of pure joy, he flattened himself against the wire. The base was embraced. After a few quiet minutes the sound of singing flowed down the line. *We will overcome* again, and he joined in with all the power he could muster.

The line of hands gradually released, and they all began to embrace each other. The man next to Ewan fell on his knees, and dropped his head in silent prayer. Ewan felt he should be doing the same, but the woman on his other side, who was crying openly, flung her arms around him. 'Those that can do so much do nothing,' she wailed, 'and those that can do nothing do everything they can.'

It was coming home later in the mini-bus that the idea was first mooted. The senior photographer, Jacob Poznanski, was a middle-aged, heavy-featured man, whose English reflected the deep, guttural accent of Eastern Europe. From his jacket pocket he produced a flyer, handed to him by a group of American Jesuit priests. It was fronted with a classic painting of Christ on the Cross; a solitary, hanging figure with no Madonnas, Magdalenes, or large cast of attendant saints. Beneath the figure was a short text: *Jesuits minister to those who are voiceless and those whose values are undermined by contemporary culture.*

In the fading light, Jacob passed it to Fanny. 'I was approached by the leader of Scarlet Gate,' he said. 'Her group are a devout Christian faction who want to use the crucifixion as a symbol of peace. She had a crazy idea that I should set up a photo shoot with a crucified woman hanging on a tree. You know. Symbolism. *'She died to save us all'.* That sort of thing. What do you think?'

'I think the sight of a rag-bag hanging on a tree would do nothing to capture the imagination of the unconvinced, or do the cause much good.'

'What about a Christie Brinkly type, then? Cover her in flimsy gauze. Long silky hair hanging down like an angel.'

'You mean a long-limbed lovely? Far too page three. The women would love that. Not!'

'No, not sexy. I mean ethereal. The innocence of the youthful maiden.'

'Oh, yuck. You might as well stick up a Cicely Mary Barker fairy.'

'Crap idea, then. I'll forget it.'

'Not entirely. I like the idea. The religious ethic passes me by, but I think it would work better with a man. I don't mean beefcake. I can see a young, lean guy with good cheek bones. A sensitive depiction of the modern Christ would really underline the passive stance. Next week I've got eight pages of the Sunday Supplement to fill on Greenham, and I really need something mind-blowing for the front cover. It'll be the last issue before Christmas, so perfect timing on the

Christ front. Think you can give it a go? I'm sure I can rely on you to find a suitable boy.'

'How long have I got?'

'Next Wednesday lunchtime at the latest. In the meantime, I'll have time to work on the editors. *The Courier* can't become the official mouthpiece of the movement, but it would certainly cause some outrage from Tunbridge Wells. I'll think they'll buy it.'

Once back in London, the minibus parked at the rear of *The Courier's* offices in Fleet Street. The tired group of reporters and photographers got out, wearily flapping their arms in an attempt to produce some adrenaline for the several hours of work they had before them. Fanny, who was clearly the most tired of them all, turned and waved a spidery hand of fingers at Ewan. 'Bye, Ewan. Keep in touch.'

He nodded. 'Thank you, Fanny. It's been a life-changing experience.' She began to walk away, but with a rare bravado, he ran to catch her up. 'Stop, please. I don't want to be overheard.' She stopped. He diffidently hung his head, and moved his feet around on the tarmac of the car park. 'The photograph. The one you were talking about. The Crucifixion. Can I do it? I must be anonymous, so you'd have to hide my face in shadow or something, but I want to do it.'

'You! Good God! Today *has* made a difference?'

'Today a woman grabbed me, and she said, "Those that can do so much do nothing, and those that can do nothing do everything they can." When she said that, I realised that what she said was true. I *can* do something. Then later on, after my ordination and the time's right, I can confess my identity and get a platform for my mother's vendetta.'

Fanny straightened up, seeming to forget her fatigue. 'I'm getting fired-up with this idea.' She stepped back to look at him. 'Take off your anorak and sweaters.' Despite the cold, he did as she asked. She then turned him round, and looked him up and down in the light of a street lamp. 'I must admit you're exactly what I had in mind.' She called over to Jacob, and the photographer ambled over with his cameras and light meters slung over his shoulders. 'Jacob. The Crucifixion photograph we talked about. Do you think Ewan might fit the bill? He's actually a Catholic priest, so he could be bare chested and wear a dog-collar. It would be a great take. I think he'd be perfect.'

'My face must be hidden,' Ewan said. 'I'm to be ordained soon so

I mustn't be identified. My lip. . .'

'Yes, I understand,' said Jacob. He stepped back to view Ewan slowly from the front perspective. He moved forward, ran his hands over his shoulders, lifted an arm and held it up at full length to the side. 'How tall are you?'

'Six foot one.'

'I think you are thirty inch waist, yes?

'Yes.' The photographer then stepped back to examine him again, as if he were viewing a painting. Just at that moment a squall of icy rain sent Ewan's long hair in a wet sweep to the side of his face, and he veered his head sharply to the side.

'I agree, Fanny. He's perfect.' Jacob then reached into his jacket and handed Ewan a professional card. 'Here is my studio address. Will you come on Tuesday morning on the dot of nine? Please do *not* wash your hair or shave again before then as I wish you to be seen as a suffering subject. And bring a dog-collar.'

Travelling back to the seminary Ewan's euphoria was so great he felt a type of terror, wondering if he seemed outwardly changed. As he entered through the front door Father Ronald was crossing the hall. 'Ah, Ewan, good evening.' Ewan waited, sweating, holding his breath, waiting to be asked where he'd been, why he was dressed so differently, and why he looked so flushed. But just at that moment, Damien, a fellow seminarian, hurled himself noisily through the front door, dropping his rugby kit on the floor with a loud clunk. 'Victory,' he shouted. '42-11.' Father Ronald raised a fist, and became engaged in a lively, animated discussion of the game with the young sportsman.

Ewan, unnoticed, and having no part in the conversation, slipped away, as invisible as he'd always been.

Chapter 33

At 8.00 a.m. sharp, Cora Feather arrived at the back door of The Manor, holding two plastic bottles of milk she'd picked up from Mr Bhatti's. 'How's the patient?' she demanded, rolling up her sleeves. 'I'm used to all this, you know. I do two afternoons a week at the Sinking Sun Nursing Home.'

'Tim's not had a very good night, actually,' said Roger briskly. 'He had a bit of a nightmare and I had to call Dr Gibson out, but fortunately he calmed down and went back to sleep. Obviously, I'm hoping he'll be fit enough to attend his mother's cremation tomorrow. Once we've got that out the way, I feel sure he'll pick up.'

Cora gaped. 'Are you telling me that I've only got twenty-four hours to organise a funeral reception?'

'Nothing to do, Mrs Feather, nothing to do.'

'What do you mean, nothing to do! There's caterers to organise, and a buffet to choose, and glasses to hire. . .'

'None of that nonsense needed. Tim won't be up to it anyway, so any mourners who want to pay their last respects can gather at *The Dog and Duck.*'

'*The Dog and Duck*! I beg your pardon, Mr Fuller, but *The Dog and Duck* won't do at all. Lady P was a brave and gracious lady, what deserves a proper, refined send off, and if you think. . .'

'I don't actually care a tuppeny toss what you think, Mrs Feather. I shall ring Trevor Frogett and book the taproom at the back. It can accommodate thirty at a push, so it should suffice. I'd be grateful, though, if you can spread the word. It's at ten-thirty at the Crem on Three Mile Hill.' Cora stood stunned and open-mouthed while Roger slipped on his jacket. 'I've agreed with Dr Gibson that I'll give work a miss today, but your services are still required, at least for this morning.'

'You promised me double time until seven.'

'Did I really? Well, there's been a change of plan. I'm off home now to answer my emails and attend to my post. Tim knows you're coming, and he's very pleased. You'll find him in his mother's bedroom. He'll need a bath, and then make sure he has a shave and gets dressed. I looked in on him two minutes ago and he'd gone back to sleep, so it would be a good idea if you got his day going quite soon. Oh, and by the way, there was some nonsense talked last night about him wanting to talk to a priest. Just a spur of the moment panic, but it's all sorted now. If a Father Ewan rings, can you politely explain that his services are no longer required?' With that, Roger strode out of the kitchen, heading for the front door.

Cora fizzed. What appalling manners from them what were supposed to be the elite of society! What did he think she was? Some sort of curtsying servant. If it weren't for him upstairs, she really would walk out, and never come back. Mind you, much as she had respect for dear Lady P, all this baloney was probably her fault for spoiling the little toad. In her opinion, he hadn't been given enough smacked bottoms, and as for sleeping in his mother's bed. . . There was something very iffy about that!

At that precise moment Andrew Gibson phoned. Cora, in high dudgeon, ear-blasted him with a verbatim report of Roger's appalling manners, and her serious disapproval of *The Dog and Duck* as a venue. 'It's outrageous!' she fumed. 'Now he's swanned off home.'

'Bear up, Cora,' said the doctor. 'He's got to attend to some urgent business, so I'm terribly grateful you're there. A motherly presence is exactly what Tim needs. What's he doing now?'

'Still in bed. His Nibs says I've got to get him to have a bath, and get dressed.'

'If you can achieve that it'll be an excellent result. I'm very anxious to see him eating normally as well. Tim's suffering from a very peculiar condition I suspect is something called post-traumatic stress disorder. You might find his behaviour's more than a bit odd, so once he's up and about try and get him to concentrate on simple things. Perhaps a look at the morning paper, but no TV. Those morning chat shows just throw personal angst in one's face like a bucket of water. Maybe he could pop down to his greenhouses for a recce, and get some fresh air. Anything to continue his normal routines. I'll call in as soon as I've finished morning surgery, but do ring the Health Centre if you're at all worried. Oh, and you'll be getting a phone call from Father Ewan, Marina's special priest. He's coming down later on to give Tim some counselling.'

'Mr Fuller said that was all off.'

'Oh? Perhaps Tim's changed his mind, then. Can you find out and let me know sharpish? No point in dragging the poor man all the way down here if he's not required.'

Cora set-to to prepare Timothy a tasty breakfast, but a search in every nook and cranny could only turn up one cracked egg, stuck to the box, and two stale crusts skulking in the bread bin. Cora tightened her mouth like a buttonhole. Obviously, a certain person had sat on his fat arse all weekend, and hadn't been to Sainsbury's. Oh, well. Her kids had gobbled up egg-bread, so egg-bread it would have to be.

She carried the tray upstairs and set it down, but when she drew the curtains, and Timothy slowly turned his head, she caught her breath. He was hardly recognisable. Dark bags hung below bloodshot eyes, he had a two-day growth of beard, and an angry rash had broken out on forehead. His pallor was jaundiced, and he had the expression of a zombie. 'Nice pot of tea and some egg-bread,' she said, 'and you're lucky to get that. There's still not a crumb in this house, but the swing-bin's full up with wine bottles and them silver take-away boxes. Your friend doesn't stint himself, and neither does he know how to wash up.'

'Not hungry,' Timothy said flatly.

'Nonsense. It's a fair bet you've had nothing since I left on Saturday. Now come on. Be a good boy, and eat up.' Timothy slowly managed half a slice, and sipped the tea. 'I hear the cremation's arranged for tomorrow, dear,' she said, attempting something that might pass as normal conversation.

'Is it? Are you coming, Cora?'

''Course I am. There'll be a big village turn-out, too.'

'We'll all be there, won't we? Me, and you, and Pa and Morgana, and Roger.'

'Oh, I expect so.'

'I really wish I knew where to find Patrick. I know Mumma would like him to be there.'

'Who's Patrick?'

'He was my friend. I think he used to live with us, but I can't *actually* remember him being there. When I was little Mumma talked about him all the time. She always laid a place for him at the table, and if we went shopping, we would buy him a comic. When we went up to town to buy new clothes at Harrod's, Mumma used to say, "Wouldn't Patrick look really smart in that?" or "This colour would really suit Patrick." I'd really like to find him. Perhaps Father Ewan knows about him. He's coming to see me later on today.'

'Mr Fuller said that if he rang, I had to tell him he was no longer required.'

Timothy shot forward in the bed, spilling the remains of the cup of tea. 'Well he *is* required! I need him! He *must* come!'

'All right, ducky. Don't upset yourself. I know just the thing to calm you down. How about a nice bath? It'll do you the world of good.' Cora moved into the adjoining bathroom and turned on the taps, confirming the benefits of hot soapy water as an aid to recovery.

'Put in some of Mumma's Body Shop Strawberry Bubbles,' he called out languidly. 'Then will you give Roger a shout? I want him to come and wash me.'

'''Fraid it's only little old me you've got,' Cora said, coming back into the bedroom. 'Your friend's gone home.'

'You're a liar!' he shouted. 'A terrible liar, and God will strike you dumb. He wouldn't go out and leave me. If he's not here, he'll have gone to Sainsbury's.'

'Oh, yes. So he has. I forgot. I get so muddled up in my old age. He's gone to Sainsbury's, and he'll be back in the shake of a lamb's tail.'

'Then will *you* wash me?'

'Don't be daft. You're a grown man, and grown men can wash themselves.'

'Please, Cora. You've got such big strong hands. When Roger washes me, it's just blissful.'

'I don't understand the likes of all that,' she said. 'Not that you can't do what you want behind closed doors, but I'm glad your dear

Mum never knew. Saved her a lot of heartache, I'll be bound.'

'There was lots she didn't know about me. She came back in the night, and sat on the bed. I tried to tell her my big, bad secret, but I just couldn't find the courage.' Cora sighed. Came back in the night, did she? Her and Elvis Presley that would be. He certainly was cracking up.

'Pop yourself in the bath, dear. There goes the phone. It might be that Father Ewan.'

When she returned Timothy was lying back in the pink sudsy water with his eyes closed. 'That *was* him,' she said. 'He'll be down around six. He said he's praying for you.'

Timothy smiled contentedly. 'Oh, that's wonderful, Cora. He's coming to hear my confession. I know he'll forgive me, and then we can talk about the Kingdom of Heaven. By the way, did you manage to make the fairy cakes?'

Chapter 34

Sally's surge of love and passion for Ewan had strangely seduced her to a full night's sleep, entertained by crazy, sensuous dreams of him. They'd soared high over rural Suffolk in an air balloon, made aggressive love up against a tree, and crawled naked through wet, sulphurous potholes into a fur-filled womb of safety. She'd awoken with a sense of soft-bodied joy, the real feel of his lips on hers, and a desperation to fall back into the magic, but the scenes disappeared amorphously into the inexplicable world of night madness.

It was now nine o'clock on Monday morning, and she was once again sitting opposite Ewan; he in his American rocker, she in the Edwardian armchair. Today, he was dressed in his Priest's cassock, and yet another atmosphere prevailed. Something was missing that she sensed as keenly as a hound. The fire was lying in a collapsed heap of cold ash, and there'd been no bobbing and weaving of social ritual. Perhaps, being the first day of the working week, a different set of rules and expectations had destroyed the rapport of the weekend. The 'Monday morning' syndrome of being thrown awake at dawn by a bleating alarm; a full diary; a pressurised clock-watching day, and all semblance of leisure denied. 'Good morning, Sally,' he said, but his face was solemn and pale, and he looked even more exhausted.

Sally was momentarily self-conscious. Were her eyes shining too brightly? Was she projecting her craving for him as boldly as a searchlight? Please God, her expression wasn't one of dopey adoration. She took charge of herself to present a detached, but attentive, persona, and laid her hands primly in her lap. She rapidly scanned him, and as he lit his first inevitable cigarette, she immediately saw he was no longer wearing the gold ring on his left hand. Now why was that?

'You still don't look very well,' she said.

'I feel fine.'

'I'm a nurse. I know you're not well.'

'I know myself. It's nothing. In any case, I've no time to be ill. I had a phone call early this morning from your medical colleague, Dr Gibson. It seems Tim's in a very bad way emotionally, and he's asked to see me. It sounds like a real emergency so I've arranged to go down this evening.'

'Poor Tim,' she said, with genuine sympathy, 'but it's only to be expected. I hope you didn't tell Andrew I was here.'

'Absolutely not.'

'Thanks. I really don't want to be found and have to explain myself. After our talk yesterday I decided I would definitely go back to see Roger. The thing mostly on my mind is Marina's cremation. It must be soon, and I should be there, but I'm not really ready yet. I need to get psyched up.'

'Then you're rather forced into making a snap decision. Dr Gibson told me the cremation's been slotted in for tomorrow morning at ten-thirty. I promised Marina I'd attend, so I'll be there to try and get Tim through it all as well.'

She sighed. 'Tomorrow's really far too soon for me.'

'I agree that a few more days would have been better but. . . something's happened.' Ewan leaned forward in his chair, clasped his hands, and looked Sally very firmly in the eye. 'Sally, the Doctor said that Roger's been trying very hard to support Tim, but he's had very bad news himself. I wish I wasn't the one to have to tell you this, but I have to. Your dog's been run over and killed. A petrol tanker on Saturday afternoon.'

After two seconds of open-mouthed shock Sally's careful composure collapsed. She began to cry, with a sudden, spontaneous whoosh of tears and noise, that one would usually associate with an abandoned child. Indeed, she felt exactly like a small child, seeking the comfort of laps, and arms, and the shushing noises of understanding. Ewan got up, walked over to her, knelt down, and took her hand. 'I'm so sorry, Sally. It's a bitter blow, isn't it? I've counselled a great many patients who've lost pets, and I've never treated their loss in any way different from the human kind. Do cry. You know it's good for you.'

She felt his warmth hanging like a blanket before her, and saw the blurred outline of his domed head. Holding her fingers within his palm, he gently began to stroke her knuckles with his thumb, but she felt no jolt of desire, or yearning to prolong the intimacy. The news had destroyed any other feeling other than that of deep shock.

After Ewan returned to his chair she wept openly for a little longer, shook her head, sniffed loudly, and straightened up. 'At least I've been forced into a decision. No matter what I think of Roger, be it love or anger, Finnegan's death is a tragedy for both of us. There's no choice now. I must go home straight away. Can I drive you down?'

'It would be practical, but I've got patients all morning, and I have an important meeting in London this afternoon.'

'So will you stay at The Manor tonight?'

'I've only spoken to the housekeeper, and she didn't mention anything. I suppose they might be expecting me to stay, but it's better if I don't. I'm not really a family friend in the true sense, and I'm sure Roger won't want me muscling in. Is there a local hotel you can recommend?'

'I'm not sure if this is appropriate, but would you consider staying at my house? I've got four spare bedrooms. They're all en-suite so I can offer you complete silence and seclusion.'

'Thank you, Sally. It's most kind and considerate of you. I accept with pleasure.'

'So what will your role be at Marina's cremation?'

'She asked me to bless some personal affects, and to make sure they accompany her, but otherwise I promised her faithfully that God would be left at the door. I'll take it upon myself to give a short address, as an old friend who knew her well, but apart from that, I'll be just another mourner.' He suddenly lowered his head. He said nothing. He swallowed profusely, and his breaths were short and sharp. The silence lasted far too long to be a respectful pause, and was only broken by Lucifer's loud mewing. The sleek black cat snaked and twisted his supple body through Ewan's feet, seeming to impose the sixth sense of knowledge and sympathy only conferred upon cats.

Sally was thrust into a dilemma that had to be resolved with a split-second decision. Talk of Marina's cremation was clearly affecting him deeply, and her mind tried to focus on this peculiar new shift. Should she try to develop the situation with words of comfort, or should she quietly leave? Inquiring words, no matter how sympathetic or brief, would have compelled some sort of explanation from him; something she was too nervous for in case it led to a cold request to leave him alone. But hadn't he leapt to his feet only minutes before to soothe *her*? Ignoring him would have been callous, and not the actions of an experienced counsellor, especially one who was besotted with love for him. She moved to stand in front of him, and slowly lay her hands on the top of his bare crown. Her palms were ice cold against his warm skin, but he didn't flinch. She left them there until both head and hands were of the same heat. 'Until tonight, then,' she said, taking one of her one of her professional cards from her bag, and laying it on his table. 'Ring me on my mobile when you're through with Tim. Good bye, Ewan.'

He didn't answer. As she left Lucifer jumped up onto his master's lap, but got no response.

Chapter 35

After his bath, Timothy withdrew completely into childhood, and to Cora's horror, wrapped himself up in Lady P's kimono. Again he asked for Roger, and when Cora told him that he hadn't got back yet, burst into tears. Thereafter, all suggestions for reading the paper, or a walk in the garden, were ignored. He stayed in his mother's bedroom to play with a wind-up toy, and to talk to her photograph. He held conversations with the mysterious person called Patrick, and mumbled about sinning in God's sight and being no more worthy to be called his son. Cora, not knowing what on earth to do, phoned The Dower House several times in an attempt to summon Roger, but with getting no answer, rang Dr Gibson's surgery to demand an emergency home visit.

When he arrived Cora babbled with bewilderment. 'Tim's gone quite off his chump. He started off being a bit dreamy and dippy, talking to his mother, and rambling on and on about someone called Patrick, but then he got very agitated when I couldn't produce Master Fuller. I made up a lie he'd gone to Sainsbury's, but after that he went completely off the rails. He said his mum had come back in the night, and he wanted to tell her some big bad secret about himself.'

'Yes, I actually knew about that. Mr Fuller called me out in the night because he thought Tim had had a nightmare. I diagnosed it as a psychotic illusion.'

'Well, I think I'd better tell you what this big bad secret is.' Cora paused for effect and took a deep breath. 'You won't believe this, but him and Mr Fuller are a pair of nancy boys. What do you think of that, then! No one else knows but me. Even Lady P never knew.'

The doctor stared with popping eyes and an open mouth. 'Are you sure?'

'Positive. Been going on years. You look shocked, Dr Gibson.'

'I must admit I'm quite bowled over.'

'Well, it's true.'

'Good God. I had absolutely no idea. I've always thought Tim was rather fey, but Roger Fuller doesn't seem the type at all. Do you think Sally knows?'

'Search me, but it seems strange she hasn't shown her face at all around here, 'specially as she's trained up in all this grief wotsit stuff.'

'According to Roger she's gone away for a few days, but that might be a blind. Her presence is desperately needed, but if she *does* know then it's the last place she'd want to be. Oh, dear. This really has put me in a difficult position on patient confidentiality terms. Thanks for the info, though. All Tim's ramblings yesterday about confession have fallen into place. Do you know what his current thoughts are on the priest?'

'Definitely wants to see him.'

'And has the Father rung to confirm?'

'Yes. Said he'd be down around six. I told Tim and he was ever so pleased. That was before he went all peculiar.'

'Excellent. If he feels the need to cleanse his soul then confession may be invaluable. In the meantime, I'll get him back to bed and try some sedation. After the priest's been I'll re-assess the situation, possibly with the help of a colleague. If there's no improvement, I might be forced to admit him to a psychiatric hospital.'

'That bad, eh?'

Together they went up to Timothy, who was lying curled up in Marina's bed, sucking his thumb. 'Tim, old son,' said the doctor carefully. 'You're really worn out, aren't you? How about a nice bit of shut-eye?'

'Yes, please. I'd like a good sleep before Father Ewan comes.'

'Here's a couple of pills to help. When you wake up try a little turn around the garden, and get some deep breaths of fresh air.' Timothy obediently swallowed the tablets with a sip of water, lay down and turned his back.

As they left the room Andrew Gibson looked at his watch. 'Just gone ten-thirty. He'll be right out of it for at least three hours. Did Roger Fuller say what time he'd be back?'

'No, he didn't. Just booked me for the morning.'

'And you say you've had no replies from his land-line? I presume you haven't got his mobile number?'

Cora bristled. 'No I haven't. Being on-call's not part of his plan, is it? Selfish so and so.'

'I was aware that he had some very urgent business to attend to. That's why I was so grateful you were going to be here. Oh, well. I'll be passing The Dower House on my way back to The Health Centre, so if his car's there I'll pop in and explain the situation. If he doesn't turn up in the fullness of time, and you really can't cope with Tim when he wakes up, ring me straight away.'

'Dr Gibson, if these tablets are going to knock him out cold, can I call old Mac's taxi and do a quick whizz up to Sainsbury's on the ring road? There's not a crumb in this house, and Mr Bhatti's just won't do. I'll be ever so quick.'

'As long as you really *are* quick,' he said, 'but it's only right that we tell Tim. Best let him know what's happening. It's all part of respect to the patient, and I'll write it up in his notes '

They quietly entered the bedroom again. 'Tim,' Cora whispered, patting his hand. He blearily opened his eyes. 'Listen, I'm going to call old Mac and nip up to Sainsbury's.'

'No need. Roger's been.'

'Er. . . no. He rang to say he's not actually had time yet. He's still at home doing a bit of sorting out. You have a nice sleep and I'll be back long before you wake up.'

'OK, but bring me a packet of Quavers and a bottle of Merlot. Father Ewan will need them to give me communion. Oh, and before you go, can you look out Morgana's bag for him?'

Cora looked blank. 'A bag that belonged to his little sister,' mouthed Dr Gibson. 'Some talk of blessing. A request of Marina's. Nothing to concern yourself with.' Timothy sighed deeply, turned back over, and began to breathe evenly. They both stood looking at him for another minute. 'Spark out,' said the doctor.

'Right,' said Cora. 'I'll get old Mac on the blower.'

Chapter 36

Ewan's front door clicked shut as Sally left, but he didn't hear it. His ears were aching with tension from the restraint he'd had to exercise. He felt Lucifer's pushing demands against his brow, but as he attempted to fondle him, the cat twisted and leapt away. He gritted his teeth, berating himself for his weakness. It *must* have been obvious to Sally that his emotional reaction was much more than that of a mere therapist. As a fellow grief counsellor, she was trained to recognise signs, so what explanation could he offer if she tried to draw out his feelings further tonight? Her natural duty was to counsel, and wasn't this what he craved?

The imprint of her fingers remained on his head, and an irrational thought jerked through him. That he should run after her, call her, make her return, allow himself to collapse and reveal himself, as surely he had to for the sake of his future sanity. Her Madonna's arms would hold him, and her cool hands would massage his bursting head. Why did he see himself kneeling at her feet, and kissing the smooth skin of her ankles? Fearful of madness, he forced his mind to swing to the higher plane of suffering and denial to which all priests are conditioned.

With gritty resolve he folded his hands together, and prepared to continue his odyssey, noticing the smooth, white indentation on the finger that had held his ring. Its skin was shedding like a snake's.

DECEMBER 15TH 1982

As directed, Ewan arrived on time at the address stated on Jacob Poznanski's business card. Alma Terrace was one of the many narrow side-streets that made up the congested area of South Hackney. The entrance to number nine was not what he expected, being an archway fronted by a high pair of rusting iron gates. He lifted a stiff latch, pushed his way in, and found himself in a scruffy courtyard that fronted a seemingly derelict warehouse. It was built of dull, yellowy London brick, blackened by the polluted air of steam trains, factory chimneys, and exhaust fumes since its Victorian inception. Roof water ran down a loose drainpipe, straight out onto some uneven, green-slimed cobbles, and a precarious looking fire-escape hung ominously to the side of a fifty-foot wall. He looked up to see a row of sad, cold pigeons, puffed to the size of chickens, clinging to the gutters. With no signs of occupation, and with all the window panes either cracked or cobwebbed, he was sure he'd come to the wrong place. But then he noticed a standard bell push, positioned beneath a small painted notice board: *Jacob Poznanski. Photographic Studio.*

He hovered, shifting from one nervous foot to the other, suddenly realising the extent of his commitment. This whole thing was a folly; a bizarre derangement he had no moral right to be even contemplating. A lurch of diffidence shook his body, but as his fingertip hovered over the smooth plastic button, he was compelled to press. He gave it one short pulse, hoping perhaps that the bell was faulty. That he could truthfully say he'd turned up, but having got no answer, had left.

Jacob immediately appeared at the top of the fire escape. 'Up here, my dear boy,' he called out. 'In penthouse suite.' Once Ewan had climbed to the top of the wobbly metal staircase, Jacob led him into an echoing, high-walled space that measured perhaps sixty feet in each direction. Clearly, it had undergone an extensive conversion. The smooth walls and ceiling were painted with bright white emulsion, the floor was covered with shiny black vinyl, and on one side – the north facing side – a wholly glazed wall afforded a far-reaching view of the green-swarded London Fields. Jacob introduced him to two young men who were busy setting up the shoot. Gary, his technician, and Max, an artistic assistant. 'This is David. A young friend of mine who has never before been involved in the madhouse of photography.'

The two men smiled, and said, 'Hi, David' in a friendly fashion, and although they'd obviously been told that the model coming had a cleft-lip repair, they looked at him as most people did; a split second too long, followed by a dropping of the eyes, and a turning away.

'Right, gentlemen,' Jacob announced. 'What I've got in mind is purely a work of art. The crucifix is in place and the wind and rain will be provided by high tech equipment.' He laughed. 'A hairdryer and a plastic spray bottle of water. David, your own jeans are too new for the effect I want to portray, so I've acquired some old worn ones for you to wear. Your boots are just fine. I want your upper body naked apart from. . .' He lowered his voice. 'Did you remember to bring the collar?' Ewan nodded. Jacob then turned to his assistants.

'We are going to create David as the modern day Christ,' he announced. 'The boots will need some paste to dirty them up, he is to wear a dog-collar around the neck, and on the brow the barbed wire crown Max has made. I want the jeans to have a low waist, with a tight crotch and thigh. In this picture I wish to create a tableau of beauty, virtue and piety, but by Christ this guy could shag his arse off if he weren't dying.'

Once Ewan was dressed to order, Max examined his arms, and finger-pulled his long hair into various positions. 'Jacob, do you agree to shaving of arms only?' Max asked. 'His chest hair is excellent, and upper body very beautiful. Skin quality is quite flawless. Beard stubble can be untouched, but I might tidy the neck up a bit.'

Jacob stepped back and thought carefully. 'Fine to leave stubble and to tidy up neck, but otherwise disagree. Shave off all visible body hair and rub in baby oil. No make-up at all on the face, and absolutely no hair gel or lacquer. I want the so-called rain water to run off the tips of his hair and trickle down his chest. With oil on skin it will run like tears.'

The Crucifixion cross had been borrowed from a theatre company production of 'Jesus Christ, Super Star,' so all restraining shackles had been proved safe. Shaven and oiled, Ewan mounted by a stepladder and was manipulated into position. Concealed clips were attached to his jeans, the heel of a boot was placed on a hidden platform, and his flopped, manacled hands were able to rest on discreet spurs. But, despite this element of safety, it was a scary and uncomfortable position that required a great deal of his own strength and concentration to maintain.

After Polaroids were taken, the three men debated and argued technicalities amongst themselves. With all dissent resolved, Jacob then worked with great energy and deliberation, giving precise instructions as to how he wanted to involve both artificial and natural lighting. Spotlights went on, spotlights went off. Blinds went down, blinds went up. The team worked with balletic precision, involving diverse angles, several reels of film, and numerous changes of camera. After ten minutes, Ewan was beginning to tire, and feared he might slip. 'Please, Jacob,' he called. 'I'm exhausted. May I come down for a rest?'

'The more exhausted you look the better,' Jacob called up to him. 'I am selfish old sod. Just one more reel and then we have lunch break, yes?'

Eventually shooting stopped, and Ewan was helped down, but his body was as stiff and cold as an effigy in a church. While Gary disappeared downstairs to the dark room with the shot reels, Max passed him a candlewick bedspread to wrap himself in, and led him to sit before a two-bar electric fire. 'Get warmed up, David,' he said. 'I'll nip out and get us all some sandwiches, but perhaps this morning I should ask for loaves and fishes?'

Jacob laid his cameras down and walked over, rubbing his hands together. 'I think we have done good work,' he said, bowing slightly. 'This image will be something special.' He then moved to stand behind Ewan's chair. 'I think your neck will be stiff and sore. Let me ease your muscles.' As his fingers worked and kneaded he spoke gently. 'You are very beautiful young man, Ewan, or perhaps I should really call you David. Looking at your body I think only of Michelangelo's David. The perfection of Renaissance man. The models that the master used for both painting and sculpture were labouring men, you see. Not lazy sons of merchants, or fat cats. Builders and stonemasons with tight muscles and sinews. They led physical lives. They worked hard, using the strength of their bodies to earn their livings, such as their livings were. In those days the priests would have been very fat and flabby.' He then leaned forward and kissed Ewan's bare shoulder.

Ewan instantly recoiled, and shot forward with shock. 'Don't be so shy, dear flower,' Jacob continued. 'What does the big book say about hiding lights under bushels? My light shines like the sun out of my big bushel. I feel huge passion for you.'

'I'm not. . . I'm not what you think I am,' said Ewan.

'I know that you are priest, and I guess that you are virgin?'

'Yes, but I'm not gay.'

'Ah! Then if you know you are not gay, you must know that you are straight?'

'Yes. I know that, but I've chosen to lead a celibate life.'

'Is it because of your looks? Your lip? Do you think women will not want to kiss you, or sleep with you?'

Ewan flushed, and fumbled for words – for the right words – feeling a sense of fury. Why did he always have to explain himself to people? 'I've chosen the life of a priest because I love God, and I want to be his disciple, and I can try to do so much good in the world. It's *my* life. I've the right to choose and I've chosen.'

Jacob moved round and sank down heavily on a scruffy chair beside him. 'Forgive me, please. You have humbled me to shame. My behaviour was disgraceful. Can we shake hands? I promise I behave myself now.'

'Of course,' replied Ewan. 'I extend to you the love of God.' The two men shook hands. Jacob then leaned back in the chair. 'The right to choose your life's path in this country is your birthright, and I sometimes forget how lucky I am to be here. I am refugee, you see. Polish Jew. My father was a doctor, and we lived in a small town near Warsaw. We had big house, fine furniture, large garden, and servants. One day I had been out with our old gardener to pick up wood for our fires – a regular treat I greatly enjoyed as we would travel the surrounding area with a pony and trap, and stop to have our bread and cheese under the watery sun. On that day, when he brought me home, the house had been wrecked. Ripped through as if by bomb. My parents, my two brothers, and my sister had all disappeared. I was only five-years-old, but I remember that scene as if it were yesterday. They had been taken away to death camps, like thousands of others. After that, I stayed with the old gardener and his wife.' He shrugged. 'They had no choice but to look after me.'

Ewan, with immediate sympathy for Jacob's suffering, was compelled to hear more of his terrifying story. 'Please, tell me more. Much more. How did you survive?'

'There's not much more to tell. No, of course that is not true. There is much, much more, but my short story is that the three of us were taken soon afterwards to the Jewish ghetto in Warsaw. The old couple quickly grew weak and ill, and were unable to care for me, so I joined a band of other abandoned children. We were like feral dogs, hanging on to any one who took us in, but who were only keeping themselves alive by scratching and begging. By the time the war ended we had had very little adult care or education. We were bordering on little savages, but we learned to look out for each other, and love each other. I was rescued by a British charity, and brought to UK in 1945, when I was aged ten. I was adopted by Anglican family, the Wakefields. They took me to their lovely country house, and gave me privileged life. Private education, holidays, horses, and the same love and attention they gave to their natural children. I was absorbed into their lives as if I were an ingredient in a cake, and indeed, when the cake was baked, there I was. Jack Wakefield. New English boy. Ewan, never could I be an English boy, so out of respect to my roots I work under my birth name of Poznanski. My Wakefield family is proud of me, but they accept me for what I am. They know I still belong to Poland.'

'Have you ever been back there to look for your family?'

'Once, about ten years ago, but in my heart I knew that searching for them was madness. I managed to find the place where our small town used to be, but it was wholly changed and there was nothing left of the community. Our house had stood alone, surrounded by forestation and fields, but the area had been razed and was part of huge factory complex. All records had disappeared, and what chance did I have of finding anyone who knew us?' He raised his arms to demonstrate hopelessness. 'We were Jews, my dear. In the war, if a Polish Jew was not herded away to a death camp, he did the smart thing and ran away. Things being as they are, I've no chance of ever finding out their fate.'

'But things are changing for Poland today.'

'True. Today there is a real wind of change in my country. The Pope and Walesa are doing everything they can to cry freedom, but you note that these men are Catholics. Poland has a great Catholic tradition, and I thank my God for them, but the history that hangs over me and my people is a closed door.'

Jacob then shut his eyes and began to sing in a strange language; a song that sounded like a lullaby, even though his voice was a deep, bass baritone. He sang three verses, and then opened his eyes. 'You see. Still word perfect, and still exquisite words. *Rozhinkes Mit Mandlen.* Raisins and Almonds. *In the temple corner sits a widowed daughter of Zion, rocking her only son. She sings, 'Someday you will trade in raisins and almonds... that will be your calling. Sleep now, little one, sleep.'* I can still remember my Mamush holding me on her knee, and singing that little song.'

Jacob then jumped up out of the chair, and his voice strengthened. 'That is it. That is enough of Jacob and his broken heart. We will have good strong coffee now, my friend.' He turned and walked over to a table that held a kettle and mugs. 'Ewan, the prison of my sexuality means I will never have my own child on my knee, which is an even sadder tragedy for me. You, my dear boy, have the good fortune to have those joys and rewards of life, but you choose to join a prison too. One day you will find that love and passion shouts out to you, and you won't be able to shout back.'

Ewan pulled the bedspread tighter around his shoulders, recalling the sad strains of Jacob's singing. From the shadows his own five-year-old self began to scramble up onto his own Mammy's knee. 'Mind your sandals, darlin'. Those sharp old buckles will ladder my best nylons.' Her skirt felt rough and tweedy against his bare legs, but she smelled of flowers, and her long silver-blonde hair brushed his cheek. Ewan could never understand why he then said the words he did. To tell a complete stranger something that he'd never discussed with anyone else, other than the few brief exchanges he'd had with his adoptive mother, but the words blurted out. 'Jacob, I too was adopted. I was only five-years-old, but I too remember my mother's knee and her closeness.'

Jacob returned without the coffee, Ewan rose, and the two men clasped hands. 'We will talk,' Ewan said. 'I intend to make my career in bereavement counselling. My old school, The Abbey at Waldringhythe, has just been refurbished. I've known the Bishop since I was a child, and I've asked if I can be appointed as chaplain so I can set up a grief-counselling centre. Jacob, I'm studying hard. Philosophy, psychology, counselling skills, and the physical effects of grief, but in order to qualify I've got to produce a portfolio of cases. Will you be a case for me?'

Jacob laughed. A loud giant's roar that Ewan was to come to know as so much a part of Jacob's personality. 'Everyone who knows me says I am suitable case for treatment. I will be pleased to be suitable case for you.' He then cocked his head and winked. 'The fire escape is rattling. Here comes my bagel.'

After lunch the photo shoot continued, but this time, to take his mind off the pain of his stretched muscles, Ewan too began to sing. A song he recalled his Mammy singing to him when she put him to bed at night.

'*Heavenly shades of night are falling, it's Twilight Time*'

Chapter 37

DECEMBER 16TH 1982

My dear Ewan

Once again I apologise for my selfish behaviour yesterday. I know we have parted friends and, as I so wish to keep you as a friend, I must forget how much I am attracted to you. Your offer of talking to me about my yesterdays will be gratefully accepted, even though I'm now a man of forty-seven, and my troubles are deemed to be far behind me. As you know they are not. They are, and forever will be, following my every footstep.

In the post-war world, no one had heard of counselling, or emotional support to children such as myself. I was one fucked-up kid. When I was first brought to this country all I remember was strangers, whispering amongst themselves in a foreign language, and being busy around me. They smiled sweetly, patted me on the head, and made noises like sad birds. They scrubbed me clean, they deloused my hair, they fed me orange juice and cod liver oil. They offered kindness, which is the only thing they knew, but it was many years before I recognised it as such. I had no feelings, you see. I had been conditioned not to feel or trust. I so look forward to talking with you, and if it helps me to cope with the theft of my past then our Gods will be as one.

Now. News of the photographs. They are truly exceptional. One above all others is superb, and I think the best thing I have ever produced in my career. This afternoon I have spoken with Fanny, and it is all agreed at The Courier. On Sunday, you, my dear boy, will be my Crucifix Man, but you must not worry that your identity will be revealed. Only Fanny and I know who you really are, and the editors are aware that you are to remain anonymous. That is, until you choose to reveal yourself.

We will see each other soon, yes?

With much love, of the purest kind,

Jacob

DECEMBER 20TH 1982

Jacob's pride in his work had not been exaggerated out of conceit. *Crucifix Man,* as illustrated on the cover of *The Courier's* Sunday supplement, was a stunning work of emotion. Shot in the style of a classic Edwardian sepia print, the Christ figure hung as a single spectacle of suffering. Beneath the rib cage, a deep hollow dished to reveal a lean waistline above the low-slung waistband of the Levi's, and the wide stretch of the arms showed the undulating curves of the shoulder muscles. Against the soft-brown colour wash, minute droplets of water on the torso resembled golden pearls.

The body was, indeed, of great physical beauty, but it was the sheered head that even more positively drew the eye. Although wet hair obscured all facial features, a wide central gap allowed the viewer to admire the high cutting angle of the cheek-bones. The barbed wire crown was fronted with the CND logo, and from it a dark rivulet, of what was intended to be blood, ran to the top of the left eyebrow. Above the head a piece of simple white parchment was tacked onto the cross, and hand written with the simple words, '*Save Us All, Sweet Jesus.*'

From the moment *The Courier* hit the news-stands their office phones were jammed with messages of praise and outrage in equal proportions. The publicity generated was indeed unique, and within twenty-four hours there were global headlines declaring, '*Anger and Praise for Nuke Shock Crucifixion Snap.*' Thus, every major newspaper, and television news programme in the world, featured it as a controversial talking point. From then on all bodies of the three estates argued either its artistic beauty, or blatant heresy, and, especially with Christmas imminent, a shoal of articles, of both admiration and castigation, appeared. The furore caused was unprecedented, and a mystery began as to the identity of the Christ figure. The Christ figure chose to flee.

3RD JANUARY 1983

My Dear Ewan

I write to thank you. Could anyone have thought that the immoral, predatory creature that I am could spend ten happy, celibate days in the beautiful isolation of a cottage in Scotland with a priest? The first time for nearly thirty years that I have taken myself away, and left my cameras at home.

Can I convey to you the sheer joy of those ten days? Rising in the dark to watch the pale dawn come up over the Atlantic, and then sitting with you, in a perfect companionable silence, to eat porridge and drink strong, sweet tea. Putting on our spiked boots, and padded jackets, to hike up the hard, frosted hills, and eat our packed lunches. How will I ever forget our afternoons? Sitting like two old men beside an open fire with our drams, and a Christmas TV diet of James Bond and 'The Generation Game.' The fun of our Hogmanay evening in the crazy, drunken bar of the McCraigan Hotel, when we told everyone we were father and son. Oh, that you really were my son, Ewan! What pride I would have in you.

All the time we talked and listened to each other, dragging out our fragments of childhood memories with fine tweezers. We talked of Poland and Albania. We puzzled, we gave our opinions, and we sympathised. We commented on our similarities, and sank into our own silent thoughts. Perhaps we said many things that in the cold light of normal life we have no strength for. When we parted you were contemplating whether to search for your birth mother. If you do so, then all my support and help is here for you.

I've come home a much-changed man. After our time of closeness and bonding, you will now understand what I say, without fear, or recoil, or disgust. Ewan, I love you. The genuine love for man and woman, and man and man, is the same. I love you from the tops of my ears to the tips of my toes.

Yours, with every scrap of love and affection I can find,

Your Jacob

Chapter 38

Within ten minutes of leaving The Manor, Cora was powering a shopping trolley round the air-conditioned aisles of Sainsbury's. Now, unloading at the checkout, she stood boldly with self-congratulations. Spare staff were summoned to pack, and the village taxi was loaded up by an acned youth with far less strength than Cora. She looked at her watch. 'Good timing, Mac. Wagons roll. You'll come in for a cuppa won't you?'

As the taxi reached the top of The Manor House drive she slapped the sides of her seat so strongly old Mac was forced to swerve, narrowly hitting a lamppost. 'Ha!' she shouted. 'Meladdo's back, and not before time.' Roger was observed removing several very large Marks and Spencer's bags from the back of his car. At first she was compelled to forgive him for being absent. He'd been shopping for food after all. She'd jumped the gun, and judged him too quickly, but it was soon obvious that his bags were much too large, and not full enough to contain food; the soft and swingy variety that held clothes. There were at least ten bags, and even a zipped suit-cover over his arm. Cora could contain her fury no longer, and struggled inelegantly from the car. 'Where the hell have you been?' she yelled. 'That poor troubled soul upstairs, going from crisis to crisis, and all you can do is swan off. He was acting up so queer I had to call out Dr Gibson. He was extremely concerned, Mr Fuller. Extremely concerned, and none too pleased that you'd done the disappearing act. The only thing he could do was get him back to bed and knock him out with pills. Some friend you are.'

Roger placed his bags down on the drive, and squared up to her. 'Mrs Feather, Andrew Gibson was fully aware that I had urgent business to attend to. In any case, it's absolutely none of your blasted business what I do, or where I've been.'

'Ah, but that's where you're wrong,' she bellowed. 'It is my business. It's my business to tell you that you're a selfish sod. There wasn't a scrap of food in the house, but did you care? Did you buggery. You'd have been better off going around Marks with a food trolley instead of treating yourself. I've just been to Sainsbury's to make sure the poor boy doesn't starve, and don't think I give a monkey's what happens to you.' She then turned and shouted to the taxi driver. 'Get the boot open, Mac.'

A red-faced Cora, who was near to tears, snatched out each bag of groceries, and threw them down on the drive for maximum impact and damage. To underline her attitude, she gave a couple of them a firm angry kick across the shingle. She then scrambled in her handbag for the till receipt, and stuffed it on top of a bunch of bananas. 'Right. Now get me what you owe me, Mr Fuller. That little lot was a hundred and thirty six pounds, 68 pence, plus Mac's fare of twenty with the tip, and while you're at it you can pay me the eighty quid what you told me I'd earn today. That makes a grand total of two hundred and thirty seven to my reckoning. Then I'll be off, and I won't be back. At least while you're still around, I won't be.'

'Mrs Feather,' seethed Roger, 'that's the best news I've heard in my entire life. You're a vicious old cow who assumes far too much importance in this house. I'm delighted to see the back of you.' He produced his wallet, and counted out two hundred and fifty pounds, in crisp new notes. 'Here you are, with interest. Any unpaid wages will be sent to you, and I'm sure Tim will be pleased to supply you with a basic reference, despite your numerous shortcomings.' He walked forward and stuffed the money in her hand. 'Now piss off and good riddance.'

As the taxi retreated down the drive, Roger's heart beat fast, his breathing was laboured, and the smell of fresh sweat radiated from his armpits. His fury was such that he could have cheerfully swung a cricket bat round the old trout's head, and been grateful to see her felled to the gravel in a bath of blood. Fucking bitch! Now he was faced with the humiliating task of clearing up the drive. As he wearily picked up the first food bag, it split from underneath. The contents fell out covered in tomato ragout, with a broken glass jar showing the red-stained face of Lloyd Grossman. Not one food bag out of twelve had escaped being plastered with damage, ranging from broken eggs, washing up liquid, salt, flour, milk and Worcester sauce.

It was a full ninety paces from the front of The Manor House, to the hinterlands of the scullery door, and carrying the detritus through the house was not an option. Feeling hot, clumsy, and exhausted, Roger carefully placed his personal cargo of new clothes in the portico by the front door, and went to find a wheelbarrow.

On his return his spirits sank even further to see a visitor had appeared. 'Father Joseph,' said Roger, with a tight-lipped attempt to hide his fury. 'You've called at a very inconvenient time. Tim's sound asleep and I've got my hands full as you can see.'

'Well, many hands make light work, Mr Fuller. Let me give you a hand.'

'That's very decent of you. Thanks very much.'

Together they loaded up the wheelbarrow, and trundled it around to the back of the house. Once inside, dishcloths were found and taps run. Items beyond saving were thrown away, and the rest were washed, dried and packed away in the larder, or the fridge. The weariness Roger felt was overwhelming, and all he wanted to do was to sit down completely alone, and pour a glass of something large and alcoholic, but he was obliged to offer the old man a reward. 'Amontillado, Father? I think we both need one.'

'How kind, how kind.'

Roger took the bottle from the pantry, glugged out two large sherry glasses, and opened a packet of delicate cheese straws that had miraculously come through the assault perfectly intact. 'Help yourself,' he said, lifting his own glass, and sinking half of it. 'I'll go up and see if Tim's awake yet,' but within a minute he was back. 'He's deeply asleep. He's actually been rather distressed this last couple of days, and I think Dr Gibson's medicated him.'

'That's why I'm here, Mr Fuller. I had a phone call from Father Ewan McEwan. You must have heard the family speak of him. He's quite a star of the priesthood. He's coming down later to counsel Tim, and he rang me to ask if I'd pop in to keep a weather eye on things.'

'With the greatest of respect, Father Joseph, the famous star won't be needed. Could you contact him to that effect? If you've got his mobile number I'll do it myself.'

'Sorry, Mr Fuller, but I've no contact number at all. I suppose you could always ring The Abbey, but I know he had an appointment in London this afternoon.'

Roger swallowed another large draught. 'This is all getting out of hand. I've just *got* to get Tim through the cremation tomorrow. I take it you've been informed?'

'I've been informed, but I've also been told by Arthur Fullylove I'm *persona non grata*. Lady P left strict instructions that I was unwelcome to officiate.' He shrugged. 'I was never very popular with the lovely lady, but I still have a duty to Tim. I can't just walk away. Father Ewan and I will do all we can to help him through the trauma.'

'Look, Father,' said Roger, unable to keep his exasperation to himself. 'I've got to get Tim there in a sensible state, and he's in a bad enough way without the interference of grief therapy.'

'Oh, Mr Fuller, you've absolutely nothing to fear. I can guarantee that any therapy will have a miraculously calming effect. There's no one more apt to steer Tim through things than Father Ewan. He's a truly wonderful practitioner. After the family tragedy I was convinced that Lady P was going to disappear into permanent melancholy, and I was the one who recommended that she should consult with him in the first place. I'm delighted to say he was solely responsible for keeping her spiritually nourished and sane. I'm sure you must have heard of his book, *'Hand in Hand With Your Inner Self'*?'

'I have actually, but I've never read it.'

'Well, you must. It's a life-changing classic. Rest assured, Mr Fuller, Father Ewan's a latter day saint.'

Roger slumped his shoulders. Knowing he was defeated he couldn't be bothered to prolong the conversation, and looked at his watch. 'What time's he coming?'

'Around six. In the meantime, I'll hang on to support Tim when he wake up?'

'Father,' Roger said, restraining himself with great difficulty from grabbing him by the scruff of the neck, and physically ejecting him. 'I hardly slept last night, and Mrs Feather has just been hideously unpleasant. I need something that's known these days as a little head space.'

'But I assured Father Ewan I would stay in attendance until he arrived.'

'Well, I'll be here. He won't be abandoned. Why not pop back around four.'

The priest looked dejected, and sighed wearily. 'As you will, Mr Fuller.'

As soon as the old man was on his feet Roger steered him firmly by the shoulders up to the front door. Again, Roger felt like swinging the cricket bat and leaving another corpse lying on the drive alongside the Feather cow. As the old Morris chugged away he vowed that Saint bloody Ewan would be the third.

Chapter 39

Ewan sat in his consulting room in the Chapter House, discreetly looking at his watch. Eleven o'clock. He was finding concentration difficult, but the sad man facing him required his full attention. It was only a half-hour follow-up; a referral back from a colleague who'd taken Arthur Evans on, but was finding great difficulty with the man.

'Father, I despair of life having no purpose,' the sad man said.

'The dictionary calls that nihilism,' Ewan replied, 'but I prefer to call it a temporary glitch. The meaning of life is so abstract and vast, pondering its existence can only drive you mad. You're facing a big hole; a metaphorical grave, and my part in your recovery is to provide a safety net.'

'But Father, Barbara's been dead for three months, and I still feel hopeless.'

'Arthur, it's not a competition. You and Barbara were unique, and you must never compare yourself with any other person, or feel inadequate. Please don't try to rush through your stages, and don't forget the key text. *To know yourself is to understand yourself, and memory is the only key. To go back in time, to the beginning of your life, and work forward in strict narrative order*'. Where have you got up to in your journey?'

'My National Service days in Africa, Father.' The sad-faced man then began to talk haltingly about his days spent in the shadow of Mount Kilimanjaro, but Ewan hardly heard a word. He nodded and agreed, in what he hoped were the right places, but his mind was elsewhere. He finally drew the meeting to a close and stood up. The man too stood up, came over, and clutched Ewan's hands. 'This session had been invaluable, Father. Talking to you has opened up my mind. Thank you so much.' The man left with renewed strength, but Ewan knew he'd said nothing useful, nor made any helpful suggestions.

Back at his house Ewan went up to his bedroom and removed his cassock, knowing that he'd never wear it again. He dressed completely in black; tight jeans, a T-shirt, Spanish-dancer boots, and a leather jacket. He brushed his hair to hang loose over his shoulders, and placed a moleskin fedora on his head. Before putting his car keys in his pocket he idly contemplated the key fob. TVR. Metallic grey. Smoked glass windows. Driven in the face of his Bishop's disapproval, but knowing he'd never be admonished, due to the vast sums he donated to the upkeep of Waldringhythe. Yes – his car was the impressive sleek machine of the spoiled playboy, but he desired it in much the same way as he'd desired Marina. Only last spring she'd sat beside him in the passenger seat, wearing her long, camel cashmere coat, and Gucci sunglasses, her voice screaming with mock fear as he'd accelerated up and down the twisting lanes of Cornwall to find their hired stone cottage. The four days spent in the harmony of long, meandering clifftop walks, indulgent and boozy pub lunches, and hard passionate nights.

After putting his overnight case in the car he set off for the Abbey cemetery, to join the same narrow lane he'd walked down on the day he said goodbye to his father, and on the way back virtually said goodbye to his mother. That day he'd been a schoolboy of eighteen, brutally jerked out of a warm cocoon of family love and security. Suffering not only bereavement, but the sight of his mother, racked with misery, and confessing his adoption. The day she went mad. Yes mad it was, but a strange kind of madness that allowed her to distance herself from life, and inhabit an insular world to which no one had the key. Thereafter his eventual attempt to pursue her demand for justice that led. . . That led precisely nowhere. Now, thirty years later, here he was again, moving down the unchanged lane. But this time he was a bereaved priest, suffering a confusion of the mind that was his own sort of madness. As he strode out his inner self joined hands with the lonely youth, and the youth, in turn, joined hands with the innocent five-year-old child that had been himself. The little boy's voice spoke out from the past.

'Where am I going, Mammy?'

'Somewhere lovely, Patrick. There'll be other boys and girls there, and you'll have lots of fun. Father Ignatius is coming over to get you.'

'Will it only be for a little while?'

'Just a holiday, darlin'.'

'Why are you crying, Mammy?'

'I'm not. I've got something in my eye. Now you've to be a very good boy.'

'Of course I'll be a good boy.'

'I know you will. You're always a good boy.' She'd grabbed him, and clasped him so tightly she hurt his chest.

He entered the churchyard and wove his way across to the two matching marble headstones, side by side beneath the shade of a large oak tree. The more weathered one of his father.

Duncan McEwan
A dearly beloved husband and father
Head of English at Waldringhythe Abbey
1965-1978
Taken from us on July 18 1978
Aged 51

In a fairer world this kind, modest man would still be here. Perhaps frail, leaning on a stick, wearing a hat, muffler and gloves, feeling the spring sunshine on his face, and enjoying the easy familiarity of his middle-aged son's company.

The one less weathered of his mother who died of natural causes, falling into her permanent sleep whilst sitting in her small bed-sitting room, hunched with a bowed back, and knitting a tea cosy.

Jean Anderson McEwan
A dearly beloved wife and mother
Taken from us on April 4 2005
Aged 75

To the day she died she attended mass on two sticks, and was still word-perfect in her prayers and responses. Miraculously spared cancer. She, too, should have been here, unafflicted by neurosis, and playing Joan to Dad's Darby.

Ewan took his hat off, and stood in reverent repose to begin his silent soliloquy. 'Your dream, Dad, was that I should become an academic. Your dream, Mum, that I should become a family man. Instead I chose my own path in life, but today I've stopped walking. These last four days my life story's been going round in my head, like two noisy trains circling in opposing directions. The first five years, of which I know so little, and the last forty-three, of which I know so much.

'Mum, my apologies. I never did get 'the buggers' for you, did I? I chose cowardice, and a spoiled, easy life. Now I can't lie and deceive myself any longer. All my delusions about being a good priest, and giving myself up to the selfless service of the bereaved, are a nonsense. My vows pledged me to sacrifice, poverty, obedience and chastity, but it's all been a sham. Judge me as you will, but rest assured that the book will be re-opened soon. Oh, and if both of you really *are* up there looking down on me, please will you look after my beloved Marina, until such times as we are all re-united?

Ewan ran his hands along the castellated top of the gravestones, fighting his admission that he was talking to the trees.

The Courier May 10, 1983

'Jacob Poznanski, the photographer of the stunning *Crucifix Man* (pictured left) has been nominated for two major awards. It was announced today that he is a major contender for The Silver Lens, the top British award for achievement, and The Prix Sans Frontiers, the American photography equivalent of the Oscars. A spokesman from *Photography Today* praised him as one of the finest craftsman in the world, and said he is the clear favourite to win both awards. As a Polish/Jewish war orphan, Poznanski was brought to the UK in 1945 by an Anglican charity, and grew up in Dorset. His long career has included much memorable and groundbreaking work, including the war zones of Angola, Vietnam and Northern Ireland, worldwide political protests, and the famines of Africa.

Poznanski said last night, 'All photographers want to produce work of an exceptional nature, but winning prizes should never be the goal. However, I am honoured and delighted to be nominated.' When asked to reveal the identity of *Crucifix Man* he said, 'I respect the young man's wishes to remain anonymous.'

11TH MAY 1983

My dear Ewan

A little letter from a very happy and hung-over Jacob in Los Angeles. I do so wish you had been here to celebrate with me last night. I could have held up your arm and proudly paraded you. As for me, you would not have recognised the handsome man in a white tuxedo. A lady asked me if I was Victor Mature. Ha! I had to remind her that the real Vic would now be nearly seventy, so perhaps not such a good compliment.

Over the years I've picked up a few minor awards, but I have forgotten all about them, and continued to get on with the job. As for the international prizes, I've always thought the plaques awarded were no more than doorstops. A large stone was all I needed, and the beautiful chunk of Scottish granite I brought back with me in January has pride of place on my sitting room carpet. Well, the dazzling piece of crystal I received last night is no doorstop. It will be given a place of supreme honour in my home, and when I'm dying, I will look at it to remind me of this happy time in my life, and of my love for you.

It has been six months since I declared my love for you, and not for one second has my passion for you been truly out of my head. How can I quantify what I mean? Tonight I'm off with my camera to document Bishop Tutu, and his South Africa. When I get on the plane I will be watching the other male passengers like a buzzard, watching for a lift of a chin, a sideways glance, and the raise of an eyebrow. After several brief, meaningful looks, a voice-less deal will be struck with a stranger. When we get to the airport we will share a taxi. In the hotel room we will fuck like rattlesnakes, and exchange not one word of affection. With every sordid movement my eyes will be closed, and I will be thinking of you. Your body, your face, and the aura of your whole beloved being. For me, sex is a drug of the loins. I'm an addict - a mainliner. I'm continually searching for the dragon, but in my heart and with every part of my mind, I always think of you. A love that _can_ speak its name, but never will.

Your Jacob

25TH MAY 1983

My dear Ewan

Where are you? Since I've been home I have rung you at Waldringhythe constantly. Please, when you get this letter, ring to tell me that you are all right. I must guess that you are not answering your phone because you think it might be the newspapers hounding you. Maybe you have gone away again, perhaps to hide in Scotland until all the fuss is over. I have just spoken to Fanny. She too is trying to reach you, so can you please contact her as well?

It must have been such a shock, and a tragedy, to find yourself plastered all over the most despicable tabloid of them all. The Daily Record is nothing but a down-market rag, famous for its scandalous cheque-book journalism, and although it will be of no comfort to you, I've sourced the leak from my contacts in the publishing world. The person who betrayed you was Max, the stylist on our photo shoot. It was just sheer bad luck. He saw you on a tube train one afternoon, dressed as a priest. He followed you back to your Seminary, and casually went in to enquire after the young priest with the lip repair. Of course, in all innocence, they revealed your name. He has kept this knowledge to himself, waiting for his time to be right, so he can scoop up some cash. I will now trash his name around the trade, and make sure he never works again.

I am hoping so much that the elders of your church will not accuse you of sin or betrayal, and that whoever deems to judge you, can stand back and see what a fine young man you are. Please, dear boy, put me out of my anxiety and contact me.

With much love and affection, and my undying support.

Your Jacob

Ewan was asked to wait in a small reception room. His heart thudded, vibrating through the whole of his upper body, and his face burned. Hot trickles of perspiration ran from his armpits, and down the small of his back. A feeling of wanting to cry and scream with shame held at the back of his throat, but most of all he felt defiled; a latter-day Judas, covered with the dirt of betrayal, and knowing he'd been summoned to be castigated and vilified.

A young African priest entered, and spoke with cold efficiency. 'Father Ewan, please come with me?' Ewan followed him up a wide curving staircase to the first floor. The young man knocked on a door, and left without saying a word. The door was opened by another African priest who could have been the twin of the first. 'Come in, Father Ewan.' Ewan entered, thinking, as he always thought on his rare visits to the Bishop's private apartment, that he was entering a Royal household. Cream walls, a thick red carpet, crystal chandeliers, and vast gilt mirrors. Grotesque French ormolu furniture, and hideous Rubenesque oil paintings of flabby women and flying, naked putti.

The Bishop was sitting in a large velvet armchair, and was surprisingly dressed in a light summer suit. He remained sitting but looked up, smiled and extended his hand. Ewan dropped to one knee, and kissed the offered hand. 'Your Grace.'

'Take a seat, Father Ewan. Sit opposite me.' Ewan sat, while the Bishop dismissed the attendant priest with a mild wave of his hand. 'I must apologise for any noise and disturbance. We have an American contingent visiting. Their lunch party is lively, to say the least.' Ewan smiled back politely in an attempt to hide his terror, peering to look out of the window where, on the Palace lawn below, a happy lively throng were attempting to balance plates and glasses. The Bishop then lifted a copy of *The Daily Record* from a side table, with the headlines clearly visible: '*Crucifix Man Named As Catholic Priest*'. 'Father Ewan. You must know why I've summoned you?'

'Yes, Your Grace. I've seriously violated the bounds of our moral code. I'm so, so sorry, and I deeply apologise for bringing my career into disrepute.'

'Do you think you have?'

'Only if you think I have, and I'm sure you do.'

'Then can we focus this debate onto its true crux? You're proud of your CND stance, but if I show my condemnation, you'll immediately capitulate. That's not the reaction of a true radical. It's the answer of a coward.'

'Your Grace, I did what I did with true motives of dissent, but I had no idea that the result would be so. . . I think word I'm searching for is humiliating. I'd planned to reveal myself in the fullness of time, but only in a dignified way. This cheap exposé is degrading.'

'Ewan, when I was your age the Second World War was raging. You may have thought I'd have been a conscientious objector, but no. I was a Padre in the army. I spent nearly four years in France and North Africa, despatching brave young men into the hands of God, and trying to give spiritual support to the ones that lived. I became so enraged with what I saw as the insanity of it all I ended up being relieved of my duties. I was flown home to rural Somerset, officially to rest, but un-officially I was showing signs of instability and collapse. The futility of war was slowly driving me mad. Please believe me when I say I understand your horror of the nuclear age. However, I think I really know much more about your true motivation, and it's not wholly about cruise missiles, or CND, is it? There's something of a hidden agenda. A personal crusade?'

'How do you know that, Your Grace?'

'Just before you entered your training you were in serious confusion and turmoil, having not only lost your father, but having to bear your mother's mental collapse. I personally guaranteed to fully fund her care for the rest of her life, and it was I who took Sister Concepta to meet her in the hospital. Your mother was ranting loudly to you about 'getting the buggers', and urging you to read something that she'd written about it all. Can I ask you if you read that material?'

'Yes, I did, Your Grace.'

'Ewan, I'm aware you're an adopted child. I'm also aware, through my discussions with Father Paulinus, that your mother only confessed this fact on the day of her breakdown.' Ewan nodded. 'And what you will have subsequently discovered, from reading the material, is that your mother had known great sadness in her life.' Ewan nodded again.

'Then its time I revealed to you what I know. Just after your father was appointed to Waldringhythe I met your parents for the first time. They kindly entertained me to tea, and a very fine tea it was. You were there, of course: a charming, well-mannered little child playing quietly on the floor with a jigsaw puzzle, but then you became tired. You eased yourself up onto your mother's knee, and fell asleep. It was while you slept they revealed to me, in the strictest of confidence, that they had only very recently adopted you. I was incredibly surprised, as I remember thinking how easy and comfortable you all were together after so short a time. You called them Mummy and Daddy – you laughed – you asked questions – you presented as a very happy and united little family.

'In time I bade them farewell, and I possibly wouldn't have recalled the afternoon so vividly had not your mother written to me a few months later asking for an audience. She arrived alone, dressed in a formal suit, seeming nervous. I put her at her ease and asked her what I could do for her. She explained the circumstances of her war work, the loss of her naturally born son, and the conclusions she'd come to concerning nuclear contamination. She was fired up with anger, and asked me how she could get justice? I was completely thrown off guard. It was obvious she wanted me to support her officially, and to become active on her behalf, but I had to politely decline. Not that I was indifferent to her unhappiness and anger, but because it was obviously impossible for me to get involved. She left feeling very let down, but she wrote to me afterwards, enclosing a copy of the report she'd prepared for the Scottish M.P.

'Over the years all went quiet, and I assumed she'd allowed the situation to rest, but when she became so ill after your father's death, her ramblings and behaviour made it obvious that her mental state was still overflowing with her quest for justice. Ewan, I'm going to ask you bluntly. Is this protest connected? Do you intend to take this business any further politically on her behalf?'

'Yes, Your Grace. I promised her I'd take up her campaign. As I explained, I was going to reveal myself when the time was right. I've only just been ordained and the time wasn't – isn't – right.'

'Ewan, you'll have gathered that I'm a lifelong supporter of the CND and the Pax Christi, but your ill-advised entanglement – and I can only term it thus – is not just radical. It's highly personal and very public. I must therefore officially declare my disapproval and condemnation. I admire you for the exemplary qualities I know you have, but I've asked you here today to ask you bluntly where you see yourself in a career structure. As an ordained priest, you will remain thus until the day you die, but you've put yourself very firmly at the crossroads of your life. I've personally watched you grow up, and to me you are much more than just another newly ordained priest. My heart surges with pride and respect for you. At your request, I have appointed you chaplain to Waldringhythe Abbey. I've also agreed to fund your further bereavement counselling training in the United States later on this month. Now I must officially declare, that should you choose to pursue this campaign, I'll be unable to support you. I would be forced to terminate your appointment at Waldringhythe, and leave you to the mercy of your own life's choosing. I've spoken to the Cardinal and he has agreed that you be given those options. You will not be compelled to go in front of any committees, nor will you receive any further castigation, or forced to declare remorse. I'd like you now, to go away and consider your position most carefully. We will meet again a week from today.' He then looked at Ewan with a gentle, kind expression. 'Off the record, Father Ewan, the picture of *Crucifix Man* is a stunning work of art. You're a very beautiful young man. Go now in peace.'

The Bishop rang a small hand bell, and one of the African priests immediately returned. 'Father André, would you be so kind as to show Father Ewan out? I must go down now and play host to my guests.'

Ewan genuflected and left the room.

Chapter 40

Sally drove into Monks Bottom just after one o'clock. Black rain clouds hung heavy and low over the deserted High Street, giving it an eerie, day-for-night darkness, but briefly there was clear gap in the sky. Fleetingly, a fiery sun blazed down, lighting up the slate tiles on the village hall roof with a fierce, opalescent shimmering. In Sally's love-besotted head this beautiful refraction of the light lifted her to a rare sense of the spiritual, and words of the old Victorian parlour song, *All in the April Evening,* sang out to her. She began to mouth the words, and as she passed the church a choir of heavenly tenors joined her in full voice.

On approaching the village green the thatched roof of The Dower House became visible behind the towering beech tree on the front lawn. She turned into the drive, a long sweep of ancient paviers that ran to nearly fifty yards, but every inch as familiar as the contours of her own face. Was it only three days ago she'd opened up to the parody of herself in the bathroom mirror, and promised the angry, revengeful wife to find the young bride she used to be? Promises honoured. She'd returned as a soft, doe-eyed woman in love.

Women in love have the name of their lover tattooed on their tongues. They taste the sweet rain as nectar, and smell the brown earth as a sensual musk. They find beauty in every subtle change of nature that can occur in less than three days. The front lawn had become a thicket of overgrowth, interspersed with worm casts and luminous green moss. The bold, erect profusion of tulip heads were now bowed low in subservience to several heavy showers, and a few coppery beech leaves had burst open to flutter like flat tongues. She stood and stared at the garden with a weak, silly smile on her face. Closing her eyes she felt Ewan's soft beard on her face, his sweet damaged lips on her own, and his tongue entwining with hers.

Love for Ewan was turning her into a befuddled simpleton. In a visionary future life she could see them moving around each other with flawless co-ordination; walking, talking, and ageing together in perfect harmony, welded together with the symbiosis of twin souls. She left the car and walked to the front door to see a cobweb, shaking and shimmering with diamond-bright droplets of rain. Nothing unusual — the odd spider was always welcome to spin at The Dower House — but this one was over the lock. So soon. So obvious. Why destroy a thing of such perfection?

She walked round to the rear of the house, searching for her key to the back door, but as she turned the corner, she saw a freshly dug mound in the centre of the bonfire-charred lawn. The shock caused her to draw in her breath. What symbolism could she read into that choice of grave site? What thoughts had gone through Roger's mind as he'd thrust the spade into the thick, sodden layer of her furious destruction? What misery had he felt as he laid the huge remains of their beloved Wolfhound to rest?

Her thoughts immediately swung back to the day, three years ago, when an excited Roger had walked through the door holding the eight-week-old Finnegan. A surprise present for his girls, and a clever ploy to unite a house where a strange atmosphere prevailed. His traumatised wife, depressed and retracting from the discovery of Tim's invasion into her life, and his bewildered daughter, who knew that some sort of serious problem between her parents was being glossed over for her sake. Finnegan imposed harmony. Collars, leads and feeding bowls to buy, house-training to teach, grooming to learn, trips to the vet for inoculations, and obedience classes to attend. Then, at last, long family walks on the common, where laughter at his crazy, gangly antics replaced the silences and forced dialogues. Laughter now blown away. The family officially at war. Finnegan lying silent beneath the angry ashes.

The sky glowered, the rain poised for another hammering, and the first slow, old-penny-sized raindrops began to fall. Sally unlocked the door and walked into the kitchen to see the obvious signs of Roger's return. A pile of opened post, and the parish magazine, lay on the kitchen table, together with their dual goodbye notes. The chairs around the kitchen table were pulled out in untidy positions, and some used glasses and coffee mugs sat on the draining board. The room, so normally a warm and cosy Aga'd retreat, was brutally cold, and she could smell the sour waft that always came from the sink drain after heavy rain. But the thing she most noticed was the alienation of the house. From her first day as Mrs Fuller, Sally had never walked into The Dower House without a flow of gratitude that her life-fairy had given her such a beautiful home. She'd never taken her privilege for granted, but now she sensed she no longer belonged. As if the wrists of the house had been slit, and its lifeblood had ebbed away.

She turned on the central heating, but she knew it wouldn't be enough. Nights like this were traditionally accompanied by a blazing fire in the inglenook. She would light one later on, to create a warm ambience, hoping her beloved guest might not take up his option of silent isolation upstairs. She climbed the stairs slowly, wanting to spend as much time as possible in an ecstatic dream of deciding which of her spare bedrooms to prepare for him. All were decorated with her own, idiosyncratic choice of decor; the stark minimalism of white walls and heavy black Tudor beams, colliding with soft furnishings in the bright colours of fruit. The orange room, the lemon room, the cranberry room, and the lime room. She chose the lime room, with the stupid, stupid self-embarrassing notion that the colour contrasted rather well with her red hair. What on earth was she imagining? That she would be awoken in the night by a crashing electric storm? That she would rise to find a power cut, and would enter his room wearing a Victorian nightdress, holding a candle like a celestial version of Jane Eyre? That he would awake to see a heavenly vision of herself, with the neck of the nightie slewing off her shoulders, and he would throw himself out of bed to take her in his arms?

She embraced herself tightly, as a pubescent girl might invoke her pop-idol, and although she was aware that this was childish nonsense, knew it was part of the crazy love she felt for Ewan. But she was also more than consciously aware that her actions were those of lust. Lust shouted out its decadent name, but why should she be so ashamed of herself? She'd been long estranged from its delights, and her infatuation enhanced its value a hundred fold. An idiotic flightiness came over her again, but. . . Oh, but. Throughout her long drive home an anomaly that she'd refused to analyse had been sweeping round her head.

As if a drawbridge had dropped like a guillotine, the mad spinning of her mind stopped. Had he loved Marina? Loved her as 'being in love'? This morning his head had been bowed, and his silence spoke of a hidden agenda. If so, surely it had been a chaste love, kept within his own mind? On the other hand, might it have been a pure, mutual love, recognised by them both and never consummated? Or could they *really* have had a full-on, all-consuming love affair? If she, herself, felt so overwhelmed by him after just three days, of course the grieving, lonely widow could have fallen for his magnetism. Was it not also feasible that the cloistered celibate had succumbed to the stunning beauty of Marina, despite the obvious age-gap? Yes. Sally had been her personal nurse, and she knew it was more than feasible.

Her unwrinkled facial loveliness was obvious and renowned, and although Sally had secretly looked for the hairline scars of cosmetic surgery to her eyes, and behind her ears, there were none. Her body was just as fortunate. A series of thin, silver stretch marks to the sides of her abdomen were her only flaws, and to complete the hand of aces the Gods had dealt, her body was free of cellulite; as soft and smooth as that of a lingerie model. Neither had she any gravitational drooping of her breasts, no pads of flesh around her waist, or hanging slack between her thighs. Even her genitalia was blessed with neatness and perfect symmetry.

But Marina had been no china doll, with only her body and her beauty to offer. There were also the qualities and charm of her persona. Her graceful swooping movements, her soft, upper-crust Irish lilt, her ready smile, her ability to listen carefully, and her well thought-out replies. Her generosity, her sense of humour, her witty quips, and above all her complete lack of malice or snobbery. It would have been so easy for Sally to be jealous. To use the sneer of the green-eyed monster, as any other woman might, but it was not the emotion she felt. Having known the lady so deeply she recognised the emotion as admiring sisterhood.

She walked to the airing cupboard and removed a set of lime coloured bed linen.

Chapter 41

As Father Joseph's old car finally disappeared out of sight, Roger's temple throbbed like the rev of a generator, a nerve jumped in a back tooth, and he was sure he felt breathless. Was this stress? Everyone in publishing was supposed to suffer from stress, but up until now, he'd had no personal experience of it. He gathered up his newly bought clothes from where he'd left them in the portico, and stowed them upstairs in Timothy's bedroom. Or was it now *their* bedroom? Seeing as Tim and he had only spent one night there together since Friday, it had no atmosphere of joint occupancy. Desperate for calm, he went downstairs, and entered the drawing room.

Thankfully, it was the only room in The Manor that hadn't suffered the horrors of Marina's foul interior decorating schemes, retained in its original form (Tim said) as a memorial to Toby. It was nearly forty feet long, and, in classic Georgian tradition, perfectly proportioned and graciously plain. Dominated by two giant-sized Knole sofas, and matching armchairs, it was furnished with English antiques of oak, elm and walnut; a knee-hole desk, a grandfather clock, glass-fronted bookcases, and circular, tripod tables. Eighteenth and nineteenth century cartoons of the legal profession covered the walls, and over the marble fireplace was a painting of Marina, in her mid-thirties. She was reclining her sleek body on a chaise longue in the garden room, set against a backdrop of green plants. She was wearing simple black leggings, and a baby-pink cashmere sweater. Her barley blonde hair hung long and loose over one shoulder, and her feet were bare. One leg was stretched out horizontally, and the other drawn up at the knee, but her face was full on to her audience with a naughty, cat-like smile; a smile that said, 'come and get me boys, if you can catch me'. Was this the look that Toby had paid for? Dirty old sod.

But it was one of those looks in a painting where the eyes followed you round the room. Christ, was there anywhere in this house the cow didn't dominate?

He stared out of the window to watch a swan on the distant lake rear up and flap its wings. Bloody swans. Apart from the hideous cat they were the only permanent pets to grace The Manor, and its fifty acres. Bugger Tim's aversion to dogs! There was something missing without the noisy scrambling of Finnegan at heel, and he would just *have* to get another one. A sudden fear began to overwhelm him, as if he'd become a displaced person. He might grow old in this room. Only might. Probably would. He and Tim watching *Gardener's World*, and arguing about whose turn it was to set up the morning tea tray. With a heavy heart he knew he was homesick for The Dower House. Throughout every season its talking voices cracked and stretched from its low ceilings and uneven floor; its ancient beams assuring him that it was alive and breathing forth a contented, warm existence. The Manor was as abstract as a hotel, and as glacial as a church. What the hell did he want? He *did* want Tim. Yes, he was sure he wanted Tim, but not the collapsed, crazy idiot he'd become.

A turn of Roger's head showed a display of Proudfoot family photographs, but there were none of Morgana. 'Morgana,' he said to himself slowly. 'Morg-arna.' Such a lovely name, but that was all she was. A name. Poor little bitch. What did he remember of her short life? Not much. A lunch party at The Dower House, put on by his parents just before she'd been born. Marina had been heavily pregnant; she thirty-six-years-old to her husband's sixty-four. Roger himself, in his early twenties, horrified that the huge bump had been created by a union between such a beauty – yes he had to admit that much – and the pot-bellied, round-shouldered old Toby. After the birth, hearing his mother's cooing anecdotes about Marina's new baby that he didn't listen to.

What else did he remember? Apart from the fateful boat trip, only one other occasion came to mind. A village cricket match on a balmy Sunday afternoon. Marina and Toby strolling up with the child grizzling loudly in a push chair, writhing and demanding attention. Apologies made by her parents that she was a 'tired teddy'. Toby sweeping her up into his arms, her chubby little legs thrown around his corpulence, her thumb stuck forcefully in her mouth. Rumours in the village were that she wasn't Toby's child, but Roger could see that she was. The resemblance to her father was obvious and immediate, with his heavy, course features being translated, with the strange anomaly of nature, to a pert, dark prettiness.

What age would Morgana be now? Good God – getting on for twenty-eight! What would she be? An academic? A career girl? A model? A wife and mother? A whore like her mother? A crack addict? Winner – loser – happy – sad? Sad, he guessed. Her father would have been long gone, and her mother would have just died. Her older brother would have been her tower of strength and rock to cling to. Would he fuck!

From upstairs, Roger heard a door open and a vague, creaking movement. He wearily rose to his feet, and climbed the stairs.

Chapter 42

Ewan stood on a pavement in Belgravia, staring up at the imposing Gothic mansion; an address that any man in the street would always follow with a whistle of envy, and a bemused calculation of the area's market value. Manicured shrubs, in all variations of new and old green, were landscaped into the small paved facade, with not one dead leaf or twig-stalk daring to drop.

He walked towards a pair of heavy glass entrance doors, through which he could see a formal mahogany-fitted reception area. A muscular Afro-Caribbean concierge, attired in full morning dress, stood regally in attendance, fronting a range of intimidating surveillance equipment. As Ewan walked in the man gave a theatrical half-bow, and crossed himself. 'Father Ewan,' he said deferentially. 'You are expected. I will programme the lift.'

'Thank you, Titus,' Ewan said, signing the proffered visitor's book.

The lift smelled of cigar smoke, and inexplicably, of money. He exited at the top storey, but he had no need to ring a doorbell; the whole of the penthouse suite was Jacob's domain. The reception hall was large, full of natural north facing daylight, with every inch of the walls show-casing a stunning record of Jacobs's life's work. Sharp, monochrome images covered the global history of the last half-century. The war-torn zones of Angola, Vietnam, Northern Ireland, The Falklands, Iraq, and Afghanistan, depicting soldiers and civilians in varying states of filth, despair, and injury. From the starving African nations, both pot-bellied and stick-thin children stared without seeing, their huge eyes encrusted with flies. A skull pile in Rwanda. Political protests from the first passive, duffle-coated Aldermarston marches, to the Paris student demos, the miners' strike, the Greenham Common campaign, and the London poll tax riots. In a separate section was his last work before illness overtook him; a portfolio depicting the face of New York's grief, taken only a few short hours after the devastation. One rare portrait showed the ageing photographer himself, taken at the foot of the twin tower carnage, with his cameras slung over his shoulder, and his creased, craggy face in a pose of bewildered desperation; the image that had fronted *Time* magazine. And then, with dedicated space and display, a whole wall devoted to the single work he considered to be the pinnacle of his achievement, and loved above all others: *Crucifix Man*.

To Ewan's surprise Fanny appeared, wearing a long, figure-hugging black tube, and dangling gold earrings. How changed she was from the brash young woman who had clattered her stilettos up to him on that first night in the church, her heavy breasts bouncing in a cheesecloth blouse, and dark curls falling over her shoulders. Today's woman was a dominatrix of the media, lean and lined, with a platinum-blonde crew cut, and cubicle-enhanced tan. 'I wanted to be here for you,' she said. 'I'm so, so sorry, my love.' She kissed his mouth, but with neither the tenderness of a mother, nor the energy of a lover. An invisible, close-stitched, unity of long friendship.

'How is he?'

'Terribly weak and a bit confused. He had morphine shot about an hour ago.'

'So there's no pain.'

'Only the mental kind. How long since you've seen him?'

'Over four weeks. I'm so sorry it's been so long, but I've been selfishly absorbed. . .'

He and Fanny slowly embraced. 'What can I do to help you?' she asked.

'This,' he replied, pulling her into his chest, and tightening his grip. 'This. I ache for her.'

From a distant room a distressed, feeble voice called out a string of muddled words. The voice that in health had been as loud as boots crunching on gravel, but now hadn't the strength to crack eggshells. A smiling nurse appeared, wearing a white dress uniform. 'Hello, Ewan. Can you hang on a minute? He's not quite ready.' Within two minutes she returned. 'All done. You can go in now. I'll put the kettle on.' She lowered her voice. 'I've had to draw the curtains. He says the sun hurts his eyes, but actually he can't bear anyone to see him in full daylight, especially you.'

'I'll go into the kitchen and talk to Sarah,' Fanny said. 'You need some private time with him.'

As Ewan entered he gagged as he inhaled the powerful pungency of the sick room; a sweet and sour mixture of disinfectant, surgical spirit, urine, vomit, sweat and the heady perfume of some lilies in a vase. The bed was raised on blocks, and a cylinder of oxygen stood alongside. On the wall that faced the bed hung a three-quarter-size depiction of *Crucifix Man*, and at its foot a small shelf held a large piece of crystal, mounted on a plinth. The patient, his weakness obvious, was propped up on a bank of pillows. Attempting a gesture of welcome, he raised a bony, wavering hand, disfigured with large purple blemishes. Ewan quickly crossed to the bed, and took the offered hand. 'Jacob.'

Jacob pulled the hand to his mouth, and greedily kissed the palm. 'My dear boy. My old heart is breaking for you. How can I help? Come talk to me.'

'You know I'm not used to talking,' Ewan said. 'Only listening.'

'If you're still not ready to talk I'll respect your silence. Just let me take you in my disgusting old arms.'

Ewan sat on a bedside chair, leaned his head down to rest against the skeletal rib cage, and folded his arm over the scrawny body. Jacob's skin smelled of his usual Diorissima female fragrance, but overlaid with the faint, sour odour of a fermented dishcloth. 'How do I begin?' Ewan said. 'The first thing I always ask my patients is to say the name of their lost one.'

'Then say her name. Say it. Your beautiful lady of the water.'

'Marina,' he said, whispering dryly. 'Marina. My love. My life. My wife.'

Jacob's wavering hand clumsily reached out to stroke Ewan's hair. 'Your sorrow destroys me, but you had the comfort of being truly loved for so many years. Your people would say it's a sin, but the sane amongst us will say that it's a virtue. What is the saying? *'Man cannot live by love alone'*. Well, perhaps he can't, but it goes a long way to make it worthwhile. Ewan, when I declared my hopeless passion you could have run away in horror, but you did not. You threaded us together, like two beads on a necklace, and thenceforth we hung round each other's necks with another sort of love; a declaration of devotion in the name of Plato. Talk to me, my lib. Make use of me while I'm still here to hear you.'

Ewan, with a swollen throat, and barely moving lips, continued. 'The term used in my work is anticipatory death. Of course she gave me full notice of her leaving, but it was no buffer zone. Now I want to cry my misery from the rooftops. I want to shout, and scream, and publicly applaud her life. The dictum of my life forces me to silence, but I can't hold it in any longer. I'm burning with duplicity. I'm a fraud, Jacob. My cloth has become a burden, and I've resolved to leave the priesthood.'

'So your God has left you?'

'I no longer wish to serve him, but I shall always love him. We've spent so long hand in hand, I'll feel lost without him.'

'Is he helping you now?

Ewan shook his head. 'He's testing me.'

'The fucking Gods don't test you, my boy. They put lead in your shoes. They're the law, the judge, the justice, and the jury, so they never lose.' Jacob then laughed, but it was a dandelion puff compared to his old giant's roar. 'Fanny will give you double-spread and exclusive interview. I can already see the headline. *'Crucifix Priest Loses Faith. The Road To Damascus In Reverse'.* With his exhaustion obvious, Jacob laid his head back on the pillow. 'Soon, very soon, I shall be gone, and everything I have will be yours. This apartment, the house in Capri, my money, and my negatives. Then you will be able to go forth in comfort, and take a little bit of me with you.'

'Jacob, we've discussed this so many times. I can't accept such wealth.'

'Without office you can accept everything. I love you, and I have no other heir. *Crucifix Man* has made me a fortune, so it's only returning to its rightful owner.'

'Then I'll accept your wonderful gifts, but be assured I'll use your riches wisely to benefit my fellow man. Thank you so much, my dearest, loyal friend.'

Ewan leaned down to kiss Jacob on the lips. The dying man pressed his weak hand lightly against the back of Ewan's head, and closed his eyes. To this scene Sarah came in, carrying a tray of tea, but without interrupting, or seeming surprised, she poured two cups and left the room.

'You're so beautiful,' said Jacob, running his desiccated finger across Ewan's scarred lip.

'Marina told me I was beautiful.'

'And you most certainly are. Now will you pass me my tea and I will show-off that I still have the strength to lift a cup to my mouth.'

With the tea drunk, Jacob again collapsed against the pillow. 'Ewan. It makes me happy to know that you will have both personal and financial freedom when I'm gone, but you will be completely alone in the world. My next question is the inevitable. Will you now resume your search?'

'Jacob, somewhere there are, or were, my birth parents. The feisty, loving blonde, and the absent fishporter. Perhaps they're still alive. The blonde maybe back on her knees scrubbing floors. Maybe the fishporter is still humping fish. I wanted to begin to search for them, and you promised to support me, but the coward in me couldn't do it. I was too scared.'

'Then you must overcome your fear, or be content to live the rest of your life in ignorance. You are now forty-eight years old, Ewan. Poznanski's law says that time is the destroyer of all procrastination, and it will soon be too late. Come, my honey. Let's sing. Let's sing as we sung on the top of that big, grey mountain in Scotland on Christmas Eve all those years ago, only this time it's a duet for one dying and one bereaved voice.' With wavering voices they began.

'Heavenly shades of night are falling, it's Twilight Time'

Chapter 43

On hearing Timothy's movements Roger had gone upstairs to find Marina's bedroom and bathroom were both empty. 'Tim,' he called. 'Where are you?' There was no answer, but across the landing a door was open; the one Roger had never been through and was usually locked. The nursery overlooked the panorama of The Manor House gardens; a tidy shrine wallpapered with Beatrix Potter characters, and untouched since the day of Morgana's death. A row of soft toys sat fixated in the window-seat, and a faded collection of mobiles and marionettes hung lifelessly from the ceiling.

Timothy was sitting on the floor, wearing the black kimono, his back against the wall and his head bowed. He was holding a large purple handbag, and singing softly to himself: *'Heavenly shades of night are calling, it's Twilight Time'.*

'Tim,' Roger said evenly, 'are you OK?' There was no answer. 'Tim, I heard Andrew came back and gave you some tablets to calm you down. Have you slept well?' There was still no answer. Beginning to feel exasperated Roger tried to firm up his questioning. 'Now look here, Tim. This weird behaviour's really spooking me, and it's got to stop. I'm serious.'

'This used to be my room,' Timothy said, without lifting his head. 'When Morgana came I had to move out so she could sleep near Mumma and Pa. This is her bag. The one Father Ewan's got to bless. What time's he coming?'

'For God's sake,' Roger pleaded. 'You don't need a priest. You've got me.'

'I don't want you. I want Father Ewan.'

Roger chose, and said, every word of his reply carefully, trying to maintain his patience, but his jaw was taut with frustration. 'Angel. All we've got to do is get through tomorrow, and say goodbye to your mother in the way she wanted. Then things'll start to get better. It's all going to take a long time to get over, but we don't need the Holy Joes. We've got a new life to look forward to, and we must both be strong. I'm as confused as you are, but if we don't work hard we'll lose each other.'

'Go away and leave me alone,' Timothy said coldly. 'I've got a headache.'

'A headache!' Roger shouted, with a final loss of control. 'The only reason you've got a headache is because you've done nothing for three days, except moody around and sleep. I've already had a mother-fucker of a day. I've done a full shop at Sainsbury's, I've traipsed miles to Wycombe to buy some clothes, and I've had a humdinger of a row with the Feather-Bitch. I had a motherfucker of a weekend as well, and all you can do is play the invalid. Now get up and stop pissing about with that bloody bag! If you don't get up right now I won't be responsible for what I do to you.'

Timothy threw himself forward, and rolled into a ball. 'Don't hurt me,' he screamed. 'Don't hurt me.' Roger turned round and pressed his palms hard against the wall, knowing that his boiling anger had to be diverted somewhere, or he really *would* hit Timothy.

Lying curled up on the floor, and with his eyes closed, Timothy started to fiddle with the clasp of the bag. 'You don't understand. I'll be much better when I've seen Father Ewan. He's got to hear my confession. My big, bad secret.'

With uncontrolled fury, Roger strode over to Timothy, hauled him to his feet, and flung the bag into a corner. He pulled him roughly out of the room, thrust him into the guest bathroom, and pushed his face to the mirror. 'The only confession needed is to yourself,' he seethed. 'Who do you see, Tim? Do you see a man in his forties, or do you see the jealous, screwed-up boy of eighteen, who took a boat trip on a lovely summer's day with his little sister? His innocent little baby sister. You may think I'm completely oblivious to what's going on in your head, but you're wrong! I know everything! I've just kept my gob shut all these years because I loved you. Tim, you're not saying one word to that frigging priest. When he turns up, I'm getting shot of him. End of story.'

Timothy was ashen, his shoulders shook and his lip trembled. 'You've always known, then?' he said.

'Go back to bed, Tim. I'll go downstairs and put the kettle on.'

When Roger returned with a tray of tea, the black kimono was on the landing. Timothy was back in Morgana's room, sitting naked on the floor, with his hands capped over his knees. Roger placed the tray on the floor, and knelt down at his side. 'Judges and juries aren't in the room, honey,' he said gently. 'I just want you to get better.'

'And you won't ever mention it again?'

'No. Never. Past history. Chapter completely rubbed out.'

'So you still love me, and everything's going to be the same?'

'Exactly the same,' said Roger, leaning forward to slide his mouth over Timothy's eyes, his nose, and finally his mouth. 'I adore you, Tim. Always have, always will.'

Timothy began to mutter, dropped his hands to his groin, and ran his fingers, like a flautist, along a burgeoning erection. He fixed eye contact with Roger and smiled, but there was no need for words. At last, thought Roger. At last the familiar road was going to be travelled, but there would be no time for the foreplay of the tart-mother's satin thong, or the slow mantra of their usual, dirty-worded talk-up. Just a manic rush to disrobe himself, and to complete the swift, clumsy act they'd refined over so many years, when passion was overflowing, venues were restricted, and time at a premium.

Post-coital affection had never been sweeter. They enfolded on the soft carpet, and words of love flowed back and forth. 'We've turned the corner, Angel,' Roger said. 'We'll go arm-in-arm to the crem tomorrow and announce that we're a couple.'

'Oh, Skipper. We are, aren't we? We've just had a hiccup.' They lay becalmed in silent bliss, but their descent back to earth was interrupted by the shrill summons of Roger's mobile phone. On seeing the number of his caller, he practically yelped, and flung it to his ear.

'Sally!' he gasped. 'Oh, thank Christ. Don't talk about anything. I'm on my way. I'm at The Manor and I'll be straight round.' He immediately leapt up and began to dress. 'That was Sally. She's back. I really must go and sort things out with her. You'll be all right for a bit, won't you? Actually, you can come as well if you want to. Whatever

I've got to say to her is for your ears too.'

Timothy shook his head dreamily. 'I'll be all right here. I'll have a shave and tidy up.'

'You're all right? I mean. . .' He tapped gently on Timothy's brow. 'In there.'

'Calm as a millpond. I feel wonderful.'

'You *are* wonderful. For God's sake, don't let's ever lose touch again. Sure you're OK, now?'

'Yes. Really, I'm fine, but don't be long.'

'I'll try. She doesn't know about Finnegan yet, so I'll be treading on egg-shells.'

'I've made things so tough for you, haven't I? I'm really sorry. Give my love to Sally. I mean it. I want her life to be as happy as ours will be.'

Chapter 44

Jacob, with his arms still embracing Ewan, suddenly fell asleep. Ewan carefully disengaged himself, and walked to the kitchen where Fanny and Sarah, having dispensed with the teapot, were imbibing large slugs of Southern Comfort. 'Forgive me if I slip away,' he said, 'but I'll come back soon. Very soon.'

'I'll see you out,' said Fanny.

'Is there anything I can do?' she asked, once they were standing alone by the lift. 'I know that's your cue to say butt out, but if there *is* anything. . .'

'There is. Can you get a wreath sent to Fullylove's, the undertakers in Henley? I want red roses in the shape of a heart. I know it's a naff choice, but it's what I want for her. I'll settle up with you later.'

'They'll ask for a message.'

He thought carefully. 'No message. She'll know they're from me.'

Rain slashed in a blinding sheet as he joined the relentless thrust of traffic on the M40. He looked at his watch. Not even four o'clock. It would take less than an hour to reach Monks Bottom, and he wasn't due until six. Not good to arrive early. A vulnerable patient always mentally prepared for therapy, and if they were caught off guard it could destroy what little confidence they had. He would stop off in Henley and kill some time in a coffee shop.

Thirty minutes later, the rain was replaced by clear blue skies, and the blinding power of the sun glared up from the wet tarmac. Now, on quieter roads, the landscape had changed to rolling fields and woodland, with far-reaching views over the county. But then he saw the flash of an over-sized green signpost, and a right hand arrow that pointed to Hurley Village. A place name that rang out with the clash of a cymbal, and he was compelled to investigate. He turned into a long village road, fronted by a mix of house styles. Once past an old timbered pub, the road petered out into a narrow, uninhabited lane, and a sign pointed to, '*Boatyard. The Lock. Summer Parking*'. From there a single track snaked down between sheep-filled meadows, to the rain-swollen Thames. He got out of the car and walked over to the sodden edge of the riverbank, prompting a dozen resting ducks to flee with much quacking and splashing. It was here. In a weir near Hurley Lock. The place where Morgana's body had been found.

He crossed the river over an arched bridge, and sat down on a wooden bench. Staring at the water he reprised the story she'd told him once, and only once. So many years ago, but every word remembered.

SEPTEMBER 1983

Fifteen months after the death of her daughter, the lonely and depressed Marina Proudfoot had come to Waldringhythe to be counselled for her enduring grief, but she confronted the young priest with cynicism and despondence. She stood before him with a bold, haughty posture, and a look of indifference. 'I've been sent here by my feeble parish priest,' she said. 'He hasn't a clue if you're any good, of course. He's only heard of you because of that notorious photograph. Do you know what I think? I embarrass him, and he wants to off-load me onto anyone. I've already tried no end of nonsense to please him, but nothing's been of any use. I think all therapy's a load of eyewash actually, but now I'm here I suppose I'll have to give you a chance.'

Choosing his words with both skill and firmness, Ewan replied. 'Lady Proudfoot, it would be foolish to waste each other's time with such obvious resignation in your heart, but I agree with you. As with any relationship, a chance is something we both have to take. If I'm to help you, our journey will be long and hard. There'll be many miles to travel together, and collaboration will be needed over the map reading. Only then can we reach the end. Otherwise, you're free to leave.'

She fixed him with a swan's stare, but her composure was threatened, and she became flustered. It was the first time, since her tragedy, that she'd been challenged or confronted with anything other than cautious, pussyfooting subservience. She was humbled to apologise. 'I'm sorry. I must have sounded very pompous. It's just that it's all going to be difficult, and I'm afraid. Will you accept my limitations, and in return I'll try?'

'Say your daughter's name.'

'I can't.'

'Please try.'

'I can't!

SEPTEMBER 1984

A year later. It was the afternoon of an Indian summer, and the session had, as usual, been without form or direction. Over the previous year, despite her declaration that she'd try to involve herself, formal counselling sessions had proved impossible. There'd been no advancements, no revelations, and no declarations of inner thoughts. Not even the occasional anecdote of her life with her husband and daughter. Ewan's standard method of going back to her earliest memories were completely ignored. She talked entirely in the present, with rambling references to the news, the arts, the media, seasonal changes in the grounds of her home, and her daily domestic life with her son.

'. . . Tim's had some huge greenhouses built. He says he can even grow peaches. . . Tim's gay, but I'm not supposed to know. He's in love with a man called Roger Fuller, but Roger suddenly upped and left him and went to America. . . I've read a wonderful book called *The Color Purple*. . . Tim's slashed and burned three acres of our jungley land. He's going to turn it into a market garden. . . Roger Fuller came back to Monks Bottom when his father died. He didn't come to see Tim, though. . . I rather like Michael Jackson. He moves like a machine. . . Roger Fuller's mother tells me he's getting married to a very nice girl called Sally. Tim's terribly quiet and depressed – I wish I could tell him I know his heart's broken. . . Princess Diana's got so thin, I wonder if she's worn out by the baby?. . . My heart breaks for Tim. We've had invitations to Roger and Sally's wedding, and he's putting *such* a brave face on it. . . The market garden's doing really well. He says he's going to go in for a 'pick your own' scheme next. Raspberries and strawberries and asparagus to start with. . . I saw a really excellent film called *The Dresser*. . . Tim's still terribly depressed but he's thrown himself into another project. He's creating a grassy island in the middle of the lake as a safe haven for swans. . . The village shop's been taken over by a very friendly Asian man called Mr Bhatti, and it's now full of lentils and strange pickles. . .'

Today's talk had been the progress of several pounds of damsons to a perfect jam. A jar brought for Ewan, together with a large bunch of dried thyme to hang in his kitchen. He'd long expected her to suddenly cease coming to Waldringhythe, but perversely she'd continued to book in once a month. Their relationship was so frustrating to him that he'd moved their sessions from his counselling suite in the Abbey's Chapter House to the comfort of his own sitting room. His hope was that a less inhibiting approach might soften her into an outpouring.

On that afternoon she'd become restless, and even more uncooperative. She got up and sat down several times, and eventually insisted they sit outside in the warm sunshine to do a crossword from a tabloid newspaper; a pastime she usually completed over morning coffee with Cora, her daily help. 'My brain's like porridge today,' she said. 'It must be the heat. Four across. Five letters. Clue. ' A peach of a singer.' Fourth letter B.'

'Melba?' Ewan volunteered.

'Oh, you're sooooo clever!' she cried, filling in with her ballpoint.

He'd often wondered over the months if she was more than slightly psychotic, but despite his inner concerns for her mental health, he knew, as he'd known for many months, that he was in love with her. His thoughts had started as those of innocent day-dreaming, that became forbidden night-dreaming, and had now turned into an all-consuming obsession. Thus he allowed full license to her strangeness.

'Six down,' she continued. 'Nine letters. Clue. 'A swimming rapier. Second letter W. Sixth letter F.'

'Swordfish?'

'Oh, you're sooooo brilliant!' She fixed him with sparkling eyes, and smiled widely; a lasting smile of simple, genuine happiness that she probably had no idea she was projecting. Each tooth perfect and pearlised. The fine laughter lines at the side of each eye flaring, and the eyes themselves the colour of cornflowers.

The September sun was beginning to lower behind her shoulders, covering her in a flow of golden light. There was probably four feet between them, but Ewan felt the space arc around them like an invisible shell. He could sense she felt the atmosphere change, but she showed no sign of discomfort or unease. Her smile gradually dropped, and she continued to look at him with an unhurried expression. 'Perhaps I should go now, Ewan,' she said. 'Is that the best thing?'

His speech faltered. 'I've no more appointments. Perhaps. . . perhaps you might like to stay. . . for tea. I rarely have tea with anyone and I'd very much like. . . I'd like you to stay.'

'It's probably best I go.' She got up.

He rose to join her, and they walked inside the house where she picked up her handbag. 'Are you sure I can't persuade you to stay?

'Thank you, but no.'

It was their habit to shake hands formally at the end of every session, but on this occasion the hand of the priest clasped the elegant, manicured hand of the widow for two or three seconds too long. There was going to be a kiss of sorts. It should have been an indifferent air-kiss peck of parting acquaintances, but they became magnetised. Their bodies grew larger, seeming to black out the daylight. The inches between them lessened, their feet stumbled together, and a magnet pulled. A slow, adult kiss that was his first.

His actions then became rushed and clumsy, covering her with wet, flowing kisses, running his mouth down her neck, and closing his hands diffidently over her breasts. But she suddenly sought his hands, held firmly onto his wrists, and pulled his arms to his sides. 'So you want to make love to me?' she said. 'You want to wreck your vows and become a man like any other.'

'But that's just it. I have to pretend otherwise, but I *am* a man like any other.'

'Of course, you are. Oh, Ewan. Of course, you are.' She drew him back into the sitting room, ordered him to sit in his rocking chair, and knelt. 'Do you know what I intend to do?'

'Yes, I think so.'

'And do you want me to do it?'

'Yes.'

Her head filled his lap, and her long, flowing hair dropped like a veil to mask the act she performed. He had no will or ability to resist, and the station clock ticked in unison with the faint squeak of rocking springs. But then all sounds disappeared. He had reached a plain; a silent plateau on the top of a mountain, where there was no light, and no oxygen, and he was sucked into a black vacuum. He threw his head back, and closed his mouth, trying to muffle his crying out, but he heard his own alien voice forming a sound of terrifying, melancholy sadness.

Loud sounds returned. The clock's tick, a seagull's caw coming down the chimney, the rustle of dry clematis leaves skimming the window panes, and the sharp gasps of his own laboured breathing.

Slowly and silently she sank down to sit on the floor. 'Now I'm ready to talk to you,' she said.

'Then talk,' he replied. 'You may pause as often as you need to, but I won't interrupt. Just tell me when you've reached the end.'

She took his hand, and leaned her cheek against his knees. He pulled her hand to his face, and kissed her fingers. After taking several seconds to compose herself she began to speak. Halting. Hesitant. Her voice soft and diffident.

'You'll remember I told you about Tim being in love with Roger Fuller, don't you? We'd known his parents for years, as part of the Monks Bottom dinner party set. Christina was sweet, but Toby and I weren't particularly fond of Alex. Anyway, he was a lynchpin of the village, so we were rather stuck with him. He'd just acquired a re-fitted Dutch barge, *The San Fairy Ann*, and of course he wanted to show it off. A large Sunday lunch party had been organised, and the idea was that we would glide elegantly up the Thames, posing as seasoned sailors. We all gathered on the riverbank at Henley, and Alex welcomed us on board shouting, "Ahoy there, me hearties," or something just as stupid. Roger Fuller was being really daft as well, wearing a stolen Ark Royal Captain's hat, and organising the seating like a manic game-show host. He was really going over the top, but he was always a good sport.'

"'Good morning, Monks Bottom!" Roger shouted. "As you know, I'm normally protecting the Queen, but today I'm Skipper of *The San Fairy Ann*, so you'd better behave or it's the Tower for you." That was followed by loud booing. "Seating has been organised and your names are on the seats."'

'Toby and I were placed at the stern, but he shouted out to Tim, "Tim, if you and Shirley Temple take the little curved bench opposite the wheel-house, she'll have room to play." When all thirty guests were packed in I stood up and peered at the bow.

"'Be firm with her, Tim,"' I called, '"you know what a fidget she is."'

"'I've got her straps, Mumma,"' he called back. '"She's looking for fish."'

'Toby got to his feet and smiled at our darling daughter's rear view. She was wearing red sandals, blue-striped Osh-Kosh dungarees, and a white T-Shirt. Around her chest was buckled a set of old-fashioned reins. You might remember the sort, made of leather, lined with sheepskin, and attached with tinkly bells. They were so old I'd had them for Tim, and they were really useful, but, oh, how she hated them. The performance we had when she saw them coming, you'd think we were trying to get her into a strait-jacket. The enormous purple handbag she carted everywhere lay on the seat beside her. On that day it was bulging with an *Action Man* doll, a plastic gun that whizzed out sparks, and a little Fisher Price musical box that played '*Old MacDonald Had A Farm*'.

'Roger then demanded our attention again. "Right, we'll be travelling slowly up river and docking at Cookham for lunch. In the meantime, Dad will serve snifters, and Mum has prepared some rather more-ish canapés." He then moved to the wheelhouse, the engine revved, and the boat swayed. We were off and a big cheer went up.

'I stood up again and called to Tim, "Whatever you do, hold her straps. It might be a good idea to get her to have a little nap before lunch. If the sun goes in, pop her cardi on." Then I called to her. "Look at Mummy. Now be a good girl for Tim," but she didn't look round. She was still kneeling on the bench, looking in the water, with her bottom in the air, and her dark, curly head out of sight. Later on, as the novelty wore off, Tim laid her down on the soft leather bench and she went to sleep. I smiled and waved. He waved back.

I then turned to socialise. Some of the company were people I knew well, some were strangers, but it was a very merry crowd. We sipped chilled cocktails, snacked on Christina's fussy fancies, told funny stories, and put the world to rights. But then the whole company started to laugh, and turned to watch, as a jolly old chap called Jack Wood rolled up his trouser legs and began to dance a hornpipe. Then another couple of the men jumped to their feet and joined in, whistling the theme tune to 'Blue Peter'. The laughter became louder and louder, until it turned to helpless hysteria and clapping. Then a sudden lurch of the boat, a splash, and a shout of, "Child overboard."

Roger rushed from the wheelhouse and hurled himself into the water.

Toby followed him in nanoseconds.

Tim briefly stood transfixed before he dived in too.

Then all the other men, both young and old, tore off their ties, and jackets, and shoes, to join in. The women were screaming but I was silent and calm, knowing it was just a question of the first good swimmer to reach her.

There was a real panic around the bow, with too many rescuers getting in each other's way, but Roger's strong crawl gained ground over everyone else. "Where was the splash?" he shouted.

"Over there! Over there!" thirty voices yelled back.

"Where for fuck's sake's over there?"

He dived under the water time, after time, after time, but it soon became stirred up into a muddy sludge. He tried, and tried so hard, but each quest became shorter and more desperate.

The women were now silent and holding disbelieving hands over their mouths. *The San Fairy Ann*, with no one in control, slewed a wayward course and collided hard with the river bank. There was a cracking and crumpling sound of glass breaking, and metal twisting, and those of us left on board were flung on our backs.

No one wanted to be the first to admit it was a hopeless cause, but in the fullness of time, when Roger conceded failure, everyone in the water began to gasp and scramble for dry land. The women were now openly sobbing, and rapidly abandoned ship to assist their menfolk. I was left to stand alone.

The place she'd fallen in was now as still as a millpond, and the normal life of the riverbank had already returned. A heron hooked a fish with the plummeting beauty of its large wings, a pair of swans led their cygnets in a slow, weed-trawling glide, and the wind swung the willows. It was only then that I screamed. I screamed so loudly I didn't make a sound.'

She then stopped speaking, slowly raised her head, and looked up at Ewan. 'My daughter was drowned. My husband was drowned. There's no more story to be told.'

'Say her name.'

'I can't. I've not been able to say her name since.'

Ewan reached down to hold the sides of her head within his hands, and to forcefully sound his words. 'Say. . . her. . . name.'

'Morgana!' she shouted. 'Morgana! The word lashed out of her as if she were filled with hate, and her face remained suspended, in an expression of shock, for several seconds. After taking time to control her breathing she elegantly levered herself to standing, bent down to kiss him, and to run the tip of her tongue over the fine scar on his top lip. 'You're beautiful, Ewan,' she said.

'No, I'm disfigured,' he replied. 'Deformed. Ugly.'

'No, Ewan. You truly are beautiful.'

'Can you accept that I'm in love with you?'

'Ewan, I accept your love with great honour and delight. I too, have hidden my own obsession for you, but if we're to become lovers you must commit yourself to me. Not just your body but your mind. I'm a widow, and I can do what I like, but you'll have to bear the burden of your so-called sin. There can be no half-way house. Our devotion to each other must be free of demons. Don't answer now. We've got another appointment tomorrow afternoon at three o'clock, and by then you must have decided if you want me or not.'

She rose and left without further comment.

Chapter 46

Timothy lay, flat on his back, on the floor of Morgana's room. A feeling of calm was washing over him, but it was more than the normal release of coition. He couldn't quantify it, but his heavy black overload had disappeared, and there was a comforting slackness to his bones. He got up, stretched his neck from side to side, and wandered around the room. It was a large, light room. A perfect nursery, being shaded to the south by the fully mature walnut tree some thirty feet away. *Juglans regia*. Bare-branched, and currently flowering its long tasselly catkins. As a child in bed on April mornings, he would watch its shimmering fingers shake in the wind. He would then bounce on his mattress like a trampoline, until Mumma came in, pretending to be cross, but he would laugh, and then she'd laugh, and he would leap from the bed into her arms.

He wouldn't come into this room again. He'd lock it, and ask Roger to hide the key. Morgana would never be mentioned, or intrude into his mind again. Her ghost finally exorcised. On turning from the window he picked up the purple handbag from the floor. He would throw it away. Stash it deep down inside the wheelie bin, and eliminate every last scrap of the vile child. 'Sorry, Father Ewan. No handbag found. Mumma must have changed her mind. Thank you, and goodbye.'

He carefully shaved off his heavy three-day overgrowth with an open bladed razor, showered, and washed his hair. He then threw on the kimono, walked back to his mother's bedroom, and sat down at her dressing table to study himself in the mirror. Dark shadows had formed beneath his eyes, and a florid blotch of *rosacea* covered his forehead. Picking up a pen brush of *Touche Eclat*, he carefully applied its smooth, beige cream to hide the flaws. His comfortable, dreamy state had become a surge of euphoria, fuelled by love. He loved Roger, he loved Mumma, and he loved the happy man who now looked back at him from the mirror. He stood up and walked down to the drawing room, clasping the purple bag, deemed for disposal. Although the central heating was turned on, the room felt empty and alien. He would light a fire. Roger had been to Sainsbury's and was bound to have planned something extra special for dinner tonight. They could eat it on trays, and relax before its cosy warmth.

Timothy knelt and arranged shredded paper, firelighters, kindling wood, and some light, dry logs. He struck a match to the paper and, as smoke and flames began to draw up, he sat down on one of the giant sofas, and looked up at the painting of his mother, hanging over the mantelpiece. 'Everything's going to be all right, Mumma,' he mouthed. Outside of his sanctuary the wind made a panting sound. The wild weather was returning, and a surge of hail-filled rain smacked against the window, like hurled gravel. He snuggled down, moulding his body to the feather cushions, with unprecedented joy. With no particular purpose he idly began to examine the bag.

Horrid bag. Horrid colour. Scuffed all along the bottom where the repulsive child had dragged it on the ground behind her. The clasp of the bag was a pronged metal twist. He clicked it open. Anything inside? Yes. A cream A5 sized envelope, written on with Mumma's hand. *To Ewan. Personal and private. To be read only after I'm gone.* It was sealed shut with one of her bespoke address labels stuck over the flap. Clearly there were some documents inside, but how could they be personal and private? *He* was the only person of importance in her life. Father Ewan was only a priest with whom she'd had a detached relationship. Priests were never personal friends. Anything she had to say to Father Ewan could be shared. He ran his thumb under the envelope flap and removed the contents.

Chapter 47

Sally heard Roger's key in the lock, a sound normally accompanied by scrambling paws, and deep, excited woofs. 'I'm in the sitting room,' she called. He entered but neither spoke, each waiting for the other. It was Roger who found his voice first.

'Sally. I'm so grateful you're home.'

'I'm not home, Rog. I'm just back for a short time. To tie up ends with you, and go to Marina's cremation.'

'Are you all right?'

'Yes. And you?' He nodded. 'Roger. About Finnegan. I already know.'

'How do you know?'

'I've been staying at Waldringhythe Abbey. I'm going to work there as a counsellor, but don't cross-question me. I don't want to talk about it. Andrew Gibson rang Father Ewan about Tim. He mentioned it, and obviously Father Ewan passed on the bad news. I'm devastated. Poor Finnegan. What happened?' Her eyes blinked tears, and she held a hand over her jaw.

'It was all my fault. I left the front door open. I'm so sorry.'

'No blame, love. No hair shirt. You had a lot on your mind.'

'I buried him in the er. . . in the ashes on the lawn.'

'Yes. I saw the mound. I'm sorry I burnt your clothes, but I was angry.'

'You'd every right to be.'

'I'm not angry any more. I accept everything. Can we still be friends?'

'After what we've been to each other, Sal, friends seems a strange word.'

'But we're not in love any more. How can we be anything more than friends? We can stay fond of each other, but we must give all our energies to our future lives.'

'I suppose. But surely we can have a hug for Finnegan's sake?'

'Of course.'

Sally rose, moved to Roger, and they embraced. How strange he felt. The familiarity of his girth and height was not forgotten, but the man she now desired was leaner, and finer-boned. Her arms around Roger were too stretched, he was too solid and it felt wrong. Their awkwardness was obvious, and they drew apart. The first brick laid onto the mortar of their permanent estrangement. They both sat down.

'How are things? With Tim, I mean. He's in a bad way, isn't he?'

'Things are suddenly better. Much better. A miracle, really. A complete turn round back to normal, thank God. Did that priest McEwan tell you he was coming down to see Tim this evening?'

'Yes he did.'

'Well he isn't needed now. Can you contact him and cancel?'

'I can't, Rog. I've no idea of his mobile number, but surely he can still see Tim and at least have some sort of a chat? He was coming down tonight, anyway. He has to bless some of Marina's effects, and attend her cremation tomorrow.'

Roger sighed, loudly and deeply. 'With the greatest of respect to the chap, I don't want him interfering in case he stirs up Tim's anxiety again.'

'But he's a superb practitioner.'

'Sorry, Sal. Everyone says he's the cat's pyjamas, but. . .'

'Then when he arrives at The Manor will you give him directions to come here? I'm putting him up for the night.'

'That's sweet of you. I suppose he's your sort of employer now.'

'Yes. Waldringhythe will be my home. Hopefully for a long time.'

'Are you positive about selling up?'

'Yes. Soon as possible. You *will* arrange the deeds of transfer, won't you?'

''Course. The house is yours with my blessing.'

'Thank you, Roger. Thank you for your generosity. I intend to buy Louise a flat, by the way. She won't be homeless.'

'Sally, we must talk about Louise.'

'She has to fight her own way through the maze of our mess. It won't be easy for her, or for us either, but it's the way it has to be. We must behave like grown-ups. Don't throw blame. Give each other a good and respectable press. Be tolerant of her anger. Make sure she knows we love her.'

'I'll do my very best, I promise.' Roger breathed evenly and smiled at Sally with kindness. 'You're lovely, Sal. I'll really miss you. I hope you'll be happy.'

'I am happy. Very happy'

'You look it. Abnormally so. Is there someone else in your life?'

'Yes, there is.'

'I see. Will he look after you, this man?'

'The relationship is very new, but I hope one day. . .'

'But you're in love?'

'Yes. It's good that we're both in love. It helps to equalise things.'

Roger then looked at his watch. 'Oh, Lord. Look, I'm really sorry but I've got to go. I've just remembered the Proudfoot's parish priest is coming over to poke his nose in. The man's a confounded nuisance, and I must deflect him as well. All I want to do is get tomorrow over. After that, I've decided I'm going to take Tim away. Somewhere warm so we can really laze up and relax. Barbados I thought.'

'I'll see you tomorrow at the Crem then, Rog? Do we go back to The Manor afterwards, or what?'

Roger groaned. 'Fuck! I was going to book the taproom at *The Dog and Duck*. Oh, well. I suppose we can take *vox pop* that we mosey back there anyway.'

'Shall we talk here afterwards?

'We'd better. After that, who knows when we'll see each other again? I hope your new thing – the new man in your life works out.'

'So do I.'

'Anything else we should talk about now?'

'Not really.'

'Best be off, then. Tim sends his love. Genuinely.'

'And give my love to Tim. I mean it too. I'm glad he's better.'

'Bye, then.'

'Bye, love.'

Roger made to go, but turned back. 'It was good, wasn't it? Most of it.'

'All of it was good, Rog. All of it.'

'We went through a lot, didn't we. The babies, I mean.'

'Treasured bonds, Rog. Nothing can break them.'

'You are happy, aren't you?'

'Blissfully. After rain, flowers grow.'

'I'm glad.'

'Bye, Rog.'

'Bye, Sal.

Chapter 48

Timothy's face had frozen, and the fingers of both his hands clutched tight to the written pages. He stared hard at the familiar script of loops, and swirls, and dots and crosses, that she'd shaped with the nib of her gold fountain pen. Shiny black ink on cream parchment. Consonants and vowels fitted together in every combination of correct positions; the words formed to be read with animation and resonance. The prose roared off the page, seeming to form a fist that struck out and hit him on the jaw. Something crawled out of his eye, and slithered to the cavern of his ear. Smack-smack went his hand as he tried to rid himself of the irritation. He looked down. The pages were moving; an undulating wave caused by a myriad of wriggling, thread-like worms.

He dropped the pages, and fell out of the sofa onto all fours. He'd become an alien; a nothing; a homeless nomadic creature; a filthy reptile crawling through the mire of life's detritus. He leaned onto his knuckles, with nausea rising in his throat. He began to pant loudly, hearing the resonance of his lungs gasping over the crackle of the fire, but he soon became aware that there was another sound in the room. A loud rustling. He turned to find himself being stared at by a group of sinister, shadowy strangers. 'Pathetic clown,' jeered an old woman in the front row. 'Thinks he's Fauntleroy, but he's only a slut's brat.'

Also in the front row stood a little boy. A little boy he'd just been reading about, afflicted with a cleft lip repair. Patrick. Bastard number one. Patrick, who he thought had been his friend. Perhaps he *was* his friend, in unity. Removed from the harlot for his own care and protection. In the back row he saw the fishporter, Patrick's father. Stank of fish. She too stank from the touch of his fishy hands, and he could smell the oil of herring plastered on her body. Alongside the fishporter stood the rotting Rabbi. The filth that had created himself. Bastard number two. Food and dribble stains down the front of his black jacket, and a frill of greasy dandruff on the collar. His beard encrusted with food. His rancid sweat, his foul breath, the pissy stink of his lousy crotch.

'Listen, Timothy,' said the old woman. 'Can you hear the sound? Boomp-boomp-boomp. That's my body bouncing down the stairs. Kicked hard and pushed down by the hysterical doxy. Murdered by the whore, but no hangman's noose or stoning for the sly beauty. No incarceration to pay the price for her sins. Rescued by a short, portly Quasimodo. Gratefully grabbing herself a rich sugar daddy. She'd have shagged the devil, that one.'

Saliva dripped from his mouth. The colours of the room faded away to a cold, hard grey, but the smells remained. He sank down, curled himself tightly into the foetal position, and crossed his arms tightly against his pounding chest.

'Despair. I must end my pain. There is no hope. My future squeezed onto a narrow shelf where falling off is certain. I have fallen. I have fallen into a big, cold, dark cavern. All is negative. No earthly chance of positive. No options. An unrelenting, oppressive sadness. Trapped in a deep black hole. No heaven exits. No relief. The pain will never end. Tomorrow will be the same, or worse. The urge to die, intense. The only way to find complete peace. No reason to live. Nothing matters. The deep, black hole getting deeper and darker. A sharp dagger thrust into my heart. My heart has died. Life is a paralysis. The song of her lies shouts my death knell. I have no thoughts, or wants, or dreams. Only hate is left. Death is my only escape, but no trace of her, or the filth of her past, must remain. They must not know my shame.'

He lifted the cream vellum pages, and the envelope, and placed them on the fire. They immediately caught flame to become a hot blaze of yellow, scarlet and leaping streaks of blue. The degradation taken up the chimney, and spat out into the wet night. Soon, all that remained were delicate grey flakes, shaking and fluttering on the tops of the logs.

Timothy rose. He opened the casement doors that led into the garden, and went out into the teeming rain. He kicked off his mules.

He walked onto the long lawn and tore off the kimono. He walked down, and down, until he reached the lake. He waded in. The water lapped warm around his thighs. There was the loud noise of an angry swan flapping its wings, a warning, hissing cry, then just the perfect comfort of the watery haven.

Chapter 49

Roger sped up The Manor House drive to find the old Morris Minor was already parked up. Bugger! He would have to firmly deflect the old pest, but the black-frocked figure was rushing towards him, his arms waving, his cassock wet from the thighs down, and his feet splaying beneath weak knees. What in God's name was the silly old fart doing? He approached Roger, gulping and shouting long before there was any chance that he'd be heard. When he reached him he sobbed, clutched his head, and rocked it from side to side. 'He's in the lake! Tim's in the lake! Nothing I could do. Help, Mr Fuller. You're stronger than I am. We must pull him out. I've called an ambulance.'

Roger fled down the long lawn, with the old man puffing behind him, gasping his story. 'I rang and rang the doorbell but I got no answer. You weren't here, were you? Oh, Mr Fuller, you said you wouldn't leave him alone. I went around the side of the house to try and find Tim. The drawing room doors to the garden were wide open, and there were some leather mules on the terrace. A black garment was in the middle of the lawn, and in the distance I could see a head bobbing on the water. I couldn't believe anyone would take a swim. . . Not in this rain.' He repeated every word of the story again, and twice more. Roger wasn't listening. His legs were charging down the squelchy skid of the grass, his body jerking with an electric shock of pain that shot from his hip-joints, down his calves, and through his Achilles tendons.

Timothy's body was floating, face down, in the centre of the lake, but as Roger started to wade out, there was a rearing of strong, white wings. 'The weed-pole, Father Joseph,' he shouted. 'Quick. Hand me the weed-pole.' Roger grabbed the pole, and swung it like a Samurai sword at the threatening creature, while Father Joseph threw pebbles, and made pathetic shooing noises. In fear, the swan took flight, accompanied by its mate. Roger then waded out to grab the floating shoulders, and towed hard towards the bank. 'Help me, Father Joseph. You must take an arm.' Together they tugged and heaved the inanimate, naked body face down onto the grass.

'Is he alive?' Father Joseph shouted. 'Oh, Mr Fuller! Please let him be alive!'

'He's not alive, Father Joseph.'

'A chance. A chance. The ambulance is here.' The old priest ran up the lawn again, flapping his arms. 'Drive down to the lake,' he shouted at the paramedics. 'Quickly. The kiss of life may save him.'

Roger knelt over Timothy's body, and pulled him over. His dead face was blueish-grey, and covered with small red wounds. His eyes were closed, and his expression was one of peace. Green weed lay like shanks of embroidery silk on his head, and thick, muddy slime trickled from his hair. He knew he should yell and shout. That he should throw himself over Tim's corpse, and howl his grief, and take his poor dead face in his hands, and talk to him, and kiss him, and rave with hideous wailing, and to ask why? Why? Why, for God's sake? Tim, you had recovered. Fully recovered. You were completely back to normal. But Roger showed no loss of control. No shouting or histrionics. Only the repression and holding in of grief; the reaction an observer would translate as intrinsic to an ex-Guards officer, but which only Roger knew as the mask of cowardice.

The paramedics flew from their vehicle, pushed Roger aside, and rushed to work, while Father Joseph repeated his story again. The pulse was felt for, and a stethoscope placed on the heart. Then energetic mouth-to-mouth procedure, and bearing down on the chest. Electric defibrillators to both chest and throat were grabbed from the ambulance, and three attempts at resuscitation made. But after several minutes of frenetic activity, they stopped. 'I'm afraid there's no point carrying on, Sir. Who's his G.P.?

'Andrew Gibson, at the Health Centre on Stonor Road.'

'I'll get our control to bleep him. The body has to be officially declared dead at the scene by a doctor before we can take him away. The police will have to be called as well. Sudden death. Just routine.'

Roger rose, walked around to the other side of the lake, and vomited into the bulrushes. He knelt down behind a wall of Gunnera leaves, feeling as if he were teetering on the edge of the world, looking down into two craters separated by a million miles, knowing he would fall into one of them, and also knowing that he had the power to choose which would claim him. One had wide, winding steps that led down to a green, flower-filled garden. The walls on either side were painted a sunny yellow, and below he saw a running video of familiarity. The spread russet ribbons of Sally's hair on the pillow, the jade mirrors of her eyes, and the intimate, comely feel of her body. Sun-dappled Sundays on The Dower House lawn. Lying on a blanket, and staring up at her freckled profile, while she read a novel in a deck chair. One especially bad winter, both of them with shovels, intent on clearing snow from the drive, but ditching them at the first opportunity to pelt each other with snowballs. Louise joining in, and taking Sally's side. Both of them overpowering him until, totally conquered, he lay laughing on his back to allow their game of burying him alive.

But there were also boxes hanging on the walls. Not window boxes filled with flowers but locked boxes, created by his infidelities, and lies, and addictions. Each holding a secret, known only to himself. There was also the huge, closet-size box of which Sally was well aware. Dearest Sal. The sweet guardian of his weakness, who had never exposed him, loyally keeping him warm, and fed, and housed, whilst shouldering his rejection of her. She was standing at the bottom of the steps, wearing her wedding dress, and looking up as Rossetti's *The Beloved Bride*. Innocent. Trusting. Loving. Passionate. Now she herself had fallen in love with another. Soon to be carried off and owned by a stranger.

He pulled back his gaze and looked down into the other chasm. It was a view down a long, dark tunnel into a telescoped landscape – a barren, treeless field of ploughed brown. No birds, no sounds, no leaves, no flowers. No music, no laughter, no friends. Only the turned, rejecting backs of heterosexuals marching away from him. He was compelled to draw back a thick, black curtain. Behind it was a huge football crowd of men, seemingly happy, laughing and joking with each other, but hiding the sad fact that most of their alliances were of faceless ships that passed in the night. Smiling salaciously, the massed throng waited to be picked up in the gay lending libraries of bathhouses, and tawdry basement clubs. On the sidelines its saddest victims. Lonely, desperate, shuffling old men (such as he must inevitably become), offering the riches of Croesus to the greedy, the faithless, and the diseased. In the hard grey sky above him white swirling lines of plane trails were forming words. 'Faggot. Queer. Poofter.' 'I'm sorry, Tim,' he whispered. 'Oh, my love. My Tim. I'm so sorry.'

He composed himself and walked back, his eyes smarting, but his back ramrod straight. 'You all right, sir?' one of the paramedics asked.

'Sorry. The shock hit me. Had to puke.'

'Are you a relation?'

'No. Roger Fuller. A very old family friend.'

They all then looked up to see Andrew Gibson walking down to the scene, accompanied by the wet and bedraggled Father Joseph, again telling his story with much gesticulation. Nodding to Roger, and swatting off Father Joseph, Andrew attended to his duty. Five minutes later Timothy's body was shrouded, and transferred to the ambulance. 'I'll accompany him,' said Father Joseph. 'It's the least I can do. Poor Tim. Poor, dear boy. Please can you apologise to Father Ewan for my absence?' As the ambulance drove slowly away up the long lawn, Roger and Andrew stood in respectful contemplation.

'What on *earth* can have happened?' Andrew said, shaking his head. 'I can only relate my involvement today. Mrs Feather called me out on an emergency visit around ten. She was in a right old state. She'd found him delusional and incoherent, but there was nothing to indicate I should be worried for his safety, *per se*. Medically, I had two choices. Arrange to admit him, or sedate him. I chose sedation. I thought it better to play it by ear until he talked to the priest. As I'd heard nothing more, I assumed he was being manageable, but I was going to pop in this evening for an update. What time did you get back this morning, Roger?'

'It must have been around eleven-thirty.'

'How did you find the situation?'

'I had a major bust-up with Mrs Feather, and she flounced out. Tim was sound asleep. Father Joseph can confirm that, as he turned up not long afterwards. Tim eventually woke up around two. He was a bit stroppy for a bit, but then he bucked up completely. What amounted to a full recovery. I mean *absolutely* back to normal. I popped home for less than half an hour, and left him in very high spirits. He was going to have a shave and get dressed. That's the God's honest truth.'

Andrew breathed out and dropped his shoulders. 'His condition was very precarious, and very complex. What you saw was probably a manic phase that gave all indications of normality. You weren't to know. I can only guess that his thought processes flipped back again after you left. Did he leave a suicide note?'

'I've no idea. I've not been back in the house yet. Actually, I must go in now and get into some dry clothes.'

'Best I accompany you, and we can have a look round together. The police will be here soon, and they'll need our corroboration. I shall firmly assure them that his mental state *could* have been conducive to suicide, but there were no obvious indications. No point them nosing around and suspecting foul play.' He looked at his wrist-watch. 'Just gone four-thirty. Father Ewan's due to turn up at six, isn't he? Can you stay on?'

'I'd rather I got over to the mortuary to be with Tim.'

Andrew patted him on the shoulder. 'I understand, Roger. I mean, I really understand, but someone needs to be here.'

'Sally's back home now,' Roger said, brightly. 'I'll ask her to come over.'

Chapter 50

When Ewan arrived at The Manor House Sally ran out to meet him. 'Come into the drawing room,' she said. 'There's been a tragedy.' With the story told, she sloppily poured two glasses of wine, and gestured for him to sit in an armchair, but before he could sit down, he was obliged to remove a large purple handbag.

'The police have only just left,' she said. 'They had a good look round, and took basic statements from Roger and Andrew. What did Andrew tell you about Tim's mental state when he spoke to you yesterday?'

'An admission to A & E on Saturday, with a diagnosis of panic attack. Then a build up of psychosis on Sunday, with psychosexual and religious features. He initially diagnosed PTSD, but he hoped there'd be an improvement after he'd spoken to me. Otherwise, he was considering admitting him, either voluntary or otherwise.'

'Andrew confirmed that story to the police, but Roger was emphatic that Tim returned completely back normal after lunch today. So much so, you weren't required. Andrew's opinion was that Roger saw a period of elation, as a manic change from the deep despair, and a psychotic state Tim had developed. Something very simple could have tipped the balance back into reverse. The police seem satisfied it was suicide, and they're not treating the death as suspicious, even though there was no note found. It's so sad. Roger was adamant that the fire in here wasn't even laid this afternoon when he left, but a fire was found burning brightly, so Tim must have lit it. He'd also had a shower, and a shave. The blade of his open razor was laid out to dry, and even the wet towels had been neatly folded over the radiator. Real signs that he was behaving normally. We'll never know what happened, will we?'

'And where's Roger, now?'

'He's gone to the mortuary to be with Tim. As far as tomorrow's concerned I asked the police if Marina's cremation could go ahead, and they said there wouldn't be a problem from their department. Andrew's going to inform the family solicitor, so I guess we should check with the undertakers first thing tomorrow. Look, I know you didn't want to stay here, and I don't want to leave you on your own, but I must go. I've made Roger promise that he'll come straight back home, when he can do no more for Tim.'

'Of course, I'm happy to stay here. There are nine bedrooms, and I'm sure I can find an empty one. How *is* Roger?'

'Devastated of course, but he gave his statement as if he was just a very concerned outsider. He really loved Tim, Ewan, and they did intend to 'out' tomorrow. I'm sure he'll crack up tonight, so I must be there for him. Our marriage might be over, but our past love still remains. Probably always will. Can you understand that? I'm not even sure that I understand it myself.'

'There's so much about life, and love, and ourselves that we're never likely to understand, isn't there?' he said.

'Marina,' Sally said. 'You were in love with her, weren't you?'

A shudder shot through Ewan's body. He stiffened, as if his body had suddenly grown a hard metal shell to prevent his inner self escaping. His stomach dropped like a block of ice to his bowels, and prickles rose in his neck and face. The only confidants to his love for Marina had been Jacob and Fanny, but their knowing was never a threat to his security; in fact they were the steam valves in his pressure cooker of concealment. He shook his head, swallowed hard, and forced out a few stilted words. 'No, of course not. Our relationship was wholly professional.'

'Dear Ewan, I can tell you were. Call it sixth sense, or a woman's intuition. Your body language screams it out. Your desperate sorrow. The look in your eyes when you talk about her. Looking back, the withheld, dreamy expression that came over *her* face when she talked about you. You've no need to explain.'

'Of course, I wasn't in love with her...'

'I'm not chastising you, and it won't go any further than these four walls. Admit it for her sake, even if it's only to me, and allow her memory to emerge into the light. Admit it for the sake of your future life, and to celebrate the one she's just lost.'

With a sudden burst of energy, Ewan's body unlocked, and his resolve evaporated to become a proud outing. He was free! Being free of his cloth, and free of his chains, he could now hold up his fist of admission. 'I must admit it, then. I loved her. I loved her for most of my adult life, but it was a love for all the right reasons. Passion, companionship, fidelity, and comfort. To someone like me, our kind of love is a venal sin, and a betrayal of my vows, but she will always remain seeped in my bones, and embedded in my flesh. Are you disappointed with me, Sally? Do you judge me as a faker and a fraud.'

'Of course not. I'm not bound by the demands of your faith. I'm an atheist, remember, but can I offer to counsel you? Please let me help you in the way that you've helped so many others to recover. My ears can hear you, and my hands can hold you.'

'Thank you for your kindness, Sally, and please forgive my lies. Perhaps we can talk again tomorrow. With an evening alone ahead of me I'll have the luxury of protected time to reconcile my thoughts.' He laughed nervously. 'I'm afraid this is the only way that priests ever get around to deciding anything.'

Sally rose to go. She poked the slumbering embers of the fire, and threw on a couple of logs. 'You'll find everything you need here, but if not, or you've got any problems, phone me. Andrew's taken Marina's cat, by the way. He says he's happy to offer it a home, but you know what cats are like. It might just turn up. The central heating's on, and there's plenty of food in the kitchen. By the way, Ewan. Morgana's handbag. The one Marina wanted you to bless. That's it on the chair.'

'Yes. I guessed that,' he said. 'Should things be allowed to go ahead tomorrow I'll go down early to the chapel of rest in Henley.

I'll see that it goes into her hands, and I'll escort her safely to the crematorium. I can then get straight off after the ceremony.'

Sally paused nervously. 'Oh, well. So that's it, I suppose. Goodnight, Ewan. Please sleep easy, and be assured that there's no sin called love.'

'Good night, and God bless you, Sally.'

She went to go, but she found that her feet had become as heavy as lead, and seemed magnetised to the carpet. She stood still, waiting for him to prolong the conversation, but he said nothing further.

As she dragged her feet to move she begged, with what she hoped was thought transference. 'Please ask me to stay,' her silent voice cried, but he'd turned his back and was looking up at the painting of Marina.

Chapter 51

Roger shut the front door and walked to the kitchen where Sally was sitting at the table, staring into a large glass of gin and tonic. She got up and steered him to a chair. 'Do you need a drink, love?'

'I do. A beer, please. I'm so thirsty I could drink a river.'

'Shock has a wide range of affects. Can you talk about it?'

'I can talk about it, but I can't cry.'

'It often happens.'

'Tim was the same on the night Marina died. He couldn't cry either for a while.'

'Then you know it'll come, Rog. It's all in a box, waiting for its time.'

'Is that what they teach you? This grief stuff.'

'That, and a great deal more.'

'You know I've always thought it was a load of hippy shit.'

'Listen, love. I'm going to read to you.' She picked up a book.

'No one prepares us for death, so when it happens we don't know how to react. We have no rehearsals, no guidelines, no crib sheets. The way we usually conduct ourselves is the way we've been conditioned to. It's likely we've been disciplined into feeling that there's something weak, or demeaning, in venting our emotions for public display; the stoicism of the stiff upper lip. Perhaps, on the other hand, we can't hold it in, and we break down. Most likely, at the same time, we'll be apologising to make our audience feel less embarrassed, and promising we'll pull ourselves together as soon as possible. The first lesson to be learned is that it's permissible to grieve. It's allowed and it's natural, and it's also permissible to grieve loudly and publicly.'

'I suppose that's the Father Ewan school of thought.'

'Yes. The quotation's from *Hand in Hand*. His basic text book.'

'Sandridge Fuller turned it down. Did you know?'

'I did know, actually. Father Ewan told me.'

'It was me who rejected it. Just me. No one else saw it. I thought it was a right load of bollocks, and it wouldn't sell a single copy. My '*Beatles Moment*', as they say. Life's a fucker.'

'We all make mistakes.'

'Me more than most. Tim really *was* back to normal when I left him, Sal. I know I'm a selfish bastard, but he really had completely recovered. No one will believe me, though. Andrew's been very fair and professional, but old Father Fuckwit will make sure my name's dragged through the mud.'

'Let me try to help you through this, Rog?'

'What's the point? You'll be off tomorrow afternoon. Off to your new life. Sorry. No bitterness intended, but it's true, isn't it?'

'I have to go.'

'I know.'

'Another beer?'

'Another, and another, and another. It's all I know.'

'Will you say something, Rog? Say this. I love you, Tim.'

Roger leaned forward to lay his cheek on the cold wood of the kitchen table, but a few stray crumbs imprinted grittily on his cheek. He lifted his head to brush off the discomfort, and looked at Sally. The harsh light of the overhead neon tube cruelly showed every small line on her face. Her hair was mussed into a wild, unkempt bush and mascara was smudged beneath her eyes. She looked tired, and one of her pearl earrings was missing. But he thought she'd never looked lovelier.

Roger made a bridge of his fingers, pressed his nose with his thumbs, and sucked in his breath. 'I've got something to tell you, Sal. It's been a cruel cross to bear for all these years, but I can't hold in any longer. Morgana. Tim hated her. He was insane with jealousy. On the day of the drownings everyone on board was laughing like hyenas at some silly old pillocks dancing. Then the boat lurched. I think it was a speedboat roaring past, and I had to grab the wheel with both hands to take control. For a moment, I was fully occupied, keeping the boat on a straight course, but then I saw it all. The child was sound asleep, lying flat on the bench behind Tim. He reached back with both of his hands, and blindly rolled her through the narrow gap in the safety railing. She was only tiny, you see. A tiny, innocent, sleeping child. It only took two seconds. Of course he had no idea that I'd seen what he did, but it all went horrendously wrong, and his father died as well. He worshipped his father – just worshipped him in the same way that he adored his mother – and he never recovered from his loss. But he never showed any remorse for Morgana's death. He truly hated her.'

Sally sat with her hand over her mouth, stunned into silence.

Chapter 52

Ewan gave Sally a few seconds to vacate The Manor before his hand leapt to the purple handbag. He wrenched the clasp open. Empty! Empty! His heart beat rapidly. As if his eyes had deceived him, he thrust his hand inside and roughly searched. Nothing. There was a wide zipped compartment on one side, and a deep, open pocket on the other, but not a line of writing did either hold. Not even a note to say she'd changed her mind, and there was nothing for him to read after all. His last precious line of contact with her gone. Gone. Blown away.

His breathing began to calm. Things would remain the same, then. Perhaps it was for the best. No revelations, no pleas for clemency, no taint on her character, or loss of face. Their perfect love would remain intact, with no murky shadows, or reading of the runes. This was her house, he was alone in her house, and he had the freedom to try and find her essence. From above the fireplace her glorious cornflower blue eyes looked down at him, and he stood, contemplating her soft loveliness, for several minutes.

He got up and walked out into the hall, hoping that voices of her presence would whisper to him from the walls, and evocations would be round every corner. Through every door he went; the garden room, the morning room, the formal dining room, and the library, but there was no sound of her merry laughter, no swish of her skirt, and no click of her heels.

A long corridor led to the kitchen, and he stood within its cream walls. Free-standing units resembled a French farmhouse, with an Aga and a walk-in larder. Gingham curtains of pale blue and mauve. Brass pans on hooks. Swathes of dried herbs, and hops, and lavender hanging on the walls. A bookcase of recipe books. He turned and walked back up the corridor to find the front staircase. Once upstairs, he searched for her bedroom. When he found it, he turned on the lights, and closed the curtains. Some three years ago, when decorating this room, she'd gone into intense detail for him. 'It's really retro fifties,' she'd enthused. 'Sooooоо old-fashioned, but I adore it.' The wallpaper was of cerise cabbage roses, the curtains thick, flouncy drapes of blush-pink velvet, and the deep pile carpet a greeny-cream. A mirrored dressing table was adorned with cosmetics, and perfumes, and a collection of family photographs. Several of the poor, troubled man who was her son, in various ages and poses. A postcard of *Crucifix Man*. How gratified he was to know that when she awoke every morning her eyes had alighted on himself. No image of her daughter, but two of her dead husband.

From an ornate silver frame, the grisly judge stared out, captured in sharp-focused monochrome, with the curly sheep's ears of his wig resting on his shoulders. A bulbous nose, and each bagged eye etched with deep crow's feet. The chin neatly bearded, the neck short, the years obvious. The face was hard-set, terrifyingly austere, and powerful enough to put the fear of God into any felon shaking in the dock. Ewan stared, trying to find the man she loved, which was immediately obvious in the kind eyes that no severity for the camera could ever disguise.

Her wedding photograph was more beguiling. She was so different, so young, so innocent. Her face showing the soft, rounded curves of a youthful chin, and cheekbones that would refine, and surge, into the timeless beauty she became. Her sweet, unadorned face, looking at her new husband with obvious adoration.

He undressed and got into her unmade bed. The ascetic, cold comfort of the cotton sheets shocked him into his usual shivering, and he trembled under the counterpane until he was warm. It was here she had breathed her last breath. He gathered up the lace fabric with both his hands, and held it to his face. At last it was her time.

SEPTEMBER 1984

Her appointment was for three, but she arrived at nearly twenty past. His face showed a grateful relief. 'You're late. I thought you weren't coming.'

'I'm deliberately late. I've given you a little more time to wrestle with your conscience.' He was aware of a sharpness in her voice, and a distinct change from her softness of yesterday. She looked at him with her familiar swan's stare, and an aloofness that seemed to convey she had no real interest in the matter. 'For God's sake, Ewan. Do you want me or not?'

'I want you,' he said. 'I think of nothing else but you. I'm in love with you. Those that judge me will declare my love for you is a sin, but it's one I must commit to survive my calling.'

'So I take it you intend to remain a priest?'

'I do, so our love must be carefully concealed.'

'Oh, thank God for that,' she said. 'I had a terrible dread you might reject me, and then a worse horror you might want to leave the church and marry me. You see, I realised that you weren't the only one with a crisis of loyalty. I accept I must share you with God, but you in turn must share me with the treasured memories of my dead husband. Are you still sure you want me?'

'I'm quite sure, but only if you really love me. You talked yesterday of obsession, but it has to be love.'

'I love you. The love I have for you is one I've never known before, but be assured, it's a true and devoted love.'

Ewan's bedroom was plain, and white-painted, with no evidence remaining of his childhood and boyhood. The windows had been tightly shut all day, and the hot September sun had boiled the room to an airless heat. It smelled of clean linen, and an embedded sea-sidey smell that had been absorbed over a hundred years of winter mists and summer winds from the estuary. His bed was a large French antique, with head and foot boards of intricately carved walnut. Two matching wardrobes filled the entire length of one wall and on the opposite side was hung the room's only affectation: a life-sized reproduction of *Crucifix Man*. At the side of his bed stood a small shrine for the Madonna, twisted prettily with a rosary.

Nakedness between first-time lovers induces shyness and fear of disappointment. Bodies that look so standard when clothed, reveal unexpected surprises. The distribution of surplus flesh, imperfections of the skin, the first sight of the genitalia, the obvious deviance from the stereotyped perfection of the Hollywood beach movie. Marina's skin was pale cream with the surface of smooth wax. She was lean, but athletically curved. Her breasts were firm and elliptical, but seeming too heavy for her narrow rib cage. Long silvery splits on her abdomen led to a sparse pubic triangle, and long, slim-thighed legs. After a few seconds of silence, she took his hand. 'Look at your body, Ewan. You're a beautiful young man. By rights, you should have a young girl to make love to, but I'm far from that.' She took his fingers, and ran them gently over the weak gouges of the silvery splits. 'See these. Feel these. The damage of my babies. You must look at me, and touch me, and really love what you see and touch, or this whole thing will collapse into farce.'

Her words were unheard and unheeded. He had no need to examine her for fault or comparisons. He was in love with her. He bowed down to kiss each side of her abdomen, and to press his tongue deeply into the damage. He then laid his palms upon her, sliding his hands around her warm skin, following her lead as she stretched and shimmied against him, forcing him to bend, and crouch, and twist, into contortions of discovery. Their long hair rasped together; her flowing corn silk against his own, darkest brown, but already heavily shot through with white. He was vapourised and weightless; acting with the unconscious impetus that before had only come in dreams. His hands cupped her breasts, holding them, and weighing them, as they sat heavily in his hands, losing all sense of gentleness as he took her nipples into his mouth. As he drew them in, they hardened, and lengthened like rose hips. His eyes were open and alive, as his body leapt out of his holy vows without reticence or shame.

She raised her knee to rub the underside of his erection, and took his hand again, but this time she led it to the mysterious, complicated, and frightening place that was now open and wet to his fingertips. She guided, defined, and encouraged his gentle searches, and then reached for his penis, now strong, and inflexible, and threatening dispersal. Her leg wound around his thigh, she leaned back and, with no warning or instruction, slid him inside her. Trapped now, within her tight, ribbed walls, he found himself crouched over her, hard held, imprisoned, and forced to take her weight, but he was empowered with a peculiar freedom. To indulge in this hammering, shaking thing that romantics such as himself referred to as making love. Ewan *was* in love, but he knew that he was fucking. It surely had to be the most perfect word constructed to describe this magnificent convulsion; to indulge in this powerful, primordial force of procreation. With no hope of delay, and having neither the skill nor need for restraint, a magical, musical overflowing possessed him. A man fulfilled like any other.

Seeking her own gratification, she was strong and mechanical, programmed to complete, hanging heavily onto his neck while he fought not to drop her. She cried out, each wordless sound ascending in pitch. She grabbed the back of his thighs, pulling him tighter inside her, seeming to try to consume him. As her own climax overpowered her she screamed like a rabid witch.

Now still, and breathing hard, they stared blearily at each other. Conjoined twins. Flushed faces, two heads of hair in birds-nested chaos, rivers of dripping sweat, limbs threatening collapse. Each dizzy with the glory of saturating satisfaction. With ungainly shuffling, and not bearing to pull apart, they put themselves into his bed.

Chapter 53

In the dull light of early morning Roger woke in the lime-coloured sheets of the spare bedroom, wishing he could sleep forever. Last night he'd made apologetic excuses to Sally and had gone to his study. She'd pressed Father Ewan's textbook into his hand, and although he'd kissed her, and thanked her, he discarded it as soon as the door was closed. He'd slumped down on his swivel chair, and reached out for the whisky bottle; the only friend he wanted, but one with no wise counsel to offer. He could only think of Tim's cold body, lying on a refrigerated mortuary trolley, with a label tied to his ankle. The words declared the body to be that of Timothy Tobias Proudfoot, but the beautiful man, so identified, would never have recognised himself. Roger opened his eyes, and watched the cold morning air gently fluttering the hems of the curtains. His inner self began to invade, but he pushed it away, unable to contemplate its findings, knowing he had no hope of ever perceiving Tim's despair, or his own part in it.

There was a sound of movement from the corridor, the door opened and Sally entered, wearing blue jeans and a red sweater, holding a tea tray. 'Did you sleep at all?'

'Suppose I must have, thanks to Scottish malt. What time is it?'

'Just gone nine. I'll pour you a cuppa.' Roger struggled to sit up as Sally placed a large mug at his side, and packed a bank of firm pillows behind his back. After pouring one for herself she sat cross-legged at the end of the bed.

'What I said last night,' Roger said. 'About Tim and Morgana. It really is true. I knew it was wrong to conceal what I knew, but how could I expose Tim? I must be guilty of some sort of chargeable crime, even now. You won't ever tell anyone, will you?'

'Of course not. What would be the point? Tim's dead. He's paid his price. No one will ever know, or need to know now, but it's an horrendous crime. Poor little kiddy. And poor Marina, too. How blighted her life was. It's all too dreadful to contemplate.' She sipped her tea, thinking ruefully. 'I remember the first time I met Tim. It was in *The Dog and Duck*. June 1983. After a village cricket match. We'd just got engaged, and I was so in love with you. You said, "This is Tim, my oldest friend," and I remember thinking how dazzlingly good-looking he was, but he seemed so dull and bland. Then you told me afterwards he'd lost his father, and little sister, in a drowning accident the summer before, and you'd saved his life. When I tried to discuss it with you later on, you clammed up, and it stayed that way, didn't it? I thought you were just being heroic or modest.'

'A topic too delicate for discussion,' Roger said.

'I'll leave it that way, I promise. And I promise I won't ever blab that you and he were. . .'

'Thanks.'

'I'd better go and phone the undertakers now to see if the crema-tion's still on.'

'If it is, I won't be coming. I know it's the done thing to turn up, but I can't face it. In any case the fuzz, are coming back to rubber stamp my official statement.'

Ewan rose and drew the curtains. As he returned across the carpet, his bare toes closed over something hard and sharp. It was a small child's toy; a clockwork tin chicken. He reached down, picked it up, and smiled with nostalgia. He knew he'd had one exactly like this as a child, but although it was far, far back in time, he could still remember playing with it. 'Does the key hurt the chicken when you wind it up, Mammy?'

'Of course not, my lovey, but it will if you wind it too tight. All his insides will go ping, and he won't be able to peck, so you can have two more goes, and then we'll pop him back in the box for a rest.' Ewan wound the key carefully, placed it on the dressing table top, and watched the frenzied display until it wound down and fell over. He picked the toy's box up from the floor, put it safely away, and placed it in his overnight bag.

He then washed and dressed, knowing that his outfit would cause comment at the cremation service, but he had dressed only for Marina. As promised, he would attend as her lover, and not as her priest. After telephoning the undertakers, and receiving confirmation that the cremation would take place, he spent no more time in nostalgia. Before leaving the house he removed the painting of his love from the drawing room, carefully folded it up in her lace counterpane, and carried it to the car. Perhaps it was stealing, but he didn't care.

Sally came to stand at Roger's bedside, dressed in a plain black trouser suit. 'All systems go, Rog. I'm just off to the Crematorium.'

'Will you come back here afterwards? What I mean is, will you come back here to say goodbye before you head off to Suffolk?'

'I'll come back to pack some clothes, but I'll be leaving when I've done that.' She then opened her handbag, and withdrew an envelope. 'I forgot to tell you about these,' she said. 'Did you know that Marina had requested that Father Ewan bless a handbag that belonged to Morgana?' Roger nodded. 'It was in the sitting room last night. I opened it, and found these snaps inside a zipped pocket. I know I should have left them, but after what's happened, I thought you might like them.'

Roger took the envelope from her. It contained a thick collection of old photographs, wound round with a loose elastic band, and he slowly examined them. Most were of Timothy. As a baby, as toddler, and as a happy, animated little boy. He soared on a swing wearing Wellington boots and a bobble hat; dressed as a cowboy, he pointed a toy gun to pose as a tough guy; he waved from Noddy's car on a fairground roundabout; he hung upside down from a tree branch. And there were also some of the child, Morgana, in various poses. She'd been such a pretty little girl, but there were none that showed her smiling. A cross face, with a creased brow, and a look of disdain to whoever was trying to encourage her to pose and laugh for the camera. One of Toby, as a twenty-something young man, slim and beardless in wig and gown, holding, presumably, his final qualification scroll. Another of him taken forty years on. Rotund and florid, cigar and wine glass in hand, wearing a Panama hat and cream linen suit. A faces-only shot of Marina's wedding day, and a standard postcard of

Crucifix Man. One of an unknown child sitting on a beach, holding a Labrador puppy in his arms. Wearing glasses. Something wrong with his face.

'I wonder who the strange kid is?' Roger said. He turned the picture over. 'It says, *Dearest Patrick. Wherever. Aged 5*. That ties up, actually. Tim was getting very worked up about finding someone called Patrick, but Andrew thought he was just an imaginary childhood friend. I guess he must have been real after all.' Roger then looked reminiscently at the images of Tim again, separated them in a dedicated pile, and placed them, without further comment, on the bedside cupboard. 'Thanks for saving them, Sal. I'll treasure them.'

'What about the rest of the snaps? Shall I take them to the cremation?'

'No point. Coffin lid'll be firmly nailed down, won't it?'

'What shall I do with them, then? It seems sacrilege to throw them away.'

'Oh, Christ, Sal, I don't know and I don't care. I really haven't the nous to get my shoes on the right feet today. Sorry to be so arsey, but I feel like shite. Chuck them away.'

'O.K.'

Ewan arrived at the undertakers, but he lacked the strength to view Marina's body. He blessed the purple handbag, and gave instructions that it be placed within her hands.

'Father McEwan, the Proudfoot's Solicitor, has rung,' Mr Fullylove simpered, twirling his black-gloved hands. 'A Mr Mount. He's sorry that he's not able to attend, and I've also had apologies from Father Joseph McCarthy who is feeling unwell. I understand that there is to be just the one piece of music to be played. *Twilight Time*, by The Platters.

Ewan nodded. 'Yes. It was a favourite piece of hers. And mine too.'

He drove behind the long, black Volvo to the crematorium, watching his heart-shaped wreath of red roses, her only floral tribute, lain on the coffin lid. On arrival, he found Sally was already waiting outside. She came to stand beside him, and took his arm. With the cremation being so hastily arranged, and no social grapevine informed, only two other mourners arrived. A stout, elderly lady hanging weakly onto the arm of a middle-aged, nondescript man. Sally whispered their names. Cora Feather and Andrew Gibson. Both parties nodded to each other, and moved forward, but no one smiled. Introductions and handshakes were made. Ewan thanked them both for their superb care of Lady Proudfoot, and all four of them respectfully expressed their profound shock and sorrow at the news of Timothy's death. The undertakers were now assembled to carry Marina into the chapel, and the small party followed on.

Ewan moved forward and knelt in front of the coffin. He prayed silently and returned to sit by Sally. He then put his hands together in prayer, and muttered quietly. After a statutory time of silent reflection, a pair of red brocade curtains automatically closed in front of the coffin, and a gentle clunk announced its slow journey to the pyre. After a few seconds the dark brown sugar voices of The Platters began to sing. *'Heavenly shades of night are falling, it's Twilight Time.'*

Roger opened the front door to a uniformed policeman. 'Colin,' he said wearily. 'We meet again. Terrible business, isn't it?'

'It certainly is. The Inspector on the case knew I was personally involved when Tim Proudfoot collapsed on Saturday, and he asked me to pop down for... well... a bit of a chat.'

'I thought it was just a question of crossing T's and dotting I's?'

'Well, it is, and it isn't.'

'I'm in no mood to protract all this, Colin. Sorry to sound callous, but I'd rather get it over and done with. Come on into the sitting room.'

The policeman stepped heavily, and diffidently, into the house. 'Can I have a glass of water?'

'Would you like some coffee? I can quickly get a pot on. Tell you what. Come on into the kitchen. Then we can talk at the same time.'

Now, with mugs in front of them, and seated at the kitchen table, the two men were both aware of an embarrassed silence. 'So,' said Roger. 'Let's get on with it.'

'It's about the P.M. The post-mortem. They're still running some tests – just routine – so the finding won't be officially out for a bit but...'

'But *what*, for God's sake?'

'They sent me down because I know you. I'm a mate. We need some info.'

'That's no problem. Tim and I were friends for thirty years. There's nothing I didn't know.'

'It's actually about. . . er. . .your. . . er. . . friendship. Look, there's no evidence at all to suggest that he didn't commit suicide, but. . . look, I've got to spit it out. The physical findings showed that he'd had sex – gay sex – some time very shortly before he died. A sweep sample of the. . .er. . . you know. . . showed – oh, this is all so bloody difficult – a very lively sample, if you get my drift.' The policeman cleared his throat several times, and took a long gulp of his hot drink. 'I'm not well acquainted with the forensic findings in technical terms, but they know the contact happened shortly before his death. We know the estimated time of death as about ten minutes before he was found, but there are pieces of the puzzle that we have to fit together for the inquest. We know for sure that there were three males who visited the house yesterday. Dr Gibson, Father Joseph McCarthy, and yourself. Dr Gibson's visit was supervised by Mrs Feather, and quite early on in the morning, and Father Joseph – well he's more than a long shot in anyone's opinion. That only leaves yourself. Unless of course there's a fourth we need to know about.'

Roger had been slowly stirring his coffee, and staring at the table, but then he lifted his head. 'And is contact, as you term it, suddenly a criminal offence between consenting adults?'

'No. Don't be stupid. It's just that if there was a fourth person involved, we need to know, and find him. The inquest demands that we need to be in charge of the full facts. Look, Rog, we don't want to hang this out any longer than you do. The next step is DNA testing, and what we're really trying to doing is to wrap things up before the file gets ten feet thick.'

'There wasn't a fourth person involved, but you already know that, of course.'

'Needed confirmation, that's all.'

'Then you've got it. Something juicy to splash around the station locker room.'

'I give you my word it won't come to that. I'm sure the result of the inquest will be the usual. That he took his own life while the state of his mind was disturbed. We promise you complete confidentiality. My sister's boy. He's – you know – that way as well. I'm not a complete bastard.'

'Thanks, Colin. You're a true friend.'

'Funnily enough, I always wondered about you and that Indian referee a few years ago. The one from Middlesex what wore a turban. He did a lot of standing around and staring in the locker room. You get to know the signs. He could never take his eyes off you.'

'Sanjay,' said Roger wistfully. 'The silky skin of the beautiful Sanjay. You're right, of course. Did you ever wonder about me and Tim?'

'I haven't lived in the village since I was a lad, so I'm not much into local life any more. Didn't even know you and he were friends. Crossed my mind when I saw him on Saturday, though. He had that girly look, didn't he? Face just like his mother's.'

Roger stared straight ahead of him. 'Face of a fucking angel.'

Ewan felt Sally's hand take his elbow as they left the chapel. The tradition was that mourners filed out in convoy to view the wreaths, but there was only the one floral tribute, placed outside the door. Red roses from an unknown source. 'They're lovely, Ewan,' Sally said. Andrew Gibson and Cora Feather approached, Andrew now clearly supporting a very distressed and openly sobbing Cora. 'Both of 'em gone,' she choked. She shook her head, clearly unable to say more. The doctor nodded in agreement and sympathy, but chose not to add any more words of wisdom or comment. Ewan stood for a long contemplative stare at the wreath, and began to walk away at a snail's pace. Sally accompanied him until they were standing on a bland patch of grass that fronted the car park.

'My day is done,' he said. 'I'm going back home now to prepare for great changes in my life.'

'I'll be back at Waldringhythe later on tonight,' she said. 'I'll be ready to counsel you when you feel the time is right.'

'I wish I could say that I'll be taking up your kind offer, Sally, but I won't be able to. I'll be blunt. I'm giving up the priesthood and leaving The Abbey for good. By the time you get back tonight, I'll have left. Like you, I suppose, I'm running away.'

He didn't notice her jerk of shock, or the flush that came to her face. Neither did he notice the crinkle of misery around her mouth, her shaking jaw, or cry of desperation in her voice. 'No, Ewan. You can't leave. Please don't go. Please don't. You're not alone. I'm here. I understand everything. Let me help you.'

'I don't need help,' he said kindly. 'I have a whole new life planned. Soon I will be very wealthy. So wealthy as to be immoral, but I will use the money to benefit my fellow man. I intend to become an ambassador for the anti-nuclear movement, and I'll be staging a high profile political enquiry. Sally, the misery of my lost love remains, and always will, but for some strange reason, I'm suddenly happy. These last four days, I've been practising what I preach. I've been on an intense odyssey around myself, and I've come home. It's as simple as that. Now it's time for me to be strong, and grow, but thank you for caring.' A rare, wide smile came to his face. 'As Marina said, the true meaning of life is to love, and to have been loved. That must be my last word. Goodbye, Sally.'

Sally watched him as he walked away. His head held strongly, his leather jacket loose, and his fedora in his hand. The broad shoulders held stiff, his lower body rolling in his unique Salsa-dancer way, and his Spanish dancer boots clicking on the tarmac. Toes slightly turned in, the buttocks firm in his tight jeans, his long legs moving forward with swinging, confident strides. Although the view of his car was half obliterated by the hanging branches of a yew tree, she saw him open the door, jack knife his body in, and sit down. He removed the band in his hair, and shook its length free. He was still smiling. As he drove off, he didn't look back, or wave.

Her moment of despair was invaded by Cora, still holding heavily onto Andrew's arm. 'That's 'im, then,' she said, with renewed strength. 'That Father Ewan. What a shock. He's nothing like a priest. Looks more like one of the BeeGees.'

'I'll take you home, Cora,' said Andrew. 'You're done in. Sally, might I invite you and Roger around this evening for a drink? I'd like to talk a bit more to Roger about Tim's psychosis. His condition was most complicated, and I'd like to enlighten him further.'

'Not tonight, Andrew,' said Sally kindly, 'but thanks for asking.'

'Another time then. By the way, the cat seems to have settled in. I'll be making a donation to the RSPCA.'

Sally returned home. A fire burned in the inglenook, and there was a smell of freshly brewed coffee. Roger got up, kissed her on the cheek, and helped her off with her jacket. 'Sit down, love. You look exhausted. Can I get you a drink?'

'A coffee, and a very large brandy please. I'm shattered.'

'Well, I'll be leaving you in peace soon. I'm driving up to Worcestershire. I've turned up a Wolfhound breeder with a litter. I've just *got* to get one. Can't stand the silence. Suppose you'll be gone by the time I get back?'

'Change of plan, Rog,' she said. 'I won't be leaving after all. I'm not going anywhere. I'm staying here.'

'I see.' Roger paused diffidently for several seconds. 'Suppose you don't fancy coming with me? That's if you feel up to it.'

'Yes, I'd like that. I'd like that very much.'

Roger paused again. 'The puppies. They're eight weeks old. Ready to take home. There's the choice of a dog or a bitch. What do you think?'

'I think we should take them both.'

Ewan drove away from the crematorium in a state of inexplicable joy. The TVR responded to the pressure on the accelerator, and all around him the sun shone, and the signs of bursting spring lifted him to even greater heights of ecstasy. His freedom soaked into him, as if he were immersed in warm wax. When he saw the turn off for Hurley, he again followed the village road, until he was parked, as before, down by the Thames. He left the car and walked to the same bench, overlooking the lock. From his pocket he removed the often-read medical report, concerning *Child Ref: 6543M* – the only historical piece of his past he possessed. 'Sleep, sweet, little child,' he said. 'Sleep sweet.' He wouldn't tear it up. That was sacrilege. He knelt down and placed it on the bobbing surface of the river, and watched it as it floated downstream. It would, in time, be taken up by the water, but *Child Ref 6543M* wouldn't drown, as Marina's tiny child had drowned. *Child Ref: 6543M* would live, as he, himself lived. Ewan McEwan. A man like any other.

The Epilogue

The Tales From the Purple Handbag had burned into sooty, microscopic molecules. Absorbed into the hot swirl of wood smoke they'd flown up the wide Georgian chimneystack, to be absorbed into the tempestuous night rain. Thus, they began a long journey. Carried, by the high-powered force of howling wind, they dispersed over both the village and the county, settling in a fine layer on dark fields and gardens. With plough, and rake, and spade, they would gradually become absorbed into the earth as the whole process of decay and rebirth began again. The Tales From the Purple Handbag can never die. In giving sustenance to new green shoots, they are born forever on the cry of life.

THE PRIEST'S TALE

This is your story, Ewan. A story as joyous as a bird singing from a treetop on the first day of spring. Today, I'm having what I joke with Cora as 'a long lie-in'. Truth is, I'm tired. So tired, I can hardly hold the pen. Forgive the shaky words. After today I'll have no more to write, and the end will come – or perhaps the start of what comes next for me. When I started these scribbles I forewarned you it would be a confession. There was never any guilt concerning our love, but perhaps, as a final rounding off, I might be able to proffer one last apology for the retention of the truth about myself.

You know I only came to Waldringhythe to get rid of Father Joseph. Oh, he meant well, but his creeping platitudes were driving me mad. He wasn't too keen on me either, since all I did was scream at him to go away and leave me alone. My pain had become so much part of me that in some weird way I'd become so accustomed to it, I couldn't let it go. I had a recurring dream that I'd look out of the bedroom window, and Toby would be standing under the lime trees, holding the hand of a fractious little girl wearing Osh-Kosh dungarees that had never seen a drop of water. And in the distance, walking up the drive, smiling and waving as he always did when he saw me, was the other lost part of my life; a thin little boy with a cleft lip repair.

The first sight of you, Ewan was a shock. Priests didn't wear blue jeans, or have long hair past their elbows. Of course, as soon as I caught a full view of your face, I had instant empathy, but it was a terrible jolt. Your surgery was excellent, and virtually hidden with that Zapata moustache, but I could still tell. As if you had deliberately put the lip on, thrust yourself in my face and said, 'Suffer! Every time you look at me I'll stick my knife into every festering, miserable memory. I'll make you spew out all your secrets and confront all the demons you try to hide.'

'Go back in time and work forward' was your philosophy. What a stupid illusion! Me! How threatened I was. In those days, the devil sat on my shoulder and made me nasty, but you had such quiet patience. You never gave up on me, but my secrets remained hidden, as deeply as a Roman ruin beneath a car park. Can you now understand, my dearest Ewan, why I refused to pull off the mask? How could the refined Lady of The Manor suddenly reveal her deception? You loved the lady you thought I was. Forget sin and redemption, and all that atonement crap. I left the whore and the killer behind me with such gratitude. Ewan – you loved *me?* Not *her.*

My hand aches so I'll have to stop this mad scribbling, but before I do, just one more thing I know will cross your mind. Why did I not try to find Patrick? Answer in one line. I don't know. It's like that game we all played as children; 'Dare you to jump over a big black hole, scaredy-cat.' In your dreams you're lifted up, and you soar over the danger like an Olympic long jumper. The other children cheer and clap, and you land as gracefully as a fairy on the other side. In reality, your heart pounds, your feet are leaden, and your soul lacks the bottle. You think about it, but you know you can't do it today, so you put it off for tomorrow. You just don't do it. I'm a shallow, cowardly woman. Of course Toby would have supported me, but what of Tim? How could I have let him discover the painful truth about me?

Today, my love and apologies go out to everyone, not least to that dear, sweet little boy I lost. His small face and innocence fills up my heart. I loved him, but I had to let him be. Patrick. My son. Please God that he has had a happy life. That must be my last word.

Here endeth The Priest's Tale